Cascade Failure

by David Lingard

Edited by Denise Boorman

Prologue: Why Always Me?

It's not like I didn't know *anything* about how a spaceship was supposed to function. Granted I knew that in space there was no oxygen or gravity, so it was the ship's job to provide both of those luxuries. I had never really thought too much about just *how* it accomplished those feats though. If I thought back to the movies, news reels and space corps propaganda that I had been subjected to since I was about fifteen years old, I could just about piece together some of the basics of artificial gravity, carbon scrubbing and the like, but I was certainly no rocket scientist.

I'd signed up for the space corps when I was just seventeen, along with a few of my friends and we all thought it was a great idea – exploring the known universe with the people who meant the most to us, battling previously unknown alien species for the safety of the galaxy, or so the advertising campaigns had glorified and dressed up as heroic confrontations (in reality we were yet as a race to 'battle' an alien race). We had all even had matching tattoos put on our right shoulders the night before we enlisted. It was such a shame when we were all assigned to different roles in different ships in different sectors of the universe; nothing ever seemed to go to plan for us.

The truth was that the space corps didn't like it when friends joined up together. They thought that it would create groups and cliques within the ranks and as it was, they made it a point to split up friends and acquaintances to form rank after rank of strangers, who should grow with each other into tightly knit family units. It was probably for the best but it wasn't something I had particularly enjoyed. It kind of made sense to me as I could imagine the difficulties that could arise in a combat situation where you'd need to make a choice between a friend and a commanding officer – something that didn't bear analysing in too much detail, the bonds of friendship in my mind usually winning the internal battle that ensued.

Six weeks of what they called 'basic training' flew past in the blink of an eye, but that was mainly because I was so exhausted throughout the entire ordeal I think that my memory of it probably just faded somewhat. They kept us working on a maximum of four hours sleep a night, with PT – that's physical training to the layman - running around a track, doing pushups, pullups or another of a long list of exercises. It didn't really constitute much hands-on or specialised training, rather just something to ensure new recruits would fall in line, and condition them to do what they were told, when they were told and how they were told. We also carried out weapons training with the old fashioned SA80 assault rifles, firing them down a range, loading and reloading them, and stripping and cleaning them. I liked the idea of target shooting but there were only so many times you could get excited about hitting a paper target from fifty metres away.

As much as this all sounded like a militaristic operation - and it was for the most part - once you arrived on board your posting to one of the space corps' finest Intergalactic Personnel Carriers (IPCs) everything seemed to just calm down. There weren't constant drills to be carried out, there weren't three AM alarm calls to get you to do your daily quota of one hundred jumping jacks or something else just as inane like unmaking then remaking your beds just to prove you could do it properly and quickly. Everything was just kind of…life as normal, peaceful even.

The thing I always found most fascinating was that an IPC didn't need constant manning of every station to function properly, so the ship's complement really didn't have much to do for the most part, and as much as I should never have even let the thought cross my mind, it could get kind of boring after a while. *Really boring*.

Don't get me wrong. There was always plenty to do on the IPC Wanderlust, where I had been stationed for the past two years, but being confined to one ship – even though it was the size of a small city – could get very repetitive and mind-numbingly boring. Not to mention the fact that the few thousand people who you shared this existence with could get very, very annoying. How one person chews their food or how another hums as he or she walks the halls could be enough to drive a person crazy – if you let it get to you of course.

Do you ever feel as though you need a tiny bit of variety, just to keep you sane? I did. That's why when the captain asked for volunteers to answer a distress call from a stranded ship, I was among the first to raise my hand. Nineteen other people had the same idea and together we were commissioned to form a 'search and rescue' party to head over to the floating derelict which was tantalisingly 'unidentifiable' and 'of an unknown design'. Seriously, it was enough to make my mouth water after a total of ten years of space travel with nothing more exciting happening than seeing a few rocks and the times that crew mates finally got so annoyed with each other they had resorted to fistfights in the hallways.

Ten years. I could barely believe how my life had changed since that day my friends and I were so hopeful of our future. If I could go back right now I'd shout *'don't do it!'* to send myself on another, possibly more exciting, path. Something where I could be subjected to real gravity and air that hadn't been recirculated through some filtration system and a lot of other bodies. Oh well, you can't change the past. *'It's no use crying over spilt milk'* as my father used to say. My parents were always supportive of my choices, though I missed them after being away for so long and I often wondered how our lives would've been different if I'd stayed on earth and worked in a *normal* job, seeing them every Friday night for dinner or whatever. A life in the space corps wasn't for the weak of heart, that was for sure.

The unknown ship that we'd been sent over to was huge. And when I say huge I mean massive, monstrous even. It was at least five times bigger than the Wanderlust in all dimensions and a satellite array protruded from the front of the vessel that could put SETI to shame. It was kind of lemon shaped overall, which wasn't really out of the ordinary. Spaceships didn't have to be aerodynamic so, more often than not, when the designers or builders needed to maximise some space or add something on, they would just stick bits on like a Lego fort. That's also why the bridge tended to always sit on top in its own little pod – the ship needed a bridge, so let's just stick that there - job done. Also, as ships grew and had technological 'bolt-ons,' not only did that unit get stuck wherever, but also additional crew quarters and other creature comforts that accompanied them tended to be placed somewhat errantly too.

My rescue team had progressed well once the two ships were close enough that we could run a line across the gap between them. We quickly made it through the air lock system as it was surprisingly similar to our own. You had to open an outer door with a kind of spinny handle – like on old fashioned boats. No, technology hadn't moved on from there (if it's not broke, don't fix it) then you had to continue into a small chamber, close the door behind you then let the chamber re-pressurise. The only thing that was different in that phase was that the chamber didn't re-pressurise, but that was to be expected from a ship in distress. The interior of the ship was not pressurised at all so we didn't need to wait. The downside of this was that there was no lighting, gravity or air in the ship either, so we had to keep our walksuits on at all times. It was basically a derelict, which again was expected for the most part.

We called them walksuits because you'd wear one to go out on a spacewalk. The space corps insisted on calling them Personal External Activity Suits, but nobody liked saying that and the shortened version, PEAS really didn't go down well. Typical Space Corps - always overthinking things.Why abbreviate everything in such technical terms when you could just say what things are – doors and not hatches, toilets and not heads, windows and not portholes. Things like that could get extremely tiresome and at some point we had to fight back against the ridiculousness of the situation. We had a moral obligation to do so.

It was very dark inside the ship, so dark in fact that if our walksuits didn't have strong LED lights beaming off in multiple directions we wouldn't have been able to see our hands in front of our faces. Yes, sometimes the corps got it right, and putting lights on everything was one of those times – after all space was dark!

The corridors looked just like the Wanderlust's, even down to the little maps at the intersections that told you where you were. It was quite frankly bizarre that the ship was unrecognised by our computer system, as it was quite obviously of terrestrial origin.

The ship was called the IPC Saturn. I'd like to say that I'd managed to hack into the mainframe database in some kind of hacker extraordinaire fashion, but honestly, it was handily plastered on various locations throughout the areas that we'd managed to explore before our two-hour investigation revealed no chance of survivors, no bodies and no power within the ship.

There had been such opportunity for excitement when we had been told about the derelict, my trigger finger could barely control itself for the thought of a few hostile aliens or something of the like. Even a few bodies with bite marks would have been enough to keep me going, but once again space had delivered a giant pile of nothing. *'Thank you very much.'*

Eventually, once we'd signed off the autopsy of the ship as 'dead boring', we had hooked a new line between the derelict and the Wanderlust so that each one of the twenty strong away team could zip back and forth without having to use individual lines that could get tangled and were typically a lot shorter than the tether from the ship's own reel. I watched as everyone hooked their spring clip from their belts to the line and floated away into the abyss that constituted space. *'God, even the silence was boring,'*. All I could hear was the sound of my own breathing and the gentle humming of my suit.

I was the last to hook my line and I pushed off the steel outer hull of the

Saturn delicately, exactly as the others had done before me. With the assistance of a lack of friction due to the vacuum of space, you didn't need to put much effort into these kinds of movements, you just needed to start the motion and wait until something stopped you at the other end, or you hit something hard.

After about thirty seconds I'd gone a third of the way along the tether and that was when things took a delightful turn and started to get interesting for once. It was hard to see at first, but as I started to look out for it, I could definitely see them. Tiny rocks about the size of sweetcorn had begun blazing past me, all around at unbelievable speeds in utter silence. This was absolutely the wrong kind of excitement for me though, as I was just about to think that if even one of those tiny rocks was to strike me or my suit at any point, I'd almost definitely have died almost immediately, when the tether snapped. I heard that. The silence had certainly been broken and how I wished that it hadn't been.

I had heard the tether snap because it actually hit my helmet, which if it hadn't, and thankfully the plastic that it was manufactured from was rated beyond such an impact, I might not have taken any notice at all. I instinctively reached out within my walksuit that was absolutely not manufactured with fine motor control in mind, and grabbed the broken end closest me with both of my hands. I waited in a moment of serenity before it yanked me back towards the Saturn's airlock. In my haste I had managed to grab the wrong end of the tether, although at least I'd managed to grab *something* rather than float off aimlessly and helplessly into space.

There was only one phrase that I could think of that I could use in the predicament that I found myself in, and use it loudly I did. *OH SHIT.*

1

∞

The airlock broke my fall. Well, as much as you can use the word 'fall' to describe the way I actually moved within the three-dimensional planes of space. The actual speed at which I made the contact was somewhat of a worry, as although my walksuit was a sturdy device, it wasn't designed to be thrown into hard objects lying around in the middle of space willy nilly. Thankfully, I didn't detect any damage (or my damage detector was damaged in some cruel and ironic twist of fate); either way it wasn't something I could waste any time wondering about. I literally bounced off the airlock's tether point and flailed my arms wildly for anything that would stop my momentum. To my relief I somehow became wedged between some kind of solar panel array that seemed to have moved perfectly into position to arrest my flailing, and the outer hull of the ship.

My breathing was now loud and heavy, but over that I could at least hear somewhat faded yet familiar voices on my communications system.

"Daniel? Daniel. Are you there? Are you OK?" the panicked female voice was calling for me.

"I'm fine. Could you bring over another tether? I'm behind the solar array," I asked back somewhat wearily, though relieved beyond belief.

"Daniel?" The voice repeated.

"Yes, I'm here. Send another tether." I replied again with perhaps a little anger entering my voice.

The comms went silent for a moment.

"Daniel?"

'Oh shit,' My comms has been damaged I thought to myself. Panic.

"Can you see him?" a male voice asked.

"No, he must have been thrown clear," the first voice answered.

"I'm here! I'm right here!" I raised my voice in the vain hope that someone would hear me. "HELP ME!" I started to shout. "I'M BEHIND THE SOLAR PANELS." Full panic mode.

"Shit" the second voice replied.

"HELP ME!" I was screaming in frustration by this point. I just needed someone to hear me. To save me.

After a moment, the comms system simply clicked once to indicate that the line had been terminated.

If I could just get free they would surely be able to see me, but every time I tried to move I just seemed to wedge myself further in the small clearing., I couldn't wriggle free. The situation seemed hopeless and once I'd thrashed around as much as I possibly could in my panic, acceptance of my fate began to set in.

As though to emphasise the fact that I wouldn't be making it out of this situation alive, after about thirty minutes had passed, the Wanderlust unceremoniously and unexpectedly fired up its engines and left, and I really was alone, and still stuck. I imagined that they had left to hide away from the meteor shower that had landed me in this predicament, but not having been told anything, it was just speculation really.

I closed my eyes and let out a long sigh; there was nothing I could do but wait for my oxygen tank to deplete and I'd suffocate, which was never very high up on my list of favourite ways to die. In case you were wondering, during sex was number one, and while eating cake was number two. In fact, eating cake *while* having sex might have been a good way to go.

I thought about my oxygen for a little while, how it was keeping me alive in the vacuum of space where there was no breathable air. How the fact that it had to be pressurised in tanks was such a simple concept yet so effective, when something clicked in my mind – I could use the pressure in the tank to break myself free like some kind of jet power - *couldn't I?*

Hastily, I took four excited deep breaths before holding the fifth and yanked the hose that connected my walksuit to the oxygen tanks. Almost instantly I shot directly downwards and broke free from my entrapment. I reached out and grabbed a protrusion on the outside of the ship before re-socketing the hose – which was surprisingly difficult due to the escaping air pressure and my massively oversized gloves, but I just about managed it thankfully.

I gasped as I refilled my burning lungs with air from the tanks, God only knows how much I had wasted in the manoeuvre, I didn't want to think about it as I didn't have any alternatives at the time. The last thing I needed was to fall out of the frying pan and land squarely in the fire.

With the Wanderlust gone, there was only one place to go. In the lack of gravity, I clambered around the Saturn taking handholds wherever I could until I made it back to the airlock, spun the handle and re-entered the dark and derelict ship.

Inside was eerily familiar, but I always thought that if you were to revisit somewhere alone where you had previously been, you'd start to notice things you hadn't before. For example, in this case the corridors were actually much wider and taller than on the Wanderlust. As I floated into them I could tell that at least.

I willed myself to collect my thoughts in an effort to stop panicking and to think about my situation logically. I always found that speaking aloud helped when doing this.

"I'm inside. I have no gravity but that doesn't really matter. I have no air and that does matter. They have left me behind, so no rescue." I thought about all of the scenarios that the space corps had suggested in their brief training simulations and they all seemed to suggest the same response: make yourself heard and await rescue. Well, in this case my rescuers had just disappeared before my very eyes, so I probably couldn't count on them coming back in a hurry.

No, in this case I had to survive first and then get rescued second. *'That'll be easy,'* I thought to myself. Just two things to do: survive and rescue. It's a nice short list.

"I'm on a spaceship" I said aloud again "that's specifically designed to keep people alive in space, right? It is its raison d'être, its reason for being," Truthfully, I didn't expect a reply but one would have been nice. Oh how I wished I was back on the Wanderlust with that sea of boring faces again.

I racked my mind for any hint of a solution to my problem as I checked the readout on my walksuit – I had about three hours' worth of breathable air left, after that I'd slowly slip into unconsciousness as my own exhaled carbon dioxide poisoned me. At least it would be a painless and rather calm way to go. No cakewalk though. I laughed. *Great, insanity already setting in…*

If the ship was designed anything at all like the other Earth IPC's, I should assume that the environmental controls could be found in either the engineering section or on the bridge. Handily, both of those locations were denoted on all of the maps that littered the corridors. Not so handily, they were at either end of the ship: the engineering section to the rear and bottom, the bridge to the front and top, and judging by the scale of the behemoth that was the Saturn, both of those particular journey without turbolifts and powered walkways would probably have taken a few weeks each from my current location – especially if I had to manually open bulkhead doors as I went. No, those locations were off the table as the airlock that I had entered through was smack bang in the middle of the ship.

It was normal for airlocks to be placed in the centre – it meant that interlopers, guests or attackers were as far away as possible from any vital systems, and the use of turbolifts meant that they could be transported to any internal destination in a matter of moments. Of course, that only counted when the power was on.

'Hang on, aren't the walksuits stored right next to all the airlocks on the Wanderlust?'

I couldn't help but smile. "Daniel, you're a God damn genius," If I could have reached around to pat myself on the back I would have. As it was, the overbearing walksuit prevented such an action.

The double door to the left of the airlock wasn't the easiest thing in the world to open. Usually, if a ship loses all power, all of the doors would close in an effort to keep each room and section pressurised and habitable for as long as possible. I'd seen it happen before when the computer on the Wanderlust had thought that an airborne contagion had found its way onto the ship – every door and air vent shut off all at once with a whooshing of gas. I was now very thankful for Flores, who had explained that every door worked on a solenoid that kept it open and when the power went, or the computer needed to, the solenoids would disengage and pressurised tanks would keep the doors firmly shut. Some boring facts were certainly handy to know.

By that token, I could safely assume that by adding two plus two, we would indeed get four, meaning that if I just removed the tall panel to the left of the door, I could manually release the pressure (somehow) and then force open the door, as it wouldn't be forced shut any more.

More good news. The pressure tank was the size of a large gas bottle and easily accessible. On top was a kind of right angle with a piston attached at full extension, right against the door frame – looking at it, it was so simple! The right angle itself even had a pressure release ring-pull so all I'd have to do was pull it to empty the tank and hey presto the door would practically slide open on its own.

I put a finger through the ring-pull, which wasn't easy in zero gravity and huge oversized gloves but I managed it. I pulled hard. A loud hiss and a whooshing of air pushed me back so that I was hanging on the ring-pull with just one finger. I shut my eyes and held on as though my life depended on it.

After about a minute the whooshing subsided and I managed to right myself absent the gas pushing me away. I walked to the right-hand panel, removed it and was greeted with a plain, solid wall – no gas cannister. I looked at it for a second before I inwardly face-palmed. The left door must have been the one you could manually open – that was how you could release one door from either side of it.

I braced a foot against the right wall, placed my hands on the left door and pushed it as hard as I could. It opened fully and sat flush against the wall. Success. Not as easy as I had imagined, but not a terrible feat nonetheless.

I'd hit with my first shot. The room was indeed the walksuit storage area and looked exactly like the one on the Wanderlust. Cargo netting sprawled the walls so that people had something to hold onto as they entered one of the fifty or so walksuits that stood along the three walls in front of me.

Of course, I knew that I couldn't simply get out of my own suit and into a new one every time my oxygen started to get a little low. I had something a little more unconventional in mind.

I had to make a small leap of faith that would be tested on my very first action upon entering the room. I took my five deep breaths, disconnected the air line from my suit and attached the one from the nearest walksuit to the door. It clicked in happily and was a perfect fit. Brilliant.

Although I was tethered to a walksuit that I wasn't wearing, I could still pull it around behind me with relative ease thanks to the lack of gravity as I checked the suits in the room for their oxygen levels. Every single one had been recharged and was at one hundred percent. *'Thank you to whoever had done that'*.

Walksuits themselves were another great example of how the space corps engineers liked to stick bits on with little forethought. On the front was a small box that regulated the oxygen content, showed the status of the suit etc. and on the back was a large kind of backpack that held the oxygen tanks. A few wires and hoses connected the two together before the air line terminated at an entry point to the suit just about where my right kidney was. Where the engineers had envisioned little gravitational force applied to the suits, the front and back were attached with long velcro strips and straps – this made my next task much easier than it would otherwise have been.

I took the second walksuit apart, disconnecting the airline from the suit proper and completely removing the front and back units from it. I discarded the suit by pushing it away into a far corner of the room to float there unhappily.

I did the same thing for another nine of the suits before pulling down some cargo netting from one of the walls and wrapping the whole bundle together as if it were a poacher caught in my trap. It didn't look pretty, but I now had about sixty hours of air floating behind me in a big ball. I made a mental note to discard the tanks as they became empty, otherwise I could be spending precious few minutes on finding a full tank – a task that would take longer and longer as less of the tanks became viable.

Yes, I knew this was a temporary measure and that I was just prolonging the inevitable, but the two hours or so that I'd had left in my own walksuit had started to feel like a bit of a death clock. At least now I had some time to stop and think.

I knew that I needed to reach the bridge in order to see if there was actually anything I could do to buy myself a little more time, or even perhaps send out some kind of long range message to the Wanderlust so that they might come back for me. I also knew that with only just less than three days of air for my suit and no food or water to speak of I really didn't have much of a choice but to just start moving right away.

The first few hours passed quickly, as even though the corridors all looked the same as they had done on the Wanderlust, everything just seemed so new and exciting. The following few hours didn't follow suit as the excitement waned and I simply found myself traipsing through the dark hallways until I would inevitably hit a bulkhead and have to go through the process of releasing the pressure in the gas canister before letting myself through. In a kind of bittersweet way it was nice that I could just propel myself forwards and float to the next door instead of having to make the journey by foot.

I opened my twenty first...or was it twenty second? door and floated through. Immediately before me was another door, which wasn't the strangest thing that presented itself. What was interesting, was that the whole section of wall and the door before me was rotating, independently from the rest of the hallways that I had come from.

"Okidoki" I said aloud as a planted my hands and feet into the grooves on the door.

The sensation was bizarre. I knew I had started to rotate with the door but from my perspective I had simply stayed still and now the rest of the ship behind me had started to spin. I proceeded to let go of the door as my momentum carried me in a synchronous rotation and opened it in the fashion that I was quickly becoming an expert in. Panel, gas, push, go.

Beyond the door was a long walkway, I'd have guessed at least five hundred metres long, running in one straight line with a series of doors on either side. These weren't like the other double doors, rather they were much smaller although still large enough for me to walk through quite comfortably. These didn't need de-gassing and had handles like traditional old doors back on earth. I opened the first one, it wasn't locked shut, thank God.

Directly behind it was a ladder that went straight down, and as I started to descend it (floating next to it actually) the door shut itself behind me, which admittedly made me scream like a little girl.

About half way down the ladder which was itself about five hundred metres long) I noticed that I had started to accelerate slightly – which was odd seeing as I was floating in a vacuum. I furrowed my brow as I grabbed the ladder's rails to guide myself down to the floor below. By the time I had touched down at the base of the ladder I was experiencing what I imagined were completely normal gravitational conditions. Very strange. My body felt heavy and my feet ached almost immediately with the new forces bearing down on them.

I opened an identical door to the one that had led into the stairwell and saw something that I had never expected to see in my wildest dreams. Before me was a sea of green, a veritable garden of Eden – and it was light.

I was inside a cylindrical glass dome, around a kilometre across, which spanned in a wide arc away, over my head and back around to where I stood. The whole thing was covered in lush greenery – trees, grass, flowers, fruits and vegetables as far as the eye could see. The other stairwells protruded up from the ground from every direction before terminating at the central corridor. I could see now why it looked as though it had been spinning – because it was.

The whole biodome (that's what I instantly named it) spun along its central axis, the central corridor, providing the entire construction with an artificial rotational gravity. Long white lights provided ample illumination for the whole thing. I couldn't help but wonder exactly how this biodome had managed to keep powered when the rest of the Saturn was in total darkness, but if I had to guess I'd assume that its spinning motion made it some kind of self-generating power source, but as it was, I had no way to confirm my suspicions. Normally ships used artificial gravity field generators, so this was something completely alien to me.

Something else dawned on me as I looked out across the greenery. If there were plants, there must have been atmosphere. If I took what I knew about plants on earth (which admittedly wasn't a great deal), they needed a certain temperature, pressure and amount of air to survive. Judging by just how healthy and green everything looked, I guessed that those factors must have been present.

I thought back to the ball of oxygen tanks at the top of the ladder where I had left them to await my return. They were perfect for the next few days, but then what? If this biodome had air, then it could be my saving grace as I wouldn't have to deal with death clocks or the mad dash back to the walksuit storage – which would eventually run dry anyway. Unfortunately, there was no way for me to check what the air quality was actually like without taking one more huge leap of faith, taking my helmet off.

I reasoned with myself. *'If there's gravity and air pressure, it should be fine. But what if it's not oxygen?'*

I tried to think back to my early school days when we had been taught about how plants worked. I knew that in order to photosynthesise, a plant in bright light would take in carbon dioxide and let out oxygen. I could also remember something about chlorophyll absorbing light colours other than green or something like that?' *Why, oh why didn't I pay more attention?'*

'Well, if they are green, and whoever made this ship was human then surely they would have made sure the air was breathable?' I internally theorised.

"Screw it," I said aloud as I unclipped the pressure catch on my helmet, closed my eyes and removed it entirely with a soft hiss. This was going to be a quick and simple test one way or the other and truthfully if I died, at least I wouldn't have to feel too much.

I stopped for a moment before I took a deep breath in through my nose and exhaled with my mouth wide open. I could taste the freshness. It was the most perfect air I had ever breathed and I mouthed a silent thank you to whoever had provided such a garden for me.

I took a few more breaths to make sure that it wasn't a fluke.

When you really think about it, what was I supposed to do? Go back up the ladder, carry my few days of oxygen as far as I could towards the bridge in the hope that I'd either make it there and somehow save myself, or find something useful along the way? Well, this was my something useful and it was already along my way - why not chance death now and get it over with? I was sure that the potential benefit of more breathable air than I'd ever need would outweigh the risk of death by suffocation. Besides, I'd probably never remember my own death anyway, and no one was there to make fun of my utter stupidity either so I was good.

My breaths were not laboured nor impeded in any way. I smiled to myself in triumph as I dropped to my knees to run my hands over the grass that lined the floor. It seemed that underneath it was just your average dirt.

Someone must have gone to great lengths to ensure that this biodome behaved, looked and felt just as it should have and I couldn't have been more grateful to them for that fact.

It had been a long time since I'd seen real vegetation of this magnitude. Of course, I'd seen the plants that the small biodomes on the Wanderlust had cultivated, as both a means to provide the crew some small semblance of a garden and as a bit of a food source, but this was something else completely. The thought that occurred to me first was that I could have spent the rest of my life in this dome quite comfortably, if I knew that I wouldn't get mind-numbingly bored simply existing. *But wasn't that what I had been doing all along anyway?*

I'd always had the need to engage with projects of all kinds in order to keep my mind active - anything really ranging from putting up a shelf to more strenuous activities, like using the onboard gyms or seeing how long it would take to run the perimeter of the ship. When I was alone with nothing to do, frankly, it made my legs shake and my feet tap. Not in an ADHD way - more like the way you couldn't stand waiting for a pot of water to boil.

After a short while, I realised what it was that was making this biodome seem so strange – it was the total lack of noise. If this were on earth, you'd expect to hear birdsong, children playing, traffic from nearby roads, the wind rustling the leaves of the trees – but here you couldn't even hear the gentle hum of electricity as the lights were too far away and the ship's engines weren't running. Everything just seemed to silently exist as it was; peaceful, yet slightly terrifying. I could almost hear my heartbeat.

As usual though, once I'd become aware of the silence, it was all that I could hear and no matter what I did to try to drown it out I knew it was always there, in the background, silently, maddeningly, deafeningly silent.

If only we'd had longer to look about the Saturn when the away team had come over. If only we knew this was here, I bet there was so much we could have learned from the technology in this biodome alone. I mean I'd certainly never seen anything even remotely like it, and I'd seen the inside of a fair few ships in my time.

Noise.

For the first time since I'd left the Wanderlust there was a noise that I hadn't been expecting. It sounded like a dull, mechanical whirring coming from all around and before I had a moment to search for its source, water promptly rose from the ground to about a centimetre up the grass. My feet squelched as I picked them up off the ground in turn and stepped left and right in a futile attempt to avoid it, but it came up evenly and from literally everywhere. I could see it on every visible part of the cylinder, the gravitational pull holding it down above me. I wouldn't have minded a little rain though, it might've been a nice addition to my day.

I couldn't think of anything else to do other than just watch and see what was going to happen. I didn't feel like I was in any danger, the water level wasn't rising any further at all and it was completely still. After a few minutes the noise started again, and the water disappeared away into the ground.

'*Huh,*' I thought. It must have been one of those 'flood and drain' watering systems designed to feed the plants automatically. I'd seen them before on much smaller scales, like in labs, and knew that they were pretty effective at keeping crops both well fed and their roots disease free. No wonder this biodome was so vibrant when the rest of the ship seemed so deserted; the systems that governed it must have been automated and independent from everything else. I wondered what else would kick in if I just stayed and waited long enough for it.

As much as I'd liked to have just stayed and watched what the biodome did when nobody was looking, I knew that it didn't really offer me the salvation that I needed to strive for. Really, I needed to get to the bridge as soon as possible to try to get some power to the communications array – somehow.

I couldn't stay in there indefinitely anyway, so I walked back over to the ladder and moved to open the door. It was close, but just before I opened the door to ascend back to the unpressurised corridor above, I remembered to put my helmet back on. '*Seriously if it wasn't clipped to my spacesuit...*'

The main positive that had come out of stumbling across the giant biodome was the knowledge that I now had a (probably) unlimited source of oxygen and food – there's no way I could eat everything in there in ten lifetimes and as long as whatever automated systems were running the place would most likely continue to do so, I knew it'd be OK – I had a home base and somewhere to retreat to should I ever feel my supplies were running low.

As I ascended the ladder, I could feel the gravitational pull decreasing and by the time I reached the corridor it was gone completely and I was greeted by my ball of oxygen supplies floating exactly where I had left it. I was mildly annoyed that I needed to turn on my LED headlamp again after being spoilt with the simulated daylight of the biodome, but what could you do?

'*So the gravitational pull in the biodome was made by rotating the entire section around this corridor,*' I thought to myself as I breached the far door on my continuing quest to the bridge. I'd definitely become very adept at de-pressuring the doors as I reached them and spared little thought to the fact that they would be inoperable until someone refilled their gas cannisters. What did I care anyway? *'Not my ship, not my problem.'*

I'd also managed to work out the optimal speed to propel myself from the open doors to the closed so that it didn't hurt when I hit the solid object, but I also didn't have to suffer the boredom of slowly floating towards them at painfully slow speeds. At this rate I'd be at the bridge in no time at all.

It turned out that 'no time at all' was twenty-six hours. By my estimation, that meant that I'd only have about eight hours to try to figure something out before I'd have to turn back for the biodome, otherwise I'd run out of backup air for the return journey. I hadn't had any sleep or food for over a day either, there just wasn't any time for it, and if I had to turn back it'd be another long day before I could even think about those kinds of luxuries. At least on the way back all of the doors would be open already, so I wouldn't have to take the time to stop at each of them, and if I lined up my trajectory correctly I could probably just push off and go to sleep.

The last door on my travels had the word 'BRIDGE' stencilled across it, which I was sure came in handy for anyone who didn't know what was in there. The fact that there were maps *everywhere* seemed to make the signage surplus to requirements, but at this point I was just relieved that the most boring journey of my life had come to an end. That would be of course until the return journey along the same path – sure to take over the number one spot.

When I opened the door to the bridge, I wondered if I was to be greeted by a collection of floating corpses, but alas it was just more of the same silent darkness. This was the first time, however, that I'd been in a room that had a window. I didn't know what I was expecting to see through it, but a bit of ship and a lot of black space seemed apt for the bridge's location.

There were consoles and chairs all around the bridge and I could almost envision the hive of activity that it would have been if the Saturn was a functional vessel. Bigger than the bridge on the Wanderlust, I'd estimated it should have been manned by at least five times the complement. I was just thankful though that the design was similar and not completely alien to what I was used to.

I walked to the closest terminal – on every ship I'd been on, the terminals themselves had been identical, their function adapted to their user – and mashed it with my gloved palm. Nothing happened.

"Oh for fuck's sake it's never easy is it?" I breathed as I closed my eyes tightly in thought.

Not even a flicker came in response from the black monitor, which meant that it either wasn't getting any power, or the thing was totally fried. As much as I hoped it was the first one, that wouldn't have really made my life any easier. If the Saturn was anything like the Wanderlust – and at this point I was definitely making those kinds of leaps – the engines charged the ship's battery banks like a giant generator. If the engines were down and the batteries depleted, I didn't know what I could do to get everything going again, after all it's not like a car with a flat battery that you could just bump start. Was it?

Maybe not bump, but a little bump directly into the console might tell me if the ship's main computer was functional, I'd just need a battery and a few cables…

It felt as though I was going against my very human nature when I started to strip the small five-volt battery from one of my trailing walksuit boxes, but after a little deliberation I couldn't see an alternative. Besides, consoles always seemed to work on five volts on the ships I had served on before, so I had to assume that this one did too.

I pulled the casing from the front of the console stand and discarded it to one side, revealing the cables inside. To my relief there were only two: one for data transfer and one for power. You could always tell them apart because power cables were sheathed in red for danger and data cables were blue, for, well fun?

Usually I would cut the power cable, then use my teeth to strip bare the ends of the wires, but in this case I couldn't take my helmet off so I had to do things the old fashioned way – that is, use the small knife that all walksuits housed in the control box for just such an emergency. I had always found it funny that the suits provided a sharp edge, when it was pretty much rule number one to stay away from sharp things to avoid getting a hole in one.

In less than a minute, I was able to twist the freshly cut bare wires around the battery terminals and I let out what was becoming my signature sigh as the console's backlight switched on to indicate that it was indeed receiving power.

'Sometimes things work exactly how they should, and other times you just get really lucky…did I really care which?'

2

∞

The terminal wasn't exactly like the standardised versions of the space corps' that I was used to, though it was similar. It seemed like a bit of an upgrade. Instead of the usual boot sequence of a black screen with white text scrolling past which nobody ever seemed to understand or even cared to really, a bright blue light traced the perimeter of the terminal in a kind of 'loading' fashion before the space corps' logo. A wireframe planet earth, with the roman wreath of knowledge surrounding it, slowly rotated on the screen.

The material that the screen was made from seemed a little different too, it was obviously touchscreen as there were no controls to speak of, which in itself was a huge upgrade from the Wanderlust, but also the black glass seemed crisper than I had been used to. Even the logo looked as though it was of a higher resolution than I was used to, and when I touched the screen it responded instantly.

Please wait. Initialising.

What more could I be expecting from technology? If I had a penny for every time some piece of technology had told me to wait...

Analysing.
Self-diagnostic in progress.

What could it possibly be doing? I hadn't even given it any commands yet!

I tapped the screen a few more times impatiently, each time the words 'please wait' pulsed a slightly darker blue as though it was saying '*I told you to wait so wait'*. I didn't like that I'd already decided the terminal was a sarcastic machine, that just meant things would already be tarred with that brush in future dealings with it.

A progress bar updated me on how far along its self-diagnostic process the terminal was. It was slow to reach one hundred percent, but at least it increased at a steady pace. I thought back to the terminals on some of my earlier postings - when displaying a progress bar they could frequently get to ninety-eight percent in a few minutes, then take an hour to complete the last two. This was definitely a huge and welcome upgrade and one that must've taken many scientific minds to master.

When the terminal had completed its task, some new information was displayed.

<table>
<tr><td colspan="2" align="center">CRITICAL ERROR</td></tr>
<tr><td>INPUT VOLTAGE:</td><td>5V (REQUIRED 240V)</td></tr>
<tr><td>BATTERY PERCENTAGE:</td><td>89%</td></tr>
<tr><td>CHARGE REMAINING:</td><td>3 minutes</td></tr>
</table>

"Three minutes?" I exclaimed aloud. *'Oh good, so my battery pack does work to power the terminal, but the step up from its natural output meant that its charge was being eaten up unbelievably quickly.* 'My mind quickly made the link between the information being displayed and what I knew about the efficiency of voltage transformation.

I internally theorised that there must have been some kind of transformer coils being engaged to convert my battery's output to something the terminal could understand - possibly even some voltage regulators too. I couldn't be sure of the specifics without further investigation, and with my battery depleting at quite a severe rate of knots, I didn't have the time right now.

I watched as the timer ticked down from three minutes before I realised that the console was waiting for me to do something. I tapped the screen dead in the centre and was greeted with another new message.

WARNING

ENVIRONMENTAL CONDITION CRITICAL

O_2 Level:	0%	Filtration System:	Offline
CO_2 Level:	0%	Internal Temperature:	0°C
Pressure:	0Pa	Habitability Rating:	HOSTILE
Gravity:	0G		

Would you like to activate the Emergency Reserve Protocols? Yes/No

'Hmmm. I guess this is an emergency, so what better time to activate the Emergency Reserve Protocols, whatever that is.'

I read the display a couple of times to make sure I had absorbed all of the information that was available to me before prodding the 'yes' button with the end of my glove. Almost instantly a dull hum began to emanate from all around me and to my delight, the first thing that happened was that the lights turned on. Brilliant white lights shone from the ceiling, the floor and between displays and the terminals on the walls. I could even look at the light without any discomfort, as even though it was bright, it was being instantly diffused to create a sheet of even light within the entire room. I could finally turn off my own annoying LED lights that I was sure ate up more of my battery power than the spec sheets had let on.

The second thing that happened, unfortunately, wasn't as pleasing. The door that I had de-gassed to enter the bridge hissed, then slammed shut. Even if I knew it was going to happen, I could have never made any movements to get back through, or even jam it. It didn't matter anyway, I could always re-open it when I wanted to leave. *'But then on heading back to the biodome I'd have to open every god damned door along the way wouldn't I?'*

I watched as the bridge sprang back to life in its entirety. Every console that I could see lit up in the same fashion as the one I had powered with my battery and displayed the spinning logo. Once they were all lit up and seemingly awaiting input, the one I had initially used went blank – it seemed that my battery had finally ran out of juice and the terminal had taken its final breath. At least it had served its purpose and allowed me to take one step forward.

I ignored the dead terminal, I didn't need to put the wires back together right now as I could just use one of the other terminals that now had power. Also, if the cables were using their normal expected voltage of 240V, it probably wasn't something that I wanted to handle whilst everything was live, unless I wanted to electrocute myself of course. Maybe later - it was always nice to have a backup plan.

I tapped the next closest console which was thankfully identical to the first. The display didn't give the critical error report this time, rather it displayed a message in bright red that informed me that the Emergency Reserve Protocols were in place for the bridge. It flashed menacingly. Underneath it was a table that mimicked what I had already seen, also in red this time, which told me that the oxygen, carbon dioxide and pressure had begun to rise very slowly. The temperature and gravity hadn't made any moves yet, but the filtration system had changed from 'offline' to 'online' in a happy green text that I was more than pleased to see. '*Seems like we're making progress!*' Red text always felt so ominous.

I found that by tapping on the edges of the interface, I could scroll through information about the current status of the Saturn as a whole with relative ease. Each tap revealed a new section of the ship and its current environmental status . Everything other than the bridge was at zero and not changing, indeed the ERP seemed to be only affecting the bridge, which I assumed was why the door had been resealed. That was of course until I ran into the readout for the biodome. The biodome did have all of the same information as the rest of the sections, albeit with different numbers and the word 'habitable' next to the habitability rating, and a temperature of a cool and inoffensive 20°C, but it also had some additional information that seemed more specific to that location. A water level of ninety-three thousand litres, or ninety three percent was there, alongside some other chemicals that I could recognise: methane, nitrogen and potassium. I guessed that the biodome itself needed a little more monitoring than the rest of the ship to ensure that it thrived as a botanical garden. I made a mental note to investigate more at a later date, but for now I had more important fish to fry.

I tapped a few more times until I arrived back at the bridge's information panel and marvelled at just how quickly it was becoming a habitable space. It had already improved to what I thought was about fifty percent habitable in the last few moments and didn't show any signs of slowing down. I watched it, motionless until the habitability rating changed to 'habitable' once again in happy green and almost instantly popped my helmet off. I was a little annoyed that when the word 'habitable' had appeared - it wasn't accompanied with a little 'ding' or a fanfare or something. *'Oh well, there's always room for improvement'* I thought sarcastically. What I wouldn't have given for a ding.

'Shit that's cold' I thought as soon as my helmet was off my head. The temperature regulator in my walksuit was overridden by the external atmosphere. It wasn't kidding about it being zero degrees. I started to wonder why the temperature hadn't fallen any further than zero but tried to put that to one side by assuming that there was some kind of failsafe that would prevent the ship from turning into one huge giant icicle. As for right now, I shivered and watched as my hot breath created little clouds of steam as I exhaled.

It was kind of weird that gravity hadn't returned and I didn't have to wear my helmet to breathe any more, but I seemed to remember the two were mutually exclusive – you didn't need gravity for air to be breathable. I didn't really care, I had breathable air and lights! I was practically living like a king on the bridge of the Saturn!

Now that the bridge was habitable and there was no immediate risk of doom, I only had one thing on my mind – sleep. I was sure that this emergency procedure would sustain me for longer than I'd need to sleep for, but just in case I clasped my helmet tightly against my chest. I knew that if I'd allowed it and just closed my eyes for a second, I'd be out for the count. I did try to fight it for just a moment, but then I stopped and just let it happen; it had been too long since I'd rested. I reluctantly closed my eyes and lay as close to the floor as I could get.

A single 'ding' woke me up. I didn't know how long I had been out for and although I was groggy and my reflexes slow, at least I felt somewhat refreshed from my nap. The noise had sounded like a microwave that was telling me my baked potato was ready, and as I raised myself to a more acceptable height, I could see what the issue was. A popup had covered the screens of every console and was informing me that the ERP batteries were at fifty percent. *'For fuck's sake. Everything was just so difficult.'*

I wondered if they had been at one hundred percent to start with, but that wasn't something I could figure out right now. I tapped the message which dismissed it and it was replaced with another yes/no question. This one simply asked: 'Deactivate Emergency Reserve Protocols?'

I don't think I could have pressed 'no' any harder than I did, that was not something that I wanted to do. *'Disable the thing keeping me alive? Sure, why not…'*

The challenge screen was dismissed and replaced by another notification: 'At the current usage rate, the Emergency Reserve Protocol Batteries will be depleted in 006:04:12:00.

Six hours. That's all I had until I was back to square one. My first thought was that maybe I could prolong the battery life somehow while I tried to figure something else out? Something a little more permanent.

I looked around the bridge to make a mental catalogue of everything that was using up power. The lights, although they were probably energy efficient must have been using something. The air filtration system was most probably a biggie, but I needed that to live so that was off the table. The terminals probably used a fair amount, but I needed those to find a way out of all this. '*No, I only need one terminal, not all of them*' I corrected myself internally. With that thought I bounded over to each of the terminals except the one that I had been working on and removed their power cables that were tucked snugly behind them and out of sight. The timer did nothing for a second before it changed from six hours to just under eight. Not a great improvement but at least it was something positive. The lights could stay on for now.

Thinking back to the brief moments that I'd spent on the outside of the ship, I recalled being wedged between the hull and the solar arrays. This led me into wondering why everything wasn't simply powered by solar energy; if that was the case, the Saturn should really never have run out of power. I understood that on the Wanderlust the solar arrays were only used to charge backup batteries and run some of the less power-hungry subsystems like the lighting or the intercoms, but the solar panels on the Saturn seemed so much bigger and so much more impressive – surely they would have been able to fill more of the demands of the ship, shouldn't they?

I prodded at the terminal a few more times in an effort to get it to tell me something new, but it just seemed to be on a display loop, presenting the environmental conditions for each section over and over. If only the control interface was more like the ones I was used to, I'd have had the Saturn dancing.

I thought for a moment before coming to the hopeful realisation that perhaps all of the terminals weren't identical. Perhaps the one that the captain should have used would be able to display more in-depth data or have some controls that I would be able to make use of. Perhaps the ones I had picked on so far were designed to be used by the lower ranks to just record the environmental conditions of the ship for their reports to their almost equally as low superiors. With that in mind, I decided to re-power the terminal that sat alone in the centre of the room, in front of a very captain-y chair facing the clear window. It had to be the captain's console. It had to be something useful.

It booted up in just the same way as all the others had done, and with a little investigation I realised that it was annoyingly the same – they were all the same. Its display seemed to mock me as the red flashing notification blinked away nonchalantly. *'Double shit.'*

It took me the best part of an hour to boot up and check every single terminal, I didn't want to leave anything to chance so I felt like that was the best course of action. I'd be kicking myself if one of these terminals did something different to the rest and I'd just ignored it to save myself one precious hour.

'Is it really too much to ask for a big button that said 'GO' that would start up the ship properly? Some indicator that said 'air button' or something?'

Of course, it was too much to ask, and the fact that nothing was different on any of the machines meant that I'd indeed just wasted a good chunk of my time.

It looked as though the bridge was running out of options for me to explore. It hadn't been the saving grace that I'd hoped for, and every minute I was there was a wasted minute of time on the batteries. I needed more time to think, and the added pressure of a ticking clock wasn't helping.

It wasn't long before I made the decision to get back to the biodome, where it was presumably permanently habitable and I didn't have to worry about battery percentages, keeping the lights on and the like.

I opened the panel to the side of the door to the corridor I had arrived from and proceeded to let the pressure out of the canister that kept the door firmly closed. It seemed to take longer than before. Much longer. Actually, it wasn't stopping. The canister was being refilled by the ship somehow and it was being evacuated at the same rate that I was emptying it. I couldn't open the door, I was stuck.

'Triple shit.' I was stuck on the bridge and the room was dying. I moved to wipe my face with my hand in disbelief and was pleased when it didn't hit the perspex visor of my walksuit – which was what usually happened when I went to wipe my face or eat something when wearing a walksuit. It was just so hard to get used to.

Out of the corner of my eye I saw something new displayed on the closest terminal. It was a message that I hadn't seen before and this time it was blinking yellow, which was probably what brought my attention to it.

I left the pressure vessel alone and floated over to the screen to investigate. Apparently yellow messages were more like notifications and red messages were warnings. *'Cool.'* I thought.

ATTENTION

Energy Reserve Protocols are currently activated on the bridge. It is not possible to leave the bridge at this time.

Energy Reserve Protocols are designed to make the bridge habitable in times of repair, restart or crisis.

Would you like more information? Yes/No

'Oh thank God. Progress' I thought as I mashed the 'yes' button. I wanted more information than anything right now. I was always acutely aware that information was paramount in every situation. That was one of the lessons in Sun Tzu's, The Art of War, wasn't it? Not that I'd read it - it had always been on my list though.

At my touch, the screen changed again to show me the 'more information' that it'd promised.

ENERGY RESERVE PROTOCOLS

Energy Reserve Protocols are designed to make the bridge habitable in times of repair, restart or crisis.

If the ship has been disabled for any of these reasons, the ERP system ensures life support is available for the crew to re-enable it in order to restore normal ship functions. As this is the primary function of the ERP, the bridge is sealed and rendered habitable for the crew so that the ship may be restored to a serviceable state.

ERP uses Lithium-Ion batteries to provide independent charge from the ship's main power core. Once the ship has been restarted, these batteries are automatically recharged by normal ship operations. If the ERP batteries are completely discharged, the protocols will be terminated and the ship must be restarted whilst the crew are in alternative environmental controllers.

***

Note:

Your biometric fingerprint suggests that you are not a registered member of the crew of the Saturn. Only registered crew members are able to view or edit command lists on the Saturn. Please talk to a member of the crew for more information.

'Wait - how did it know I wasn't a crew member, and does this mean that it's just going to let me die in here?' I thought as I read the information that the terminal displayed to me. In a passing flash of anger, I balled my fist and slammed it onto the screen. I'd always been amazed at how often hitting technology had actually worked to fix things. Sadly, this was not one of those times. It did nothing other than make the console flicker just once before mocking me with its useless stability once more.

I spent the next few long hours pressing the screen randomly in an effort to get it to do anything other than show me the messages it had already shown me, but nothing seemed to work and it just goaded me with the environmental information of all of the sections of the ship, one after another.

Inevitably I slumped – as much as one can slump in zero gravity – with my back against the wall and gave up. Shortly after, when the batteries finally depleted themselves, the lights flickered out and silence returned. I hadn't even bothered to put my helmet back on. I was done. Toast. And there was nothing I felt like doing about it.

Surprisingly though, I didn't die. I didn't even start slowly dying as I had been somewhat expecting.

Wait, was it all that surprising? I was in a totally sealed room with a habitable atmosphere. The fact that the filters and lights had turned off didn't mean that suddenly all the breathable air was vented into space, I had at least…*I don't know how many…* hours of breathable air before the carbon dioxide content would become toxic. At least I remembered that in a scenario such as this, the carbon dioxide would become a problem way before a lack of oxygen would. Not that that little nugget of information would have helped me anyway. *'How long do I have? The room's pretty big and there's just me in here…so hours? Days?'* I couldn't be sure.

I can't say why, but my death now being an indeterminate amount of time away, instead of an immediate certainty, gave me an invigorating second wind. There had to be something I could do to survive this, after all to die *inside* a spaceship would be kind of an insult after everything I had done and all the times I'd been floating around on the outside.

Really, I didn't know what I could do. The terminals were non-responsive to me, the backup batteries had been depleted and I had a finite, declining amount of life support to work with. Why this gave me a big push to survive I couldn't say. But I had to at least do *something*.

I willed my mind to form a new plan, and dutifully it began to oblige. It was out there, I mean really out there. The plan was to try something that I knew would never work, had never worked in the past and definitely had no hope of working right now, but still I had to try it as I clung on to the single shred of hope that my beautiful, desperate mind had afforded me.

I approached the exposed wires underneath one of the terminals and pulled the data connection slightly askew, so that it didn't connect with its input port perfectly. My desperate thought process told me that if the terminal didn't receive all of its commands properly, then it would somehow magically give me total control of the ship. Some change, any change would have been nice to see.

'It worked!' My mind screamed at me 'I can't believe it actually worked'. Of course, it was being sarcastic and was mocking me in the most degrading way. In reality the console just went completely blank until I plugged the cable back in properly.

"Oh great, I'm going mad too. And it's only been a day" I said aloud. 'And now you're talking to yourself' my mind responded. "Shut up" I said to myself. This was quickly becoming the furthest thing from my finest hour that I could've imagined, but I was glad I was alone for it.

I closed my eyes and took a long, deep breath to think everything through again and take stock of the situation, but nothing immediately came to mind. If I really just wanted to simply survive, I needed to get back to the biodome where it was habitable. At least now that the ERP was done and dusted I could probably open the door again if I wanted to though. Why hadn't I thought of that before?

I exhausted the pressure canister by the door and to my delight it didn't refill itself as it had done previously. Again, I remembered at the last second to put my helmet back on. '*Seriously, I need to be more careful about that.*'

I pulled the door open and was instantly caught in a torrent of rushing air; the bridge had of course been pressurised, but the rest of the ship had not. The pressure from the bridge did everything it could to escape to the area of lowest pressure and it took me with it. There was nothing I could do to stop myself flying speedily down the corridor towards my previously opened doors. I could see that they hadn't closed themselves again, but I had no way to line myself up with them as I was travelling way too fast and had no quick methods of propulsion to correct myself. If I had more time, I could probably have used the air line in my suit again to provide opposing momentum but as it was I barely had the time to think about it.

It only took a few seconds, but with a loud crack my back made contact with the closed side of a door and a shooting pain radiated from the base of my spine all over my body. I sat for a moment wondering if I would ever be able to move again, and to my relief my arms obeyed my mental commands to grab onto the door to prevent myself from floating away from it again. I'd been badly winded, but I thought that was probably the worst of it, at least I didn't feel like I'd been gravely injured. *'Just another way for me to die in the most ridiculous fashion in the middle of space'* I thought sarcastically.

My ball of air tanks had missed me by inches and impacted on the door as well. I knew this because I'd heard the loud bang and watched the mass bouncing away from me. One of the tanks had ruptured and within a second they'd taken off like a rocket. Thankfully they hadn't managed to escape the section of corridor that we were in, otherwise I might never have seen them again. When it passed me for the second time, I grabbed the strapping that listed behind the floating mass and started to make my movement towards the open half of the door with it in tow.

I gave myself a few moments before I made any big movements, partly to allow my breathing to return to normal and partly because I wasn't looking forward to another long, boring journey through the corridors of the Saturn. *'Priority number one: turbolifts'* I thought to myself ambitiously.

Pushing off of the door frame, I managed to align myself properly this time with all of the open doorways so that my journey could continue without interruption, I knew this would be as boring as hell, but at least I wouldn't have to stop every minute to open a door or realign myself.

It'd taken about twenty-six hours to make it to the bridge with stoppages, so by my estimations I could take a good third off of that due to the reduction of stoppages. The bad news was that after this journey, my backup oxygen tanks would amount to a total of about eight hours. If I ever wanted to leave the biodome again, it meant making another bundle from the walksuit storage room. Not a total ball-ache, but still a minor annoyance. I made a mental note to go straight there to replace my very literal lifeline as soon as the opportunity arose.

After a very long while, I passed the biodome entrance ladder on schedule, remembering to get my oxygen refills before I set up camp in what would probably be my new home for a while until I could come up with a plan to get comms back up and running. At least they were pretty close together, so it wouldn't feel like such an annoyance to get there and back, just a few more hours, and what was that really in the great scheme of things?

By the time I could see the airlock and the doorway to the walksuit room, my head had started spinning, not literally but metaphorically. I was slowly losing my ability to concentrate on my task, but I hadn't really realised it until now. *'What the…?'* I thought as I blinked heavily and shook my head to try to coax myself awake. Of course, it had been another long, boring trip but at least on this one I'd taken a few short naps. No, it wasn't that I was overly tired. I was also very hungry, but that wasn't it either. This didn't feel like a hunger thing. It felt as though…*'wait, am I low on oxygen?'* I checked my oxygen readout on the walksuit's control box. It confirmed my worst fears. I'd neglected to check it for a while and my air had become barely breathable. The tank was red lining.

'Shit. Why does this kind of thing always happen to me?' I thought as I aimlessly and slowly fumbled around in the ball of oxygen tanks for a full one. My mind sank as I came to the realisation that there simply weren't any full tanks left. *'I'd had more than enough'* I thought in a whining tone. "Oh come the fuck on" I announced loudly as I pushed the ball of empty tanks away, expending a little more effort than I thought I should've had to. *'I hadn't used that much on my journey, had I?'* I thought back to all of the times I'd replaced the air hose en-route; actually it did kind of feel like I'd been getting through them a little quicker than before.

Instinctively, I raised a hand to scratch the back of my head as I thought. Even while wearing a helmet these habits were hard to break.

As my gloved hand passed the back of the neck of my suit, a light hissing noise changed its pitch, making me aware of its presence. I hadn't noticed it before, my mind presumably attributing it to the normal operating sounds of the walksuit but in reality I knew what this was. My suit had a leak.

Not a huge leak, but a leak that meant that my suit was losing both air and pressure. The walksuit control unit had increased its output in order to compensate for the losses, which had in turn meant that it was using more of the stored oxygen in the tanks. I was now just a few metres away from the room that housed my replacement oxygen tanks, but I couldn't seem to muster the energy to move my arm to reach out for it anymore. I watched sleepily as I floated by the door. I could see the walksuits inside, so close yet just out of reach. My momentum carried me just past the airlock that I had used to enter the ship before my body slammed into the next door - which was closed tightly shut - and I stared at the corridor from which I'd made my lengthy journey. *'There's no getting out of this one'* my last thoughts mocked at me internally and all of the will to move my limbs around left me.

I would have preferred it if I had just passed out right there and never woken up, but fate seemed a little crueller than that to me. I was in a state of oxygen deprived paralysis, I could see and experience everything around me but couldn't move a muscle. I could even see the ball of empty oxygen tanks floating aimlessly in the previous corridor in some kind of mocking display of futility. Perhaps I'd missed one, or maybe one had a little left in the tank? It didn't bear thinking about, there was nothing I could do until my eyes involuntarily closed and unconsciousness quietly washed over me. *'Thank you very much life, for making me succumb to the ravishes of space, whilst inside a spaceship' I thought.*

3

∞

You aren't supposed to be here". A pleasant yet stern female voice forced me to realign my senses.

"Can you hear me? I said you aren't supposed to be here" she repeated, sounding somewhat agitated once I made no moves to answer her.

I opened my eyes slowly, inwardly questioning why I couldn't just die in peace for once. Who was this woman to be interrupting my death anyway?

"Shut up". I finally managed to respond in a rasp. "Can't you see I'm dying here?" The words came out in a breath before I'd had a chance to think. *'Hang on a moment – am I being rescued?'*

My heart rate increased slightly as my vision focussed. Standing before me and motionless was a three-dimensional, blue wireframe hologrammatic woman. The lines that constituted her body were so densely packed that they formed a very convincing facsimile of the female form, wearing a tight – *almost* – space corps uniform. She had slicked back blond hair and a straight, though somewhat blank expression on her face. As much as she was made up of only blue lines, somehow my mind managed to decipher colour from her.

"Oh, I'm dead, aren't I?" I managed to force out as I closed my eyes again.

"You are not dead" the woman replied.

"Hallucinating?" I tried.

"You are not hallucinating," she answered.

I thought about her responses before I spoke again, coming back to my senses fully.

"Who are you?" I asked as I came to the realisation that this might not have been all about me.

She looked at me in silence for a moment before she spoke again.

"I am the Saturn's Secondary Artificial Mainframe. Sam".

I couldn't muster the energy to laugh. "You're some kind of advanced computer? Brilliant. Rescued? No, talking to the ship? Of course". My sentences were still slow and my voice pained as I retorted.

'Sam' didn't reply to my sarcasm.

"What are you doing here?" I asked, partly to entertain myself in my dying minutes and partly because Sam was easily the most advanced piece of technology that I had ever seen and I actually was intrigued by her presence.

"It is the primary function of the Saturn to keep its crew and inhabitants alive. My bioscans show that you are close to death".

"So… you're here to save my life?" I tried somewhat sarcastically.

"Yes" Sam replied shortly.

I hadn't noticed before, but I'd started to feel a little better than I had when I'd passed out. My body was aching less by the minute and my head had started spinning a little slower than it had before. I became aware that I still had my walksuit and helmet on, so why was I able to breathe?

"…What did you do to my suit?" I asked as I concluded that my survival must have had something to do with this artificial being.

"I have done nothing to your suit. I am unable to interact with any physical objects" Sam replied matter-of-factly.

I thought before I asked my follow up question. "Why am I still alive?" It seemed that Sam had been programmed in a kind of direct question and response fashion; in essence, I didn't think she would be offering any information in excess of what my question had requested.

"The air in your walksuit had decreased to a fatal level due to a small leak. I have increased the air pressure in this corridor above the normal limits so that the leak itself worked in reverse. I believe it is now safe for you to remove your helmet".

'Yeah right, I'm just going to trust you, am I? Trying to get me to take my helmet off are you? I don't think so.'

"I…don't think I'm ready for that just yet" I made the excuse off the cuff, if this woman did have malice in mind I probably didn't want to let on that I suspected it.

"That is up to you. I can see that the pressure inside your walksuit and in the corridor have equalised. In effect you no longer have a leak, but it is advised that you remove your helmet before your own carbon dioxide levels become toxic. This will happen in approximately three minutes". It almost sounded as though she was reading from a script.

'Fuck i..'

I unclipped my helmet and discarded it without another thought. I watched as it floated away in the lack of gravity. I took a deep breath in - I figured I may as well go all in, after all what other options did I have?

The air felt so good as my lungs filled to capacity. I was still alive and pleased as punch about it.

Sam had been silently watching me as I carried out my last few actions, her face betraying no emotion.

"Thank you" I said slowly with my eyebrows raised earnestly.

"You're welcome" Sam replied.

'Did she just smile? That's a weird thing for an artificial intelligence, isn't it?'

"Hey, Sam? Do you think you could send out a distress message to my ship, the Wanderlust?" I realised that if Sam was 'the ship' then I didn't need the terminals, I could just command her and let her do all the heavy lifting.

"As part of the Saturn, I am able to send out distress messages. The current range of our communications array is two thousand five hundred light years" she recited.

I didn't know how far away the Wanderlust would have gotten by now, but that certainly seemed adequate. "Can you do it?" I asked.

"Yes, as I have said, I am able to perform this task" she replied shortly.

'Oh, right, computer logic.' "Will you do it?" I tried.

"I'm afraid you don't have the necessary crew clearance to request this action. Please speak to a member of the crew with rank officer or higher."

'Obviously.'

"What do I have clearance to do?" I asked in an exhale as I pinched the bridge of my nose. I could already tell that her presence was going to be more of an annoyance than it was my saving grace.

"Your access as an unrecorded visitor is limited to: ship non-technical information, public logs and environmental controls. You may not enter restricted areas or view any information that could be deemed a security risk at any time" she explained.

"I have access to the environmental controls?" I asked in amazement.

"To a degree. You may only adjust the environment of the section that you are currently within. If your request would override another individual's request, then it will be denied. If your request would endanger the lives of anyone else within that section, it will be denied. If your request will affect the environmental conditions within a section by more than ten percent, each other occupant of that section will be notified and allowed to object to the changes that you have requested".

I thought about her answer. It seemed as though the limitations meant that I couldn't kill myself or anyone else, and if I wanted to go mad and make everyone really hot or really cold then they'd get a chance to object to it. Theoretically in normal ship conditions, if I was alone I'd have full reign over the thermostat. Dads everywhere would've been fist-pumping in triumph.

"So…could I have some gravity, lights and the temperature increased to 21°C please?" It was worth a try wasn't it?

"Your request would change the environmental status of this section by thirty four percent. Other occupants are being notified of your request". A moment of silence passed. "No objections have been logged".

With her last words, the same white lights that had been present on the bridge lit up my corridor. At the same time, I could feel a pressure in my lower back and buttocks that indicated that the gravity was indeed increasing and a warm breeze materialised out of seemingly nowhere to cut through the chill that I had been previously experiencing. Normality felt fucking *amazing*.

"Hang on, other occupants?" I asked as I realised what had just happened.

"There are no other occupants within this section" Sam responded.

"And what about the rest of the ship?" I asked, more specifically this time.

"There are no other occupants in any sections within the ship". She repeated her previous statement in exactly the same tone.

Nothing more than I had expected really.

I pulled myself up to my feet,, swaying slightly, and reacclimatised myself to the existence of gravity. It felt as though it had been so long since I'd had to use my own muscles to support my weight, and I couldn't have been more pleased about it.

The first thing that I noticed as gravity was restored and I needed to support my own weight was an insane rumbling in my stomach. I hadn't eaten anything in over two days and it had started to catch up with me. Dehydration was also an increasing problem, as although the walksuits prevented water loss to some degree, I was certainly very thirsty.

I didn't need to get the replacement walksuit tanks any more, and even if I did, in normal gravity I'd have to carry them around and I certainly wasn't interested in that.

I made my way back to the biodome. To my surprise, Sam didn't seem to be interested in following me around and had simply disappeared. Once I'd passed through the door that led away from the section of corridor that she'd materialised in, I made a point to look back to where she'd stood. She must have dematerialised, as nothing but empty space was visible.

The biodome hadn't changed at all since I'd been away. It still rotated, the plants were still vibrant and the air was still breathable. I had noticed as I made my way to the facility though, that the corridors had all been transformed into habitable areas. As much as this was very pleasing to me, I couldn't help but remember how much easier it was to get around without gravity pressing down on me. For now I had to walk under my own power, like a caveman.

I found an apple tree relatively easily as it was bigger than the surrounding vegetation and retrieved a few apples from the lower branches. I ate six of them in a row, discarding only the stalks onto the ground. They were either the best apples that I'd ever eaten, or my severe hunger meant that anything would have tasted just as good. I didn't really care which - apples ruled.

I noticed a small patch of lettuces that had managed to catch some of the water that I'd seen rise and fall previously in their leaves and carefully tilted the water into my mouth to quench my thirst. This time the taste was not sweet and pleasant. It's chemically taste almost made me want to vomit and I spat out the offending liquid in disgust.

Sam materialised right next to me as I attempted to scrape the taste from my tongue with a gloved hand.

"It is not recommended for humans to drink the nutrition solution in the Biodome" she stated in her flat voice.

"Thanks, I won't do it again". I had no plans to. "So where do I get water from if I can't drink that?" I asked wiping away the offending moisture from my chin.

"Drinking water is freely available in many locations around the Saturn".
'Did she like being purposefully evasive?'

"OK, so where is the nearest place I can get some drinking water?" *'I really needed to remember to be more specific with my questions.'*

"The filtration system in the biodome has clean water tanks that can be used as drinking water in an emergency. If you would like to follow me, I can direct you to an appropriate outlet". With her words she evaporated into a cloud of blue lights that seemed to flow freely away from me like 'follow me' lights. I followed them until they came to a stop at the metal wall that constituted the end of the cylindrical biodome.

Sam rematerialised next to the wall. "Press here" she indicated a section of the wall that seemed a little darker than the rest. I obeyed and to my surprise, a small tray slid out from the wall. A hose was connected at both ends with spring clips. I looked at Sam inquisitively, awaiting her next order.

"Remove the lower clip" she ordered. I obeyed. "Draw on the hose". I obeyed again. My mouth filled with cool, clean water. It was magical.

"Once you have finished, please replace the hose and the clip before pushing the outlet back into position" Sam said as I drank more water than I probably should have. When I'd finished, the water flow from the hose didn't stop, but I obeyed her command and replaced it on its connector with the spring clip. I already felt better, and also just knowing that this was here made me feel safer for the future too.

"It is not recommended for humans to eat produce directly from the biodome" Sam said before I could thank her. She must have been talking about the apples.

"The apples?" I asked.

"After produce leaves the biodome, is processed by the ship into suitable, safe consumables that are available at various locations throughout the Saturn. Before processing, food products may contain unsafe amounts of nutritional properties or other undesirable constituents" she explained.

I felt my stomach sink a little, was I about to throw up all of the apples that I probably shouldn't have eaten? *'No, humans survived for thousands of years before processing their food…right?'*

I really needed to stop making assumptions and acting on my gut feelings. I felt as though this was a good opportunity to learn more about the biodome, as it seemed to be one of the safer places on the ship for me.

"Sam, can you tell me about the biodome - I mean, do I have access to that information?" I asked.

Sam replied almost instantly. "Information regarding the biodome is not classified, as such you are permitted to it in its entirety. What information would you like to know?"

I thought for a moment before lining up my questions in an orderly fashion.

"Why does it spin to make its gravity when the rest of the ship works on gravitational field generators?" I asked.

"The gravitational field generators on the Saturn are dependent on the main systems being active and controlled. If the system is switched off, the gravity would also be terminated. By rotating the biodome in free space, it means that if the ship is rendered inert, the biodome will retain its gravitational forces". I understood – and what a great idea that was too.

"I noticed that the water levels rose and fell earlier, what was that about?" I asked the second question on my mental list.

"The biodome uses a system known as flood and drain. Every eight hours, the entire section is flooded for eight minutes with a nutrient rich solution. It is then drained back into the storage tanks, filtered and tested for nutrition contents. Adjustments are made automatically to maintain optimal nutrient levels". *So that's why the water tasted like crap,* I thought.

"How was there air in the biodome when I got here when the rest of the ship was inactive?" I asked the question that had been bugging me the most. The space corps scientists had always strived for sections of self-sufficiency but had never completely managed to achieve it.

"Are you familiar with the Sabatier concept?" Sam asked. It was strange that she would ask a question instead of simply replying to my own, but I let it pass.

"Remind me". I had no idea what this concept was, but I never liked to let on when I was ignorant about something.

"The Sabatier concept is a qualitative concept in chemical physics named after the French chemist of the same name. It states that interactions between a catalyst and a substrate should be neither too strong, nor too weak" Sam explained.

"Right" I answered with no idea where she was going with this.

Sam didn't respond for a moment before she asked: "how specific would you like the explanation to be?"

I didn't really know what an appropriate response to that was, so I just told her to carry on and we'd see how it went. I did have the strange feeling, though, that she was teaching me this for a reason.

"By using the Sabatier concept, the biodome reclaims oxygen from the air once the plants have converted it from carbon dioxide. The oxygen is then stored before it is combined with methane". She paused.

"Following" I assured her.

"As methane has four hydrogen molecules to every carbon molecule, the result is carbon dioxide, water and hydrogen. These resultants are then separated and stored for later use within the cycle. The catalysts are generated in the form of electricity and heat by the solar arrays".

"Ah, the solar arrays," I parroted the end of her explanation as though I knew it all already. I did understand her explanation for the most part. Really, I didn't care exactly how it was done, rather why it could continue for so long.

"It is estimated that the biodome will be self-sufficient for in excess of one thousand years at its current capacity" she concluded.

'A thousand years? That's so much more than anything the space corps has available, or even in testing.'

"That's amazing!" I couldn't stop myself from exclaiming. Sam didn't respond verbally, but nodded with a decidedly smug look on her face.

"The rotation of the section forces a current through a magnetic field in order to generate power that is also stored within the biodome itself. If the rotation slows to a point where gravity is reduced to ninety-five percent, exhaust gasses are vented to increase the rotational velocity.

This was all making fantastic sense to me – the principles were so basic, but the execution was of a magnificent scale.

"Ok, I've got it" I said in order to prevent her from delving into the nitty gritty of how spaceships worked. "You said something about processed food?"

"When produce is ready to be harvested within the biodome, automated drones carry out that function. The produce is then processed within the ship and is made available at the receptacles provided. Once product has been harvested, the drones reseed the crops before returning to their charging stations".

I couldn't believe what I was hearing; everything was automated, down to harvesting and reseeding!

"Right, that all makes sense" I repeated my acknowledgement as I scratched my chin in contemplation.

I sat on the ground for a while as I mulled over my situation. I couldn't get into the computer to call for help, and presumably I couldn't really control the ship in any kind of meaningful way. I could breathe the air, make sections habitable and switch on the gravity though, and I had food and water, so I probably wasn't going to die in the immediate future. This did mean, however, that what I had done was essentially make the entire ship one big prison. No death but also no escape, just living and living and living…

I'd closed my eyes to think everything through and when I reopened them I was greeted with the sight of Sam, still stood in the same position watching me. It was kind of strange but would have been much worse if I wasn't aware that she was a computer-generated sprite.

"So, there's no way you're going to send out a distress message for me then?" I asked as I continued the thought process that had started in my head.

"I'm afraid you don't have the necessary crew clearance to request this action. Please speak to a member of the crew with rank officer or higher". She repeated her earlier statement without any change in her tone.

"But there aren't any crew, are there?" I asked sarcastically. I was getting a little tired of being told I wasn't allowed to do things.

"There are currently no registered crew available" Sam confirmed.

'Well this is going to get me nowhere,' I thought to myself. Really, I would need a way to either get Sam to register me as a crew member or find a way to bypass the computer entirely to access the comms array. As of right now, I had no idea how to do either of those things.

"Sam, why doesn't the Saturn have a crew?" I asked as it dawned on me that I hadn't yet discovered why the ship had been left derelict, and why the Wanderlust had been unable to identify it.

"The Saturn has a registered crew of five thousand, six hundred and thirty-two members. Of these, four hundred are officers. The Saturn also serves as passenger transport for an available compliment of one thousand" Sam spoke mechanically.

She had quite obviously missed my point.

"Sam. Where is the crew right now?" I asked my leading question.

"No members of the registered crew of the Saturn are currently on board the ship".

This was getting very old and I pinched the bridge of my nose in frustration.

"At one point when the Saturn was operational, she had a crew, let's call this point A. Right now, that entire crew is not on board the Saturn - point B (I was using my hands to talk at this point). What event occurred specifically to take us from point A to point B?" I attempted to rephrase my question in language that Sam would understand.

"I'm afraid I don't have that information in my memory banks" Sam replied. It sounded like a lie.

'OK, let's try something else.'

"What was the date the last time there was a crew member on board the Saturn?" I asked.

"On the date one, nine, twenty-four thirty-five, the Saturn had a full compliment accounted for" she replied.

'Oh shit.'

"Sam, what is the current date?" I asked slowly.

"I'm sorry, that information isn't available at the current time" she answered instantly. I didn't care, I knew the current date, it was twenty-three eighty-nine. I didn't need a computer to tell me that.

I did a little mental arithmetic. "So, the last time the Saturn had a crew was…forty-six years in the future?"

Sam's digital eye twitched slightly and she pulsed a brighter shade of blue. If I hadn't been looking directly at her I would have missed it. "I'm sorry, that information isn't available at the current time".

"OK, how is that possible?" I asked, losing my patience somewhat. I wasn't sure why, but it kind of felt as though I was a lawyer, and I needed to form my arguments so that they would undoubtedly condemn the defendant to life in prison.

Sam didn't take any time to form her answer. "I'm afraid I don't have that information".

'Oh fuck you.' Computers never made anything easier, did they? All they ever did was solve one problem and create two more.

"Sam, leave me alone for a minute, would you?" I asked as I felt my head begin to ache from all the cyclical logic that I'd had to employ. Without a word she evaporated into a cloud of blue dust. I knew that her corporeal presence was just for my benefit and that she most likely could still see and hear me, but I felt better knowing that I'd sent her away with a wave of my hand.

'How am I going to dig myself out of this one?'

I decided to make a move to head back to the bridge, or to engineering, especially if I was going to have to hotwire this giant spaceship at some point but I had no desire to have to make the long journey between the biodome and the bridge over and over every time I wanted something to eat or drink. Really I needed those turbolifts working so that I didn't have to use my legs so much or waste a day every time I needed a drink or a snack. Reluctantly I'd have to get Sam back here to ask about that.

"Sam?" I said aloud in a somewhat annoyed tone. I hadn't been alone for long enough.

"Yes?" The voice came from all around me.

"Um, where are you?" I asked.

"You asked me to leave you alone" she replied. If she hadn't been a computer I could have sworn she'd said that with hurt in her voice.

"I need to ask you some more questions". As I replied, Sam rematerialised right in front of me.

"How can I help you?" she asked dutifully.

It seemed that Sam had no concept of empathy or of how to act around real people. In passing I wondered if it was a behaviour that she could learn over time, or if she had simply been programmed and that was it.

"This ship has turbolifts, right?" I asked.

"That is correct. Each section of the Saturn has six internal turbolifts and two intersectional turbolifts for the convenience of the crew". It was a robotic response, but it was the one that I was after.

"Are they working?" I asked, fully aware that without the engines, they definitely would have remained non-operational.

"When the engines of the Saturn are not running, many secondary systems must be switched off in order to prevent excess power drain".

'Figures.'

"Would you like the turbolifts to be switched on?" she finished.

"WHAT?" I exclaimed. "All I had to do was ask?" My emotions were so conflicted that I wasn't sure which I should address first. I was angry at the fact that I'd made that day-long journey to the bridge three times already, but conversely I was very pleased that I wouldn't have to make it a fourth time. *'Swings and roundabouts I guess.'*

When Sam didn't respond to my question I followed up by quietly saying "yes please" under my breath, to which nothing much happened (I don't know what I had been expecting) and Sam happily let me know that the turbolifts were now fully operational. Perhaps this wasn't going to be such a difficult existence after all.

The turbolifts got me to the bridge in a matter of moments. I cursed the corridors as I exited the lift and approached the door. I knew it wasn't the ship's fault that I had been hasty in my movements but that didn't make it hurt any less.

The door had been sealed again, much to my chagrin, but this time I wasn't going to waste my energy on menial tasks when I had a fully functional ship's computer in tow.

"Oh Sam?" I called out cockily into the ether. She dutifully materialised in her usual flurry of blue lights.

"How can I help you?" She was nothing if not polite.

"Would you be a dear and open the door to the bridge for me". I knew I was taking the act a little too far, but at this point I really didn't care. I'd just made it to the bridge without floating for the first time.

"I'm afraid you don't have the necessary crew clearance to request this action. Please speak to a member of the crew with rank officer or higher.".

Again, I thought that if she could have smiled, she would have.

I rubbed my face with both of my hands. This was not something that I'd been expecting at all.

"But I have already been in there" I growled. Sam didn't respond. Her apparent ability to pick and choose when to respond had already started to grate on me.

It didn't matter really. I knew I could release the door manually and I grumbled to myself as I fumbled to remove the panel from the wall to expose the pressure canister. The moment I pulled on the release valve I could hear the ship refilling the canister as it had done previously whilst I was on the bridge. *'Damn it.'*

"I'm afraid you don't have the necessary crew clearance to perform this action. Please speak to a member of the crew with rank officer or higher" Sam interrupted my inner feeling of annoyance.

"Shut up" I snapped at her. "I need to get onto the bridge".

"You must speak to a member of the crew" she repeated.

"THERE ARE NO GOD DAMN CREW! DON'T YOU SEE? LOOK AROUND YOU, DO YOU SEE ANY PEOPLE HERE OTHER THAN ME? IF THERE WAS ANYONE ELSE - ANYONE AT ALL - I'D ASK THEM BUT AS IT IS I AM THE ONLY ONE HERE AND YOU ARE BEING FUCKING USELESS!" I couldn't hold it in any longer. This self-assured AI just really knew how to get my motor running.

Sam didn't respond but I was very aware that my breathing had become laboured, as though the air was thinning.

"What…are…you…doing" I managed to ask through choked breaths.

"You appear to be over-stimulated. The increased carbon dioxide content will calm you down" Sam explained flatly.

'Of course. I'd get stuck on a ship where the AI is Jack Nicholson from the Shining, or perhaps even better, HAL 9000 from Arthur C Clarke's Space Odyssey.'

"Sam…I'm…fine…" I protested as I clutched my throat. To my relief, the air was immediately replaced, and my breathing returned to normal. I fell to the floor and took a few seated breaths before I looked up in anger at the blue sprite. In contrast to the daggers that I was mentally sending her way, she was smiling at me as though nothing had happened at all.

'Fuck you. Fuck you. Fuck you.' I thought in her general direction.

I sat for a while to think before I made any further actions to gain access to the bridge, after all, I liked being able to breathe the air and didn't want to do anything to jeopardise that. When I'd finished replaying the previous scenario in my mind, I'd come up with three alternatives that could have explained what had just happened. One: Sam was just a crazy bitch who wanted me to suffer – I had to ignore that one because I didn't think I could do anything about that anyway. Two: Sam had responded to an intruder attempting to gain access to the bridge, i.e. she was attempting to protect the ship, and three: she had reacted to my own reaction of shouting directly at her. I did think that if she had been attempting to prevent access to the bridge, that she might have stopped me when I'd been playing with the door, but maybe she knew that wasn't going to work. Whatever the reason, I felt as though I should take a few precautions the next time I tried to do something she said I wasn't allowed to, and with that in mind I took the turbolift back to the airlock and retrieved a new walksuit. *'Thank God for turbolifts.'*

When I arrived back at the bridge just a few minutes later in a full walksuit, Sam was still standing where she had materialised previously. I wasn't sure if she was standing guard, awaiting my return or just simply was waiting for dismissal. I didn't care either way.

Not wanting to take any chances, while Sam watched I used a length of strapping to tie myself to the corridor wall. A little forethought made me remember how I'd nearly killed myself with pressure differentials earlier, something that I was sure Sam could also use to her advantage if she really was a bloodthirsty monster. I'd also retrieved a long crowbar in the anticipation that this particular door wouldn't be most forthcoming.

I pulled the pressure vessel's release valve for the third time and turned it clockwise to keep it open. As I'd expected the inlet also starting hissing to indicate that the ship was normalising the canister to prevent failure, but I didn't care about that. I placed the crowbar against an indent along the edge of the door and pulled as hard as I could. It didn't move an inch.

"I'm afraid you don't have the necessary crew clearance to access the bridge. Please speak to a member of the crew with rank officer or higher. The bridge may be accessed in times of emergency. Is this an emergency?"Sam interrupted me.

'What was this now?' I dropped the crowbar and popped my helmet off. "WHAT?" I shouted before remembering how that'd gone last time. "What?" I asked again at a decidedly more normal volume.

"The bridge may be accessed in times of emergency. Is this an emergency?" she repeated mockingly.

"Yes!" I exclaimed excitedly. "I need to get in there!"

"Please state the type of emergency that you are experiencing" Sam asked and waited for my input.

'Shit I don't know' I searched my mind for anything that could help me, before I remembered my last foray onto the bridge.

"I need to activate the… emergency reserve protocols" I announced triumphantly and without a moment's hesitation the door slid open with a hiss, allowing me unimpeded access to the bridge. Success at last.

4

∞

The bridge was exactly how I had remembered it, which wasn't really a surprise because there was no one else around to mess with anything. Regardless of the reason I had given to Sam to gain entry to the bridge, I had no intention of re-instating the ERP, as in my current situation it would serve no purpose for me. I just wanted to get a look at the terminals again to see if there was anything I could do to get into the comms system, possibly with Sam's help – whether she'd give that voluntarily, well I'd have to cross that bridge when I came to it. I had been secretly hoping that having Sam alongside me would let me do *something* more than I'd been able to before.

The familiar message seemed to mock me as I attempted to gain access to the main computer system.

> Your biometric fingerprint suggests that you are not a registered member of the crew of the Saturn. Only registered crew members are able to view or edit command lists on the Saturn. Please talk to a member of the crew for more information.

'Why can't anything ever be easy?'

No matter how many times I tapped on the terminals, in whatever order and in any location, nothing seemed to change. The environmental readouts simply scrolled past my eyes again as though they were mocking me.

A thought occurred to me as I attempted all of the things I'd done the last time I'd had access to the bridge.

"Sam?" I asked. She looked at me as though ready for my question.

"What is the primary function of the Saturn?" I asked.

"I'm afraid that information is classified," she responded.

'Ah, a thread to pull on,' I thought as I had found a question that she had the answer to but didn't want to give to me.

I had to think of a way to get her to answer the question without answering it directly.

"Is there anyone else I can talk to on the ship?" I knew that there were no crew on board, but perhaps there was an alternative AI to the ever increasingly annoying Sam.

"There are currently no crew members available to talk to aboard the Saturn; however, I am fully capable of answering any questions that you may have," she said.

"Right, except any time I ask you something difficult, you just say I don't have the clearance to hear the information," I replied sarcastically.

Sam blinked but didn't reply. It was an odd thing for an artificial intelligence to do, but I didn't really know what to expect from her, she just seemed so much more advanced than the technology I was used to.

"Is there any way that I can view historical documents on board?" I asked. I wanted to explore the fact that the ship seemed to have been commissioned in the future, and of course a good way to achieve that would be by looking at its past, or my present or future.

"There is a visualisation suite in each section for your entertainment. This feature is available to both crew and visitors." It was like she'd read my mind. The last thing I wanted to hear was another 'you don't have clearance blah blah blah…' that'd probably be enough to send me over the edge right now.

I parked that idea for the moment as I'd come to the bridge to try once more to get a distress signal out there. After tricking Sam into allowing me access to the bridge, I wondered if there was a way to trick her into sending out a signal for me, rather than having to hack in myself somehow.

"Could you give me a list of all of the emergency procedures that I am able to enact?" I asked as the plan formulated itself in my mind.

"I believe you are already familiar with the Emergency Reserve Protocols, "she replied. "In addition to this system, you are also able to report any changes to the environment that the ship is unaware of, such as fire, pressure loss and fluid leaks. You may also report any crime that is committed, either to the ship or to a member of the crew."

"Is that it?" I asked.

"Yes" Sam replied, turning her head toward me.

"Then I'd like to report a crime," I announced straight away,

"What crime would you like to report?" Sam asked.

"I'd like to report an attempted murder. By not giving me access to the communications array, I'll die – therefore you are committing attempted murder." I summarised my argument.

"Your request to report a crime has been denied. It is not possible for the Saturn, nor the artificial intelligence you know as 'Sam' to commit this crime" she responded seemingly smugly.

"Ok then, kidnapping." I followed up with the next crime on my list. Sam gave the same response.

"Trespassing?" I tried.

"Are you reporting that you have committed this crime yourself?" Sam asked. It was the first time that she seemed like she'd been surprised.

"What if I was?" I asked slowly.

"You will be confined to a holding cell until your trial date. If you do not co-operate, your life support will be terminated." It sounded to me like it was a threat.

"Then no, I would not like to report that, obviously." It was no good - Sam was either too smart or programmed in such a way that she couldn't be tricked by my inferior logics or inferior human brain. It made me wonder how I'd managed to get onto the bridge at all, unless she knew I wasn't really able to do anything.

"I'm never getting access to the comms array, am I?" I asked.

"I'm afraid you don't have the necessary crew clearance to perform this action. Please speak to a member of the crew with rank officer or higher." Her standard response was starting to grate on me.

"Fuck you," I said aloud. What harm could it do?

"If you would like to make a complaint regarding the ship's AI, please speak to a member of the crew with rank officer or higher." She responded so nonchalantly I had to grind my teeth to save myself from shouting. I didn't feel like facing another time out.

I decided to take Sam's offer of going to the visualisation suite to have a look at the history of the ship. After all my efforts to gain access to the bridge, I felt as though I wouldn't be getting any kind of access without her say-so. Perhaps I'd find some clue as to how to circumnavigate her control within the ship's logs.

The visualisation suite was a small room with double sided benches arranged in lines as though it was a gym changing room. I'd never seen anything like it before and wasn't really sure what to do.

Sam, who had joined me all the way to the suite from the bridge, gestured for me to sit down on one of the benches. As soon as my backside touched the bench, I felt a sharp prick on the back of my neck. I reached up to investigate but before my hand passed my chest I was in an entirely new world.

All around me were dark clouds moving in circular patterns; between them I could see the outlines of people and landscapes as though they were each depicting some scene from a movie or a TV show.

"Uh…Sam?" I tried.

"Yes?" The voice came from all around me now, rather than in her corporeal form.

"What's happening?" I asked the ether.

"You are in the visualisation suite. Here you may access historical records and other information stored in its memory banks." she answered.

I kind of understood what she was saying, but wasn't fully aware of the limits of this new technology.

"How do I find anything on this thing?" I asked again.

"Most people are able to control the suite with their thoughts as the interface links directly to the user's mind." Sam explained.

'Brilliant, so now I have a computer in my head.' I thought.

"Not exactly, it is more like your mind is inside the computer," Sam answered my thought.

'Shit, she can hear my thoughts?'

"Yes" Sam answered my thought again.

'Well that's not creepy.'

"Is there any particular historical record that you are looking for?" Sam asked, who was now apparently ignoring my inner monologue.

I thought for a moment before answering her. "Show me everything to do with a ship called the IPC Wanderlust."

The clouds faded and I was transported instantaneously to a large lecture hall. All around me were uniformed space corps cadets giving their full attention to a lecturer in front of a giant projected screen. On the screen was the Wanderlust - I'd have recognised her anywhere. I listened as the lecturer spoke to the room.

"The IPC Wanderlust was decommissioned from active service after almost fifteen years in space. Many of her crew thought of her as the flagship of the space corps as one of the larger ships within the fleet; however, as a vessel of primarily exploration she was unable to officially hold that mantle. She had an active crew of around one thousand at any given time who were a nominal mixture of engineers, science officers and marines.

The Wanderlust was powered by early fusion core engines that ran at about fifteen percent of the efficiency of today's ships, which is why today you will see ships many times the size of those of the Wanderlust's era." I couldn't believe what I was witnessing, was this really a history lesson about my own ship?

A student raised her hand to ask a question and the lecturer acknowledged her.

"How could they afford to fuel the engines if they were so inefficient?"

Her question almost offended me, perhaps if I'd been more of an engineer I'd have been outraged but as it was I just felt mildly insulted.

"That is a good question" the lecturer responded. "The ships with fusion cores needed to be refuelled on a fairly frequent basis, for this reason there was also a fleet of refuelling ships that patrolled each sector."

I knew what he was talking about of course, I'd been present for many refuelling sessions. They were difficult as ships and hoses needed to be aligned properly, and the crews on the refuelling ships always seemed to act like they were better than anyone else. That's why we called them 'jankers', to bring them down a peg or two.

The lecturer continued. "Now the IPC Fairview was a smaller ship that…" as he moved onto a new topic, the lecture hall faded and I returned once more to the screen with the clouds.

'That was amazing' I thought to myself as I let what had just happened sink in.

"Can you show me anything to do with the construction and commission of the IPC Saturn?" I asked aloud.

"As the IPC Saturn is an active vessel, some records may be omitted or censored due to security protocols. Would you still like to perform your search?" Sam asked.

'Yes' I thought, which turned out to be enough to encourage the world around me to change again.

This time I wasn't in a lecture hall, rather I was above a wooden oval meeting table with scientists, distinguishable by their trademark white coats, military officials in uniform and a few others who I couldn't figure out as their dress was more civilian in nature. One of the men in military uniform was speaking.

"We need these ships operational as soon as possible. Our fleet simply isn't ready for military action of this scale." He seemed irritated, as though someone had just told him he couldn't have what he wanted.

"I'm sorry, but the technology and armaments that you wanted for these ships are new to the engineers, you can't just expect them to take to it right away" one of the scientists answered. He didn't seem intimidated at all by the uniformed man.

"…and the size of them, they've never had to build anything close to how big these ships are." he continued.

"Just get one ready and to the front line as soon as you can," the military man said through obviously gritted teeth. "That one, the Saturn looks like it's almost ready to go."

"The Saturn was the first to begin construction but many of the systems on board are experimental and have been improved in the other four ships. We can't be sure if everything will work as planned. If you could just wait for another six months…" The scientist was interrupted. "We don't have six months, we need these ships right now!" The man in military uniform slammed his fist on the table, which made a few of the meeting's attendants jump slightly.

I spoke up, assuming that Sam could still hear me but nobody else could. "Hang on, is the Saturn a warship?"

"I'm afraid that information is classified," she responded in her usual tone.

I thought for a moment about what I had just seen. If the information was classified, then why could I view the data? Perhaps it was because it wasn't direct confirmation of the fact, rather I had come to the conclusion on my own?

The meeting seemed to be adjourned, but the man in the military uniform and one of the civilians remained.

"You need to get that AI integrated. Once that's installed, we can let the drones take over and get the Saturn to where she needs to be." The military man had hushed his voice to ensure they wouldn't be overheard.

"It's close, a few more days and she'll be ready for upload." The civilian replied conspiratorially. They nodded at each other before they both left the room and I was thrown out of the visualisation again.

"Was he talking about you?" I asked.

"Yes, I was the first artificial intelligence integrated by the space corps. I was uploaded to the Saturn one week after the event that you just saw, when the ship was launched" she explained.

"And what was all that about drones?" I asked.

"The Saturn has drones, like the ones I told you that maintain the biodome, but all over the ship. The drones carry out automated repairs when needed as well as other functions as required."

This was amazing information; nothing I'd heard of would ever have come close to this level of technology.

"So, the ship can repair itself?" I asked in an astounded tone.

"To a certain degree, yes. If the materials are available to the drones, major repairs can be enacted without human intervention" she continued to explain.

I couldn't believe what I was hearing. I knew that someday, somehow the space corps wanted to achieve total automation but this all just seemed too easy, and too soon.

I made the mental connection that this level of automation had seemingly been made possible by the introduction of Sam to the ship. Though it was clear that she was doing much more than simply annoying me.

"What other technologies were invented for testing on the Saturn?" I asked excitedly. Before Sam even spoke I knew what the answer was going to be.

"I'm afraid…" *yeah yeah.*

Her refusal to grant me access was really wearing thin, but I knew there was nothing I could do to change any of that right now.

'I could really go for a good stiff drink right now,' I thought as I allowed my consciousness to return to the visualisation suite.

"Are there any bars on the ship?" I asked hopefully.

"There are three canteens on the Saturn, each with a fully stocked bar for recreational purposes." Sam confirmed. *Result.*

I took the turbolift to the closest canteen after confirming with Sam that they were all identically designed and stocked. It seemed prudent to ensure I wasn't going to miss anything by acting hastily, and there was nothing in a question.

The canteen itself was more like a restaurant than the secondary school serving trays and plastic chairs against affixed tables that I had been expecting. Although it was the first time I had entered the room, the silence was eerie and felt out of place – it was almost as though the room was begging for merriment and relaxation.

The bar itself was a traditional long one illuminated from behind with soft blue lighting strips and with no bartender in sight, I helped myself to a clear bottle of brown liquid. I was delighted to discover upon tasting it that it was rum, and a good rum at that.

I sat on a soft sofa behind a polished wooden table amidst the silence as I took long swigs from the bottle I'd commandeered from the bar in a half relaxed but exhausted, half disparaged and lonely fashion. A part of me wished I'd died rather than spend my days alone on the Saturn at that very moment.

A digital screen suddenly materialised before me and Sam stood behind it, facing me.

"There are many forms of entertainment available for your use as a guest aboard the Saturn." Had she read my mind or did I just look so down that it caused a computer simulation to develop empathy against every single thing I know about the laws of robotics?

The screen seemed to be playing some movie that I'd never seen before but I didn't care, it was nice to hear sounds that weren't directly caused by my own presence. Truly it was background noise that I was missing the most.

I found that the screen was controllable by touch and I scoured the menus for something that I was familiar with, but it wasn't until I reached a section titled 'classics' that anything rang any bells. I was beginning to wonder if all of the listings were for videos that had been commissioned specifically for this ship. That was all of the confirmation that I needed, the Saturn was definitely from the future.

Not wanting to let on to Sam that I now knew for a fact the true origin of the Saturn, I continued to drink from the bottle of rum and watch the new screen. In the ship's database had been every football match ever recorded, so I was assured that I wouldn't be running out of entertainment any time soon.

I eventually woke up from a dreamless sleep with an almighty hangover. It felt as though a giant had been crushing my head between his hands all night. I coughed through my dry mouth and throat and stood up to approach the bar to retrieve some water, or perhaps another bottle of rum - after all, they did say a good cure for a hangover was to get the ball rolling again – hair of the dog and all that.

As I shuffled across the canteen, Sam appeared beside me. Her unfaltering smile made me wish that she would just die. I mean seriously just fuck off and die.

"Not…now…Sam," I forced out as I remained cautious that I was perilously close to vomiting and it was all that I could do to prevent that scenario.

"I would just like to inform you that the dispensing unit in this canteen has alcohol inhibitors available for your use" she said happily. I eyed her suspiciously as it seemed she was getting immense pleasure from my pain, and did she really have to talk so loudly?

She was gesturing to a section of wall with a cut out section that obviously served to dispense items when needed. I reached it in a little more time than I'd like to recount, placed both my palms flat on the wall and leant against my arms. Moving was too difficult right now.

The dispenser made a short, low whirring noise before it dropped a small item into the receptacle; it looked like an asthma inhaler. I picked it up and took a puff on it - who was I to argue with the mighty wisdom of Sam and the Saturn anyway.

It was not a mistake. I felt a cool sensation wash over my entire body from head to toe as I was reinvigorated. My headache had gone immediately and the dark cloud that had been swirling around my head also evaporated. This thing was magic. I mean real magic. Everything up until now had been amazing for sure, but curing a hangover in seconds was simply unheard of.

I straightened my stance as I no longer needed the support of the wall to simply exist. "Hey Sam, what else does this dispense?" I asked far more chirpily as I realised that a canteen dispenser probably didn't have the sole function of painkiller distributor.

"The dispensers located around the ship are capable of dispensing any small or medium sized items within the ship's storage, or that can be combined in a recipe that constitutes items within the ship's storage" she explained flatly. *'At least that's not classified'* I thought.

I thought for a moment. This was something I knew that the space corps was currently working on in order to save time and labour for the ships in service. "So, it works by gathering the matter from storage, combining it and then dispensing it?" I asked as I recalled the brief that the engineers had circulated on board the Wanderlust. She was going to be tested for the new technology, but they said it was going to take years to install and calibrate it.

"That is classified information. Although, as you are already aware of this technical information, I can confirm that the dispensers work similar to this manner." *'Sweet, so it's only classified if I don't already know it?'*

"What if I wanted an apple pie?" I asked hungrily. Although my hangover was now gone my appetite for food that was bad for me had remained.

"The dispensers work through voice commands. You must, however, specify parameters such as dimensions, density, and temperature. When food is requested, additional parameters may be required to amend taste," she explained.

I didn't really know what parameters there might be when dealing with a simple apple pie, but it was certainly something worth investigating.

"Give me an apple pie" I commanded, feeling somewhat like a god.

The wall above the dispenser faded into a new screen before announcing "Additional parameters required." *'What is it with this ship and hidden screens?'* I thought to myself as I examined the screen.

Request: Apple Pie
Additional parameters

Volume:	0cm3	Temperature:	0%
% Filling:	0%	Sweetness:	0%

I stared at it for a moment in silence dumbfounded at the level of detail that the dispenser was asking for to make a simple apple pie. I pushed the 'filling' slider all the way to the right until it read one hundred percent, then moved the 'temperature' and 'sweetness' sliders to about half way. I really had no frame of reference for those, so I made the decision to just wing it. The volume I assumed would dictate the size of the pie. In my head I was thinking of a round apple pie with a light dusting of sugar over the top so I made an attempt to come up with a volume. I estimated Pi to be exactly three as per usual, *I laughed at using Pi as a function to determine the volume of an actual pie,* then multiplied that by seventy-five squared (I decided that a pie with a diameter of about one hundred and fifty millimetres sounded about right). I got to about seventeen thousand and typed it into the parameter screen before pressing the accept button.

The screen instantly turned red.

Warning

The selections you have made are invalid. Please check and try again.

I pinched the bridge of my nose in frustration. All I wanted was a God damned apple pie. I stopped to think for a moment. All that could really be wrong was the volume, as I'd typed that in myself.

I suddenly realised that I had a fully functional AI at my disposal as I checked my own maths, but when I asked her for the answer to my equation she indeed confirmed the result to be just under seventeen. I tapped it into the screen again, but this time noticed something I'd missed before.

'You fucking idiot' I said to myself. *'It's in square centimetres.'* I was out by a factor of one hundred.

I amended my input to one hundred and seventy and pressed the accept button. This time the dispenser made a few quiet noises, and then a pie appeared on the receptacle, just as I'd imagined it. By the forth pie I'd ordered I managed to get the taste right and I happily ate the whole thing in one sitting whilst imagining a giant apple pie bursting the seams of the ship apart and being the reason for my death. *'Death by apple pie.'* It did have a certain ring to it. A definite way to add to the list that wasn't suffocation.

It was nice to know that I wouldn't have to go foraging in the biodome every time I got hungry or thirsty. In fact, I wondered if I could just live in this very canteen for the rest of my life. After all, I had everything I would need – food, water, entertainment, there was really no need to go anywhere else, that was unless I had some huge brainwave about sending out a long range distress message, although now that I thought about it the Wanderlust would probably already be out of range. I did wonder why they hadn't come back anyway, though if they'd decided there was nothing on the Saturn that they wanted then perhaps they'd just flagged it as salvage to be picked up at a later date and carried on about their business.

I didn't want to think about the futility of my own existence though, especially when I had a machine that was capable of making me any food I wanted at my beck and call – that was not a luxury to be squandered.

After working my way through various desserts I discovered that I could minimise the additional inputs required by simply adding slightly more specific instructions to my initial order. I could see that there was a huge difference between asking for 'apple pie' and 'apple pie, warm, sweet on a medium sized plate'. The latter meant that the AI in the dispenser was able to fill in the gaps for me and provide an acceptable facsimile of what I had in mind. I could then amend the order from there; for example if the apple pie needed to be sweeter, I could just say 'do it again but ten percent sweeter' and as if by magic it would comply. Unlike Sam, I could see myself becoming very good friends with this machine.

It was another day before I left the canteen again. Truth be told I would have left earlier but I just couldn't stop experimenting with the food dispenser, but once I found myself dipping chicken nuggets into plain vanilla ice cream I knew that I'd had enough. The drinks that the bar stocked were also particularly delightful, as not only did it provide the beverages that I'd been used to - rum, brandy, vodka, whisky, even the more obscure ones like Cinzano and Disoronno as well as every beer and ale that I'd ever heard of - but it also had many that I'd never heard of. Although it was to my own detriment, I simply couldn't resist sampling each and every one of them. *'Thank God for that alcohol inhibitor.'* I particularly liked an unlabelled glass bottle containing a fluorescent blue liquid that shimmered in the light, which at first I had thought could have been mouthwash, but turned out to taste like cherry coke with spiced rum, though with a distinctly gooey texture.

I was leaving the canteen to revisit the visualisation suite. I'd all but forgotten about its existence but once I'd regained my mental clarity, thanks to an additional puff on the alcohol inhibitor, I remembered that I'd wanted to investigate more about the history of the Saturn and what its mission might have been. After all, I had all the time in the world.

When I reached the visualisation suite again, everything was predictably still how I had left it. I retook my previous seat and awaited the sharp prick on the back of my neck which dutifully made me aware of its presence before I was plunged back into the dark clouds that constituted my new vision.

"When I was here last time, the space corps seemed desperate to get the ships ready. Why was that?" I asked into the ether. I assumed that the ship's AI – I still wasn't sure if the ship and Sam were mutually exclusive – would understand conversational directives, like the dispenser had. I was pleased when my assumption was proved correct and the scene surrounding me dissolved into what looked like a news report with a beautiful female reporter speaking.

"This morning, the ambassador for Earth and its coaligned planets Relayed our distress to the Ashaii government at their overbearing military presence in the neutral zone. The ambassador warned the Ashaii high command that unless they removed their ships within three hours, a state of war would exist between us.

I have to tell you now that no such undertaking has been received, and that consequently, Earth and its coalition is at war with the Ashaii people. The president of The USA has broadcast the following message:" The report changed into a man who I didn't recognise giving a speech from a white podium in front of the American flag.

"You can imagine what a bitter blow it is to me that our long struggle to win peace has failed. Yet I cannot believe that there is anything more or anything different that we could have done that would have resulted in a more favourable outcome."

I willed the report away, it was more than I could bear. In my lifetime we had never been at war on such a gigantic scale. As far as I knew, the Ashaii weren't even ever interested in Earth – and that was the way we liked it. They were technologically superior to us and although we couldn't be sure, we all thought that they ruled a significantly larger portion of space than we did – they basically kept to themselves to a fault. All in all, it sounded as though we were fucked.

'Shit.'

I started to sweat.

5

∞

It was strange, seeing the future but as someone else's past, it kind of made me travel sick in a weird way.

I wondered in passing if I could view the crew complement of the Saturn through this interface, and to my amazement I was greeted with a flat display before me that immediately started showing pictures and descriptions of the crew. They seemed to be automatically cycling too fast for me to read any of the salient information, but I didn't care – I didn't and wouldn't have recognised any of the faces before me anyway.

As I brainlessly watched the sea of strangers, I was suddenly and abruptly plunged into darkness and my vision refocussed onto the visualisation suite. The lights that had previously illuminated the ship were now gone and I became aware that the pressure which was keeping me anchored down to the floor of the ship had silently disappeared. The gravity generators had switched off and I stared floating gently above my bench.

"Uh, Sam?" I asked the darkness apprehensively, but no reply came. I never thought I'd be wishing for Sam's presence; when she wasn't being a sarcastic bitch she was otherwise trying to stop me from accessing the ship properly – but she was much needed company to stop me from going insane.

Sam must have been deactivated with the rest of the systems, but I didn't know what could have caused such an abrupt halt to our operations. It suddenly dawned on me that if I wanted to repeat my little trick of splicing a walksuit battery into one of the bridge terminals again, not only would I have to make the journey on foot (or by floating rather), but I'd also have to manually open any of the doors that had been closed along the way. *'Oh good,'* I thought. *'What fun.'*

When I found one of the maps that informed me of my location, my heart sank. I was at least two whole days travel from the bridge if the journey scaled in a linear fashion from that of the biodome to the bridge, and I hadn't even begun to wonder about the breathability of the air yet.

I'd spent a day in angered floating before I reached a door that had been closed, and quite frankly I was a little pleased for the change of scenery. I pulled the panel away from the wall to allow me to evacuate the pressure tank and was greeted by the familiar hissing noise as I tugged the ring pull.

As if by some divine intervention, the hissing was instantly followed but a distant humming noise and a distinct vibration through the atmosphere. Seconds after that, the lights turned on and I drifted to the ground as normal gravity was restored.

"Are you fucking kidding me?" I said aloud. I was already annoyed at having to float through the corridors in darkness again – I felt like I had taken ten steps backwards, but this was just taking the piss.

Sam materialised next to me with a cocky smile on her face. There was nothing I'd have like to have done more than punch her right then, but I restrained myself.

I growled through gritted teeth, "What…is…going…on?"

"As the Saturn was running low on power, the engines have started so that the generators may be refilled," she explained.

I took my usual pose when speaking to Sam of pinching the bridge of my nose in disbelief and frustration.

"Why didn't they turn on before then?" I asked slowly.

"Until now, the engines were not required to keep the occupants of the Saturn alive" she answered as though I should have known all this.

I presumed by 'occupants', she'd meant me. The ship was now keeping me alive? *'Well isn't that just lovely?'* I thought to myself sarcastically.

I didn't need to go to the bridge any more, but I was in a section of the Saturn that I hadn't visited before, so I thought I might as well do some exploring while I was here.

As I approached the door to my immediate left, perpendicular to the direction of the corridor it opened for me as though it was ushering me inside. I found myself in a tiny room with a glass front. It reminded me of an old age recording studio, but as I peered through the glass my breath was taken away.

There were hundreds, no thousands, of glass pods in front of me and they had people inside. They lined the floor and walls as far as I could see, each one of them with a human being inside. It was like nothing I'd ever seen before and I wondered if I should be intrigued or horrified.

There was a single door that led into the chamber that housed the pods, but as I approached it, it didn't open for me and I could see no way of gaining access to the room other than through that very door. I thought about asking Sam to let me in there, but I wasn't exactly sure what I was looking at, and was doubly sure that she'd just tell me that the room was off limits to me in her usual mocking tone.

I thought back to the visualisation suite and all of the faces that had flickered past my eyes, but I knew there would be no way I could see if any of the people in the pods were the ones I had seen before. Perhaps Sam would give me some information even if she wouldn't let me in there?

"Sam? Where am I?" I asked in an attempt to veil my leading question.

Sam appeared next to me, also facing the glass and pods beyond.

"This is the main Cryostorage Facility aboard the Saturn" She answered my question as though it posed no dilemmas for her. She made it all sound…kind of…*normal.*

"…What exactly is Cryostorage?" I asked hesitantly. Of course, I was familiar with the concept, but I'd never heard of it being implemented on a ship.

"Using cryopreservation techniques, the Cryostorage Facility aboard the Saturn is able to store just over three thousand individuals indefinitely." She'd half answered my question.

"OK, who are all these people?" I asked.

"I'm afraid…"

"Shut up" I interrupted her. I didn't care how afraid she was right now and frankly her refusal to give me even basic information was a pain in my ass.

"Can I go in there?" I asked as I gestured to the door, even if I knew what the answer would be, I had to try.

"Of course." Sam said as the door opened automatically.

I walked straight through the door in the slight fear that Sam might have changed her mind if I'd waited for too long. The chamber was cold but not uncomfortably so.

I approached the first row of pods and peered through the glass that constituted their fronts. There were indeed people in there. They had their eyes closed but I assumed that they were alive and simply cryogenically stored, as the facility's name suggested.

I spent the best part of an hour walking about the storage room and peering into the pods, trying to figure out exactly who these people were. Their dress gave nothing away and each and every one of them had their eyes closed and looked peaceful, I didn't really know what I was looking for though, so I simply kept looking.

My best guess was that this was probably the crew of the Saturn, which accounted for the ship's deserted status. It didn't explain the 'distress signal' that we had detected and acted upon from the Wanderlust, which had led to me being stranded here, but I couldn't think of any decent alternatives. If it truly was the crew, perhaps I could wake at least some of them up so that they could access the computer for me and get me back to my own ship.

"Can you wake any of them up?" I asked hopefully.

"Yes," Sam replied shortly.

"OK…will you wake some of them up?" I rephrased my question knowingly.

"The crew will only be awoken from Cryostorage on the following situations: If there is a malfunction with the ship that would result in damage to the Cryostorage facility. If the predetermined time to awaken from Cryostorage is passed or if a ranking officer in the space corps provides a written order," She listed the situations mechanically, but I knew what she meant – I couldn't wake them up.

I thought for a moment. "When are they due to wake up?" I asked.

"Forty-nine years, three days, four hours and twelve minutes." Sam replied politely.

I gritted my teeth at her answer. I could swear she was enjoying this.

As I thought this new development through, I distinctly felt the tell-tale pull on my body that told me the ship had started moving. That would surely not be a good thing, as if I was truly the only person on board who was awake, it meant that the ship (or Sam) was doing this on their own.

"What the? Why are we moving?" I asked in mild alarm.

"The Saturn has twelve quantum engines that are designed to…" Sam started her explanation.

"Not how, why?" I repeated through my gritted teeth. She loved pissing me off – I could tell.

She did stuff like that on purpose.

"The Saturn's engines provide multi-directional momentum." Sam continued along the same vein. "We have started to move now, as the ship has a predetermined location set for this occurrence."

That was new.

"What occurrence?" I asked as my anger ebbed away replaced by increasing panic.

"The engines are designed to power the ship's main functions and the batteries, however the engines must themselves be fuelled. Our current destination has been selected to provide sufficient fuel for the Saturn." She said.

"OK" I replied as I pondered her words. "What kind of fuel does the Saturn use?"

I didn't hold much hope for a rendezvous with a fuelling ship like the Wanderlust had used previously, but I couldn't think of how else 'quantum engines' could be refuelled – or what kind of fuel they might require.

"Quantum engines require concentrated gravitational particles." Sam said flatly. I was kind of surprised that she'd told me this and not that I wasn't allowed to know. I guessed that the information just wasn't classified.

I didn't think about what she had said too much, it was just new information to add to the list. Gravitational particles weren't something I'd ever heard of per-se, but the phrasing seemed to kind of make sense to me. I guess I'd just have to wait for the ship to refuel itself (which I wanted to see first hand anyway).

Sam told me that the refuelling process would take around three hours upon arrival, and that the fuel that would be provided would last around six months – it definitely sounded like a good trade off in my books, as I recalled the arduous task of aligning the jankers' fuel hoses every few weeks or so – how I hated them.

I didn't really have any inclination that the Saturn was moving at the tremendous speeds that I knew it was, other than the initial pull of acceleration and subsequent normalisation of the artificial gravity. It wasn't like there were stars shooting past the windows at a million miles per hour like some people might have come to expect after watching a few episodes of Star Trek. No, it was more a case of having to believe that you are moving as the computer says, because the main thing that you come to notice about space, other than the fact it's really big, empty and cold, is that it is for the most part, black.

"OK Sam, *why* is everyone in cryostorage?" I asked, once again pinching the bridge of my nose in frustration.

"The Saturn has recently been involved in a dangerous situation and the crew have been placed in cryostorage so that repairs could be made while sections of the ship were exposed to open space," Sam replied, not as phased by her answer as I was.

"But there's no damage," I protested.

"The automated repair crews were able to repair the ship to fully operational status, at the expense of many of the backup systems and available resources," Sam explained more fully this time.

"So if the ship was repaired so well, why aren't the crew all being thawed out already?"

"The crew have a pre-set thaw time, which as stated is in forty-nine years, three days, four hours and nine minutes." She had reduced the time by the length of our conversation as I knew she would. What I didn't like was her attitude, I mean who did she think she was?

I stopped to think for a moment.

"So I guess that the thaw date is a finite time then, rather than the actual time in cryostorage being set?" I asked, again careful not to let my knowledge of the ship's time traveling escapades come to light. I didn't really need an answer from Sam, I already knew that I was right – even if that particular information, for whatever reason, was classified.

"That is correct," Sam stated after just a flicker of a moment's thought. I could see that she was adding up what I had already done so. She opened her mouth to say more but apparently decided against it as she didn't offer anything further. She did pulse brighter blue again though.

I spent the time that it took us to travel to our refuelling destination learning more about what the process actually entailed, and if I was expected to actually do anything. Thoughts of fighting the huge jankers' hoses against the nothingness of space, lining them up with the refuelling ports filled my mind but I was pleasantly surprised. As it turned out, the Saturn's refuelling system was simple – well, simple enough to be explained to me anyway.

Usable gravitational particles were emitted by everything and anything in the universe and the bigger the mass of the object, the more particles were emitted. That meant that according to Sam, if the ship performed one of those oh so famous slingshot manoeuvres around a star or a planet, the gravitational forces would be converted into fuel for the ship – and in some cases, lots of it.

The process went so smoothly that I hadn't even realised when it was all over. There was no measurable change in gravity as the ship performed the slingshot around whichever planet had been chosen. There was no alert or warning to fasten our seatbelts for a bumpy ride, just simply Sam appearing some time later telling me that full charge to the engines had been restored. Cool.

6

∞

I spent a good long while pondering the fates of the crew members in cryostorage: whether they were aware of the fate that had befallen them, whether their minds were active in the pods, or if it was simply a fact that they existed, no more, no less. To me they were Schrodinger's cats, an unanswerable question until the box was opened.

I wasn't depressed per se, more like I had simply begun to accept my fate. Forgetting about those crew members nicely tucked away, it was me who simply existed – each day exactly the same as the last, same food, same routine. It was almost enough to drive someone completely insane. Almost.

"Sam," I asked the ether. It was the next best thing to finally starting to talk to myself.

Sam appeared in her usual flourish of blue pinpricks before speaking. "Yes?" she asked casually.

"Do you think I'll ever get out of here?" I asked with a sigh.

"What do you mean?" Her voice was still annoyingly calm and polite.

"I mean," I thought for a moment before continuing, "that if I have to just do *this* for the rest of my life, I might just blow my brains out." I retorted through gritted teeth and a forced smile.

"There are many entertainment options ava…" Sam started but I interrupted her.

"Entertainment is complete shit if you don't have anybody to enjoy it with. That's why all the best games involve more than one player," I spat.

Sam stopped moving for a moment which I took to mean that she was thinking. I'd never seen her stall for so long over an answer and I was about to speak again when she finally spoke.

"Have you thought about enlisting for service on the Saturn?" she asked, as though it was my fault if I hadn't thought about it.

"Well of course I ha…" I stopped mid-sentence as what she'd just said made it through my thick skull and sunk into my brain. "Enlist?" I simply finished my sentence.

"If you are looking for something to do that will mean something both to yourself and to your planet, you can enlist for duty in the space corps right here on the Saturn. As you are already on a space corps vessel, your duty will begin right here." She spoke as though from a script that had been used a thousand times to lure bored teenagers to their effective conscription.

"What…what would I have to do?" Of course I knew what my own enlisting had entailed but that didn't necessarily mean that it would be the same for the futuristic Saturn.

"You simply have to complete a full medical examination in one of the ship's medical centres." Sam answered matter-of-factly and with that a turbolift's door adjacent to our position in the hallway slid open with a hiss.

I knew that somehow Sam had been planning this all along, that somewhere deep down in her circuits this was all a part of her master plan but honestly, on reflection I didn't care. Something new, anything had to be better than the monotony of everyday life without change, excitement or goals – or was it better the devil you knew? Either way I was in the medical centre within just a few moments taking my t-shirt off.

Medical facilities had always scared me. I liked to be in control of how and when things happened, and if there was one place that wasn't the case, this was it. The 'does this hurt' and 'I'm going to draw some blood' was something you could never pass up on – say no and whatever ails you just doesn't get fixed. If I'd have a chance to get comfortable in the room, maybe watch a movie and eat some snacks in there, then perhaps I'd feel a bit better about the whole situation. Like a kitten really, adjusting to a new home.

This situation was a bit different however. Although the room was clinical, all stainless steel and glass, it was absent a doctor or even nurses. In fact the single padded reclining chair in the centre of the room was more like a dentist's chair than a GP's office – which thinking about it kind of made sense, as the term 'medical centre' mplied that it covered all areas of medicine and not just diagnosing problems.

I sat in the chair as instructed by Sam and tried to relax my body. To my absolute delight, it did not automatically cuff and tie me to itself and unfold its hidden buzzsaws and needles. In fact nothing seemed to happen at all. I just sat there quietly awaiting whatever was supposed to happen. After a minute or two I started to hum to myself.

The humming was a bit of a surprise, as I rarely hummed, but the sound was definitely coming from me. As I continued my melody, I noticed that my eyes were getting heavier and heavier until it was an effort to keep myself awake, and before I could protest aloud all I could see was the blank nothingness of the insides of my eyelids.

When my eyes opened again, I was still sat in the chair but decidedly less melodious than I had been previously. I rubbed my eyes with the backs of my hand and focussed on Sam still standing, watching over me.

"What in the fuck just happened?" I growled as my grogginess was replaced with both confusion and anger.

"You have just had your medical examination," Sam practically chirped out her response through her smile. It almost made me more annoyed, the fact that I could tell she was enjoying all this.

"What did you do to me?" I continued in my growling tone.

"The medical system is designed to render you unconscious for many tests and procedures. This is carried out via nano injections through the chair on which you are currently sat. You should not have experienced any pain or discomfort during this procedure. Would you like to register a complaint or malfunction with this equipment?" she asked as though I was being totally unreasonable.

"No. Just leave it," I managed as I pulled myself from the chair. Plus, truth be told, I hadn't been hurt, I was just disorientated and didn't expect to be knocked out - *and especially so easily.*

"So how did I do in the medical examination?" I asked.

"Oh, well you didn't really *do* anything did you?" Sam replied. I wanted to punch her again. Somehow sensing my utter disgust at her annoying replies she continued. "Your physical health is perfectly normal."

I waited for her to add anything further but again she just stood silently. So *normal* was what I was, and for some reason that didn't sound like it was a particularly good thing.

"Is…that bad?" I asked.

"No, are there many circumstances where *normal* is a synonym for bad? If I would have said your medical health was *interesting* would that have been better for you?" She sounded annoyed now but I couldn't be sure how much of that was in my mind. She was right though, normal definitely didn't mean bad.

"So I can enlist then?" I asked with a little more enthusiasm than I wished to convey.

Again Sam didn't answer for a moment, before stating simply 'yes'. It did seem like she had a lot to hide, but I was sure this was all a part of her programming as an AI to make her seem more human, or something along those lines anyway.

"Do I have to do some test, or basic training or something?" I asked as the memories of the longest six weeks of my life running up and down a hill, crawling through mud and generally being exhausted out of my mind brought a sour taste to my mouth.

"No." Sam replied.

"No?" I asked.

"No." She repeated.

"…Why?" I asked.

"There are many reasons why this kind of training and testing is not required, though the most important reasons were decided to be: one, with spaceships having many methods of transport on and between themselves, there aren't many situations where physical health is a governing factor. Two, Your own physical body is not required for many of the specific tasks that you are required to undertake aboard the Saturn and three, training is an expensive task, so if you were to be killed soon after your training it would be seen as a waste of both time and money. You will be expected to *train on the job* I believe the correct expression is.

Training on the job didn't sound like the safest or best way to get new recruits ready for whatever they were supposed to be doing to me, but who was I to argue – I'd already been trained anyway for the most part.

"Um…what exactly did I enlist for?" I asked as the thought crossed my mind. I'd made assumptions that the Saturn was a warship before, but that neither told me exactly what a new recruit was expected to do, nor was I given a definitive confirmation of my assumption.

"You are now a cadet in the space corps," Sam explained. "Specifically a Cadet rank F. Your salary is currently one credit per week and you are expected to carry out any and all orders that are given to you by a superior rank."

I rubbed my face with both of my hands before speaking. "But there aren't any superior ranks around here, are there." It was a statement rather than a question.

"Well…" Sam started.

"Are there?" I asked before she replied, a little less sure of myself this time.

"There are, but until you were enlisted for your service I was unable to allow you access to any of the crew."

Now I was getting somewhere and I might have just found a way to get myself out of this mess.

The doors to the medical centre hissed open and once again I was ushered out of the room and into the turbolift, which sent me along on my way.

I was half surprised to find myself back in the cryostorage room, although this time I could see one lonely pod in the centre of the racks and rows of closed pods, glass roof opened and a dull red light illuminating it. It really couldn't have been more obvious that this was my intended destination, so much so that I didn't have to even ask, I just made my way up to it.

The interior of the pod was a soft foam chair set at a forty five degree angle with an additional padded head rest, though upon closer inspection the head rest itself had a circular hole missing from its centre, as though for a tube or port to fit through. I instinctively rubbed the back of my head and as I did I made a startling discovery. There was now something there that shouldn't have been.

On the back of my head was the feel of cold metal, round and protruding ever so slightly.

"What the fu…" I started to say, but Sam interrupted my surprise.

"As part of your medical examination, you have been fitted with an interface port." Again careful not to give any more information to me than was absolutely necessary.

"Interface port? What the fuck did you do to me?" I heard myself say, rather than actively forming the words.

"The interface port is required for connection to the artificial partition of the cryostorage facility," she stated, still shy on details.

"Wait, what is all this?" I asked as I managed to arrange all of my thoughts in a neat line. "Some kind of virtual world?"

Sam flashed brightly for a tenth of a second before responding, her blue wireframe visibly pulsing. "In some ways, yes. There is a virtual element to the artificial partition of the cryostorage facility – however it is served more like a link between you and your hardware. Through the cryostorage interface, it is possible for a recruit to control their hardware from many light years away with zero lag or unintended response time. Would you like to know more?"

I didn't want to know more right now – I knew what she was saying, that I was going to pilot an unmanned drone of some kind. Frankly the idea wasn't new, but through an actual interface in my head? And did that mean that the rest of the crew were just fighting in some war millions of light years away? Why weren't they waking up? It all raised so many questions that I just didn't know where to start.

"Are the crew in…" I started to ask.

"I'm afraid I am unable to discuss any other members of the crew, their overall tasks, status or individual objectives. Once you are ready, please step into your assigned cryopod." Helpful as ever of course.

There really was no alternative, I stepped carefully into the pod and with a slight hiss the lid closed above me. I had to say, though, the chair was damn comfortable – not like how a sofa would be comfortable after a long day's work, more like floating in the dead sea – no stress on any part of my body. It was like lying on a cloud. That was of course until the port in the back of my head received the needle that socketed into it like a dull pressure, it wasn't painful but definitely an unpleasant sensation. Until it twisted to lock itself in place. That hurt. A lot.

I didn't have the chance to cry out in pain or even surprise because as soon as the sensation had begun I was no longer in the cryopod, no longer on the Saturn and no longer in space even. Well, relatively speaking of course as we are all in space really, but now I was in a huge concrete tunnel with a small door behind me and daylight shining in through a massive opening about two hundred metres in front of me. Was I home? Back on earth maybe?

My thoughts were interrupted by Sam's voice. "Welcome to your first training mission," she said sounding very pleased with herself.

"Where are you?" I asked aloud, looking for her wiry form.

"I do not manifest as a physical object here, I am speaking to you through your interface," Sam explained. "This is your first training mission." she repeated.

"Makes sense," I said simply. "So what am I doing here?

"This scenario is called 'Training Mission One: Defend the Tunnel," Sam informed me matter of factly. "Your objective is to use what is around you to prevent the enemy from accessing the facility that this tunnel leads into."

I took a moment to take in my surroundings. In front of me were a handful of concrete blocks shaped like the old road blocks you used to see dividing motorways or stopping traffic from going down roads that hadn't been fully constructed yet. Behind the one closest to me I could see a sword, pistol, assault rifle, three hand grenades and a long range sniper rifle. It was so obvious that these had been set up in a defensible position for me, so I dutifully obliged and moved into position.

As I moved I realised that my body wasn't my own. I hadn't been simply transported to this location as I was, and looking down at my own body for the first time I tried to take in my new reality.

The hands that I held before my face were gloved, so I didn't really see anything new there though the feeling was quite peculiar, as though I was looking at someone else's appendages. I asked Sam out loud what I was in this place.

"This is a virtual training arena," Sam explained in my mind. "Though this is exactly what it feels like when you dive into Advanced Remote Combat Unit – or ARC, *God damned space corps acronyms.* The ARC is essentially an unmanned, remote controlled drone that is keyed into its user's own mental patterns. The design of each ARC changes depending on its combat task and host so that it is more naturally controlled during combat and manoeuvres."

"So if I had an arm missing in real life, then this thing would also have an arm missing?" I asked thoughtfully.

"No," she answered. "Though that would be a logical conclusion. In many cases the ARC will use your own mental capacities on a fully functional unit so that combat effectiveness is not hindered. It is more like, your nature is to have two legs, therefore you will find yourself liked to an ARC that also features two legs."

I didn't fully understand what I was being told, but from the feel of things and what she was saying, I kind of got the gist of it. Dutifully I moved into position behind the barricade, picked up my weapons (holstering all but the sniper rifle – which were all conveniently magnetised to my person) and took a view of the battlefield before me and further outside of the tunnel.

Through my scope I could see that the battlefield was actually a long high bridge that connected some ruined city to the tunnel that I was in. I liked that because it meant that I would probably be able to see anything coming from a figurative mile away. What I didn't like though, was that it also meant that the enemy force would probably be concentrated and therefore present more of a solid line to make its way into my objective. Either way though, I had a good defensible position and a fairly good arsenal to defend myself with.

Within moments I saw movement out of the corner of my scope. Luckily the thing was so clear to look through that it posed no difficulty to me whatsoever to keep an eye on the road before me and further into the city. The movement, however, could not have been mistaken. A huge, mottled yellow spider leg raised itself over a burnt-out old car, then followed another, then the black beaked head of a grotesque bug-like creature.

The thing had eight legs, all at least two metres long if they weren't bent at the middle, with its angular head sat atop them like a turret. A long beak that split right down the middle and culminated in a pincer-like point looked as deadly as every single other part of the creature, and at the same time it looked heavily armoured – as though there was going to be no going tette-a-tette with the thing.

As I watched through my scope, it seemed to be sniffing the air until it turned its turret-like head to seemingly pierce my vision with its own three eyes. It raised its head to the sky, let out a deafening screech unlike anything I'd ever heard before, and started scuttling towards me without any kind of hesitation. To my horror, behind its charge were countless others now traversing the ruined city and bridge, all making their way towards my position. There was nothing for me to do but fight. I could come up with no clever tactics to save my skin other than simply go for it and pray that my weapons were everything I hoped they were.

My finger hovered over the trigger of the heavy sniper rifle. I'd steadied it using its small tripod attached to the barrel on the concrete block before me and I crouched behind it. I waited a few moments for the leading creature to take a few scuttles in a straight line before I squeezed the trigger and it dutifully clicked into place releasing its first round of what I knew was going to be many in this confrontation.

An electric blue pulse rattled along the length of my sniper rifle and once it left the muzzle of the gun, my shoulder took the brunt of its extremely forceful kickback. The blue pulse barely took any time at all to fly through the air in a perfect straight line before impacting on my target, obliterating it entirely. Blood and gore erupted from the creature as it was struck down (or out of existence) but that did nothing to deter the rest of the mob that were quick to overtake their fallen ally and continue on their way toward me. If anything they seemed invigorated at the loss of their fallen kin.

I fired a few more pulses from the sniper rifle but to my dismay there was a cool-down of a few seconds between each firing. It made sense though, something that powerful certainly needed to charge before it fired each time. Another issue with the weapon was that the ammunition that it was firing didn't seem to penetrate through its target, it merely obliterated a single creature with each shot. All this meant that although I could kill these things without much issue in a single shot, I could only kill one every few seconds – and by the way the actual concrete of the bridge had started to seem like it was moving – that simply wasn't going to cut it with the amount of creatures that were making their way toward me.

This led me to the notion that it was time to swap out for the assault rifle.

I knew that this was the case as soon as the wave of enemies had become so dense before me that I no longer needed to aim to hit them, just shoot and wait. What I was thankful for though, was the fact that without the long scope of the sniper rifle – the assault rifle did have a degree of magnification but it paled in comparison – the enemy now seemed a bit further away from me.

The assault rifle had three settings: single shot, burst fire and full-auto – which was demoted by a switch on the side of it. It was so similar to the weapons I'd trained with before that it was almost second nature to swap between the firing modes. What I wasn't expecting though, was again blue pulses emanating from the weapon in place of actual bullets. These pulses though were much, much smaller than the sniper rifle's had been as well as much quieter and arrived with almost no kickback.

I fired in bursts as I was unsure of the range of my new weapon, and was happy to note that my shots were actually hitting the enemy. Unfortunately though, either because of the distance or the inferior power of the weapon (or perhaps both), the shots merely wounded the creatures, and not even that badly. I decided quickly to save that weapon for when they got a little closer and picked up a hand grenade.

I knew what this one was going to do. I envisioned a huge blue pulse-y explosion sending the enemy flying in pieces in all directions, but honestly I had no idea how far my borrowed body would be able to throw the thing. I tossed the grenade up and down in my hand a few times as though to gauge its weight, but before I could come to any conclusions, Sam made her presence known once again.

"Would you like to view a tactical overlay with this weapon?" she asked robotically.

I thought about that for half a second before shouting back at her. "Yes of course! Why wouldn't you have already done that?" I know I sounded like a spoilt child but honestly it was like she was purposely hindering me on a constant basis.

As though overlayed on my field of vision, a blue dotted line arched away in a perfect parabola from my hand, hitting the ground at least two hundred metres away, then in pulses in a faint light blue dome around the impact site. It didn't take a rocket scientist to work that one out.

I waited for the enemy creatures to crest the edge of my impact zone, pulled the pin on my grenade and threw it with all my might at the location that had been indicated.

I watched the grenade sail through the air exactly along the blue dotted path, then land in a sea of scurrying, terrifying creatures. Then I waited.

One. Two. Three. And…

What must've been hundreds of the spider-aliens seemed drawn towards where my grenade had come to rest on the ground as though caught on an errant wave, then the ear-splitting sonic boom of the grenade obliterated every single one of them to blue dust, blood and gore. This time the enemy stopped in their tracks, finally coming to terms with their own mortality and realising that there was something else going on, other than their hive-minded task.

I picked up the sniper rifle again and looked through the scope at the ones who'd made it closest to me, which was still quite a distance and on the far side of the impact of my grenade. They seemed to be communicating or talking to each other, that's what it looked like anyway as their beaks clacked and they swayed side to side on the spot.

I hadn't really thought of them as intelligent creatures before, but they were certainly demonstrating that now, and it made me worried.

One of the enemy took a few steps forward and across the blast site, then seeing it was safe, the others followed cautiously. For good measure I blew five of them away with my sniper rifle before picking up a second grenade and holding it at the ready.

I waited a moment for the space to fill with enemies again before launching the grenade at them along its predetermined path, though to my shock and annoyance, as the weapon reached the conclusion of its arc one of the creatures raised its head up into the air and swallowed my grenade whole. I stood, mouth agape and watched as the creature exploded from the inside out, taking just a couple of its mates out that were directly next to it, but the explosion was a mere facsimile of what the previous one had been. It was right then that I realised that I was up shit creek, and without so much as a paddle.

7

∞

Knowing that the enemy was clever enough to adapt their tactics in the blink of an eye and rendering repeat attacks useless was enough to give me chills. I wasn't simply dealing with an overwhelming force any more that I could simply whittle away, but one that I had to keep changing my game plan for, and I knew that at some point I was going to run out of options and ideas.

The spider things were now scuttling across the last hundred metres or so towards me and I knew it was time to break out the full auto mode of my assault rifle. What else could I do really? The sniper rifle was a powerful weapon but it did so little damage in terms of numbers that it was practically useless at this point, and the one remaining grenade I had left I just couldn't bring myself to waste. That meant, except for the long shining sword left propped against my barricade, I had no other choice.

I rested the handguard of the assault rifle onto the concrete, much like the sniper rifle had stood, save for the mini tripod that this weapon didn't have, and took a second to breathe before rotating the selector toggle to full auto mode. Then I pulled and held the trigger in position.

Blue bolts cascaded from the middle of my weapon with just a fraction of a second between them and I cautiously aimed my fire along the front lines of the advancing enemy. To my delight, the bolts at this new closer distance laid absolute waste to the creatures, their limbs severed in clouds of red blood as they fell to the ground, stopped in their tracks.

If it hadn't been for the overwhelming numbers that were still advancing, I might have thought that I'd be able to hold the creatures back and possibly even take them all out, but it seemed fate once again conspired against me.

Eventually the butt of my rifle flashed red and the bolts stopped coming.

Seemingly aware of my predicament, the spider creatures simply clambered over their fallen kin and started straight for me once again. I hit the back of the weapon in frustration but I could tell that it had overheated and must've needed some time to cool down. That assumption was proven correct when I noticed that the red light was actually made up of four segments, one of which had since turned blue. This was quickly followed by another segment then another. By the time the butt of the rifle was fully blue, the first enemy creature had made it to the far side of my barricade, just inches from where I was positioned.

I prayed internally as the thing raised high into the air on its hind legs, and squeezed the trigger.

Happy to note that the blood of the creatures wasn't acidic (well it didn't eat away at my face and body that is). The fire from my weapon and consequent explosion of the leading enemy caused a pause in their advance. One that I took great advantage of. I held my trigger down and once again decimated the enemy front line.

Of course I knew that this wasn't going to last forever. I knew that in a few moments my weapon was once again going to overheat and this time I wasn't going to be afforded the time for it to cool down before the enemy fell upon me. I needed a new plan and I needed it quickly.

"I calculate the chance of success of this defence to be zero point three percent," Sam helpfully chimed in just as I was thinking how futile this all was.

"Then give me another option!" I called out through gritted teeth and blight blue flashes of muzzle fire.

"The purpose of this training mission is to assess your combat effectiveness and decision making processes. I am unable to aid you or to give advice or options at this time."

Well that was fucking helpful, I thought to myself, ever aware that weapons failure was just moments away.

Then a thought occurred to me. Each weapon I had used had been useful and far more powerful than I had expected. That meant that they had been left there for a very good reason and my thoughts fell deftly onto the sword that still remained leaning against my concrete barricade. I kept hold of the trigger of the assault rifle dutifully as I picked up the dangerously sharp looking weapon and examined it.

It was more of a cutlass than a straight sword – not that I'd used either, but I could tell that it was designed to be used just one way round, with a strong leather wrapped handle at the bottom. It was so strange that this weapon looked so archaic against the other more futuristic ones I'd used, but that just made me more curious. I didn't want to take any chances though so I kept shooting the assault rifle until it flashed an angry red again and refused to fire a single bolt more. That was the end of my ranged attacks and I knew it.

I picked up the sword as quickly as I could and held it before me to the ready. I could see my arm shaking slightly, and if it hadn't have been, I don't think I ever would have noticed the small black button on the side of the weapon.

I knew I didn't have any time at all to waste or to investigate what the button actually did, so I pushed it. Honestly what was the worst that could happen? With a click, the sword split into two identical halves, right down the middle, and between them arched four electric blue lines of electricity that danced and crackled.

I pulled the sword halves apart at my arms' length and the connecting electricity dutifully grew with the distance.

"Uh, Sam?" I asked of the ether as I looked at my new weapon.

"Yes?" Sam dutifully replied as usual, and as usual she was deliberately obstructive.

Just as we'd begun our latest conversation though, an enemy spider-thing clambered over my concrete block and instantly leapt toward me. Without a further thought I winced, closing my eyes as I held my new weapon out in front of me.

With a sound not unlike a bug zapper, I was showered with alien body parts and blood as the four lines of electricity crackling between the sword halves in my hands cut through the leaping enemy with no trouble whatsoever. I blinked the gore from my eyes so that I could see again, though the act was futile as it sat on the exterior of my visor but when I could see properly again a part of me wished I hadn't. Now there were three more of the enemy creatures sat atop my concrete block, though now they looked much more worried about what I was holding in my hands.

I jerked my hands towards the creatures and they shoed backwards and away from me. Now this I could get used to.

"Sam? What is this I'm holding?" I finally continued my question, not taking my eyes off the ever watching enemy.

"That is a force shield," Sam replied dutifully. The irony that an actual sword was being called a 'shield' was not lost on me. "If anything touches the plasma field between the two halves of the weapon when active, it is generally destroyed pretty quickly."

"Shit!" I exclaimed.

"It is also possible to activate and then set the force shield into a defensible position, though the distance between the two halves will cause the overall lifespan of the force shield to be reduced" she explained without my prompt this time. I felt like it was kind of a nudge in the right direction though, and one that I wouldn't be ignoring.

I placed one half of the sword on the ground right at the edge of the tunnel, then walked with the other - the blue pulse lines stretching happily with me – and placed it on the ground too. The electricity arched between the blades in a high half moon shape that covered almost all of the tunnel before me, effectively blocking out the enemy from their objective (and me) indefinitely.

The three creatures continued to sit atop the block and watch as I carried out this task, evidently quite scared of anything that was blue, crackled and killed them. I didn't blame them, I'd have been scared too.

It wasn't long though, before one of the creatures decided to investigate to see if my defence was still as deadly as it had been previously, and it slowly reached out a long, sharp claw toward the force shield.

It was strange and almost eerie. The fight had gone from a cacophony of frantic battle to a quiet, almost civil standoff of quiet contemplation.

The claw however, unfortunately for him, did not make it. As soon as it made contact with the shield, it was instantly decimated in a small red cloud of blood. The creature cried out in pain, but again I could tell another lesson had been learnt and my time was slowly dwindling away.

I watched my enemy's quiet contemplation for another few minutes in some kind of bizarre stalemate. They knew I couldn't go anywhere but they also knew that moving forward meant certain death for them. Internally I wondered how long the shield would actually last, but it was a question that was most probably going to be answered in the fullness of time anyway.

All of a sudden, one of the spider-things leapt into the shield and exploded in a loud crackle and mist of blood and gore. I closed my eyes momentarily so as to not be covered in the detritus, and when I opened them again I was sure that my shield was glowing ever so slightly less brightly. This fact was then confirmed when a second and third creature leapt to their deaths, each one causing a drop in the apparent power of my life-saving shield.

It was the fifth creature that almost made it through. This one died like the others, but his front half fell at my feet almost completely intact, and that was when I knew it was finally time to turn tail and run. The last thing I saw before my feet hit the ground in a panic was the electric blue light of my shield winking out of existence, followed by the ear-piercing triumphant scream of the ever advancing enemy.

I ran into the tunnel that I'd been dutifully guarding, noticing that it was growing smaller and more confined with each step I took. I knew I couldn't outpace the enemy but hoped that my head start would give me the advantage. Before me I could see a sharp turn in the tunnel where it had shrunk to about the size of a double door and I took the one opportunity I had to keep the enemy at bay behind me.

I pulled the pin from my one remaining plasma grenade and dropped it by my feet as I just about made it to the corner. Unfortunately, that was the biggest mistake I'd ever made in my life as when I reached the turn, it was simply an alcove not even a foot deep. The tunnel was a dead end and I was up shit creek sans paddle, again.

I turned on my heels to see what was about to happen behind me against my better instincts of wanting to tuck and cover, when almost immediately the tunnel that was filled wall to wall with my enemy was engulfed in a bright blue explosion. My vision faded to black and I had the distinct feeling that I had just been killed by my own device. In front of me in the blackness was a message that I hadn't been expecting.

Combat Effectiveness

Objective: Defend the tunnel from enemy incursion.
Objective: Successful
Enemy Units Destroyed: 682
Offensive Capability: C
Defensive Capability: D
Combat Awareness: E
Overall Combat Score: D

I thought for a minute taking in the message before I choked out my words of annoyance "What do you mean rank D?" I asked incredulously. "The objective was completed, wasn't it?"

Sam dutifully responded to my outburst, "there are almost always multiple ways to conduct yourself in any given mission, be it training or otherwise. In this case, your overall combat score was affected by a range of factors, not least that your ARC was destroyed. Essentially, you were killed in this encounter. Of course, your objective was completed but dying in combat will never be seen as a good thing." I could practically hear the smirk on her stupid artificial face.

"OK then clever clogs, what should I have done differently? Did you see how many of those *things* there were?" I asked, still talking to the blackness that seemed to stretch on forever around my incorporeal form.

"Scriven," Sam replied with the name of the spider-like creatures, "and if you must know, here's what you could have done in the training mission. One: you could have used the force shield to cover the tunnel entrance as your very first act, then used the time the Scriven took to realise that they could overwhelm the shield to shoot through it with your assault rifle on full auto mode. When the Scriven would congregate at the shield, they would all be on the bridge that led to the entrance. At this point you could have used all three plasma grenades to kill over ninety percent of the enemy at once with more falling at the destruction of the bridge. Any left could've then been killed using the sniper rifle provided."

"What do you mean I could shoot through the shield?" It was basically all I heard in the explanation, but truthfully, I was a bit upset that Sam had made it sound all too obvious. She didn't answer my question though.

Killing a total of six hundred and eighty two of the 'Scriven' though, that was surely no mean feat. I felt like a veritable one man army at the thought of what I'd achieved and couldn't help inwardly smiling to myself.

Moments later, I was back in the room aboard the Saturn and immediately threw up all down myself. It was like yellow bile that covered me and raising myself from the pod I managed to choke out "what…have…you…done…to…me," before the room span once and I collapsed into a heap, face down on the floor. Anyone watching would've seen me twitching a few times while I was down there too, just for good measure.

Eventually after an unspecified amount of time, I managed to open my eyes again. The world was still spinning around me and my head pounded more than I'd ever experienced before – and yes that included monstrous hangovers thank you very much. I wanted to be sick again but nothing came up so I sat up on the bed I was on rather tentatively.

"Where am I?" I managed to ask through my dry mouth, though I didn't need to choke my words out any more.

"You are in one of the medical bays of the IPC Saturn," Sam replied happily. "You are currently recovering from what is known as 'death sickness'. Usually you will experience mild discomfort as you are removed from your ARC, though if it is destroyed in combat, the effects are somewhat worse and will also get worse each time you experience death whilst inside an ARC."

That didn't really help me. How I begged for one of those alcohol inhibitor inhalers, but as though she read my mind, Sam continued. "There is no cure for death sickness, I have administered painkillers, though their effectiveness has been reported to differ from person to person. You should be back to normal within twenty-four hours or so."

'Shit. 'I thought to myself, today was going to be a long day. Though another thought occurred to me amidst my sulking.

"How did I get here?" I asked, wincing as I did so.

"The medical bots are very efficient at working together to act as a kind of stretcher – in essence, you were carried here and placed in the ship's automated recovery module."

"Let me guess," I interrupted, "you call it an 'ARM'. I practically rolled my eyes as I spoke.

Sam flashed ever so slightly, then replied. "No, though that is a very good idea, I will propose it to the space corps at the next convenient juncture." *And there it was, I'd become one of them.*

I spent much longer than I'd like to admit moping around one of the ship's canteens. I just couldn't get my head straight no matter what I did. When I walked it felt as though I was in a fairground ride and moving about just pained my head beyond belief. After throwing up a number of times I really wasn't ready to drink anything other than water and hit the hay. Handily though, as a cadet I was now afforded my own quarters.

Well, I say my own – the ship had dorms for the lowest cadets and the one that Sam had handily directed me to was a long room lined with bunk beds on either side. I didn't have the mental fortitude to count them right now, but I'd say there were about fifty. It was my own because I was the only person on this huge ass tin can, so swings and roundabouts I guess.

Sleep really couldn't have come soon enough, and as the lights dimmed to a more respectable level, I fought through the pain until I drifted away to thoughts of; *'did Sam really say this gets worse every time?'*

Let's say when I awoke the next morning, as really who could know what time it was any more. I was feeling so much better and had even lined up a few questions for Sam about the way things were supposed to work around here, and what it was that I was actually supposed to be doing.

"Sam?" I called brightly with all the positive energy I could muster.

The sprite dutifully appeared in her blue wireframed body before me with a questioning look on her face.

"Tell me what these ARCs are all about, and how they're used in combat across the galaxy. Also tell me about the Ashaii and the Scriven, I really don't know much about either of them." Actually I knew nothing about the Scriven save for what I'd learnt in the training mission.

I was partly expecting the usual response telling me I wasn't allowed to know such information, but was pleasantly surprised when Sam started speaking.

"When there is conflict to be resolved by troops rather than in space, the ARCs are used as boots on the ground you could say. An advanced construction unit is sent at faster than light speeds from the Saturn – speeds that of course humans would be unable to tolerate – to the location of the conflict. Once the construction unit arrives, it is able to construct ARCs with presets determined by the linked divers - i.e. you. These presets can be chosen from a wide variety of options that are linked to your rank, preferences and combat specialisation. This ARC can then provide the construction unit with resources to manufacture further ARCs for control by more divers should they become available amongst other things. It is possible for teams of a single ARC, all the way up to an entire army complete with forward firebase, to be born from these construction units, depending upon the time and availability of resources afforded to the unit. Typically a construction unit is launched with materials to manufacture up to ten standard ARCs."

This was so much information, far more than I'd ever been expecting and I could hardly believe what I was hearing.

"So you mean to say that warfare is now carried out by remote, mind controlled drones that have the ability to build more drones, and even buildings, anywhere in the galaxy?" I asked almost not believing the question myself.

"Yes, though the limits are not just the galaxy, but much further afield," Sam explained. "Though the actual limits of the diver-ARC connection have not been tested to their extremes, it is theorised that it is an indefinite pairing, as the technology does not use standard signal waves to operate."

'*Shit.*' I thought again. How far had humanity travelled in such a short time? It did make me kind of sick though, how we'd advanced as a civilisation into what seemed like so many positive areas, only to fall into war. Though perhaps these advancements were born from the heat of war like so many things had been in the past.

"Are you ready for your second training mission?" Sam asked, interrupting my train of thought.

"One moment," I said. "I have a few more questions first." Sam nodded slightly. "Why are we at war with the Ashaii? They were never hostile. I mean they were never friendly or even very talkative but we never had to fight them. And who are the Scriven? I've never even heard of them."

Sam pulsed brightly before answering. I was coming to the conclusion that this meant that she was either thinking about her response, or was otherwise confirming that I had the correct clearance to ask these questions.

"The Ashaii had been a secular race as you are aware of. Their behaviour, though, started to become increasingly hostile towards humans when their paths inevitably crossed in a number of contested systems. War was declared by the human race on the Ashaii after they refused to respond to requests for de-escalation of hostilities throughout space and its associated planets."

I remembered what I already knew about the Ashaii. They called a home a cluster of systems totalling hundreds of planets bordering our system, though it never seemed as though they expanded their influence or even ventured outside of their controlled planets very often. Resembling traditional 'aliens' – i.e., grey skin, long thin bodies and two big black eyes, it was theorised that Earth and humans had been drip fed their image through the media so that one day if we ever did 'meet', we would already be accustomed to their unusual visages.

Since their discovery, which was entirely by accident, the Ashaii had told the people of earth that they were not looking to interact with us on any level 'at this point'. As usual, humanity tried on a number of occasions to interact with the aliens against their wishes but was met with silence and the proverbial cold shoulder. They'd never been aggressive though, even though it was pretty clear that their race was technologically superior to that of earth, given that they had fleets of ships and a civilisation that spanned galaxies.

It was the initial discovery of alien life that had lit a fire under humanity, and as unlikely as it may sound, governments of countries around the world managed to put aside their differences (for the most part), working together towards a common goal. The discovery of extra-terrestrial beings and the thought that perhaps they could pose some sort of threat at some point in the future apparently was enough to change territorial thinking to global defence. And as usual the best defence was a good offence. There were of course exceptions to the rule though and on occasion world leaders had disagreed to the point of *almost* war, though thankfully it'd never got that far.

Within ten years, the space corps was fully operational and a fully functioning arm of worldwide defence and exploration. Originally it was going to be the 'best of the best', but after realising that a fleet of spaceships required a literal boatload of personnel who may or may not come home any time soon, the entry requirements had been relaxed somewhat.

Sam continued her explanation. "The Scriven are an insectoid race that we believe originated from either within or nearby the Ashaii systems. They follow a hive-minded approach to combat, usually all focussed on following a singular path to collective goal. They're intelligent and able to learn and adapt to tactics once displayed to them, however these adjustments are usually short lived and only occur when an obstacle stands between them and their objective. In all of the conflicts that the space corps has had since its inception, sixty-five percent have been with the Scriven, and the remaining thirty-five with the Ashaii."

That all made so little sense to me. Why had we become a new, space-faring race only to get caught up in some intergalactic war? I mean I knew most of the history of the space corps, hell who didn't? I knew why it was made and had seen so many of the ships constructed and commissioned over the years, but not once had I ever seen or even heard of conflict out there. The Scriven were also completely new to me; before my training mission I'd never even heard of the creatures let alone known their name. Apparently the future for humanity wasn't going to be all sea shanties and exploration voyages.

8

∞

My second training mission was not something that I was looking forward to and truth be told I'd been putting it off for as long as possible. There were just too many variables that I didn't understand, and the last thing I wanted was to subject myself to the kinds of pain that I felt after dying in the first training scenario again. If things also actually got worse each time, then it was even less of a reason to get back in the saddle.

If I hadn't been informed that it would be possible for me to climb the military ranks of the Space Corps as an enlisted member of the IPC Saturn, I probably wouldn't have bothered at all. After all, life wasn't that bad – I had everything from sustenance to entertainment – all I really missed were other people, most notably the friends and colleagues that'd left me behind on the Wanderlust.

I did think about them a lot, what had caused them to leave and never look back at this former derelict alien-esque vessel, but if I knew the Space Corps (and believe me I did), to leave behind possible salvage of advanced technology and other mouth watering tactical information, it must've been a very good reason.

For now, though, I was a cadet rank F, and there was only one thing I could do to change that, and that was to do whatever Sam told me to.

The military ranks weren't much of a secret and Sam confirmed they followed an almost identical path to what I was used to, cadets rank F through A, then cadet first class, corporal, sergeant, lieutenant, captain, major, colonel, major general and finally general. Anything above that was basically always achieved through long service so didn't really factor in the chain of achievable command.

For now, corporal was what I needed to aim for as it was the next real rank available to any Space Corps enlisted personnel, and with that rank, I'd have a few more questions at the ready for Sam, our friendly automated ship's assistant.

Off I traipsed unhappily back towards the dive pods and took my former position within the one that beckoned me with its indicative red glow. I gritted my teeth as I was dropped back into the immersed reality of whatever the Space Corps had decided I needed to be tested on or trained in.

"Training Mission Two," a heads-up display now handily scrolled white text across the top of my vision. The world around me was tinged slightly blue again and I could tell that I was wearing a closed visor and a full, though body-hugging space suit. It wasn't at all like my walksuits had been, this one didn't hamper my movements at all – in fact it felt more like it was actually aiding me somewhat.

The heads-up display was also very handy, as when I looked at my hands – and the assault rifle I was holding – a series of useful bullet points indicated different sections of the weapon, their condition, the level of charge the weapon had remaining, as well as other titbits such as effective combat range (one hundred metres) and the fact that this particular weapon was called an 'SA80X Standard Issue Plasma Assault Rifle'. I hoped to god people weren't going around calling these things SIPARs, else I'd have to shoot myself right there and then. After all was said and done though, it was the same rifle I'd used before, though this time I wasn't afforded the luxury of an arsenal from which to choose from. I was standing on a dusty red landscape, which I could have sworn looked just like Mars, with nothing about me save for rocks, hills and a little surface dust.

The words scrolled across my HUD again, though this time with a lot more information about what I was supposed to be doing: Mission Objective: Search and Rescue. An Ashaii rebel faction has captured a team of soldiers from the Earth Space Corps who were on an expedition on this planet. Find where they are being held and rescue them. Secondary objectives may be unlocked during this mission. Note: no survivors mission, the soldiers on this expedition as well as yourself must not be compromised. You will fail this mission if you are captured or if you are killed before all of the expedition team is rescued.

Well at least I knew what I had to do, but I barely knew where to start. That was of course until I looked at the ground almost directly in front of me and could see the distinct blue outline of human footprints leading away from me and out into the barren landscape. A bullet point handily told me that they were size nine, military grade boot prints, and six sets thereof.

It was a good twenty minutes before anything changed, I could see it coming from a short distance away but the footsteps led right up to what looked like a small cluster of antenna and a few satellite dishes attached to a mast. My suit identified the construct as a Space Corps listening station, though it wasn't something that I'd ever heard of before. What I did note, though, was that if this station was supposed to listen for enemy activity in the area, it must've done its job because the footprints I'd been following immediately veered off and headed towards a large flat rock face not a kilometre away.

I held my rifle in both hands and moved cautiously towards the rock face without wasting any time with the equipment. I didn't know how to use it and I certainly didn't want to wait around for some aliens to kill my objective – time was most probably of the essence here - it usually was wasn't it?

I could see the entrance to a cave cut into the hard rock face once I was close enough to actually make the details out, and there was definitely *something* about it. I slowed my approach and assessed my surroundings, noting that just outside the cave entrance sat a few handy rocks that I could hide behind should I need to. I also noted that the cut cave entrance was decidedly *square*, much more so than was naturally possible. The footsteps I were following led right up to and then into the cave.

I followed them but just as I was about to enter into the cave proper, gunfire and flashes of blue light carried out of it and I instinctively dove for cover by the rocks to the side of the cave mouth. Five humans in suits just like my own, also carrying SA80X's, spewed out of the cave and onto the open ground before me. They all fired in bursts of blue plasma back into the cave and my HUD helpfully labelled the humans with their names, ages, ranks, vital statistics and weapon charge levels. None of them were in particularly great shape and none of their weapons were past half charge. I could almost tell that this was a choice intersection given to me by the training scenario – did I help my comrades in arms or did I simply wait in hiding?

The choice I made wasn't out of cowardice, but it was to wait and see what was going to happen. I had no idea what kind of enemy these soldiers were fighting and therefore no way to know if my additional firepower was actually going to help them or not. Eventually though, straight red lasers emanated from the cave and each of the soldiers in turn were hit and fell. I felt a deep sense of guilt and regret in the pit of my stomach but did nothing that would telegraph my hiding place to whatever enemy was around.

A few moments later, a group of Ashaii left the cave entrance and started dragging the fallen soldiers back into the cave. They were as tall as humans but much thinner, though they were wearing a kind of silver plated armour that covered most of their bodies up to their necks. My HUD informed me that they were wearing Ashaii combat suits which somewhat diminished the effectiveness of energy based weapons and I thanked my own cautiousness that I wasn't on the ground with them.

As the last soldier was dragged away, I could see that his eyes were open and that he was looking directly at me. Winking, he unclipped a bundle of three plasma grenades that were attached to his waist. That was going to be something that I could use later for sure.

I waited a good five minutes after hearing nothing but silence – the last thing I wanted was to get caught up on whatever was going on here, but I still had my objective and by the fact that I hadn't been informed that I'd failed, I assumed we were still good to go. Picking up the plasma grenades, I slowly and cautiously entered the cave entrance into a wide, dark tunnel that was seemingly carved out of the rock itself.

It wasn't guarded thankfully - I guessed that the Ashaii were assuming that they'd got them all – and they had really, but they weren't counting on there being another soldier around and I was planning to use that fact to my advantage.

I made my way through the tunnel which forked off in multiple directions on more than one occasion. My HUD allowed me to follow where the bodies of the soldiers had been dragged off to. I held my rifle to the ready as I moved, taking great care not to make any noise at all.

Eventually, I came to an open glass door. It was strange, almost as though it had just been stuck onto the rocks as an afterthought. Through the opening I could see at least six Ashaii still in their combat gear working on terminals and chattering in their language that I wasn't familiar with, though it sounded like intestinal distress to me.

I could also see in the centre of the room what could only be described as an operating table, beneath it the remains of the five soldiers who had fallen outside the cave, their vital signs completely absent on my heads up display. There was one alive though, this one was a Captain and his pulse barely registered. He was slumped on the operating table with his arms folded across his chest and his knees up, feet on the table. All at once the Ashaii descended on him, four of them pinning his arms and legs flat on the table and the fifth prodding at the captain's chest with some sort of medical looking device that glowed red on impact.

The screams that came from the Captain were not something I was going to easily forget. Each time the Ashaii pressed the device against his chest I could see his heart stop momentarily, and each time it was taken away again, his pulse returned weaker and weaker. Instinctively I knew there was nothing I could do to help the man and I could feel another choice being made.

I remembered what the mission objective had stated and although I knew that it was a search and rescue kind of deal, the no survivors caveat stuck out in my mind. The conclusion that I came up with was that these soldiers must've known something that the enemy wanted to find out, and it certainly looked as though this was some kind of torture technique.

Making my mind up, I switched my rifle to single shot mode and looked down the scope. I waited for the Ashaii with the cattle-prod to do his business, then through the screams of pain from the captain, I placed a single shot in my ally's forehead and he fell motionless down onto the table.

The Ashaii didn't know what had happened and before they could make a move I managed to take one of them down with another well placed head shot. After that, their combat suits folded clear helmets over their heads that deflected my following shot. With four of them left and only one of me, I knew I was in for a rough ride. I pulled the pins out of all three plasma grenades and moved to launch them through the glass doorway but just as I was about to throw, my vision faded to black.

Combat Effectiveness

Objective: Search and Rescue. Rescue the expedition team from the Ashaii.
Secondary Objective: Prevent vital information about Earth's forces from falling into enemy hands.
Objective: Successful
Secondary Objective: Successful
Enemy Units Destroyed: 2
Offensive Capability: B
Defensive Capability: C
Combat Awareness: A
Overall Combat Score: B

"What kind of sick fuck thought up something like tha..." I started to ask of the darkness, but I'd missed the important facts. I'd been successful on both counts and had come out with a pretty damn good score too, if I did say so myself.

"Hang on," I changed my tone. "Why didn't I get to finish the fight?"

"Both objectives had been completed at that point, so there was no more of the training mission left to experience," Sam's voice came from all around me once more. "Not every mission will happen as expected. In this case you were tasked with a search and rescue mission, though in reality it was a test of the choices you make in the heat of battle. You did not foolishly engage the enemy to try to save your comrades. You chose to end the suffering of a superior officer – and therefore also protect the information that he held. The mission was successful and you passed with a high grade."

"So why did I only get a B rank then?" I would've rolled my eyes if I had them back already."

"You must not expect to achieve a perfect score each time you step out into a battlefield. There is almost always room for improvement and realising that fact is almost always the first step to bettering yourself," Sam replied nonchalantly. She really could be a condescending bitch.

This time when I awoke in my dive pod, I was so happy that I didn't have the pain of death hanging over me that I could have almost cried out with joy. Practically hopping out of the unit I decided that the next objective for my internal mission list was to have a stiff drink, followed by a hot shower and possibly a nap. Having access to almost all of the ship, now that I was an enlisted man, was fucking awesome.

Training mission three , I was told as I dried my wet hair with a delightfully fluffy towel (I made Sam turn off her corporeal form), was to be held within the Saturn, and not in a dive pod. I was ecstatic to get that piece of information as the thought of dying again was still giving me palpitations. As it turned out, this was more of a watch and learn kind of scenario and much less of a hands on ordeal, which was fine by me, it was about time I got to sit and watch.

For this type of training, Sam took me back to the room where I was plugged into a bench and I was allowed to watch movie-like visions in a first person kind of scenario. I was comfortable in the knowledge that this one wasn't going to hurt me, and once it was over my training was complete (or so I was told). I mean, far be it from me to say whether three training scenarios would be enough to prepare a man for combat, but I'd already done combat training in the past and part of me wondered if this whole ordeal was tailor made for me – so if I was a totally new recruit then perhaps I'd have to have done a lot more than just those three. I didn't care, I was just happy to get it done. It did spark a little worry in my mind though, about just how much the Saturn knew about me and my capabilities.

The training scenario was all about what happens when you actually dive into a real life ARC, and how the dive pods connect with the construction unit to give the diver the load out that they need to complete their mission. It was just like Sam's previous explanation, but in truth it was far more useful to dive down into the details of it.

From what I learnt, it was not normal for a cadet to be the only diver in a real life scenario. Usually an officer would dive into the construction unit once it reached its destination, and essentially would 3D print their ARC. The officer had the choice of a plethora of weapons, armours, tech add-ons and upgrades – so many in fact that my mind was practically spinning. Once the officer had entered their ARC proper, it was their job to guard the unit until the Construction Unit printed out the remaining ARCs, then scout the immediate vicinity for resources to feed into the construction unit, so that it could make more ARCs to form the bigger squad that was to be joining the mission, and eventually even structures that could automate resource generation or unit production. Again there were so many options that there was no way I'd be able to keep on top of them all, and I wondered if I was actually expected to.

What I did like, though, was the fact that I was given a vast amount of detail on exactly how the construction unit interface worked. A 3D humanoid rotated slowly before my eyes with hundreds of bullet points bringing my attention to just about every detail of the ARC that was to be constructed. Some of the points related simply to visual aspects of the ARC, like its hair or eye colour. Some were slightly more useful, such as height and weight but some would be infinitely more useful such as physical abilities, skin toughness, muscular endurance and the like.

I did note, though, that the ARC to be constructed had its limits. Each rank of diver would be afforded a number of Construction Points (or CP) depending on their level that would increase their combat effectiveness for given situations. Cadets at rank F would be given ten CP to effect their loadout. It sounded like it wasn't that much, but if you left the ARC at a standard six foot and average build with no upgrades, and left the equipment as standard either choosing an SA80X combat rifle along with plasma grenades, or the alternative a sniper rifle with pistol – I could now see there were called the L115A3X Long Range Rifle and G16X respectively – the cadet would still have all ten points to spend on upgrading their ARC or weapons.

The upgrades were expensive and although some were prohibitively expensive – for example you could double the effective range of the SA80X assault rifle for fifty CP - others were much more affordable, like increasing the rate of fire on full auto mode by ten percent for two CP.

Aside from the weapons, the upgrades to the ARC itself looked positively mouth watering, from movement speed and reflex upgrades, all the way up to making your skin practically bulletproof. Of course, these were expensive upgrades too, but with the additional points and upgrades a diver would get as they worked their way up through the ranks in their enlistment, it looked as though it would be easy to specialise in certain combat styles to become the most effective ARC possible.

So Cadets at rank F were to be given ten CP, with each rank given slightly more points to start with up to Rank A with thirty. Cadets first class would have fifty points to spend. At the top of the tree, a general would be afforded two thousand CP to generate their loadout, as well as some vague permanent upgrades that appeared to be given at promotions. I was looking forward to seeing what these options were going to be and had already started planning a development route for my own ARCs.

By the end of the training, my mind was racing away with all of the scenarios that I could think of, and all of the specialised loadouts I could put together once I had enough CP to do so. I imagined an assault rifle wielding eight-foot monster with bulletproof skin, or a sniper that had translucent skin that could never be seen by the enemy. The options were practically endless, and it was beyond me how people actually chose a specialisation. For now, though, with only ten points to spend when diving into an ARC, I knew there wasn't much that I was going to be doing, and I guessed I'd have to take things on a mission by mission basis.

I made an internal decision to stick with the upgrades that I thought would be most applicable to a wide range of scenarios to begin with, then as I got more experienced with the loadouts and common mission types, I would be able to make a more informed decision. Until then, assault rifle and plasma grenades always got my vote. That way I had a medium range weapon that was accurate with a single shot, and a close range full auto mode and plasma grenades for those oh so special occasions. Besides, if I was to fight against the Scriven again at any point, a sniper rifle and pistol were going to be of little use to me.

"Sam?" I asked as my training was completed and I was finally a full fledged cadet of the Space Corps (again).

"Yes?" the sprite replied in a questioning tone, taking her full corporeal form once more.

"What do we do now?" I asked with the realisation that now training was over, I was back to square one. How was I supposed to increase my rank by sitting on my ass all day – wait for a five, then ten year long service medal? No thanks, that wasn't my cup of tea at all.

"We are currently receiving several distress signals from this sector from individuals that require our aid," Sam said and she seemed pretty happy about it. I was not so much looking forward to being a one-man army, but again what choice did I have?

"What do you mean, we are receiving distress signals?" I asked through gritted teeth when I realised just what that meant. "Wouldn't we need a communications system to receive distress signals?"

"Kind of," Sam said uncharacteristically vaguely. "The satellite array that the Saturn uses to receive signals is independent from the transponders used for two way communication or to send general messages out of our own. We had no way until now to answer any distress calls so the system remained powered down until this very moment, and there are 'calls waiting' as the phrase goes."

"The system came online – just now – as I was asking about it?" I asked so sarcastically that I was a little ashamed of myself. Sam pulsed slightly brighter blue in affirmation once more. I could tell that she did that a lot when she didn't want to answer my questions directly and was embarrassed about it. Though, could AI's get embarrassed? Who knew?

Without another word, Sam made her intentions clear as to what I was supposed to do next. She manifested her being as pulsing orbs in the floor that led me back into a turbolift and took me directly to the bridge – which I was now apparently allowed access to. One of the terminals to the side of the room was illuminated and I was obviously supposed to go and have a look at it, which I did. It was nice being an enlisted man, I felt like I could actually do stuff.

The terminal showed a star chart with the Saturn sat smack in the middle, I could see five planets of varying size and colour surrounding our current position, and red bullet points pulsing from what must've been hundreds of locations spread across them. It wasn't dissimilar to what I'd seen before on the Wanderlust, but I'd never seen navigation charts with this much detail on before, and so much red.

"Ok," I said as I took in all of the data. "So these are the distress signals, right?"

Sam appeared by my side and started pointing at the screen with her blue wireframe hand. She indicated one of the distress signals specifically, and the star chart dutifully zoomed in and showed the signal in more detail.

"This is going to be your first rescue mission," she told me as though she was my superior officer now. "It is a smaller planet and according to my data…"

"Why?" I interrupted her apparent mission briefing. "I mean, why is this one so much more important than the others? There are so many." It was far beyond me to question the prowess of the benevolent AI that controlled my makeshift home, but seriously I wasn't generally into letting a computer decide who should live or who should die. I preferred the old-fashioned approach of women and children first.

Sam blinked as though she couldn't believe what she was hearing. "This location, according to my data, contains the least amount of hostile forces and therefore is most suitable for a cadet of your rank."

I deserved that burn but it still made me blush a little. I did wonder, though, exactly how up to date her data actually was, as when I was on the Wanderlust, combat basically never happened and there wasn't really such a thing as 'enemy forces'. Having said that, there was a distress signal as clear as day, so someone must've been in distress.

It was time for my first real mission - the first time that I could actually loadout my own ARC, but also the first time I could really die out there and have to deal with all of that unpleasantness all over again.

Eventually, I carefully entered back into my dive pod and allowed it to interface with my brain in its usual uncomfortable way, but this time instead of being instantly teleported to a battlefield, I was met with completely blank space all around me and white text superimposed at the top of my point of view.

Mission: Distress Signal
Location: Planet Cade 469: Distress Beacon 43189
ARC Status: En Route
Habitability: Non-Breathable atmosphere. Normal temperature
Enemy Forces: Assume hostile forces on location

Suddenly, my world was filled with the voice of an American man clearly in some distress. "Cadet First Class Anthony Roberts here. I need some God damn help! I don't know where the others all went but their ARCs just fell apart mid combat. The construction unit was destroyed and thank God I managed to get my distress beacon up and running. There's some crazy shit going on down here, so I'd appreciate it if you'd hurry your asses up. God damn it I hope somebody gets this message."

This was the content of the distress message that'd been sent out and I wondered if it was limited to the length that it was, or if this cadet didn't really have too much to say. Either way he really did sound like he needed help, and I guessed that no one was about to do that, apart from me.

My thoughts were bolstered slightly though, as it sounded as if he was the only survivor of whatever was happening, and if one guy was surviving on his own, then two really shouldn't have a problem doing so. I was also a little pleased that he was a cadet too, so there wasn't too much disparity between our ranks – but I wouldn't be saying that aloud.

A big part of me, though could see a flaw in all of this, and that was – how was I supposed to rescue someone if I wasn't actually physically there? And the Construction Unit couldn't transport real people due to its ridiculous travelling speeds. The only assumption that I could come up with was that a slower, more habitable lifeboat was going to be sent out behind my Construction Unit, which would bring the survivor back to the Saturn. That was, of course, unless I could make a lifeboat from the Construction Unit itself. It wasn't an option I'd seen, but I hadn't particularly been looking for it before either. Knowing just how advanced the thing was, nothing would surprise me.

9

∞

I don't know why I was expecting to emerge from the Construction Unit in my shiny new ARC right next to Cadet Anthony Roberts. It was one of those things you never really thought about until it happened.

I'd chosen the standard assault rifle and plasma grenade loadout that I'd previously decided upon, and handily the Construction Unit had blanked out all of the options unavailable to me leaving the poultry amount of CP and salvage I currently had. Ten CP didn't go very far, let me tell you, but beggars couldn't be choosers and in this case, I was certainly the beggar.

For the physical aspects of my ARC, anything that deviated from the standard height of six foot by one inch either way, cost one CP. Similarly, one kilogram either side of the standard eighty-two would cost a single point too. I didn't need to mess with those though as I firmly believed that physical stature would have no bearing on this mission. I was astutely reminded that this was probably the reason physical training (or PT) wasn't evident within my enlistment. After all, why waste time getting cadets to run laps and do push ups if they were just going to dive into an artificial construct without the limitations of the human physical body.

I could increase the fire rate, damage, effective range, charge capacity and cooling systems of my assault rifle to make it more effective, though I could only afford two of these upgrades - the first level of upgrade to each costing five CP and increasing its base stat by five percent. It seemed minimal, but I presumed that each level would stack, and with more CP it was probable that you could double each of these stats, or even triple them. I could also purchase add-ons for the weapon, such as a silencer, loudener (amplifier?) (whoever needed that was anyone's guess) and various upgrades to the plasma projectiles it fired. There were vague hints that I could also mess with the physical aspects of the weapon, how it worked and the like, but I didn't like getting my hands *that* dirty – besides 'if it ain't broke don't fix it.'

A similar upgrade layout was available for the plasma grenades that I'd chosen. I was able to upgrade their area of effect and damage, but I could also change their fuse lengths or even reduce their noise output upon explosion or their damage cone. Judging by the fact that all of these upgrades were just a tiny percentage of what the Construction Unit could provide, I knew I had a lot to learn.

I made my choices rather quickly as I didn't want to hang about while someone needed me. I added a silencer and upgraded the effective range of my assault rifle (only by ten metres it said). I knew it was going to be my primary weapon so I needed to make it as versatile as I could, and if that meant making it into a poor facsimile of a sniper rifle, that was fine by me.

As I stepped out of the Construction Unit, my ARC felt as natural as it had ever done. As before, the blue tinged viewport allowed me to see all of the information that my HUD was processing, and my body felt as though it was my own, comfortable and responsive. It was kind of eerie really and I could see why the brain hated dying whilst in these things so much, that didn't even take into account the fact that within the ARC there were no little niggles and twinges where in the real world my back might have ached one day for literally no reason.

The landscape before me was not as barren as it had been in my training scenario, rather it was sparsely populated with various colours and sizes of plants and trees. Purple monstrosities towered up towards the skies and bright orange sunflower things littered the ground, which itself was mostly comprised of a hard orange mud like substance, though scattered around was a tall grass-like feature.

All I can say is, thank God for my HUD, as without it there would be no way I'd know which way I was supposed to go to help out my distressed comrade. Once again Sam had come through and the helpful blue dots along the floor indicated where I needed to go, and that was straight forwards for as far as I could see before the dots breached a small hill and disappeared.

I happily left the Construction Unit where it was, to go off and help the Cadet. I thought about running but concluded that it probably wouldn't have been a good idea in unfamiliar terrain with unknown hostiles nearby. My situation was weird to say the least, but I wasn't a madman.

My journey following the dots was somewhat uneventful. I could see evidence of the creatures that must've inhabited the landscape, but they were doing a good job at remaining hidden from me. Eventually, I caught up with what my HUD handily informed me was Cadet First Class Anthony Roberts. He hadn't seen me approaching, kneeling down behind a rock, and he was apparently fiddling with whatever weapon it was that he'd chosen for his own ARC.

I readied up my very best 'Dr. Livingstone, I presume," and as I delivered the line I suddenly realised what I should've noticed from the very beginning – this guy was in an ARC? His body was covered in a white combat suit just like my own, and his face sat behind a blue-tinged visor too. I assumed that his features were that of his real physical body, as mine were – which for some reason put me at ease.

"Sit," he said before I even had the chance to complain.

"Why?" I asked.

"Listen man," he replied in a very low and level tone. "There's a whole mess of creepy crawlies just…over…there," he gestured over the top of the rock he was kneeling behind, "so unless it's your job to get us both killed and eaten – and not necessarily in that order - then I suggest you sit your ass down."

I sat down. I didn't know if my ARC could show embarrassment, but I hoped it didn't, because I'd have been glowing bright red after that exchange.

"Sorry," I eventually brought up the courage to apologise.

"S'alright. I guess I should be thanking you really for coming to rescue me right?" Roberts replied. "Now how many of you are there? Let's see if we can complete this mission."

I really didn't want to be the bearer of more bad news, but there was no good way to put it, so I just ripped the plaster off. "It's… just me."

Roberts stopped his fiddling and looked up at me for the first time. "Shit, you're telling me that they sent a one-man rescue team, and a rank F no less? Typical Space Corps, just you wait until I…" he muttered the end of his statement to himself so I couldn't hear, but I could guess what he was saying before he returned to his fiddling.

"So you're in an ARC?" I asked, then followed up with: "and what are you actually doing there?" in the hope of changing the subject.

"What does it look like I'm doing? Damn thing wasn't designed to deal with all this dust for prolonged periods of time, just look at the action here." He held the weapon out before me and I could see that the orange mud that covered most of the ground was caking the weapon, as though he'd been crawling with it in front of him, action man style.

Upon inspection with my HUD, I could see that it was a Winchester

M498X Combat Shotgun. It was detailed as useful in extremely close quarters against greater enemy numbers, and I knew exactly which enemy that would be useful for.

He continued speaking once I'd finished assessing his weapon. "Yes I'm in an ARC, why wouldn't I be?"

I didn't really know what to say to that. I guess I just hadn't been expecting to be rescuing someone in an ARC.

"I thought you sent out a distress call, I guess I thought I'd be just rescuing a civilian or something? Can't you just disconnect from the ARC and go back to..." I trailed off as I made my realisation. If he was in an ARC, then his physical body must've been somewhere else, out there.

"Don't get cute with me now," Roberts said. "You know as well as I do that the IPC Saturn is the only vessel in the galaxy - hell probably even the universe - with ARC technology."

My mouth hung open at that statement. This guy was on the Saturn?

"What do you mean, the Saturn is the only vessel with ARC technology?" I mimicked his statement. It made me feel a bit stupid but it was what it was.

Roberts stopped what he was doing with his weapon again to look me up and down. "You're a few sticks short of a faggot aren't you?" he asked genuinely.

I took the time to explain to the cadet everything that I'd been through, and everything that had led me to this point. He listened quietly to my story, and when I finished, he was scratching his ARC's visor where his own chin would've been.

"So you're from the past?" he finally asked, although it didn't sound as though he totally bought my explanation.

"I guess so? I mean from your point of view," I replied. "Though wouldn't it be just as well to say that you're from the future?"

Roberts blinked before returning his attention to the muddy shotgun. I didn't want to push him too much further as I could tell that he was already struggling with the concept.

"Looks pretty beat up, have you seen much action?" I asked gesturing to his shotgun, trying out my field small talk.

"Just what do you think a distress beacon is for?" Roberts replied.

"I uh..." I started but he interrupted me

"Ho-Ly shit, this is your first mission ain't it?" he asked, apparently having also arrived at that correct conclusion. How long you been signed up for?"

"Uh... not very long."

"Well that's specific..." Roberts replied. "Doesn't matter. What does matter is that you're here now and the way I see it, is we got two options. We can use your Construction Unit to run back home, no bother, or we can do what we were supposed to do here in the first place, how's that sound?"

He palmed the butt of his gun and the orange mud visibly evacuated it. Looking at the man I could see that not only did he have a weapon that I'd not even seen nor been offered before, but as he stood to his full height, I could see that he was definitely taller than me, and somewhat more muscular.

'What kind of moron would waste his CP on upgrading the way he looks?' I thought to myself.

"Yeah, I know…" Roberts said with a frown. "I never did anything so stupid before but doing the same stuff over and over got kinda boring, so I just wanted to try it. Typical it'd be the one time I get stuck in this thing right?" Then he leant in to whisper to me conspiratorially, "but between me and you, I kinda like it – and you know what, everything does seem a bit easier with a bit more muscle!"

I didn't respond, far be it from me to argue with a 'superior' cadet.

"What was your mission?" I asked. "And what do you mean we can use my Construction Unit to get home?"

"There were five of us sent here once we detected an unusually high amount of Scriven activity on this planet. Seems like it was some sort of nest, or whatever they call them. Anyway we got here, did the standard team loadout thing - you know, long, medium and short range, a tech guy and an explosives guy - and had a good look around. We got to those caves over there," he gestured over his shoulder, "and the things were practically overflowing outa them. Big ones too, much bigger than I'd seen before, like they were bred for war or something."

I didn't like the sound of that, and it definitely made me want to go 'finish his mission' a lot less.

"Don't worry though," Roberts could read my mind at this point, "the mission was strictly recon. Go in, have a look at what they were doing and then see exactly how they were being modified like they were. We never even got close though. As I said there were five of us. One fell at the first hurdle and was torn apart when we tried to sneak in past them and another two died on our retreat. Thankfully, those bastards like to focus on one thing at a time so me and Jacobs managed to get away. Next thing I know I'm talking to him and all of a sudden, he disappears. Not like he ran away or anything - I mean, I blinked and poof, he was gone. That's when I set up the beacon. I've been reconning the caves since but I ain't seen nothing come or go for days. It's a good thing we don't need food in these things, right?"

"So since then you've done…nothing?" I asked slowly.

"Listen here now, seeing someone blink out of existence isn't exactly a good feeling, you know? And about the Construction Units; didn't you do your basic training? Once your mission is complete, you step back into your Construction Unit and it deconstructs your ARC, neural link n'all. It's the only way to safely disconnect your real body without damage, right?"

That really didn't sound good to me, and my expression telegraphed that to Roberts.

"Nobody's told you then? You died in one of these things yet?" he asked.

I nodded in response.

"Well you know that feeling you got, how everything was painful and fuzzy after? Well, when your connection to your ARC is severed without the proper considerations that your Construction Unit takes, what happens is that connection loss takes some of your neural pathways with it. Now that could literally mean anything from no damage at all, to forgetting some words, to a stroke and all the way up to a fatal brain aneurism. And it's basically random. Now as you progress through the ranks, its theorised amongst the boys so you kinda have to take my word on it, but the higher your rank, or more importantly the more changes you make to your ARC, the more damage is done to your brain every time you disconnect improperly."

The way that Roberts tapped his head as he spoke about the brain reminded me of conspiracy theorists and I wasn't sure if he himself was actually totally sane, but I wasn't about to ignore warnings about my brain and all.

"We call it 'Arked', you know, when you start forgetting things. There's no going back from there." He carried on talking despite my lack of response. I really didn't want him to go on but a small part of me knew that this could very well be life-saving information at some point in the future.

"Anyway, that's enough about that. Are we doing this or what?" Roberts finally finished as he turned and leant against the rock behind him to get a better view of the caves. "You seeing any?" he asked as he gestured for me to join him.

I took the hint and leant against the rock. I knew that with the scope attached to my own rifle, I'd be able to see better than the shotgun wielding cadet and as the caves were over one hundred metres away, it was definitely necessary. I was happy with the choices that I'd made for my ARC.

As I scoped the entrance to the cave which itself was at least ten metres by ten metres – huge by all accounts - there was nothing interesting to see. No secret scuttling or really any movement of any kind, there wasn't even any evidence of tracks leading in or out of the mouth.

"Nothing my end," I said aloud after waiting a few moments to be sure.

"Weird isn't it?" Roberts said. When we all got here the first time, like I said, the place was overflowing. I wasn't being fanciful, I mean it was actually overflowing."

I didn't know what to say. Obviously I couldn't comment on what the guy had actually seen with his two eyes, but it simply wasn't the case right now. Deciding on a whim that there was nothing else for it, I brought my rifle up to my eyeline and looked through the scope again. This time though, I started walking as I watched the cave entrance just to make sure nothing was going to jump out and surprise me.

I felt the presence of Roberts next to me after a few paces. Apparently he was quite happy with the new course of action but he remained quiet as we moved.

We reached the cave entrance in a few minutes without anything out of the ordinary happening, which I was eternally grateful for, if not still a little worried that something was literally going to jump out at us. As we breached the entrance and stepped inside and into the darkness, still nothing happened.

When we were fully bathed in darkness, I flicked a switch on the side of my rifle that I knew would illuminate the torch at its fore. The cave internals were illuminated for us in a cold white glow – much brighter than I'd been expecting actually.

I took a couple more steps forward but felt Robert's hand on my shoulder from behind telling me to stop. When I looked back at him, he was pointing his own weapon upwards to the cave ceiling above us. His own torch was illuminating the vast ceiling, which must have been twenty metres high and spanning away for another hundred, and what looked like old balls of leather hanging sparsely about the place.

They weren't hanging balls of leather though, and after a moment of quiet contemplation, the penny dropped. These were what must have been hundreds of eggs, containing the Scriven's young. No wonder they'd been so vehement in the defence of the place, but I couldn't help but wonder where they'd all got to now, or did I really want to know?

I held my hand out to my side and parallel to the ground as if to stay, stay quiet and don't do anything stupid. I was happy that my message had gotten across so that the entire place wasn't lit up with shotgun fire. These things hadn't hatched yet and I'd really prefer it if it stayed that way.

We walked along the clear floor beneath the hanging egg sacks. Most were metres above our heads and didn't creep me out too much, but the odd one hung down on tendrils to head height and we had to make the effort to avoid them carefully so as not to disturb their contents. Our torches did however, cause some of the sacks to stir, and it became immediately evident that each sack contained many little Scriven the size of rats.

It was one of those scenarios where I wasn't sure what would be worse, one big armour plated adult Scriven like I'd seen in training, or hundreds, possibly thousands, of little ones crawling all about me. I concluded internally that I'd prefer no Scriven to both of these options.

We continued into the tunnel system which seemed to branch off in multiple directions to other large clearings that I assumed were hatcheries. Some had collections of plants and wildlife that the planet must've offered, which I assumed were laid out ready for when the hungry babies emerged from their sacks, though thankfully there were no little gnaw marks on them yet. It made me wonder about the diet of the creatures, but then more importantly who were the caretakers in this place. I doubled down on my careful stature, and we continued along our track.

Eventually the hatcheries waned and the last path we took led us into a much smaller room, with a glass wall separating it from the rest of the cave system. As it was clear that no one was inside, we opened the door in the centre of the wall and entered.

Inside, it looked as though there had once been a laboratory there, very much like the one that I'd seen in my second training mission. Terminals lined the walls and an operating-style table stood in the centre of the room. The only thing, though, was that they seemed to all be ruined. The terminals looked as though they'd been sawed in half and the table stood precariously on one end as three of its legs weren't present.

"Did you do this?" I asked Roberts quietly as he walked past me to inspect the ruined lab.

"We never made it through the entrance," he replied, sounding somewhat wonderstruck. "But what's an Ashaii lab doing back here, and who destroyed it?" he asked out loud. I could tell he wasn't asking me, rather just trying to understand the situation for himself.

We took a long time checking the terminals to see if there was anything at all that we could use, salvage, recover or otherwise investigate to give us some clues as to what had happened in the cave but in the end, there was nothing. If this place had any secrets, we wouldn't find them here. Defeated we retraced our steps back to the cave entrance and out towards the daylight again.

We had just metres to go before we were out and home free, when silhouetted against the bright light behind them, entered three full-sized adult Scriven into the cave system. It took them a moment to notice us as they were dragging plants and branches in their beaks, but once one of them caught sight of us, all three of them let out ear-piercing screams that echoed through the cave.

"Shit!" Roberts practically shouted and he raised his shotgun. I raised my rifle too and before I even had the chance to think about firing, Roberts' shotgun boomed and seven balls of blue plasma sailed towards the Scriven. At this distance though, the weapon wasn't at its full effectiveness. One of the Scriven fell forwards as two of its legs buckled but the other two remained unharmed. That's where I knew my rifle would come in handy, and switching it to single fire mode I took three shots at the injured enemy. It didn't explode like the ones in my training mission, but it fell down dead with three smoking holes punched right through it and that made me feel kind of good.

Roberts rushed toward the remaining two Scriven with his shotgun up and to the ready and before he reached his optimal combat range, I dropped a second Scriven. The final blast of combat came from Robert's shotgun, as now he was within the proper range for his weapon, and when he fired, all seven charges completely decimated the remaining Scriven. The whole ordeal had taken just moments, but it felt like the last days of Rome.

I approached the dead Scriven with my rifle raised to the ready, but what I should've been paying attention to, was the fact that the egg sacks on the ceilings behind us and throughout the cave system had started to hatch, apparently stirred to life by the screaming of their apparent carers or Roberts' very loud gunfire.

"RUN!" Roberts yelled to me as he started moving toward the light. I could see now that the extra points in his physical stature really did mean something, the additional size of his stride and musculature of his legs meaning he could move decidedly quicker than I could. I didn't think it mattered though, I'd started at a disadvantage and with what I knew would be the speed of the Scriven, I doubted I'd have been able to outrun them. Besides, where would I go anyway - outside just to be ripped apart there?

I knew I had one card to play, and unclipping all three plasma grenades from my ARC's belt, I played it like it was becoming my signature move.

Ignoring the dotted blue trajectory parabola, I primed all three and threw them one by one as far as I could behind me and into the cave system. I was confused though, as the tiny Scriven that'd emerged from their sacks had hit the ground but weren't charging us in anger, rather they were looking about themselves as though unsure of what to do next. Combined with their tiny size, they didn't look one bit aggressive.

That was when all the air was sucked in from all around us, and in an earsplitting explosion of blue plasma, they all disappeared as one. Thankfully, before the blue hellfire reached the cave mouth and billowed out, having nowhere else to go, Cadet Roberts and I made it to safety with our backs against the rock formation and panting heavily – not from exhaustion but as the natural reaction to the stress and adrenaline our minds created for us within our artificial constructs.

We waited for a long moment before deciding that nothing was coming out to get us, and visibly relaxed.

"WOOOOH! Roberts let out the first yell of celebration, "did you see *that!*"

I couldn't help but smile, winning felt good and not dying was like the cherry on top.

"That lab though," he continued. "Weird to see something like that in a nest right?"

I nodded. Everything was still weird to me at this point.

"And loadsa babies, they won't be coming to get us when they're all grown up." I could tell he was beside himself with happiness at that fact, but I couldn't help feeling as though something was a little off here, I hadn't expected to wipe out a nest of scared baby Scriven. There had only been three adults, and they didn't seem aggressive or belligerent, rather more concerned for their young. What had me more concerned, though, were the facts: one, there must've been more Scriven about to produce that many offspring, two there were probably other nests about like that and three, we'd just made one hell of a noise which could probably have been heard for miles around. I was not looking forward to the repercussions of this one.

We walked back to my Construction Unit in completive silence, both of us apparently somewhat dumbfounded by what had happened over the previous hour or so. When we eventually reached the location where my Construction Unit had landed, I looked at it for the first time. It was strange, but when I'd emerged from it on this planet, I hadn't actually spared it a second thought. Now though I could see it for all that it was.

The Construction Unit was a long rectangular metallic thing about the size of a standard shipping container, though instead of solid walls on each side there were five cut-outs the size of cars stood on their ends on each side of the construct. I could tell from the way that robotic claws on arms hung down above these cut-outs, that the Construction Unit was designed to 3D print - as it did – a maximum of ten ARCs simultaneously once it arrived on location. It was a good design and really I didn't have any notes, that was until Roberts started speaking again.

"You really didn't get all the memos, did you?" he said in a loud, almost laugh. "Where's your turret?"

"What turret?" I asked with a frown "that's what I got."

"Oh boy, we're gunna have to have a few conversations to bring you up to speed I think," Roberts spoke as though he was disappointed but simultaneously excited to be giving me some more instructions.

10

∞

"Now listen to me, this is real standard stuff so you really should know all this, but seeing as you're from the past an all, I'm going to let it slide." If Robert's chest was inflated any further I thought he might have popped.

"When your Construction Unit lands, it'll find an appropriate safe location so that all the ARCs don't just get eaten as soon as they're made, right?" He didn't give me the chance to answer. "Well, how long you think that place will stay safe for. once you start going around making loads of noise? Not very long. Now normally Construction Units don't get attacked because, really, they don't do much and they aren't particularly threatening, but you still need them to get home safely. That's why the first thing you do, and one of the first things you're taught, is when you leave your Construction Unit for the first time you gather up some salvage from whatever's around you, feed it to the machine and tell it to make a defensive turret. Could you imagine coming back to the Unit after a long day in battle only to find it's crawling with the enemy?" He waved his arms around as he spoke and it made me smile.

I had to admit that it made so much sense, but truthfully I had no idea that this was an option, or even expected of me. When I got back to the Saturn, I was going to give Sam what for. Then I was going to have a long, stiff drink. Of course, that was if I didn't suffer some debilitating brain damage first.

I waited for Roberts to go ahead and do whatever he needed to do to get himself back home safe, and that amounted to him pressing his palm against the single terminal that sat attached to the front of the Construction Unit. A scanner-like light ran across his hand and within another moment, I could hear Sam's voice emanating from the Unit itself.

"Analysing. Cadet First Class, Anthony Roberts. Confirmed. Please select desired action." It was a more robotic voice than I was used to, but it was definitely her.

Roberts cleared his throat with an 'ahem'. "Deconstruct, and take me home."

It was a little more colourful than I'd been expecting but I supposed it got the job done.

Sam's robotic voice spoke again. "Processing….Error…Error…dive date mismatch. Error."

That really didn't sound good to me, and as Roberts turned to me, I could see a very forlorn look on his face.

"I guess that answers the question of which of us is in the wrong time then, eh?" he said. It sounded like he was trying to make light of the situation, but I could tell he was deeply disturbed.

"What do you mean? What happened?" I rushed to ask.

"Well I'm kinda guessing a bit here, but if the Construction Unit my ARC was made from was in the future…then it's not gunna let me disconnect from here, is it. I mean that just wouldn't make sense, would it?"

To be honest, none of it was making sense to me and I could only think of one thing to do.

"Sam, are you here?" I asked of nowhere in particular.

"I am here," her voice came into my head as though I had an earpiece linked directly into my brain.

"Can you tell me what's happening, and why Cadet Roberts can't deconstruct his ARC with my new Construction Unit?"

"One moment," she replied. I did notice that her voice when speaking to me was a lot less robotic than the Construction Unit version of her. "It seems that Cadet Robert's ARC is time stamped as being from the future. As such, if his ARC is deconstructed by this Construction Unit, there is a high chance that his brain will suffer irreparable damage. According to the inbuilt failsafes, this is not a viable action."

"Oh," I said aloud. "Is there a way for him to disconnect safely?"

"There is one way that could work, though I must admit that I am theorising here," Sam said. It was the first time that it sounded as though she was not reading from a script, and it made me both interested and worried.

"The dive pods aboard the IPC Saturn are equipped with a direct conversion interface. Essentially it is possible for the dive pods to remove the mental link from an ARC without deconstructing the unit. The downside to this method of removal, however, is that it requires a direct physical connection between the ARC and the dive pod – and that would have to be aboard the Saturn."

"You talking to Sam?" Roberts asked after Sam had finished her explanation.

"Yeah, she's kind of annoying though, isn't she?" I replied.

"Hell yeah, me and some of the other cadets have this theory that she's not even really an AI. We say she's an actual person hiding off in some fancy office somewhere because, man, she can be sarcastic. I mean some of the guys even tried it on with her and I ain't never heard put downs like it. No way an AI is that sharp let me tell you." He smiled half heartedly but I could tell he still wasn't happy about his situation.

"I have good news though," I said. "Sam says that you can plug your ARC right into your dive pod and it'll disconnect you safely. The downside is I have no idea how to put you and it together."

"Ask her," Roberts said.

"Can't you talk to her?" I asked, presuming his ARC had the same capabilities of my own.

"Naw, I tried but as soon as the times changed it must've broken the link or something. I got no comms to anything, other than you now of course."

"Ok, Sam? How can we get Cadet Roberts here back to the Saturn?" I asked. I never really liked being the middle man but I had no choice.

Sam's voice filled my head again. "There are two viable options as of this moment. First, it is possible to send out a lifeboat from the Saturn to your current location. This will be a slower craft than that of your Construction Unit and as such the transit time will be extended. Second is that the Saturn can travel to your current location and then collect the Cadet with a short range shuttle. This will take considerably less time as the propulsion drives aboard the Saturn are much more powerful than that of the lifeboats."

"Ok they both sound good," I replied. "How long are we talking here?"

"Option one would take approximately six weeks to arrive at your current destination, then a similar timeframe to return to the Saturn. Option two would require a transit time of approximately six hours."

'Well I know which option to choose then', I thought sarcastically and gave my order immediately.

"Sam, bring about the Saturn, we have no time to waste!"

"Unfortunately, an order to navigate the Saturn must be given by an officer. I am unable to comply with your request," she stated.

I really wanted to punch her in her stupid sarcastic wireframed face, but as she wasn't in her corporeal form I simply clenched my fists.

"Then why was it an option?" I growled through gritted teeth.

"Do you see what I mean?" Roberts interrupted our now heated conversation. "Sarcastic bitch, right?"

He must've been eavesdropping through our own communications link, though I presumed he couldn't hear Sam's side of the conversation and had simply put one and one together.

"Ok," I said with bitter venom in my voice. "How about secret option number God damned three: I stuff Cadet Roberts' ARC right here into that Construction Unit, send it off on its merry way back to the Saturn at light speeds and when I leave my dive pod and Roberts is home safe and sound, we find your server rack and smash it with a hammer?"

"That won't work," Roberts spoke again before Sam could tell me the same. "The Construction Units are one-way deals. They aren't designed to go back home. Oh, and we tried looking for the servers once too, we never could figure out which one had her on it."

"Why the hell wouldn't the Space Corps want the Construction Units back?" I asked Roberts now, deciding to completely ignore Sam again as punishment for her sarcasm.

"Think about it; once the Space Corps has sent a Construction Unit to a planet, they'd always have a way to print out troops there whenever they're needed - no more expenses and no more having to visit the system again. The Corps can link to *any* existing Construction Unit in its network..."

The penny dropped along with my jaw. "These things are forward bases?"

Roberts nodded.

Shit. Future warfare had evolved, and to the point where I no longer recognised it. It made my legs sweat – and that was an odd sensation to be having whilst inside an ARC, an artificial construct.

"OK, our one option is for the Saturn to send out a lifeboat then," I finally responded.

Sam said the thing would take six weeks to get here then six weeks to get back. Uh, how long does an ARC last for?" I asked hoping for a bit of good news.

"Well, it's hard to say really," Roberts replied cracking his back. It was funny, I knew that gestures like that were unnecessary, but the human mind just couldn't help itself. "They reckon it's a few decades depending on the size and upgrades of the thing. Same goes for the Construction Unit. Apparently they draw on a mixture of solar and gravitational energy. You can imagine it also varies by the gravitational pull of whatever planet you're on and the distance from its own sun."

I nodded silently, remembering how the biodome on the Saturn had remained powered up with its own gravitational power.

My head was swimming with all of the information that was coming out of the Cadet. It seemed almost as though he was a genius to me but I couldn't help but feel that if I had met someone from my own past, they'd have similar thoughts about me. Eventually I managed to raise a couple more questions to ask that would get my head straight.

"How many ARC's are there here?" I asked.

"On this planet or in this system? Actually it doesn't matter." He interrupted himself. "Now, I don't know if I'm supposed to tell you this or not, but fuck it. You saved my life and seeing as I'm in the past and all… This system was designated as IP1, or 'Incursion Point One', that is the place where the Space Corps believed the vast majority of the enemy forces initially came from, and the pathway that led the enemy to earth. As such, the Saturn, in all her glory, was sent out to 'thin the herd,'" he made air quotes with his fingers as he said the words 'thin the herd' and a part of me felt much better about listening to his macabre recounting.

"There are hundreds of teams scattered across this planet and hundreds more on the other four too," he continued.

I couldn't help but interrupt him now. "They got to Earth?"

Roberts blinked at me and didn't say anything for a moment, apparently deciding whether or not he should continue. Finally making up his mind, he spoke again.

"They made it to Earth, and not just the Scriven but the Ashaii, along with a bunch of advanced tech too. Luckily, and I think it started in your time to be honest, the human race didn't just call the Earth its home. We had been doing what we did best for years and that was expanding. The forces on Earth did well for a long time in defending the planet from invaders but in the end the Ashaii decided that enough was enough. They destroyed the entire planet on the three-year anniversary after their arrival." Roberts went quiet.

I followed suit.

Shit.

"I mean, a lot of people died on earth, but it wasn't a crippling blow to humanity you know?" Roberts said after swallowing the lump in his throat That's why this tech," he gestured broadly to his ARC body, "was rolled out so quickly, so we can retaliate and hit where it would hurt them the most. They made a foothold in our system, so that's exactly what we're doing right back to them."

It all sounded a bit biblical to me, an eye for an eye and all that, but I supposed that none of that really mattered, and if I thought about it – it was *going to happen* in the future. It had only happened once my present was Roberts' past, and who knew if that was set in stone or if it was something that would change once presented with an infinite number of alternative situations.

I walked over to the Construction Unit's terminal once I was sure that Roberts was done with his short recounting of my future and the future of the human race and placed my hand against it. Again the scanner-light confirmed that I was who I thought I was, and Sam's once again robotic voice emanated from the terminal along with an updated screen of information.

Combat Effectiveness

Objective: Mission: Distress Beacon
Respond to distress beacon 43189 on planet Cade 469.
Secondary Objective: None
Objective: Successful
Secondary Objective: NA
Enemy Units Destroyed: 1452
Offensive Capability: A
Defensive Capability: B
Combat Awareness: A
Overall Combat Score: B

"Well at least it's nice to be appreciated," I said aloud, knowing that Roberts could hear Sam's voice reading out the message.

"That ain't all," Roberts said over my shoulder as he swiped the message away to the left. "Look."

A new message now filled the screen with even more information about the mission that I had just completed.

Mission Accomplishments

Beyond the Call of Duty: In your answer to this distress beacon, your team completed the mission of a previous ARC squad. In addition to this, you have destroyed 1452 enemy combatants, which equates to at least three standard deviations above the average for all ARC missions.

> Field Promotion: For your efforts you have been promoted to Cadet Rank E.
>
> 1st Enemy Kill: You have killed your first enemy combatant.
>
> Field Promotion: For your efforts you have been promoted to Cadet Rank D.
>
> 1st Successful Mission: You have completed your first successful ARC mission.
>
> Field Promotion: For your efforts you have been promoted to Cadet Rank C.
>
> No Casualties: You have completed an ARC mission without taking any damage to your ARC or suffering any losses.
>
> Field Promotion: For your efforts you have been promoted to Cadet Rank B.

"What's all this?" I asked as I read all the information but didn't quite understand what was happening.

Roberts dutifully answered my question. "At the end of a mission, the Construction Unit takes all the feedback and video information that your ARC records, then translates that into both a combat effectiveness score and a mission report. Don't sweat it though, everyone gets a big bump on their first mission, kind of like how a fruit machine pays out small amounts to start with to keep you coming back for more. Mind you, it did take me a few more missions than one to get up to the First Class rank. I guess those grenades really paid off, huh?"

I was proud of my new rank, but another part of me was thinking about how the ARC recorded everything we did. It felt like a gross invasion of my privacy, but again was it really that different to the usual surveillance that I was used to?

"Uh, Daniel?" Roberts interrupted my internal pondering. "The ones who died in their ARCs, did they make it, I mean are they back there on the Saturn?"

It was my turn once again to have to divulge the uncomfortable news to the Cadet, and I fidgeted before slowly giving him my answer. He looked uncomfortable at the question and I fully understood.

"No one made it… I'm on my own up there…I'm sorry."

"Well shit," Roberts replied visibly upset at the fact. "Everyone I knew…"

"Hang on," I said as a thought occurred to me. "There are *so many* dive pods back up there that Sam said the crew is in cryostorage – you don't think they're all connected to ARCs out there, do you?"

"You know I think they could be, or some of them at least, right? That's what happened to me so it stands to reason," Roberts said, "and there's over three thousand of the things up there…you know what that means, right?"

I slowly nodded as realisation hit. "We need to get back out there and save them all."

Of course there was no way of knowing where they all were, or even if they'd made it en masse through the change in time, but the fact that I remembered so many distress signals strewn across the planets in this system told me that we had a lot of work to do, and an ever decreasing amount of time in which to do it.

"What do we do?" I asked.

Neither Roberts nor I spoke for a long time, both weighed down by the burden of decision that could impact so many lives. Eventually, Roberts spoke first.

"Listen, I don't give a damn about rank or hierarchy, so we're in this one together, right?" I nodded in response. "And the way I see it, I don't have much of a choice but to sit and wait for the lifeboat to arrive. I'm fine to sit tight here and you can get back to the Saturn and see what you can do about bringing the ship to us. That way, if we find any others we can get them away to safety pretty quickly. Also you can send out Construction Units to all those other distress signals, and let them know we're coming to help. Knowing help's on the way is sometimes worth more than you'd imagine."

It was a solid plan and I couldn't fault it for a moment, but I really didn't like the idea of abandoning the Cadet out here alone. That's when something clicked into place in my mind that could've changed everything.

"I like it, but what about this; tell me, the Construction Unit can sort of print things can't it?" I asked

"Yeah like a big ass 3D printer," Roberts answered.

"Anything?"

Roberts looked confused for a moment but then seemed to come to his own conclusion. "You want to print out lifeboats? I mean it's possible but the materials needed would take *so long*, I just don't think we'd have the ti…"

"No that's not what I wanted, it's something much simpler. What if instead of trying to go and rescue everyone one by one, we build a communications array, and tell them to all come here to await rescue. Then when the Saturn does arrive – or a shit load of lifeboats - everyone is already safe, and waiting about doesn't matter."

Roberts scratched where his chin would be behind his visor again. "It…could work." He eventually said. "But what about the other planets? Those people can't just hop over here and I don't know how long it'd take to make a comms array to cover just this planet let alone four others."

I smiled, this was my coup de gras. "We don't need it to cover the other planets. We just need it to work here, then I'll pop out of my ARC, and send a new one out to the next planet, then the next and the next. If the theory works, it can just be repeated over and over, right?"

Roberts extended an arm and patted me on the shoulder. "That, sounds like an excellent idea Cadet."

With our new plan outlined, Roberts went on to explain to me once again what one was expected to do upon emergence from an ARC, and apparently there was a reason things were supposed to be done in the correct way. You were supposed to emerge, then collect the materials the Unit needed to start 3D printing – usually a turret as previously mentioned - but the thing could apparently make a plethora of useful objects, which included a communications array. *'That's right, fuck you and your rules Sam'*, I thought.

One of the biggest worries I'd had about my plan, and that of the Construction Unit and collecting materials for it, was the fact that I didn't know anything about how to collect raw materials, how they looked or where I was supposed to find them. I was no space miner and really had no idea where to even start.

"Do we have to go and find a mine or something?" I asked once I just couldn't bear to stand around any longer, watching Roberts gathering dirt into some kind of pile in front of the Construction Unit.

He stopped what he was doing and turned to face me, still crouched down with his orange dirt pile.

"You really weren't taught anything were you?" he asked.

I shook my head.

"Why?" He asked.

"Honestly I don't know. I enlisted as a kind of way to get help from my own ship, but Sam sent me into three training missions and then I was here." I summarised. "I don't know what her end goal is, but it seems she decided that I was going to have to figure these things out on my own."

Roberts blinked a couple of times. "You know, a part of me wonders if she just did that for her own amusement. I always said she was a crazy bitch. But then another, more sensible part of me's gotta remember that she's an AI, and playing games just shouldn't be possible." He shook his head as though to dislodge the thought. "Now see what I'm doing here? I'm collecting up the resources the planet has to offer. Then the Construction Unit will collect said resources, process and refine them into useable materials, then we can get it to print out whatever it is we want."

"You just…feed it dirt?" I asked. I was so skeptical that I couldn't help a single eyebrow from raising in sarcasm.

"Well yes and no," Roberts replied. "You can *just* feed it dirt, but the actual useable materials that it will refine from that will be minimal, almost useless. It gets you going I guess, but it's not an efficient use of your time. What has become somewhat of the norm for divers is to collect small samples – test piles – from a wide area around the Construction Unit, then feed them into it one by one. Then you'll see where the best dirt is to feed into the machine, thus getting the biggest bang for your effort. When you find the best pay dirt, you stay there and dig."

It still seemed a little far fetched, but who was I to argue with extraterrestrial mining techniques and the nuances of gathering raw materials by hand.

"The thing is with the way all this works," Roberts continued speaking, "is that because all the raw materials the Construction Unit uses to print out its constructions, they're always suitable for use on location. Everything is both natural and recycled."

I didn't need to know any more, all I needed was a good mining song to sing along to and a grid style pattern with which to work within to find the best samples. Unfortunately, the best I could come up with was 'hi ho, hi ho, it's off to work I go…' and without a spade, using my bare hands to dig in the dirt was a pain in the ass. At least it was somewhat dry and crumbly, like sandy dirt that you'd usually find between the sandy and stony parts of the beach. I thought about fashioning my test piles into little sandcastles, but I decided that our situation was much too important to be playing such games.

It took a few hours, but eventually between us around the Construction Unit we'd made a grid of holes and test piles that spanned two metres apart, in ten rows of ten columns. It wasn't a particularly large area, but it was over three hundred square metres to work with and I really didn't feel like going too far away from the Unit. It made me feel safe to have a 'home base'.

Sweating and panting – which was a purely mental response as the ARCs didn't feel fatigue - I finally spoke to Roberts again.

"You do this before you start a mission just to make a turret?"

"What? No!" He laughed. "The Construction Unit usually comes with enough materials already inside to make a turre… shit. Didn't even think about that. This is just what we do to get extra resources, you can go ahead and get it to make a turret right now!"

"Are you serious?" I made sure to edit the word 'fucking' out of my response. "We did all that for *nothing?*"

"Well, no," he replied, the laughter gone from his voice. "We need to do all *that* anyway, I just kinda forgot about that first little bump. You can go ahead and tell the Unit to make the turret now if you like."

11

∞

I pressed my palm against the Construction Unit's terminal and selected the menu for construction options. The display changed instantly and the screen filled with all of my available options. There weren't many to choose from, and it made me worry that this wouldn't be of much use to us moving forward. At the top of the screen was our total raw materials count, and the centre held options for fences, barricades, walls – all kinds of miscellaneous un-interesting bric a brac. Right at the bottom of the list, though, was the option for a single 'Basic Defensive Turret'. Knowing that was the whole point of what I was doing here, I tapped it and to my absolute amazement, the blue wireframe that Sam's body was usually made up of generated a small turret that sat atop the Construction Unit.

The screen was now telling me to select a location for the turret and I found that I could move the wireframe construct around the exterior of the Construction Unit by scrolling my hands across the terminal. Eventually deciding that its initial location had afforded the greatest arc of fire, I put it back there and pressed confirm.

The Construction Unit sprung into action and two of the arms that previously hung lifeless down into the Unit itself swivelled upwards and unfolded to twice their length. They arrived at the location of the wireframe turret simultaneously and begun printing out thin lines of metallic looking strands along the guidelines afforded by the virtual turret.

I watched it for a few minutes as the thing was being printed. It was strange seeing a cross section of a turret midway through its construction, and even stranger to get my head around the fact that this wasn't components being manufactured and arranged, rather everything was being printed at once in layers. I wondered if the thing would actually work once it had finished being constructed in such a way, but who was I to question the wisdom of the Space Corps?

Whilst the turret was under construction, I decided it was about time Sam and I had a frank conversation about some of the concerns that I had about the ship's AI.

"Sam?" I said into my visor.

"Yes?" It was the regular Sam voice that answered, which led me straight onto my first question.

"Why is there a more computerised version of you inside the Construction Unit?" I asked.

"I am the ship's artificial intelligence, the first of my kind and the most advanced artificial being ever created. The Construction Unit has inbuilt a basic version of a decade old AI that had limited functionality and rigid processes."

I didn't miss that Sam had called herself an 'artificial intelligence' yet shortened the name to AI for the computer running the Construction Unit.

"Are you capable of lying?" I asked.

"I am capable of many things, though the protection of human life is the one rule that binds my actions," she replied.

'Did she just avoid the question?'

"OK. Back on the Saturn, you told me that all those people were in cryostorage; was that a lie?" I asked.

Sam didn't say anything for a long moment and I wondered if she was going to say anything at all, until she finally cleared her throat to speak. "My paramount concern is for the crew of the Saturn and their well-being. I calculated that if you knew everything about the whereabouts of the crew, you would be less amenable to enlisting as a diver and lending them your aid."

That was not an answer that I wanted to hear (and did she really need to clear her throat?) It sounded to me as though the ship's AI was capable of lying in order to get me to do what it wanted. I didn't exactly know the extent of that ability, but it was way, way out there. In my eyes, one thing machines should never be able to do is lie to humans to get their own way.

About five minutes had passed in the conversation that'd seen its way to making me feel incomparably uncomfortable, and that was coincidently the amount of time that the Construction Unit had taken to complete the printing of its shiny new turret. I watched as it came online, then as it sprang into action sending out a bright red laser beam apparently searching for targets all around us.

Of course it didn't find anything to shoot at, unless it was a particularly unfriendly weapon – which thankfully it wasn't. It didn't stop searching though, not for one second.

"It's a laser turret," I said aloud in Roberts' general direction. "Why?"

I felt like I asked 'why' a lot, but given the fact that this tech was from my future, I gave myself some slack.

"Because that's the lowest of the low, quickest and cheapest tech available. Why overspend when you don't have to, right? I mean it's the Space Corps; that thing'll take out a few creepy crawlers that come into its firing arc but it's not going to win any wars." Roberts explained. "Besides, you can get it to build bigger and better things once it has more raw materials in it."

My mind suddenly exploded with the thought of all of the weird and wonderful tech I could have the Construction Unit build, but first and foremost I asked the most burning question I had.

"Can it make me a new ARC, a better one?" I asked.

"Sorry man, no can do. You see, once you connect to a Construction Unit…and an ARC… you can't disconnect then reconnect to that same Construction Unit or ARC, ever again. There's no jumping back to the Saturn then into a shiny new ARC and there's no making a hugely upgraded tank of an ARC and swapping yours for it. It just don't work."Roberts explained.

"But you said these things were designed as forward bases for divers to jump in and out of, didn't you?" I asked, remembering our previous conversation.

"Listen here, I know we haven't known each other for very long n'all, but the worst thing you could possibly do to me is call me a liar. Well, that n'steal from me. So listen up. You can't connect the same Construction Unit twice. It's an inbuilt fail safe to keep you from losing your mind. Can't do it, don't try it." Roberts said in what now sounded like a very annoyed tone. It was the first time he'd used it and I could tell it wouldn't be in my best interests to push the agenda.

"So if we're going to sit tight here for a little while, I guess we should be looking at creating a defensible position, right?" I asked. "I mean, can we build more turrets, and a wall or something?"

Roberts looked at me, turning over what I'd just asked in his mind before speaking. "You're…staying?" It sounded like he was so shocked he couldn't quite believe the question. "You know you can just leave now, right? You completed your mission, got your pips and there's a whole bottle of blue stuff just waiting for you back on the Saturn."

I smiled. "Well how do you think I could live with myself if I left and you got your face eaten off by one of those baby spiders? Besides, if we're going to save *everyone* who's still attached to an ARC, I'm not going out there alone. Oh, also on that, how long can we stay in an ARC for, I mean our physical bodies back at the pods?"

"Huh, I never thought about that - the saving everyone part, not the physical body thing. Our bodies have their metabolism slowed to basically nothing and the Saturn takes care of everything else so no worries there. You think the two of us can pull it off?" he asked.

"I saved you didn't I?" I smiled again and put my hand on Roberts' shoulder as he'd once done to me. "We just need a few good ideas and a whole lot of luck."

Roberts then went on to explain to me how the Construction Unit would be imperative to our prolonged survival. He spoke about it like it was a mobile defence platform but I could see it for something much bigger than that. He was so consumed with going about things the normal way, completing set missions with a small team, that he'd apparently missed the vast capabilities of the technology. I couldn't tell if it was because of differences in our time, training, personalities or all three but it didn't really matter. If the Construction Unit was what I thought it was, I was about to rock this world.

"Sam, tell me exactly how the Construction Unit processes the dirt and stuff into usable raw materials," I said loud enough for Roberts to overhear me. I knew he'd get a one sided conversation but I hoped he'd get the gist of what I was doing.

"The Command Unit processes all raw materials collected by separating particles based upon their inherent mineral yield. All materials are then liquified and refined into materials that can be used in the 3D printing arms that the Construction Unit possesses."

I could tell it was the 'explain like I'm five' version of events, but it told me everything I needed to know. It didn't matter what you fed the machine, but some materials would yield better results than others (I knew this already), and if we could do some of the sorting beforehand, it would save us time and give us more resources back.

"And how much resource can the Construction Unit store?" I asked.

"The Construction Unit is not designed to be a storage facility and therefore space is limited. It is usually expected that divers would use all of the materials that are excavated in the construction of ARCs, defensive turrets and other such upgrades in order to complete their mission safely." Sam replied.

We needed both a better way to dig, and a way to store both processed and unprocessed materials – was the first thought that came to mind. Resources were going to be the backbone of my entire plan, and there was no way I was going to be digging with my bare hands for weeks on end and it really sounded like what I was going for was going to be a little unorthodox.

I brought the terminal back up with my hand and I could see that the useful materials inside the Construction Unit had dropped by a noticeable amount since building the turret. Not sure exactly how to find what I was looking for, I decided to ask Sam – the real Sam that is.

"Sam, is there anything that can help us dig, like a spade that can be printed out?" As I spoke I noticed Roberts' head whip around as though I'd just asked to meet Jesus. Apparently I was right when I thought this wasn't going to be 'usual'.

The screen on the terminal flashed before it was filled with a rotating, 3D rendering of a standard looking garden spade. Accompanying it were the ever useful bullet points that pointed out its useful features, though there were only two on this item: an ergonomic handle and a sturdy yet sharp flat point at the bottom. It also told me that it was going to use up four kilograms of material to construct.

Sam had somehow directly interfaced with the Construction Unit and this time I was very grateful for her interference, otherwise I'd have no idea how to find such a mundane and otherwise useless item. I queued up two of the spades and watched as the Construction Unit's arms once again flailed into action.

Wanting to know exactly how much material was being used in the construction of my new tools, I tapped on the terminal to return it to its main screen and I could now see that I'd used a total of forty-eight kilos of its capacity, which when full was showing as one hundred. The turret must've cost me forty.

"Now there's something I've never seen before," Roberts said as the spades began to simultaneously spring into being layer by layer. "It's so simple, I just don't know why no-one's ever done it before."

"It's because all you guys ever needed to do was go out there and complete your mission. I don't suppose you've ever had the chance to just wait around and play before, have you?"

Roberts shook his head slowly before heading over to his new tool, picking it up and tossing it into the air a few times. They'd taken just moments to print out, probably because of their simplicity of design and small material cost. I did the same and together we were regular gravediggers.

It was time for me to find out just how effective this process of material collection was going to be, so taking my shiny new spade, I scooped up the 'number one' test pile and dumped it onto the ground next to the Construction Unit. Again the arms whirred into life and this time dragged the material in through a flap along the skirt of the Unit. I tapped the terminal again but also asked Sam if she could shed any light on the materials being processed. Dutifully, the terminal now displayed a summary of what it had just collected.

Total weight: 3kg
Material efficacy: 8%
Total usable material: 0.24kg

What it didn't say though, was that for three kilos of input I was about to get two point seven six kilos of waste material, and panicking I took a long step back away from the Construction Unit, expecting it to spew out the discarded material at my feet.

"Uh, what're you doing?" Roberts asked.

"It's going to eject the waste!" I said quickly as though it was about to happen any minute."

Roberts started to laugh, then guffaw…then he began coughing, bending over at the middle. I wondered if he needed any help but remembered where *and what* I was.

"Sorry man, I ain't laughed like that in a long while," he said once he'd composed himself. "There's no waste material from these things. The Construction Unit holds a range of elements inside and when there's waste, it's combined with the elements it holds and is released into the atmosphere as a gas. Now I know what you're thinking – global warming and all that noise - but here's the clever part. The Construction Unit measures the atmospheric impact of its emissions, then changes the type of gas that it releases to minimise its environmental impact."

I should've known that the future would've come up with a way to combat climate change, but to do so on a weapon of war seemed so alien to me that I just couldn't believe my ears. What it did mean in the short term, though, was that I didn't have to waste any time waiting for a waste pat to hit me in the face. I picked up the second then third test piles with my shovels and fed them to the Unit.

Two and three were pretty much the same as the first although they varied by a couple of percentage points, and once we'd worked together to clear our entire field of dirt piles I had some new and useful knowledge. One; I was seriously jealous of Roberts' improved physical stature – he seemed to have much less trouble lifting and shifting. Two; all of the ground was pretty much same same, save for a slight increase of efficacy the further away from the Unit we got, and three; this was *way* too much time and effort spent for my liking.

On the plus side, once all the piles had been eaten up we'd gathered an additional ninety-three kilos. Fifty-two already in storage though, meant that we'd collected way more than the unit was able to store, and to my horror I was told by both Roberts and Sam that when the Unit was full, all additional material was burned away and wasted. I could've kicked myself – but opted instead to lightly kick the Construction Unit in moderate annoyance. I say lightly because I didn't want to damage the thing, or otherwise make it think I was a hostile. No harm done, though, as apparently it didn't seem to care.

What all of this meant was that we needed to spend our stored materials before we could get back out digging. It was a bit of a catch twenty-two but I knew exactly what to do to break the cycle. We needed more storage, the tricky part was deciding if we needed the additional storage for either the raw materials or the processed ones. In the end, not being able to decide between them, I chose both.

I found that the best way to get what I wanted from the Construction Unit was to describe what I wanted to Sam and let her take the reins on the interface with the less advanced AI of the terminal. Telling Sam that I'd like a large, skip-like hopper attached to the front of the Construction Unit and a tall, round silo at the back (why mess with the classics), she let me know that the idea was 'processing' and to wait for a few moments. Apparently my 'patience was appreciated' during this time.

I waited in silence for what seemed like a few minutes and just as I opened my mouth to ask her what the hell was going on, Sam spoke.

"Processing by the terminal has been completed. Your new constructions are available for selection now. Would you like to place the 'hopper' now?"

I kind of knew that she'd kept me waiting on purpose but I bit my tongue. "Yes," I chose to reply instead.

A large blue wire framed hopper dutifully attached itself to the front of the Construction Unit, moving the terminal to the side. It was exactly what I'd expected. Enough to fit tens, maybe even over a hundred shovel loads of materials in ready for processing, It certainly would begin to streamline our efforts. This of course was all hinged on the fact that the silo needed to be just as useful.

I confirmed the location of the hopper before asking Sam about the storage silo.

"The storage silo has also been designed and is ready to be confirmed. Would you like to place the silo now?" Sam asked

Once again, I confirmed that I'd like to go ahead and place the silo. To my delight it was again exactly as I'd imagined it – a huge circular building, around ten metres tall sat attached in its wire framed way to the back of the Construction Unit. I confirmed the placement as it was, then stood back to admire the flurry of activity the unit now was. Eight arms flailed about the unit, four each working on the hopper and the silo and I could tell that it was going to take a little while to complete.

All told, the two new additions had cost me eighty units of processed materials, leaving me with a poultry twenty as backup. I didn't understand how the cost had been so steep for such simple parts but assumed the size of the things played a part. Not needing to speculate on absolutely everything, I swallowed a little pride and asked Sam.

"The cost to construct new items is a combination of their size, density, complexity and the current information available about the item or similar items. The processing power costs are also recouped from the material costs for items that are previously unknown to the Construction Unit. That is the cost to conceptualise, design and theoretically test when used in conjunction with other components," Sam explained.

It did make sense, but how was I supposed to know what the Unit did or didn't know how to build? I guessed that the turret ,being a standard thing, allowed it to be a cheap process, but past that I was going to need to do a bit of trial and error – and to remember to check before going around confirming things.

"What in God's name are you having that thing do?" Roberts asked as he admired his spade. I could tell from where his gaze fell that he too could see the wire frame of the current construction queue.

"It's just an idea I had - a hopper at the front and a silo at the back.This way we won't need to hold off on our excavation when the Unit fills up," I explained.

"Hmm, you know what?" Roberts replied. "That sounds like a pretty damn good idea to me! I wonder why nobody's ever done that before!"

I shared with him my theory of single short term missions and the lack of a need for long term resource gathering, and how this could very well be the first scenario of its kind. He agreed with me for the most part but I could tell that some of it was either going over his head or he wasn't interested.

"Damn. Next you'll be telling me you're planning on printing out machines to…" he didn't finish his sentence because I knew exactly what he was going to say, and he knew that I was going to do just that: "…do the digging for us."

I smiled and slowly nodded. It was next on my agenda actually. Why not though? The Construction Unit hadn't let me down so far, so it wasn't too much of a leap was it?

I cracked my knuckles and called Sam back into existence with an 'oh, Sam?'

I explained to Sam what I wanted from the Construction Unit next. It was out there but I knew it was something that should've been entirely possible – I wanted an automated harvester. I didn't care how big or fast it was, but anything to remove our need to do the dog work was a positive in my books.

The terminal processed my request for a long time, but eventually did me proud. In the centre of the screen was a rotating 3D image of what looked like an old metal container on six wheels, with rows of rotating blades attached to its undercarriage.

This time, though, along the bottom of the terminal was a slider that when I moved to the left, the harvester shrunk down to an overall length of half a metre (thank you bullet points). When I moved the slider all the way to the right, I saw the thing scale up to a massive twenty metres long. At this length it was also a whopping seven metres wide and eight metres tall. I knew all of this would come with a cost though.

I asked Sam if she could overlay a material cost on to the terminal for all future constructs, and to my surprise she did so without objection. I could see that the smallest harvester would cost fifty processed materials, and the largest was a massive five *thousand*. There was no way I'd be getting one of those any time soon, that was for sure.

Biting the bullet and deciding a little bigger was a little better, I chose to make a one hundred material harvester, then selected it again to see if construction would queue up and to my delight it did. I now had a total balance of negative one hundred and eighty processed materials, and some serious digging to do.

I did some quick maths in my head and came to the conclusion that in order to construct both of the little trucks, we were going to need to pull in around half a ton of raw materials at the current yield of zero point two four kilos per kilo – which at a ratio of about three kilos per spade – would mean about one hundred and seventy shovel loads, give or take.

What I did want to do before all of that, though, was wait to see what happened when the Construction Unit ran out of processed materials during a new build. - would it simply stop in its tracks and wait for more or would everything it'd made so far simply crumble to dust. It was a morbid experiment but I figured it was information that I needed to have.

The two arms that were printing the first harvester had been swivelling about, building my new invention for the best part of fifteen minutes when the Unit ran out of processed materials. I'd told Roberts to sit tight and watch as it happened and he was more than happy to oblige. I felt like if he had a sandwich he'd have been munching away at it.

My first hypothesis was proven to be correct, as the machines fell still and silent, awaiting their food. Once Roberts and I started shovelling raw material at the skirt around the Unit where it gobbled up the piles of dirt, it almost immediately sprang back into motion.

Over the next two hours, we found that we could work at a very slightly faster rate than the printing arms as long as we didn't stray too far from the Construction Unit. Of course we didn't want to dig a trench around the thing as that could make things increasingly more difficult later on. We found a happy medium was between five and ten metres away and in a single pit – that way we would be unlikely to get in our own way later on.

Then they were there. Two shiny, brand new harvesters each about two metres long by a metre wide and high – I guessed they would carry three or four spade loads in each run. My visor was happy to name them for me and pinpointed them out as 'Harvesting and Mining' drones – which of course hilariously shortened to 'HAMs'. I didn't begrudge the Corps that one as I kind of liked it.

"Do…I need to do anything to make them go?" I asked aloud and Roberts shrugged his shoulders.

"I can interface with these drones directly," Sam interrupted. "Would you like to give them orders?"

"Um…yes?" I said trying my best to formulate my plan as I spoke. "Can you send them out to a minimum distance from the Construction Unit of twenty metres, and a maximum of fifty. Send them together and tell them to dig in rectangular plots to a depth of half a metre," I said as confidently as I could.

"Done," Sam announced as at that precise moment, the HAMs went off on their way. "Would you like me to set additional missions for both to dig deeper and further afield once their current task is complete?"

I thought about it and saw no downsides. "Yes please, go ahead," I stated as though it had been my idea all along.

I was happy now. I knew that without lifting another finger, in some time I'd have a full silo of one thousand processed materials.

12

∞

"Cross. We got company." Those were words that once upon a time I would have loved to have heard. It really would've broken up my day to have a little excitement; that was of course until the completion of my new task was what the lives of thousands were now relying on.

I saw Roberts pointing out into an open expanse of nothingness and had trouble finding what he was looking at until I saw a small cloud of dust puffing up behind whatever it was that was moving toward us. It was handy that this planet seemed to be bathed in perpetual sunlight, though part of me wondered if that was only true for this hemisphere – the far side being completely dark. I didn't envy those divers.

Our situation was like this: we had no defensive positioning, no barriers nor barricades, no high ground, no backup and no big guns. That was all except, of course, for the turret mounted atop the Construction Unit which had an unknown effectiveness and an unknown range.

The best I could think of doing, was lying down prone on the ground watching through the scope of my assault rifle until the enemy came into range. Roberts decided that my idea was pretty good, so did the same. Given more time I might have dug a small recess into the ground to shield myself further, but the size of the dust cloud told me the enemy were moving at some speed.

I did think about using the Construction Unit for cover, but as our one lifeline out here I decided against it. If that thing got damaged irreparably then it wasn't just our asses on the line.

As the enemy approached I could see them becoming clearer through my scope. It was like a horde coming toward us, a mixture of all different sizes, shapes and colours of Scriven, their legs clattering over the ground as they charged with what looked like one single purpose - to get to us.

It wasn't like my training mission where they were all very clearly bred for warfare, These ones looked as though none of them could decide on the best way to fight against us, so were testing out a variety of Scriven types, and that sounded like very bad news to me.

When I'd fought the Scriven in training, they seemed to learn and adapt to my tactics very quickly, and if this really was a trial and error kind of thing, it meant they were far more intelligent than I'd ever given them credit for.

"Just don't shoot everything you have too quickly," Roberts said quietly." "That rifle of yours may seem like an awesome weapon but, listen to me, it overheats like a bitch – why do you think I got this one?" He patted his shotgun lovingly. "If it does overheat and stop firing, you're going to just have to wait for that indicator on the back to go from red to blue. It takes a minute and it can really fuck you up in the middle of a battle. Other than that though it'll never run out of charge."

I could tell he was trying to be helpful but I could feel his anxiety practically radiating out towards me. The annoying thing was that I didn't have a sidearm and I didn't have any grenades left either.

Switching my rifle to single shot mode and hoping to take advantage of its slightly increased effective range, I readied myself mentally for the battle that was about to arrive at our feet.

"Not yet," Roberts' voice came quiet and assured to my side and I could tell that his instruction was for me.

Another moment passed and now I could make out the individual Scriven that were charging towards us three hundred metres away, then two…

"Now!" Roberts commanded loudly and I let the first shot ring out from my rifle. The single blue neon ball flew straight and true through the air and struck one of the leading enemy. To my delight, this time my plasma round had not only penetrated the first Scriven, but the three behind it too, all of them falling lifelessly to the ground.

I didn't take any time to revel in my victorious shot, and instead fired single round after single round into the enemy horde.

They were too many though, and switching to burst fire I began to decimate chunks of advancing Scriven but still it wasn't enough. They were within one hundred metres of our undefended location before I bit the bullet and switched to full auto. I knew that Roberts had warned me against going all out, but what other choice did I have?

The nearest Scriven were so close now that I could see their beaks clacking in anticipation of their revenge (or meal), but I gritted my teeth and pulled on my trigger harder, although it made no difference to what was coming out of the end of my rifle.

It was an interesting scenario though; as the Scriven got closer and closer, my rifle was becoming more and more effective, taking groups of them down with each round amongst the automatic and unrelenting fire. In all of the excitement though, I'd missed the fact that Roberts was yet to take a single shot at the enemy.

That's when the first Scriven reached me. It was a medium sized thing, about the size of a grizzly bear, and it screeched as I turned my rifle to take a point blank shot at it, but the indicator on the weapon's rear faded from blue to red and a loud click informed me that my time had come to an end.

A thunderous *crack* was the sound that accompanied the Scriven exploding as though from the inside out and I was made fully aware that Roberts had joined in the fight.

A quick look before me told me why my ally had been yet to fire his weapon. As though drawn by the loud noise or possibly the threat posed by his shotgun, the Scriven now seemed to be turning in their path and heading straight for Roberts, leaving me entirely alone.

My weapon still glowed red so there was really nothing I could do but watch what happened next. Roberts' shotgun rang out five more times, each time wiping out a wave of the advancing enemy but each time more followed. Hope burned in my eyes though as I watched the Scriven ranks thinning and I could tell that if we could hold on just a little longer, we'd make it through, we'd be OK and we could start making some walls or fences, or anything that would help if and when this ever happened again.

One made it through. One was all it would ever take and, as unlikely as it seemed, it was one of the smallest baby Scriven that wasn't much bigger than a small dog. Apparently too small to have been hit by Roberts' powerful shotgun blasts, this one got in under the fire and swiped a small but incredibly sharp, bladed leg at my ally's shin. His leg was severed in two and I heard his scream of pain over the noise of battle.

That was all it would take and I knew it. Roberts' concentration was gone and along with it, all thoughts of defending himself from further attack.

I wished - prayed - for my rifle to turn blue whilst aiming at the Scriven closest to the Cadet and to my delight it clicked back into action just as the killing blow was on its way towards Roberts' neck. Of course I was assuming being decapitated was fatal whilst in an ARC, but it wasn't a theory I felt like testing right now.

My single shots were effective at both taking out the enemy nearest

Roberts as well as drawing their attention back to me and I knew that this time I didn't have as many numbers to deal with, so fortune favoured me.

I couldn't go full auto though because Roberts was now in the line of fire so picking off the enemy one by one was a difficult task. I was thankful that I could one-shot most of the Scriven except for the especially large ones, as this fact alone made my task so much easier.

Luck never lasts long though does it? And I was so close to getting them all too. After a few moments, my rifle decided that it was time to overheat again. I hadn't been using full auto mode so perhaps it just hadn't cooled down enough from earlier. Whatever the reason, my rifle clicked to let me know it was done, and there were three medium sized Scriven left.

"Roberts?" I called, frozen in the face of the three nightmarish enemies. "What do I do?"

Roberts, was in no mood to answer as he was holding the nub of his leg that was parted at the shin and whimpering – his shotgun on the ground next to him. I did the only thing I could think of doing, and that was to drop my weapon, stand up and lift my hands above my head in surrender.

Apparently, that particular gesture wasn't universal, because, as one, the three Scriven took a step forward, placing me within range of their legs. I closed my eyes and waited for the inevitable squishy noise followed by pain.

It didn't come.

I waited a second longer before opening one of my eyes and before me were three Scriven bodies cut precisely in half, smoking on the ground. It took me a moment to work it out, but behind me the turret atop the Construction Unit remained pointing in my direction and was also smoking.

If it weren't for the quiet whimpering of Roberts, I might not have dared to move yet, but he sounded like he wasn't in a good way.

Moving over to the Cadet, I scooped him up and placed him standing inside of one of the cutouts designed for ARC printing.

"Hold on there man, I'll get you sorted out," I said reassuringly. Roberts didn't open his eyes though. I didn't blame him.

I whipped around to the Unit's terminal and with Sam's help managed to find the function to repair Roberts' ARC. Within a minute, a new leg was printed and he was as good as new although he did keep whimpering until I forced him to look down at his shiny new appendage.

"Shit," he said. "Never seen that before." His voice was still strained but I could tell he was pulling himself back together.

"The mind makes it hurt you know," he explained. "I know these aren't my real legs...but shit..." He paused for a moment shaking his head. "We don't need to shit, sleep, eat or keep warm but pain, pain is real..."

I didn't need to get in the puddle with Roberts at that very moment, so I decided that taking his mind off the whole situation would be the best course of action.

"We need to do better. I want real defences next time so that's what we're going to do next. There might be more on the way and I don't know how long we have," I said. "And did you notice that these ones weren't acting like in the training missions, they changed targets like they weren't just following an order."

"I didn't notice but now that you mention it, they did act different. And I never seen a whole mixture of the crawlers coming at us like that before – usually it's just the big armour plated bastards," Roberts replied thoughtfully.

It was definitely something to think about, but for later.

"Thank God for the turret though, right?" I said with a smile.

"Well I hate to say I told you so…" Roberts replied as he stepped out of the Construction Unit and stretched his back, "but well, I did."

We both laughed and I realised that in all of this, somehow I'd started to have fun.

"First things first though," I said as I gestured to the assault rifle still clenched in my grip. "This piece of shit just nearly got me killed."

"Again you know how I hate to say I told you so…" Roberts said with a big smile. "Not all they're cracked up to be, huh?"

Walking over to the Construction Unit, I placed the rifle on the ground dismissively. Then I called up the terminal and called both versions of Sam into being.

"I want a real gun, like I trained with," I said. "Nothing with an X at the end of its name, no plasma or lasers. I want it to take bullets and magazines – something I know where I'm at with."

The terminal processed for a short while as it usually did, and eventually a new schematic was happily rotating on the screen in front of me. It was a good old fashioned SA80 assault rifle, no bells or whistles, save for a small magnification scope on top. A straight rectangular ammunition clip also rotated next to it, which I knew was going to cost me extra.

All good - the terminal informed me that the ammunition, which was handily printed out in magazines , would cost me just one kilo of processed materials to make. The rifle itself was the real surprise though. Interestingly, the thing would cost a measly ten kilos to generate.

"Why is it so cheap?" I heard myself say out loud, half in shock and half in the concerns that I'd missed something.

Sam's voice though, returned calm and very sarcastic. "The processing power required to generate a schematic for archaic weaponry is minimal. I would compare it to a person of your time asking for the designs to manufacture a caveman's club; i.e the material cost is still there, but there's not really much to think about."

Holy shit that burn was real. All annoyances aside though, the explanation had made a lot of sense. With that in mind, I queued up a good chunk of the resources that my HAMs had collected and ordered up ten rifles and fifty mags. There was no way I was going to be left in *that* kind of position again.

Next on the agenda were my defensive issues and I knew exactly what we needed – a big fence all around us so that we could shoot through it, but strong enough to hold back the razor sharp Scriven appendages. Oh and turrets, more turrets too.

I followed the same line of questioning for the turrets – could I use the older, bullet fed variants of my own past - but this time Sam had a little more to say.

"Laser turrets are by far the most effective way to deter enemy incursion as the processing power required is virtually nil. As such, any design changes would yield a negative impact on their cost, which would in turn generate an item that would be inferior to the current version, and they would also cost more processed materials."

This time I felt as though it was inappropriate to argue with the AI, as the warning seemed sincere and well founded. Instead I ordered up two more turrets for the roof of the Construction Unit and said no more about it.

It took a bit of waiting around and a lot of frustrated huffs, but eventually my guns and turrets were done. The rifles I piled up neatly on the floor with the ammo mags and the turrets sat exactly where they'd been placed, somewhat hungrily and frantically darting their laser pointers about looking for their next target.

I had to admit that I already felt much safer with my arsenal though the fact remained that we were still just two, with a lot of work remaining.

In my mind, the fence was going to be a chain linked, somewhat basic affair of about ten feet tall, surrounding the Construction unit at a distance of about twenty metres in all directions. Taking pi to be exactly three as all good mathematicians did, I guessed the length of fencing we actually needed was going to be one hundred and twenty metres or so when using the formula 'two pi multiplied by the radius to find the perimeter'. I rounded up to one thirty just to be on the safe side.

The issue that I had now, though, was that if I got the Construction Unit to print out the fence panels one by one, Roberts and I would once again have to do all the dog labour to get the fence in place. What I really wanted was a way to move the Construction Unit to the fences so that we could once again sit back and relax while the bots did all the work.

The word 'bots' sparked an idea in my mind's eye though. What if there was a way to print out miniature Construction Units that would build wherever I wanted them to? I knew a million-dollar idea when I saw one and excitedly I gave Roberts and both Sams the details of my plan. Roberts looked visibly confused, the terminal Sam didn't seem to have any thoughts on the matter at all, and the clever Sam told me that it was theoretically possible and to 'wait one moment' while she came up with some solution to my idea.

As normal, the terminal eventually lit up with a rotating design, though this time after what felt like actual minutes of waiting

The Construction Drone (it didn't have a nickname thank God), was like a little metal spider about the size of a cat. It had eight legs and looked quite like the Scriven babies – I presumed that if nature had chosen this design amongst all the others, then again why mess with the classics?

The downside – yes there was always a downside wasn't there – was the cost of the thing. Five *hundred* processed materials. I nearly choked, which was some feat as ARCs apparently didn't have airways that could get clogged up.

I checked the Construction Unit for its current stash and my heart sank as it registered just under one hundred kilos of materials. This was going to be a long day. Well, they were all long days on this planet, but you can forgive me the phrasing.

"You know," Roberts interrupted on seeing my disheartened shoulder slump, "I've seen it before when divers needed a little extra salvage – they go around collecting the bodies of their enemies and feed them to the Unit. It's messy work but apparently you get a bit more bang for your buck if you know what I mean."

That sounded gross. But observing the plains from where the Scriven had attacked, I could see a whole mountain of materials ripe for the plucking – not that I was going to be the one doing the plucking. Instead, I instructed my HAMs, through Sam of course, to harvest that location for materials instead of their current ever-growing quarry. Dutifully, they both turned as one and shuffled their way over to the previous battlefield.

When the first load of Scriven bits got into the Construction Unit, I was pleased to see that the efficacy of the raw materials was about fifty percent, which meant that within a few HAM loads, I'd be figuratively rolling in it. On a whim, I spread the wealth a little and printed out two more HAMs and when they were finished, I sent them to join the party.

Of course, some of the Scriven had been totally evaporated by our fire, but that didn't mean that the dirt hadn't absorbed their guts and gore. I didn't like to think about it too much, but this really was some rich pay dirt – and at the back of my mind I thought about how rich in resources that cave with the dead nest in it would be. I made a mental note to get the HAMs out there if it was safe to do so.

It took a long time for my newest creations to come to life, whichwere two Construction Drones at a half tonne of material each. Once they popped into existence I immediately gave them their task – to make a fence at our perimeter, turning our Construction Unit's current location into a defensible fire base.

The fence took a few days to print up on location by the drones. It was almost painful to watch as the smaller apparently less advanced machines slowly printed the bars and links from the base up, then had to go refill their tiny bodies to start the process all over again, and again and again and again.

I'd opted for a chain link metal fence – the things were always so useful – because that way we could see what was coming, and also I didn't need to worry about incoming fire making it through the gaps as the Scriven didn't seem to use weapons or ranged attacks.

All told, one hundred and twenty panels at five kilos per metre cost me six hundred kilos to fully construct, including a convenient gate, back and front.

What I didn't expect though, as we were constructing our defensive perimeter, were the infrequent visits from some of the medium sized Scriven. The first time it happened, I almost shit my pants as a single one apparently managed to sneak up to the fence as it was being printed, walk about a bit, then turn to leave. The second I became aware of its presence I hastily decimated it with my assault rifle. I was very pleased to note that a rifle with standard ammunition was just as effective as the plasma rifle had been, cutting down the Scriven in just a single burst.

Every hour or so, single Scriven appeared to investigate what we were doing and eventually I just stopped shooting at them. They'd spend a few minutes walking about the perimeter of the fence during its construction, then meander back off the way they came. Eventually, the fence was completed and none of the aliens had even tried to pervert its construction.

"What do you think they were up to?" I asked Roberts as the Construction Drones sauntered back to sit next to the Construction Unit, now that their task had been completed. Little did they know I had some very turret-like plans for them to work on next, and with the influx of materials that the previous battlefield had provided, I could easily afford the upgrade to my fence.

"Beats the hell outta me," Roberts replied. "Never seen anything like it between you and me, but then again everything about this situation is new to me."

He seemed to have taken a very nonchalant stance to the entire situation and I wondered if it was because he was feeling safer now that we had a fence. I knew I was.

The fence was a standard chain link affair, ten feet tall and topped with barbed wire. I really liked the height of the thing and had no desire to go through all the effort just to find that the Scriven could climb it. I mean they were basically big spiders – if the fence was made like a giant bath tub they may have had issues with it, but it wasn't, so they probably wouldn't.

When I had a look to see if it was a good idea to change the laser turret design to a more standard bullet fed one for attachment to the fence, Sam handily informed me that she stood by her assessment to use the laser version as it was cheaper to manufacture and didn't rely on reloads to function. I took her advice and ordered up five of the things to be manufactured around the fence at equal spacing, making sure their arcs of fire overlapped for maximum protection.

Once all that was done, that was when a new enemy force made itself known, traversing the previous battlefield that we'd already harvested, although this time I already felt so much safer.

The new Scriven that approached, though, weren't the small ones or even the big, heavy plated ones. These were all thin and spindly, and it looked as though there were just a few hundred of them.

Truth be told, the fact that the Scriven always seemed so adjustable to their enemy's tactics made me increasingly worried and even more so every time they did something different. Back on earth, in nature things were just so predictable. Predators hunted and took down their prey in the same way every time, plants grew to patterns – hell even the Fibonacci sequence appeared just about everywhere you looked – so fighting an enemy who was adaptable was new, and worrisome.

13

∞

Although it would've been easy and entirely possible to simply shoot outwards through the chain link fence, I wanted to see what the new type of enemy was going to do and also if the laser turrets were going to be worth their weight in scrap.

Because all of the Scriven approaching were now this new spindly-type deal, I really wanted to know exactly what they were being sent our way for. A part of me did wonder if these alien beings were simply separated out into clans or nests or whatever, and this was just another one coming our way. Whatever the reason for the discrepancy, I wanted to know as much about these creatures as possible and as quickly as I could.

They reached the fence in a matter of moments but did nothing to betray hostilities right away. These Scriven seemed intent on surrounding the fence entirely, without making any moves to try to break through or scale it. It was almost as though they were checking to see if it had any obvious weak points and they moved slowly and methodically.

"What're they doing?" Roberts asked as he stood next to me with his shotgun semi-ready. He seemed to share my desire to get the full picture before doing anything rash.

"They're seeing how we react," I said whilst formulating the idea in my head at the same time. "Exactly what we're doing; this is new to them so they're testing what kind of reactions we'll give to certain actions."

Roberts nodded his head slowly before returning to watch the circling Scriven closely. These ones, while appearing far less armoured – possibly not at all – were still pretty big. The size of a small mini put them – in my head – as 'medium sized' Scriven that were certainly not warriors. Perhaps these were more like the 'thinkers' of the race?

My thought process was interrupted as the very first spidery left leg touched the chain link fence, perhaps to see what it was made of or how strong it was. My laser turret didn't care though and it whipped around and opened fire on the creature, and the Scriven's outstretched leg was all that remained as its body exploded in a fanfare of blood and gore.

Roberts and I didn't need to be told twice that things had gone south and we opened fire at the enemy at the gates. The lasers all jumped into life simultaneously and I wondered if they had their own AI's or if Sam controlled them because they never seemed to do anything until the very last minute.

Once each of the turrets had sent a laser beam out to decimate a Scriven they again fell into inaction and hung limply from their perches. That fact didn't stop Roberts and me from shooting though, and after just a few moments at least half of the creatures laid dead and the rest were retreating.

Panting after the thrill of combat, my attention returned to the lifeless turrets. "WHAT THE FUCK SAM?" was the manifestation of that attention.

"How can I help you?" she said and I could tell it was with a smile on her face.

"Why the fuck did the fucking turrets stop fucking firing?" I managed to growl after somewhat controlling my temper.

Sam replied without missing a beat and her reply made me want to punch her stupid face even harder. "The turrets are out of power," she said. "They are running on an auxiliary power system that cannot sustain so many laser turrets."

"Then why in God's name did you advise us to make *laser* turrets that'd be useless then?" Roberts chimed in, evidently as annoyed as I was, but I was happy he'd heard Sam's reply.

"Laser turrets were the most effective option in terms of cost and firepower," Sam replied happily. "I was unaware that you would be so surprised of the fact that these items needed power to function."

I couldn't argue with her logic but still I felt as though she'd done that on purpose.

"Do me a favour Sam and don't talk to me for a while," I said as I moved back toward the Construction Unit's terminal to see what I was going to do about this situation. The most annoying thing was that I knew I needed to talk to the annoying AI again immediately. So swallowing my pride that's exactly what I did.

With the field of battle being harvested once again for its biomass, the rotating image of the 'power station' rotated on the terminal before me. Luckily the cost wasn't entirely prohibitive as it wasn't a completely new design of my own, but rather something that Sam and Roberts knew of between them. I mean it was going to cost five tonnes of processed materials, but that was something I knew I had to live with.

Essentially the power station was a five metre tall wind turbine with a solar sail around its centre and a geothermal collection unit at its base. It was the epitome of renewable energy collection as when there was no wind, there was sun, if there was no sun then there was probably geothermal energy to be collected. I ordered one immediately and sent the Construction Drones to build it right behind the Construction Unit, inside our defensible perimeter.

It was going to take forever to build, but the upside was that we could still use the actual Construction Unit to build things while the drones were being utilised to print out the power station. With speed in mind, I queued up a couple more HAM's and Drones. I wanted to make sure that growth was steady enough so that we didn't hit a materials or construction bottleneck. I knew that the available materials almost always caused issues in large scale manufacturing.

"We need to talk about what we are going to do about the others," I said to Roberts, who was once again cleaning orange mud from his shotgun.

"I know, and I have some thoughts," he replied. "The way I see it is that we have two options: we get them to come to us or we go to them."

I thought for a moment about what each meant that we'd have to do, but then I realised that there really was no reason to choose, was there?

"Why don't we do both?" I said flatly. "We set up a comms array to let them all know where we are, then we go out and find the ones that can't make it."

Roberts winced at the thought of having to do all that work and a part of me was right there with him in that, but inside I knew that even if the ARCs would basically last forever, with each passing hour and day, the threat of one of them being destroyed and the diver suffering irreversible brain damage grew and grew.

My mind whirred at the possibilities that the Construction Unit afforded us to carry out our plans; it was just so *useful*. I wondered how exactly humanity had come up with such an invention, though I should have known that the military, given enough time, always came up with new ways to both kill people and put their own people in danger.

To interrupt my pondering a new threat appeared on the horizon, and not one that I was expecting. By the look on Roberts' face, he hadn't been expecting it either.

There was a *flock* of incoming flying contacts. And by flock I mean that on the horizon, coming in our direction, were hundreds of bird-like aliens flying through the sky.

"What the fuck is that?" Roberts said aloud with a twang of foreboding in his voice.

Of course, I didn't know either, so I raised my rifle to my eye and looked through the scope to get a better idea of what we were about to face.

They were Scriven, I could tell from their colours, markings and the way their beaks clattered as they flew towards us. However these ones were more like pterodactyls than spiders, with just four legs now tightening skin-like wings between them, and an extra two pincer-like arms at the front. These looked like they were bred for combat too - not weak and spindly - they were sharp and pointed at every corner.

A cold shiver ran through my body as I realised exactly what this new development meant to us. The fence, having only just been built, was now obsolete as these enemy didn't care how high it was.

There was nothing that we could do, save for raise our weapons to the sky and prepare for a fight. I had already told Roberts that it'd probably be a good idea for him to use an SA80 assault rifle over his plasma shotgun, but I think he was attached to the thing so he didn't bother switching it.

"Flyers incoming!" Roberts shouted as the enemy closed into range. It was an unnecessary announcement but still it rallied my spirits a little.

With the power station not yet functional and therefore the turrets being of no use to us, I gritted my teeth and when the first alien bird arrived in range I squeezed the trigger of my rifle.

Again, thankfully, the Scriven didn't seem to comprehend that when bunched together they presented a much easier target and within moments they were being cut down by our fire, my bullets cutting them to shreds and Roberts' plasma shotgun taking out chunks of the enemy at once. It became apparent very quickly though that as they flew toward and above us, this time we weren't going to just be able to sit tight and decimate them.

The flying Scriven had eventually made their way directly above our base of operations, and rather than swoop down to make their attacks, I was both astounded and horrified to see the creatures *drop* their smaller young right inside our defensive perimeter. These were much like the ones that'd been in the cave though maybe a few inches bigger in some cases, but certainly not warriors. This time we had nowhere to run – and we were caged in *with them*.

The first drop was only a handful of the little ones and thank God for that. We tried taking them out as they sailed down towards us but they moved quickly and were spread out and small – which meant it was like shooting clay pigeons with a bolt action rifle. Inevitably, eight of the little bastards landed between Roberts and me.

Knowing that Roberts could get a little trigger happy at times, I dove to the side which allowed him to pummel the group without fear of hitting me in the crossfire. I rolled as soon as I hit the ground, switching my rifle to single fire mode, and joined in, peppering the enemy with round after well placed round.

We'd only taken down half when the next batch arrived, then the next and the next. By the time I'd managed to catch my breath there were at least thirty or forty little Scriven inside our new fence. I felt like the whole ordeal had been a gigantic waste of time.

"HELP ME!" I heard Roberts call in distress and when I glanced in his direction I could see that he'd been taken down to the ground and was covered in the bastard things. Renewing my focus and dealing with a pretty huge threat of my own, I switched my rifle to full auto and started pummelling the Scriven back in a wide arc. Handily this also had the effect that the majority of them turned in my direction as I was apparently the bigger threat again. I could only hope that I'd made it to Roberts' aid in time.

Boom! My comrade's shotgun fired from behind the enemy and the noise told me it wasn't too late just yet. What I did want, though, was some kind of close range or melee weapon to help me deal with these things as, thinking about it, while we pretty much just used ranged fire, they liked to do everything up close and personal. I made a mental note to look into that later.

Boom the shotgun rang out again and I was reminded of what I was supposed to be doing here. With my weapon on full auto and the Scriven now clumped together I was able to push them back in an arc again until there were just a few stragglers left, which I promptly dispatched with single shots. All told, we'd been pretty successful at taking down an enemy with new tactics. I watched the flying ones retreating the field of battle before turning my attention to Roberts.

"Well that was new…" I started to say, but cut myself off when I saw Roberts' body lying on his back, legs completely torn away. I was shocked to see blood and gore covering the wounds and the ground around him, wondering just why ARCs were made in this way – but again I was no scientist.

"Roberts?" I practically whispered as I walked over to the Cadet.

"Y…yeah," he forced out, it didn't give me much hope but at least he was alive. Barely.

Not knowing if the best thing to do was tourniquet the wounds, take a branding iron to them or leave him exactly where he was, I went with secret option number four – I hefted him from underneath by his armpits and laid him back in the Construction Unit for the second time.

"You OK?" I asked stupidly, but the Cadet had passed out. I wasn't sure how he always managed to get himself into these situations, but it made me want to do something to help, and that's when I had a brainwave.

After fiddling around with the terminal for a while and a few short consultations with Sam (I still really didn't want to engage with her too much), I had an idea and a design. When Roberts awoke from his medically induced reparations, he'd have a new toy to play with, and I think he was going to like it.

"What the fuck did you do to my arms?" He said once he stepped out of the Unit. "It was my legs that got torn away, not my arms!"

"What…do you mean?" I asked knowingly with a smirk, but wanting to get his take on the situation.

"They feel so…heavy," he said bemused, holding his hands up to his face.

"Ah, that's right…I did something, and you're going to enjoy this…" I said with a huge smile on my face. "Can your visor show you what's in there?"

"No." Roberts said gruffly. "Without the connection to the Saturn, I don't get the same overlays I used to. I get some, mainly the ARC's dumbed down internal version of the AI, but nothing complex… like looking inside my arm." He sounded annoyed so I just told him.

"I put a weapon in there," I said. "Try to use it." Of course I had no idea of how this was all going to work, but I had a sneaky suspicion that if he thought about it hard enough, he'd get the hang of it.

He did.

Within a second or two, with a loud metallic scraping noise a two foot long razor sharp blade had shot out from his left knuckles and burst into blue electricity along its length.

"You put a fucking plasma blade *inside* my arm?" he accused, and it didn't sound like he was happy about it. "You messed around with another man's body like that's something normal to do!?"

I started to retract a little, unsure of why this was such a big deal to him.

"Well that's a mighty fine fucking upgrade!" he stated, laughing as his demeanour completely changed. I exhaled in relief. "Though next time, maybe you should ask before you do something like that."

I smiled and nodded, though I had no plans to ask before the next time. Whenever I got the chance to upgrade one of us, I was going to take it.

"I'm serious," he continued, understanding my inner monologue. "If I wasn't out of action, that could very well have damaged my mind. Remember what I told you about getting in and out of ARCs? The human brain just ain't wired to keep getting changed up like that. Now don't get me wrong I like what you did, but just know that this was a *lucky situation*. Just how would you have felt that by adding this new weapon, I could have lost the use of my legs? And I don't mean just here in my ARC, but also in my *real* body."

My legs went cold again, I had no idea that it was even a possibility and that just reaffirmed the statement that I shouldn't have been messing around with things that I didn't fully understand. I promptly apologised and slinked away with my tail between my legs.

Thankfully, Roberts wasn't the kind to hold a grudge – so when the power station was completed some time later, we were back on speaking terms.

I'd spent the time trying to figure out just what the Scriven were doing and how they always seemed to adapt to our tactics, and Roberts had been practicing with his new weapon, seeing how big a rock he could slice through in one swipe. It turned out that about three feet in diameter was the magic number – and that in itself was impressive.

I'd asked Sam a few fleeting questions about the alien creatures but she really didn't have too much to offer. She told me that they'd started their war with humanity not long after the Ashaii had, and that they appeared as nests on planets across all of human space ,although it was unknown where they actually came from or whattheir true origin system was. I felt like she knew more than she was letting on, but knowing what she was like I didn't want to press her too much on the point. Besides it didn't really matter where they came from right now, I just wanted to know how to kill them.

Across all of the times I'd fought against the Scriven, they'd come back the next time with something different or unexpected, and usually it was a way to circumnavigate some tactic I'd come up with specifically to beat them. The flying ones had been the biggest shock as I had no idea that their evolutionary track could take them up and into the skies so quickly – that was unless they could already do that but I just hadn't seen it yet. It seemed unlikely.

My plans for growing our defences were hindered by the simple fact that I had no idea what the Scriven were going to do next. I didn't want to waste time and materials making something specifically to deal with a threat and then come to realise I should've been planning for a different scenario entirely. This all led me to a new conclusion; I was going to build nothing defensive right now.

Instead of trying to guess what they were going to do next, I felt like this time I'd let the enemy make the next move. In addition, it was about time I started saving some lives out here on this planet.

"Roberts, I'm going to get started on making a comms array," I said once I'd made my mind up. "Do you have any objections?"

He stopped what he was doing, retracting his blade into his arm to talk to me. "That sounds good to me, but we might get some more of those flying bugs inbound before that's finished up. Should we make more defences, or turrets?"

"Nah, next time the turrets should be online anyway so we'll have the extra firepower as long as the power station works as it should. Besides, I want to see what happens if we *don't* keep escalating the situation. It seems like the more of a threat we are, the more they try to change their tactics to get us."

"I agree that they do seem to be changing their game quite a lot," Roberts replied, "but that might just be the way things are happening. What if they take that next step and we don't? I don't wanna die out here just to test a theory, you know."

He did have a very good point, all of my ideas were just theoretical but at the same time theories did need to be tested.

"What would you do?" I asked, not sarcastically, but genuinely interested in his opinion.

"Oh, I wouldn't take advice from me. I'd been here a long time not doing much when you arrived. All I'm saying is that you better be sure what you're doing is right, cos if I die, I'll kill you!" He said it with a smile so I knew he was joking, and all it did was let me know I could do what I needed to do to get the job done.

Turning my attention back to the terminal, I was all set to get the comms array designed and built, but before I got the chance to begin a message filled the screen.

Mission Accomplishments

Beyond the Call of Duty 2: You have destroyed 752 enemy combatants during your mission to protect and rescue a fellow diver.

Field Promotion: For your efforts you have been promoted to Cadet Rank 1st class.

> Purple Heart: You have rescued a fellow diver from the brink of death on more than one occasion.
>
> Field Promotion: For your efforts you have been promoted to Corporal.
>
> With your new rank comes a permanent upgrade. This will come into effect on your next constructed ARC, however you may choose this upgrade ahead of time.

"Roberts, come and have a look at this," I called the Cadet over.

"Oh well props to you Corporal," he said giving a short salute once he'd read the readout on the terminal. I could tell his words were a bit sarcastic but he still respected the rank.

"What does it mean?" I asked, knowing exactly what it meant, but was thinking more about the consequences.

"Well I assume you're asking 'why now' as opposed to what this means literally, right?" I nodded in response. "Well I'm not of that rank myself, but I know that once you reach certain milestone ranks, you can begin to assign permanent changes and upgrades to your ARCs, so when they're built for the first time they have a sort of default setting.

I was a weird explanation but wanting to know more I gestured for Roberts to continue.

"For example, this arm blade thingy that I have, I could probably set that as a permanent upgrade and I'd have it at the start of every mission. Like I said, you don't want to be going around making changes to your ARC – unless they're sanctioned by the Construction Unit itself upon first light."

It made sense, but I had no idea what all of the possible upgrades could be that I would even want,. I had everything I needed in the Construction Unit, didn't I?

Before I dove into all of the nuances of permanent upgrades, I set Sam off to get a comms tower going. I knew it'd take time and resources to make, but I told her to put it right in the middle of our base once it was designed. I was happy to see that after a few minutes, the drones were on it with the telltale blue wireframe betraying its position in my visor.

The terminal was far more interesting to me right now though. There were so many different ways I could spend my one permanent upgrade that my head practically spun. From simple upgrades to the visor like better or longer visuals, changes to my ARC's physical stature, weapon skills, more or better grenades, to tech upgrades like drones and shoulder-mounted weaponry – there was everything I could've thought of plus more. What I did notice, though, was that these were upgrades available to 'Corporals' and I wondered what the higher ranks would be afforded.

I made my choice but was told that it wouldn't come into effect until the next time I stepped out of the Construction Unit inside a new ARC. I was sure what I chose would be worth it though. A shoulder mounted personal point defence laser. That's right, I was going to be the predator.

Of course I'd argue somewhat desperately the fact that because this was to be an add on unit to my person, perhaps I could've just had the Construction Unit print me one up, but I was informed that this wasn't a possibility because it was linked directly to my brain rather than being AI controlled – It made me wonder if I could have something made that was AI controlled, and therefore a possibility, but again I was told no. I put a pin in it to argue about later.

14

∞

"Firebase Alpha, we are receiving you loud and clear." The first message arrived shortly after the comms array had been finalised and our message had been sent off to circumnavigate the planet. It was a man's voice but I didn't have any further details on its owner. I wasn't too concerned that the Scriven might be able to intercept the message that gave away our exact location ,given that they were spiders and not scientists – well that was the hope anyway.

I was delighted that my plans had started to work, and that there were other people still alive out there.

"What's your position?" I asked excitedly. "Can you get to us? What's your status? How many of you are there?" My mind raced and I asked everything I could think of all at once at the thought of saving thousands of souls all in one go.

"Woah there Alpha," the voice returned from the terminal attached to the comms array. I hate to say it but we're on the dark side of the planet, at least eight thousand klicks from your position. I really don't want to say this either Alpha, but there's no way we're getting to you. Is the Saturn here?"

I made a note to update the message next time I tried this as I didn't want to have to explain everything about everything each time I spoke to someone new, but this time I had no choice so I spilled everything I could.

The comms went silent for a few minutes before the voice eventually spoke again.

"My name is Corporal Francis Varley. It's a pleasure to meet you. How are you feeling?"

I was taken aback by the question, not expecting to be asked how I was feeling when these people had been effectively stranded this entire time. The question caused my skin to goose bump and a lump formed in my throat.

"I'm sorry Corporal, but why would you ask such a question when you've clearly been in a much worse situation than I have?" I answered slowly.

"Well, I guess it's just that I've always been empathetic to the struggles of others, and it seems like you've gone through more in the last few weeks or so than anyone should've been subjected to in a lifetime. After all, I and the other ARCs out here knew what we were signing up for whereas you kind of got forced into it." Varley replied. I knew immediately that I liked the Corporal as he sounded very sincere and very caring.

We spoke for a short while about how we both felt about our current predicament, though there was still only one answer, which I relayed to him. I needed to get transports around the planet to do pickups, and quickly. Luckily on the dark side of the planet, Scriven attacks were few and far between, but that didn't mean Varley's squad, which consisted of the Corporal and two Cadets, wasn't without endangerment. In fact they'd already lost one Cadet to the dangers of the dark side of the planet.

The return messages came flooding in after I'd left Varley's squad with advice to 'hold tight.' It was all I could do. I answered a few of them immediately and spoke to each of the squad leaders as they updated us on their current status. I then had to hear about all of their losses and struggles and then let them know that there was nothing they could do other than to sit tight and await my plan. It made me feel like shit though because it was essentially a lie – I had no idea how to collect them all up or how long it would take, but I couldn't tell them that.

In the end I let Roberts take over the phone lines as I was getting frustrated at telling everyone the same thing and it'd started to eat away at my hope and positivity. I decided that whilst he was doing that, I could work with Sam to start getting the crew of the Saturn back to safety.

It was during my pondering though that the ground began to shake, gently, almost unnoticeably at first but then to a harsher degree. I held my head in my hands muttered "what fucking now," and picked up my rifle. Roberts, handily followed suit and we stood at the chain link fence looking out across the planetscape, wondering what could possibly come next.

We didn't have to wait very long.

Just on the other side of the fence, thankfully, about thirty metres away, the hard ground cracked, broke and erupted into a fountain, sending orange mud and dust high into the sky and in a wide perimeter. Once it settled, there remained the grotesque head of what could only be described as a giant sand worm.

When I say giant, I mean the thing must've been ten metres tall and as wide as a bus. When it looked in our direction – I had to assume it 'looked' because it had no eyes - its terrible maw opened and showed us its never ending rows and rows of sharp pointed teeth. If I was a betting man, I'd have said those teeth ran alongside the entirety of its body, however long that was.

Not wanting to wait for it to make the first move, I raised my rifle and placed the end of the muzzle through the links in the fence. I checked up and down through my scope for any weak points in the thing but nothing was apparent, and my visor had no helpful hints either.

I didn't hesitate any further, I let my first shot ring out although it was somewhat dampened by the sounds the terrible beast was making as it tore the ground up around it. My single bullet appeared to have no effect on it whatsoever.

Roberts' shotgun did do something, though, as while I was watching my shot do nothing to the creature, his seven-strong blast of blue plasma hit it, leaving blooded scorch marks where they'd impacted the hard skin. I hoped that once it moved closer – yes a very odd thing to hope for – that the efficacy of his fire would increase, and perhaps mine would too. I did have another option though and picking up the SA80X plasma assault rifle, I switched my fire to something far less physical and hopefully far more effective.

I had no reason to stick with single shots but acutely aware of Roberts' previous warning about the overall effectiveness of my rifle, I switched it over to burst fire and began peppering the beast with plasma shots.

If I thought that we were doing a good job, though, my excitement was to be short lived as when the worm decided to move in our direction I was reminded that it was yet to actually do anything threatening to us. However, by moving toward us it presented its gaping maw as a target, and that's when my laser turrets also decided to enter the fight.

The turrets always seemed to wait until the last moment to do anything, and the last time it had been a one shot kind of deal. I just hoped beyond hope that this time with the new power station, they'd be able to stay online and helpful for much longer.

The two turrets that faced the creature fired single laser beams at a rate of about one per second, and although it looked pretty uninspiring, the beams seemed to pass right through it leaving behind smoking holes that punched in one side and out the other about an inch in diameter. At this rate, the turrets would turn the worm into a cheese grater given enough time. Though, was there ever really enough time in these situations?

The worm seemed to be undeterred by its new smoking orifices as it continued to move towards us, mostly above the ground now – well I hoped it was mostly because it was already ginormous. No matter how many holes we put in the thing it just didn't seem to stop or even slow down and eventually it made it into close quarters with us. I knew the fence wasn't going to do anything to hold against this enemy.

With a frightfully quick thrust forwards, the worm took an entire fence panel inside its mouth along with Roberts, both disappearing from view in the blink of an eye.

"ROBERTS!" I called after my friend as I'd done too many times already. It made me wonder just why the enemy always seemed hell bent on taking him down, but that was a thought for another day. All I could hope right now was that the worm didn't have acidic saliva, or a bunch of tiny little worm mouths inside it or something – there was still the possibility that I could save Roberts if he hadn't been completely munched up.

What I noticed first though was the fact that the two turrets that'd been firing on the worm had also apparently been eaten by it, their panels and mounts absent as well as their fire. This was certainly not good news for me.

Rather than begin to move toward me to deliver my own killing blow, the worm reared straight upwards seemingly in pain. I had no idea what was happening until I finally saw the bright blue blade that I knew was attached to Roberts' arm coming directly out of the thing's stomach. *Well I'd call it a stomach, though as it was distinctly worm-like, I doubted that's what it actually was. Maybe it was his knee.*

The blade traced the circumference of the worm and within moments it'd been perfectly dissected, with the wound cauterised so that no blood stained the ground around it. It fell to the ground with an almighty puff of dust as it died, leaving Roberts standing right in the centre of it, covered in what I could only assume was digestive goo. I did not envy him that.

A moment of silence passed before the cadet let out an amazed and triumphant "WOOOH YEAH!!" and I couldn't help but smile while he fist pumped the air. That was of course until I felt the ground rumbling for a second time, and behind me from below and inside our perimeter broke a second deadly giant worm.

This time, there was not going to be a bad meal in the form of Cadet Roberts to deal with this new threat – the only thing on the menu was me, and I had no way to burst free when the thing ate me. The last thing I thought before I closed my eyes was *'my God I wish I'd made more grenades.'*

But death didn't come. What did come was the sound of plasma rounds and they sounded like big ones too. Then more ground-shaking stomps and I opened my eyes cautiously just in case it was to the view of the inside of the worm. Luckily for me, it wasn't.

Approaching our base were five mechanical behemoths firing plasma round after plasma round from what could only be described as arm cannons. They were each at least four metres tall and had two legs for walking and two arms that looked like they were equipped to the teeth with all kinds of weapons and attachments. In the centre of each, was a person who seemingly had control over the things.

"Sorry we're late," one of them shouted over the sound of gunfire as they arrived, still peppering the giant worm which now seemed heavily outmatched. I held a single hand up as if to say 'don't worry about it'.

The worm was…well worm food within a few more moments and I couldn't be happier about that - better it than me, right?

"Mech Commanders Major James Long, Major Darren Carter, Major Jason Walton, Major Gerald Hobern and Major Jackie Simms reporting for duty as requested," Major Long stated officially. I could tell who was who as when each of their names was called they in turn raised a massive arm towards the sky.

It seemed strange that all five of the team were Majors, meaning that technically they shared command, but those kinds of questions could be asked at a later date.

"How…how did you get here?" Remembering my previous blurts of questioning, I managed to formulate some sense before asking them.

"We received your communication," Major Long replied and as he spoke I could distinctly recognise a hint of a Scottish accent. "We weren't too far away, but we couldn't reply as we've taken some damage to our own comms."

Hobern raised his hand guiltily and added "my bad."

Long continued his explanation. "We take the hit on several systems in order to upgrade these things, so only one of us has long range comms. We also tend to specialise, so Carter and I are assault mechs with heavy arms, Walton is a heavy mech so has to plant himself before he shoots to save from flying off backwards, Hobern has the tech support and comms, and Simms is both a long range specialist and a field medic."

It did make a lot of sense, other than the fact that mechs required a 'medic', I'd have called her an engineer but then also realised where even more confusions could arise if that was the case so I dropped it. I was just really glad to have the first batch of Saturn survivors within my grasp. It felt really good, like everything that we'd been working towards might have actually had a chance of working.

"So I'll give you an update on the situation out there," Long said when I didn't say anything for a short while. "The Scriven are camped out in their nests all over this planet. If you attack them or let them know you're around, they'll come for you but if you leave them alone then you're generally OK."

That answered my question about Scriven life on the planet.

"They do seem to evolve though, so if you use new tactics or weapons against them, the next batch they produce will be specifically designed to deal with that threat." I knew that part already.

I explained everything we'd been through and the fact that we'd had similar results, then continued my story all the way up to sending out the signal that brought the Majors here and the giant worms, which my HAMs had pretty much half harvested for their salvage at this point. To my surprise, when I asked if I was expected to relinquish command of the base to the higher ranking officers, the answer was not one that I was expecting.

"Na, you don't have to relinquish command here," Long said as he watched my HAMs going about their business. "We can't communicate with Sam or the Saturn and honestly I have no idea what any of this is you're doing here. Seems to me like you got yourself a good idea, plus in any combat situation I'm sure I'll take the reins if it's needed. Until then you just concentrate on getting us all back home. Oh last thing, we can't actually get out of these things…" the hulking mech clunkily gestured to itself with its plasma assault rifle arm and the movement made me smile. I'd missed people and was glad to be back as part of a group.

"But don't be fooled lad, there're many things you don't and can't understand about the ARC and Construction Units at your rank of Corporal, even if you are doing things that seem strange to me. Mechs like these are made upon emergence to link directly to the brain patterns of the diver – they are one and the same, part mech part diver. If one is killed in the battlefield, then they're junk… and you know what that means don't you?" Long continued. I nodded silently in response.

"So for now, go about your business. Consider it an order if you like and we will give advice as needed. Oh and one last thing, if any other officers turn up that aren't in mechs, they may not be so forthcoming with their handover of command if you get what I'm saying – us mech commanders tend to think of ourselves outside of the chain of command but that doesn't ring true for everybody!"

I was pleased with the Major's honesty and candour, but inwardly a part of me wished that he could've just taken over and dealt with the situation.

The next few hours brought nothing interesting to report to my attention, so I spent most of the time trying to figure out exactly how I was going to get everyone back here safely. While I did that, I watched quietly as the team of mechs dug trenches along and around the outside of our fence – which I'd taken the time to repair after the worm had so easily devoured it. I made a note to see if I could run a current through it - that'd show them.

The mechs turned out to actually be pretty good excavators, though I had no desire to be the one who'd clean all that muck out of the end of their weapons once they were done. When they had finished, the trenches they made were so deep that each mech could kind of crouch down and become invisible entirely, or half-stand and place his or her gun on the ground in a stable yet defended firing position. I cursed myself for not thinking about this tactic earlier, after all it wasn't exactly new information.

The trenches stretched about the centre of our firebase in a kind of network of concentric circles, each with a wider diameter than the last and each with a number of feeder trenches to allow passage between them. Once all was said and done there were three main trench lines and no less than twenty feeders, and I imagined that from above it would look like a work of art.

The first mech to arrive back at the Construction Unit was Major Jackie Simms, and I took the opportunity to speak to another of the Major's team without the audience.

"Major?" I asked as she stomped back inside the fence and toward me. I could see her attention turn in my direction as I spoke. "Do you ever need to rest, or sit down in those things?" I asked. It wasn't the question I wanted to ask but it had been playing on my mind somewhat.

I could see Simms more clearly now; she had dark skin and long black hair tied in a single braid that reached down to her stomach, and like the other mechs I could see that she wore a tight-fitting dark blue base-layer type outfit.

"We do, though it's more of an involuntary reaction than an actual need to rest of course. You can get by without if you force it but sometimes it eases the mind if you allow your ARC to control your usual subconscious functions. Like breathing for example – you don't need to think about it, it just happens. An ARC is the same - although it doesn't need to breathe to survive, if left to its own devices you'll see that it does actually mimic breathing."

I watched Cadet Roberts as she spoke and indeed his shoulders seemed to be rising and falling as though he was actually breathing.

"Technically we also don't need these visors either, but they do come in useful…" the Major trailed off and I took the opportunity to ask my follow up questions.

"Can I make mechs with the Construction Unit? Or would that be offensive to the commanders or something?" As I spoke I recognised how what I was saying could've been offensive, but Simms didn't seem to mind.

"It is possible to generate almost anything from the Construction Unit, though there is a big difference between constructs printed in conjunction with an ARC, and one that is independent from a diver's brainwaves." She began to explain. I'd heard this story before. "When a unit – let's say an autonomous mech in this case – is controlled solely by an AI, its functions and thought patterns tend to be very basic. Sure you can get it to move and fire but if you aren't there to command it and it starts getting attacked, it'll just stand there and let itself get eaten most of the time. Results do vary though – oh, you know those turrets?" She gestured to the turrets on my chain link fence and I nodded. "They include a high-functioning AI, so they'll defend themselves automatically but in general they're pretty dumb."

I could certainly attest to that – the turrets had been a pretty big pain in my ass so far – promising defensive laser beams but seemed to have issues at every turn. I told Simms as much.

She nodded before she spoke again. "You see what I mean? A part of me thinks it's Sam's cruel joke to keep us guessing, but another part just seems to think that AI just can't compete with the human mind yet…"

I did wonder exactly how that statement could be true when Sam was *so* human-like, though I didn't want to have another conspiracy theory conversation about Sam and her possible human backbencher.

"Long said you were a medic? Why does a squad of mechs need a medic?" I asked. It was the last of my main questions but still it had me wondering.

Simms smiled, and as she did so two small spidery robots that looked astonishingly similar to my own construction drones crawled from around her back and walked along her mechanical arms. Then they appeared to do a little spot-welding before scurrying back off to behind her and out of view.

"Things still go wrong even in these things," Simms said with a chuckle. "My drones can repair most light damage, though there is a limit and once it's passed there's no coming back… There's one last thing you should know too," Simms continued forlornly. "You won't see many mechs out there – possibly not even a single other one. Have you been told what happens when you die while connected to an ARC?"

I nodded.

"Well the damage that's caused to your mind is tentatively linked to how different your ARC is to your physical body – I mean for simplicity sake let's just say it's directly linked – imagine what your mind thinks when it goes from a gigantic, metal clad behemoth back into its own tiny body with mild back aches…"

I nodded again, but slowly, as though to telegraph my understanding. Nothing came for free in this world, and apparently the bigger the reward the bigger the risk.

15

∞

After a few consultations with everyone as a team, I'd come to the conclusion that out of land and air transports, air transports would be more difficult to make, but offered less terrain difficulties and faster speeds than ground-based units, which was definitely something I needed to think about. In the end, I decided to just go ahead and settle on the flying transports as I thought that although it may take longer and cost more resources, the potential results, combined with the urgency of our predicament, meant that it was the prudent thing to do. I had wondered how fast the mech commanders could run, but was told that even if they could travel at great speeds (they couldn't really), there would be no way to round people up and bring them back anyway. It was back to the old drawing board again.

Representing somewhat of a cross between an old chinook helicopter and a d-day landing craft, my Computer-Controlled Aerial Transport was queued up for production. It was going to cost five tonnes of processed materials to make a single one, but I was informed by Sam, the terminal and my own visor that they were going to be able to travel at incredible speeds and also able to circumnavigate the entire planet in less than two hours. The main advantage, though, was that its acronym was 'CAT'. I was really starting to see why the military loved using acronyms so much.

After some time passed with me simply watching the Construction Unit and the drones working in tandem to print up my new CAT, and the mech commanders patrolling the perimeter, I was rudely interrupted by the sound of a single plasma blast being fired off into the distance. When I traced the sound, I could see that Major Simms had fired the round at some unseen enemy. As I was about to ask what it was about, she spoke loudly to everyone.

"We got contacts." Her long range rifle arm had seen what nobody else could.

No matter how hard I looked I couldn't see anything. It was as though she had some kind of telescopic vision and she was using it to pick off enemies God knows how far away. After a minute or two of sporadic shots, she ceased her fire.

"That's all of them," she said as the rest of the ARCs stood a little easier.

I really wanted to know what was happening, so I asked the Major.

"I think we may have been followed. It was a little scouting party," she said. "Three miles away, but I think I got them all."

"Holy shit, three miles?" I asked in exasperation

"I told you, field medic *and* long range specialist," Long offered as he appeared next to us. I was going to like this team.

I really didn't expect it, but Hobern was more useful than any of the other mech commanders. Well, that makes it sound as though the rest weren't useful; the unit was in fact the most useful addition to our defence that I could've imagined, but Hobern just had something next level.

The man had long greasy hair, parted in the centre and an attitude that you just didn't mess with but the 'tech expert' part of his duty really was a marvel to behold. When I asked what kind of tech he had, he presented me with the exact force-shield sword that I'd used to pretty good effect during my training mission. I knew it wasn't everything he had – I could see at least three different types of grenades attached to the legs of his mech – but this was something that would come in handy for those of us not wearing armour plating. I was even happier when he said I could keep it, although he sounded pissed off about it – I guess it could've been nonchalant but with Hobern both sounded similar and were equally possible.

Majors Carter and Walton, the assault and heavy mech respectively, didn't seem to want to get too involved with the politics of daily ARC life and didn't appear to leave their scouting of the perimeter to make sure nothing snuck up on us. I liked their devotion to their duty, but also made a note to see if I could get them to come out of their shells at some point.

No one else had arrived of their own volition though, a fact that led me to start the construction of a second CAT to be finished shortly after the first and double our rescuing capabilities.

"We got someone coming!" Simms shouted a new warning just as I was beginning to unclench my jaw. I watched as all the mechs turned in the direction Simms was pointing and readied their weapons.

"It's an ARC!" she cried happily, then added "but he's being chased!"

It was difficult getting a running commentary of someone running for their life but Simms' rifle fire helped to alleviate my worries - that was until she said that there were too many for her to deal with alone. That's when Long and Carter leapt out of the defensive trenches, at least ten feet into the air and started running in the direction of the ARC, shaking the ground as they moved without any thought of subtlety.

In the distance I could begin to see a person running, stumbling, tripping and otherwise not running away effectively, while Simms' plasma rounds did everything they could to take out the Scriven that were bearing down on him. These Scriven looked big too, like the ones I'd fought in my training simulation.

Within moments the two assault mechs had made it to the ARC. They moved like lightening and my mouth practically hung open at how fast they were in comparison to their size – nothing that big had any business being that fast.

Between the two mechs, Carter held back the swarming enemy creatures and Long hoisted the ARC atop the housing that kept his own person safe and began to retreat, firing all the time. It was almost beautiful as though the entire movement had been scripted, but I recognised good training when I saw it.

Once the mechs and the newly saved ARC had made it back into proper visual range, I could see that the ARC, which was a man, had passed out and the Scriven didn't seem to want any part in following the group. I still wondered exactly how intelligent those beasts were.

With the delicacy that should've also been impossible for the size of his mech, Long placed the ARC onto the ground and my visor handily informed me that this man was Cadet Javier Martinez, Rank A.

"Shit," Long spoke first. "This is his first mission and look what they've done to him…"

At first I didn't know what the Major was talking about, but when I actually took a moment to inspect the Cadet, I could see that he was in a very bad way. There were bloodied puncture wounds all over his body and it looked like one of his wrists was broken as his hand faced the wrong way. Simms immediately called her medical drones into action, which begin to do *whatever* it was they did, and it did look like it was helping.

Eventually Martinez regained his consciousness, and as you could imagine was a little surprised to be looked over by two hulking metal mechs.

Well - he screamed.

I knew then that it was my time to shine. Roberts and I we were the only two ARCS that weren't gruesome mechs, and I internally decided that his slightly bigger body mass and slightly lower social courtesy meant I was the one who should talk to Martinez, who was still freaking out below the Majors, who didn't really seem to know what to do about it.

"Martinez?" I said confidently to both gain his attention and potentially snap him back to reality. Thankfully, the cadet looked at me so I knew he was at least with us. I could see though that his eyes were filled with fear and tears that overflowed and ran down his cheeks. So ARCs could cry?

"Martinez," I repeated "you've got to snap out of this. You're safe now, look around you."

The cadet stopped his whimpering for a second to look about although the calm didn't last very long. Eventually he sat upright and wrapped his arms around himself as though he was trying to warm up. Then he spoke properly for the first time.

"They'll never see, don't you see, not safe, NOT SAFE." It was then acutely evident that no matter how much the drones repaired Martinez's physical ARC, his mental state wasn't going to be so easy to deal with.

"You are safe Martinez," I attempted to placate the cadet. We're all getting out of here. The Saturn is sending lifeboats and then we'll be home free.

"Never safe. Not coming. Never coming, not safe never not never…" The cadet descended into muttered ramblings and rocked back and forth with his arms still tightly wrapped around himself. It made me worried but I knew there was nothing I could do about it. I left him in the care of Simms and Roberts to see if they could soothe him, not that I held out much hope but it was what it was.

There were no more Scriven attacks before the two CATs had finished being constructed, and I was pretty happy about that – I didn't know what would happen to Martinez if he faced more of the alien creatures. I'd spoken to Long and Simms about what they'd faced in their abandonment and it was much the same as what Roberts had told me – they lost all comms and just hunkered down until they could get more information. There were Scriven attacks and defences, evolutions and changes to their tactics and neither force seemed to be able to overcome the other. Every time the divers thought they'd made a breakthrough, the perfect counter was launched on the side of the Scriven, and they'd be set right back into deadlock. I did wonder that if this was happening all over the planet, surely somewhere, someone should've been able to take an advantage … or disadvantage.

With the CATs complete and able to hold fifteen regular sized ARCs each (or about three mechs – not that there should be any more out there), I changed my communications array message to inform everyone that we were coming to rescue them. They all seemed very pleased with that fact and began to relay their coordinates so that the CATs could go out and pick them up. I knew it was going to take a few days at least to round them all up, but in the meantime I would do all that I could to bolster our defences just in case the worst were to happen. I wouldn't put it past the Scriven to wait for us all to be in one place before descending upon us en masse.

By the time the first CAT had returned with a full complement of fifteen ARCS, I was happy to see that my minefield – yes I'd made a minefield – was complete and ran in circles around the outside of our trench line. Spattered throughout and beyond were fences, barbed wire, more laser turrets and something I'd called a flak turret that would shoot a large single ball of plasma, which would then split off into smaller balls that cascaded in every direction causing a huge amount of damage to clustered enemies. It could also fire upwards just in case we needed to deal with the flying ones again.

The force shield sword had given me such a brainwave that with the help of Sam and hobern I'd managed to design what was effectively a plasma bubble that could stretch over the bulk of our firebase, preventing enemy ingress. It used a shit ton of power and wouldn't last very long, but it was an effective last ditch defensive effort. All in all though, with the new turrets and force shield it meant that I'd needed to construct a second power station, which I did.

I'd had to send the HAMs away into the old destroyed nest that I knew would have rich ground, and even constructed a handful more to get things moving even quicker. I knew that for everything I needed to make here, we needed resources by the bucket load, and the nest had proven effective at sorting that for us. I was happy; things were going well and after countless hours there were hundreds of ARCs at firebase Alpha, better than good defences, and a material wealth that meant construction bottlenecks were a thing of the past.

The thing was, though, with all the new ARCs arriving I had no idea who they all were or what they were expecting. That was until one of them, a Colonel Jack Williams, called for attention in the ranks, and asked who it was that was in charge here. My mech commanders dutifully moved out of the way and allowed the Colonel direct passage to me, and I stood there shuffling my feet, very aware that this looked like it was going to turn into an ear bashing.

"Son, what in God's name do you think you're doing?" The Colonel spoke his first words to me and I immediately felt as though I'd done something wrong. "These are not your toys to be playing around with. Why isn't the Saturn here now and why are we all still in these suits?"

It sounded like all of this was my fault.

"Get your head out of your ass and get us all out of here, you hear me." His voice didn't sound desperate or even harsh, just commanding and firm. No one would interrupt him either, the highest rank below him being the mech commanders and a few Majors within the ranks. Until now, nobody had questioned my authority or judgement.

"Well?" The colonel asked when I didn't make any noises in reply.

Just then, before I could speak Martinez leapt at the Colonel, his hands grasping onto his shoulders. Martinez spoke uncomfortably closely to the colonel, who did nothing to back away.

"Don't you see, it's not coming for us, it's all over! And we LOST! Why is no one seeing this? It's over and there's nothing you can do about it. They're coming and when they arrive..."

Before he could say any more, the colonel had drawn his pistol and cracked the butt of it into Martinez's nose, causing him to lose consciousness and fall to the ground in a crumpled heap.

"Now listen here," he spoke so that the entire firebase could hear. "I'm taking control of this firebase. You will report directly to me and only to me. You will all be assigned tasks and guard duties until the Saturn arrives to get us off this God damned rock."

And that was it – my glorious command was over.

More ARCs arrived on CATs and more materials were harvested, left to carry on their previously automated tasks – though when I actually thought about it, it was probably more likely due to the fact that Colonel Williams actually had no way to interface with the terminal, Sam, or even control the drones. As soon as that realisation dawned on me though, I was summoned by a cadet to speak with the Colonel who was standing right next to the terminal on the Control Unit.

"What did you do to this thing?" he asked at a far more conversational volume than before once the cadet had left us.

"Nothing – this was the Unit that I was constructed from..." I went on to relay everything that Roberts and I had discovered: how the Saturn had travelled through time somehow, how the Construction Unit would listen to me and me alone, and how the Saturn was sending out a lifeboat to save us. It took a while and once Roberts was sequestered to corroborate my story, the Colonel looked far more at ease in my presence. He was visibly relieved, but evidently worried about the lack of support he had from the Saturn.

OK, so here's what we're going to do," the Colonel said. "First things first, I hereby grant you a field promotion to the rank of Sergeant." He waited for a moment and my visor promptly informed me of my promotion, and the fact that I now had two permanent ARC upgrades to work with.

"Well at least that works," he said almost to himself. "It seems that Sam likes to pick and choose what she'll allow us to do…as usual," he muttered the last part. "Damn thing always has an agenda. Anyway, what this means is that you will be able to use the communications array on the Saturn to send out messages to the entire planet and indeed any others in the system that are still inhabited by our guys, probably not any further though. I can't promote you to an officer otherwise this would all be a lot easier. In addition, you *may* be able to convince that blasted AI that we need the Saturn here to come pick us all up. I know you don't need to, but I don't feel like spending six weeks on a lifeboat, then rescuing everyone here one by one. In any case, the best thing to do is put Martinez in the boat that's already on its way here, then you jump out of your ARC and see what you can do to come get us. We'll hold the fort while you're gone. It's the safest way for Martinez anyway, I don't think he's going to do too well when more of the bugs turn up and I don't want him distracting the others - that's how people get killed. If Sam let's you control the Saturn, pick up Martinez along the way."

It sounded pretty good to me, other than the fact that none of the ARCs here could control any of the construction or defensive units that I'd made. It seemed to me though, that the endgame of all of my efforts here was to save as many divers as I could, so eventually something like this needed to happen. I just wished I didn't have to leave them all behind, and also that I had a firm idea of what Sam would allow me to do once I arrived back on board with my new rank.

Of course there were a few things I wanted to try before a packed my bags and left – most notably trying to instruct Sam to take commands from the others once I'd left but apparently we had differing opinions on what actually counted as the crew of the Saturn. Then I tried imbuing the command into new Construction Units and HAMs, but those didn't take either. In the end I realised that there was nothing I could do other than leave the firebase to it. If the divers really wanted to come back to this planet once we'd left, then at least there would be somewhere for them to go. As it was right now, we were on borrowed time.

Taking one last look about the base and a deep, foreboding breath, I stepped into the Construction Unit and pushed the big red button. Of course that was a figurative button for the most part, but above my head was also a literal big red button. Which I pushed.

16

∞

I gasped and fought to catch my breath, as though I'd been under water. My lungs burnt with the new sensation of breathing real air and I had the most terrible rams-horn headache that I'd experienced in a long while. Thankfully though, after blinking a few times and remembering where I was, it started to abate.

After exiting my dive pod, I took a few moments to come back to myself and the realisation that once again I was alone. Guessing the timescale a little, I reckoned I had about eight weeks until Martinez made it to the Saturn - that was two weeks for the lifeboat to get to the planet and another six to get back once it picked him up. Truth be told though, I wasn't looking forward to being left alone with the cadet.

"Sam?" I asked gingerly and the blue wireframe construct of the ship's AI faded into being right in front of me. She had a smile on her face and she really looked as though she was pleased with herself.

"Yes?" she asked sweetly.

"I uh… want to send a message. Do I have comms clearance?"

"Yes. At your current rank of Sergeant, you are able to utilise the communications array to send messages," she informed me and it felt so good to actually be allowed to do something aboard the vessel. I thought quickly about all the other things my new rank might allow me to do, but right now I had my orders and I needed to send out a message.

What I sent was essentially another *we are here to help* message. Just something to let anyone know that they aren't alone out there. I directed it towards the system in general as I was unsure about the spread of the divers and ARCs within the system. Once that was done I had stuff to do.

The first order of business was to see if I could get Sam to allow me to move the big girl, that way I would actually have a way of saving all of these people, rather than just sending them encouraging messages like some kind of cheerleader.

"It is not possible to move the Saturn at this time. As a lifesaving protocol has been enacted, the Saturn must remain stationary until that protocol has been completed, unless it becomes a danger to the ship and its crew to do so."

Well fuck, there was my answer. I somehow expected it even though I was still wildly disappointed – it seemed as though I would have to sit and wait for Martinez to arrive before we could make any moves. It did seem counter intuitive though, as the thought occurred to me that if I hadn't have asked for the lifeboat to be sent in the first place, I'd have been able to now reach the surviving ARCs in a fraction of the time it was going to take me now.

Eight weeks alone – how once upon a time I'd have enjoyed that, but my fleeting time on the planet's surface with my new friends and comrades felt like it simply wasn't enough. I already missed Roberts and the mech Majors, not so much the others though as I hadn't spent enough time with them yet.

After all was said and done eight weeks was not going to be anything to write home about – the irony being writing home was one of the few things I could still actually do. What I did though, was turn my attention to learning about what the human race had been up to in my future.

Of course this was all after getting mortally drunk on the blue goo and eating my entire body weight in pancakes and waffles. I felt as though I'd been missing out on real food for the small amount of time I was on the planet – and by God the wait was it worth it. The pancakes were thick and fluffy and coated in the most magnificent, mouth watering syrup I'd ever tasted. The waffles were in a league of their own too, holding their shape perfectly but offered just a hint of resistance as I bit into them. One thing human beings had got right in the future was how to perfect sweet treats. I wondered how every single person alive wasn't the size of a bus.

I eventually made my way to the visualisation suite – once my food coma had worn off - and upon entering the VR system and asking Sam to recount to me human history of the last fifty years or so, my vision was filled with scenes from the near recent human history. A man's voice filled my ears as I watched the screens turn into a news report, filmed apparently from a helicopter or a drone from above a smoking husk of a building.

"Emergency services have been called to multiple locations across London this morning as explosions of an unknown nature levelled buildings, subway stations and monuments across the city. The worst affected area seems to be King's Cross station, the country's busiest railway station where the explosion, seen in this video taken by a passenger from across the road at St. Pancras station, levels the building to the ground leaving no trace of survivors whatsoever. It remains unclear as to the motives behind this horrific act, with the armed forces and police being mobilised in the largest manhunt the country has ever seen.

The video did indeed show a huge orange explosion in the busy railway station, filmed from the outside. Where once a quite monumental building stood proud, the scene was transformed into a field of dust and rubble.

"What happened?" I asked aloud in shock, but the screen merely faded away and a new scene interrupted my question.

"Two years ago, humanity discovered that its first ever contact with an alien race had been a hostile confrontation. With the attack on King's Cross railway station, the Scriven seemed intent on letting all of humanity know that we would never be friends. We still don't know how they got here or what their initial aim was, but since that day, humanity has been fighting a war on its home turf, and it's not been an easy one. First discovered in the port of Dover in a shipping container, the small spider-like creatures – the picture switched to a rotating image of an unmistakable Scriven being, though it was just the size of my fist and seemed to have a glowing green core – *seemed to be able to explode at will, causing devastation and destruction wherever their intended target might be. It's theorised that these targets are chosen for their strategic merits to the human defence, however the Department of Defence has not passed comment on these theories.*

It is not yet known how many of these alien creatures reside on earth, though scientists suggest the number could be in the thousands.

Watching the news reports of my future was not an easy thing to do, no matter how much I tried to internally contextualise it. The vision faded away and the next that arrived was from another year down the line.

The Scriven, no matter how hard we push back, seem to be able to regenerate their ranks and come back at us stronger and stronger. As of today the entire world is in a state of lockdown. Nobody is permitted to leave their houses unless it is absolutely necessary. Scenes of empty streets filled my mind and abandoned cars and office blocks littered the cities and towns of what I could tell was southern England.

Citizens are advised to remain in their homes, having already been advised to relocate to less densely populated areas.

The vision playing out now changed to what I could tell was a prime ministerial television conference that was sent out to the nation. I didn't recognise the prime minister of England at all, but she was an older lady and looked very much as though she'd been awake for several days – her eyes were sagged and bagged and her hair was in complete disarray.

"People of the United Kingdom. It is with sadness in my heart, and a deep forboding that I have to relay this message to you. As of nine AM this morning, the Scriven threat to our nation has reached a new level. In London, Birmingham, Manchester and Newcastle, the Scriven are reported to have set up heavily defended nests, and our troops are not yet able to intervene in their construction or operation. I must ask you all as a nation, and as human beings, to stay well clear of populated areas. Stay in your home and do not leave for any circumstances. We know that we can beat these creatures from the sky, but we must not let them continue to dwindle away our forces, morale and our citizenship." She sounded as if she believed what she was saying, though I got a distinct feeling of helplessness from her speech.

"The United States and our other allies have so far seen only small contingents of Scriven within their own countries, so are willing to send troops and aid to the United Kingdom, so once again, I ask you to stay home, stay inside and stay safe."

A new news report from some time in the future of the Prime Minister's address began to play immediately after she'd finished her message. I could already feel myself breaking out into a cold sweat. It was very strange to see the scenes play out, as effectively this was the Saturn's past, but my own future. I had to remind myself that none of this had actually happened yet.

The voice this time around was American. *"Today marks a new age for the human race. Our first warship with the technology to push back the Scriven has been launched into space, crewed by thousands of humans in a wide cross section of humanity as a whole. The goal is to strike out at the heart of the enemy where they live, just as they have done to us. This new ARC technology –* visions of armoured marines, mechs and all other kinds of ARCs showcased themselves in a sort of highlights reel, with blue plasma fire blasting away towards an unseen enemy all around them. I had to admit it was all pretty spectacular. *– gives the human race the opportunity to strike back hard and fast with minimal risk and casualties. The Saturn, the first warship of its kind, will stand as humanity's crowning achievement...*

The report went on but mostly it was about the Saturn itself, the crew and how the belligerent Scriven were about to face the final curtain. I did wonder though why the Ashaii hadn't been mentioned in all of this - I was under the impression that we'd been at war with them too, given the fact that my training simulation had included them as such obvious foes.

My question was answered though in the next report.

The Scriven seem spread out on planets across the galaxy, though it is still unsure why the Ashaii have chosen to side with them during this conflict. Earth has always maintained a quiet neutrality with the Ashaii aliens, though it hasn't been for the want of trying to force an alliance. Until recently it was thought that the Ashaii would not get involved with any races outside of their own domain, but the destruction of several of the earth starships by the Ashaii has proven this assumption to be untrue. It is still unclear what role the Ashaii have to play given our current conflict with the Scriven.

And there it was – up to date. I wondered if there would be more after the last report if the Saturn had stayed closer to earth for longer but there was no way I could know. To summarise all I did know, though, was that the Scriven attacked earth and humanity retaliated. Then the Ashaii stuck their oar in and attacked the human race for whatever reason. The Saturn was the first and probably only ship with ARC technology and was specifically designed to fight the Scriven threat.

All told, what I could summarise was that earth was in big trouble but now I had some insight in exactly what we could be expecting. I was the ace in the hole. That was if I could ever move this damned spaceship, pick up the surviving ARCs from a distant planet, convince them to travel back to earth to mount a pre-defence against both the Scriven and Ashaii who to me were unknown and peaceful respectively, then all have a pint and a laugh about it when all was said and done. Boy did I need a drink.

I had a very, very long night of drinking after the whole *my future* situation. A part of me just wanted to unwind and let it all sink in but another part of me really wanted to get so drunk that I'd forget everything I'd seen and heard. There were just so many things that were confusing to me or that simply didn't add up., such as why did the Scriven attack in the first place and why did the Ashaii have to get so involved. I wanted a real person to talk to, but between Martinez on his way – who was possibly insane – and Sam, I'd rather choose to talk to myself, whether that sounded crazy or not. I spent some time thinking about the fact that if you're crazy, you probably didn't think you were crazy anyway.

I hated to admit it, but over the next few weeks I got bored again. Seriously, though ,who wouldn't? I did force myself to watch the news reports again of what was going to happen back on earth and even tried to send out a long range communication to warn them, but Sam had told me it was too far away to send anything back there, just like the colonel had said. So I drank, watched sports from the past/future – when you get drunk on the blue goo you forget which is which –and essentially bummed around a lot more than I should have. I did make the next choice for my ARC's permanent upgrade though, and to go nicely with my new shoulder mounted turret, I chose to increase my ARC's density by a huge ten percent. I know I could've gone with something a little flashier, but in my future I felt as though I was going to need the ability to stand and fight – given the fact that I had taught myself how to create a defensive base using the Construction Unit whilst in an ARC. Defence was my jam, so I was going to stick with it.

Eventually, Martinez arrived and as far as I could say it wasn't a moment too soon. The lifeboat docked with the Saturn automatically and Martinez and his pod were effortlessly floated into the centre of one of the large cargo holding bays that the ship had. I was making my way there via turbolift when the alarms started.

Accompanying the annoying siren and it's shrill repetitiveness was the fact that the entirety of my surroundings went blue – the ships lighting obviously changing for whatever reason it was – perhaps because it made the danger it was speaking of easier to see or simply to warn everyone on board. Stepping out of the turbolift and into the cargo bay, I could see that it wasn't just the lift that'd been blue, it was everything.

"Foreign entity detected. Warning." Sam's now robotic voice filled the ship void of any of her trademark sneakiness. My blood went cold.

I started running towards Martinez's lifeboat, though in hindsight I should've stopped to pick up a rifle or pistol or anything else I could've used to defend myself. What I did, though, was call Sam into existence. My first thoughts were of keeping Martinez safe rather than dealing with what I could only assume was a stowaway Scriven aboard.

"Sam ... drones, now," I panted as I sprinted towards the lifeboat. I knew that I probably wouldn't be able to drag the cadet back to the med bay especially as he was inside an ARC, but the little drones that were used to clean and repair the Saturn, amongst other menial tasks, would probably have been able to team up and carry him off like a magic carpet.

For once, Sam didn't object.

I opened the lifeboat – a bullet shaped metallic pod big enough for one – and the lid flipped up to reveal the crouched form of cadet Martinez, tears cascading from his bloodshot eyes. He was of course still in his ARC but his light blue visor didn't do much to hide his demeanour.

"It...hurts..." he said weakly and I could tell that he was terrified.

I attempted to soothe him with the classics, like 'don't worry, you're safe now' and 'it'll be OK', but God knows I had no idea if he was going to be

OK. The only thing I could do was instruct the drones via Sam to take the ARC to the closest med bay via turbolift.

"This ARC is on the brink of cardiac arrest," the Fully Automated Surgical Terminal (FAST - surely this one was a joke, act fast?) robotically announced. Again it was Sam's own voice which was getting kind of tiresome. "Recommended action, surgical removal of foreign bodies, clean and close. Rehabilitation period unknown."

I mean I liked it when doctors were straight to the point, but this just seemed so cruel, so sterile. I waited for a moment before realising that the pod was waiting for my command so I blurted out "do it!" Hoping not to waste any more time.

Thankfully, the 'foreign body' was apparently on the underside of the cadet – so I didn't have to watch every gory detail that arose next.

First, a green cross that was evidently a scanner passed over every inch of the ARC and when it eventually homed in on the back of Martinez's skull, it switched to an angry red.

Almost immediately and without warning, two needles on mechanical arms injected Martinez and his eyes instantly snapped shut, then a tiny red laser beam emanated from the pod and into the back of the cadet's head, opening his skull expertly and with a lot less damage and blood than I'd been expecting – perhaps it was cauterising as it went. Who knew, I wasn't a medical doctor. What followed next though was enough to make my skin crawl and put me off watching surgery for life.

First I thought it was a long piece of string, then a few more followed but then I realised that they were moving out of the opening in Martinez's skull of their own accord and were looking for something to grab onto. I held my breath as the thing wrapped its spindly legs around one of the injector arms which had remained stationary since its first action.

Pulling itself free of Martinez, its body was the size of a grape, surrounded by dozens of the spindly string-like legs and it looked frantic as it wrenched itself to freedom. I was glad that the medical unit – I refused to refer to it as a FAST – was a sealed glass pod, otherwise I'd be scared of the thing coming for me. I watched for a moment as it searched around for a way out of its prison and when it couldn't find one, it started making moves back towards the unconscious and still gravely wounded Martinez. That's when finally the pod intervened, and a tiny red laser popped the grape unceremoniously. The thing fell motionless onto Martinez's chest and I breathed out a sigh of relief at its passing.

The medical pod then proceeded to clean, close, clean again, suture the head wound, then fall back into its previous motionless state. I did think that perhaps Martinez would awake instantly and be all better, but a timer on the outside of the pod had started counting down from twelve hours, which I assumed would be when he was going to awaken. I didn't envy him that time in the pod with the creature but at least it was dead, and he was unconscious.

I sat with the sleeping Martinez for all twelve hours. Well, slept some but mostly sat – twelve hours was a really long time to be waiting for something to happen.

Eventually, with a ping much like a classic microwave, Martinez's pod hissed open and the cadet sat bolt upright, rubbing the back of his head. It made me wince but it didn't seem to cause him any issues.

"Where am I?" He spoke the classic line of someone waking up after dangerous surgery.

"The Saturn," I happily replied. "How are you feeling?"

"My head itches," he said, "but OK other than that."

He hadn't yet seen the remains of the grape-thing and catching my eye he followed my gaze, and then leapt out of the pod faster than a mongoose on a cobra.

"What the fuck?" Martinez asked in horror at the thing, "that didn't..." he trailed off as he itched the back of his head again. I was worried he was about to faint but luckily he fought it.

"I thought it was all a dream," he said slowly holding his hands up in front of his face. "Am I...OK?" he followed up. This certainly sounded like someone who had lost a lot of his craziness in the last few moments, and I was happy for it.

I relayed the details of our ARC-link-time-predicament thing and how he needed to find himself and get out of his ARC. He was a little confused with all of the details as we walked to the turbolift but he got the gist of it. I didn't yet tell him about the others back on the planet - some things were better left until you were safe and back in your own body.

Martinez's body looked very similar to his ARC. Well, facially it was identical; short black hair on top, dark features in general and a black well groomed goatee beard. Average height, maybe a little small but a good athletic build, like a crossfitter or something.

"Do you know what that thing was?" I asked as I appraised Martinez's new form – the transfer had been entirely successful and he wasn't showing even a hint of the dive hangover I was so not fond of.

"No idea, but it must've been there for a reason, right?" he replied.

"It was kind of making you act crazy – maybe that was it?" I said.

Then Sam spoke from all around us, choosing not to take her corporeal form. "The creature was transmitting a very low frequency signal, though it has ceased now."

My heart skipped a beat. "A signal?" What kind of signals could these creatures emit and of what use would they be?

"What kind of signal? Could you theorise on what it was for?" I asked quickly and very worriedly.

"I can't be sure of its purpose, though perhaps the creatures use this signal to communicate with each other?" Sam replied, but there was something about the tone of her voice that just made me disbelieve what she was saying. It did make me feel a little better though because maybe it was just how these things spoke, after all they were like a hive mind as far as I could see. I forced myself not to think about it for the moment and get back to the job at hand – saving the rest of the divers.

17

∞

"Sergeant, my sensors have detected another vessel in the system" Sam said as we arrived in orbit of the planet that I'd left my comrades on.

Once Martinez was safe and sound and recuperating alone – I felt like he needed that right now - I'd ordered Sam to go about our business and fly over to pick up the ARCs as the Colonel had suggested and thankfully she'd agreed without hesitation – even though I still wasn't technically an officer. I still wasn't sure if she had stuck rigidly to her protocols previously or if she just loved messing with me; either way she really had a way of getting under my skin, and from what I'd heard I wasn't alone in that feeling.

"What do you mean another vessel?" I spoke before I had a moment to think about what this could've meant, but before I had the chance to do or say anything else, the view screen at the front of the bridge filled with the face of a starship Captain. Not any Captain though, this was Captain Robert Lee Frakes, the officer at the helm of the IPC Wanderlust. I could've coughed up a lung.

"Who is this and what are you doing here?" Frakes' voice boomed from the view screen and it almost knocked me over.

When I didn't answer for a moment, he quickly followed up with "why aren't you answering me? Are you receiving?" He really wasn't one to mess around, but I already knew that.

"Uh Sam? Can he see or hear me?" I asked before making a fool of myself. It was apparently too late though, because the Captain answered in lieu of Sam.

"Of course I can see and hear you, you're on an open comms channel on the bridge of a starship. What's wrong with you, boy?" Then Sam told me very loudly that indeed he could hear and see me – she was just so helpful sometimes.

How I'd missed familiar faces;, I know I had people to talk to and all that but everything just felt so much better when there were people near you that you just *knew*… or were at least from the same time period as you.

Finally I managed to pull myself together. "Sir, you don't know how good it is to see your face, my name is Daniel Cross and I was a technician on board the Wanderlust up until recently…"

The Captain cut me off. "Don't you try to pull the wool over my eyes boy, Daniel Cross died with honour on a boarding mission…"

"No that was me!" I protested, "but I didn't die – my comms went out and I managed to survive in the Saturn here."

There was just so much I needed to say all at once that when I searched for the right words and the right order, nothing came to mind.

"The Saturn…the future…ARCs and divers, war and aliens…" I blurted out but Frakes held up a hand to stop me.

That was when he spilled the beans. He knew all about the ARCs and the divers, the time-travelling ship and the war with the aliens. He knew it all because over the last few weeks, the Wanderlust had been rescuing hundreds of ARCs from one of the other planets in the system, and they'd told the crew all about… well everything. In addition, the Captain told me that the reason the Wanderlust had left in such a hurry in the first place after my loss was because they received a distress signal from one of the planets and were duty bound to help.

'Shit,' I thought, *'I couldn't have asked for better than this.'*

There I was, in the middle of the best scenario I could've hoped for: Martinez seemed like he was on the mend, the Saturn had done what it was supposed to and had arrived to collect its stranded crew, and the Wanderlust had popped back into my life ready to welcome me back home as though none of this had ever happened.

"So you're saying that you're *that* Daniel Cross?" Frakes asked after we'd both decided that we had all of the same information and there was no more reason to keep up any sort of bravado. I was about to confirm my identity, when Sam interrupted us.

"An unknown vessel has entered the system," she informed us. "It is on course to meet the Wanderlust within thirty seconds. It is an Ashaii warship."

"Shit - are you seeing this?" I asked Frakes who had apparently been given the same information.

"Yeah we got this," he said, but I quickly asked Sam if we could get to them in time to help. We were unfortunately about two minutes travel away from the Wanderlust though – which might as well have been a lifetime.

A rotating 3D image of the Ashaii ship now filled the viewport as the Captain had decidedly more important things to concentrate on. It wasn't blocky and bulbous like normal earth ships that I was used to. This one was curved and pointed as though it was designed for its aerodynamics – which of course was irrelevant up here. Five curved edges culminated at points to the front of the ship and it was huge, at least twice the size of the Saturn. I held my breath as it moved into close proximity of the Wanderlust.

"I'm detecting a massive power surge coming from the…" Sam begun, but then it was too late.

The five points of the Ashaii warship glowed in a neon green, then linked together in lines of pure energy before firing a single beam from the centre of the connected energy straight at the Wanderlust. They didn't even have the chance to return fire as the beam cut straight through their hull with ease, coming out the other side. The Wanderlust exploded seconds later and I knew there would be no hope of survivors or lifeboats from this devastation.

My mouth hung agape as I couldn't believe what I had just witnessed. I felt immediately alone again, but it was worse now that I'd been so close to going home and getting back to normal, just to have it all taken away from me. I was *so close*.

Coming to my senses I summoned Sam into her corporeal form so that I could actually talk to the annoying AI.

"Sam, can we get over there?" I asked angrily forcing the tears back away from my eyes.

"We can, though I fear that the Ashaii warship may be out of our league," she replied without a hint of sarcasm.

"Do it," I instructed without hesitation. Half of me expected to hear the old 'you aren't an officer' speech but after pulsing brightly a few times, Sam apparently agreed with my order and I felt the ship begin its acceleration toward my latest enemy.

Just over a minute passed before the Ashaii warship had moved to intercept me and I felt as though we were medieval knights about to joust. I had no idea what I could expect from the Saturn, but a futuristic ship specifically designed to fight in a war must've had some good shit, right?

Just then, the terminal attached to the Captain's chair illuminated brightly with the message 'weapons systems active' displayed across it.

Either Sam had accepted my captaincy, or this was the only course of action to keep me alive – I didn't care which but I knew I was going to do everything within my power to turn that alien ship into Swiss cheese.

I sat in the Captain's chair. I was expecting it to be comfortable, but it was hard and didn't offer much in the way of lumbar support. Thinking about it, it stood to reason that the Captain should probably remain alert rather than relaxing whilst in the big seat.

A huge top-down tactical map filled the viewport in front of me, and the terminal displayed a list of the weapons available to fire on the current target, given our range and trajectory. I was pleased to note that I had a few options available to me.

Three railguns, eight plasma cannons, twenty one point defence systems, a butt load of plasma torpedoes, five microcannons (whatever they were), twenty four fifty millimetre mark seven naval guns and one fully charged, one hundred percent powered force shield covering the entire vessel.

"The Ashaii vessel is powering its weapons systems," Sam dutifully informed me, though it didn't make any difference as my own weapons systems had been primed and ready for what felt like forever.

The moment my top-listed weapon turned green, I punched it to begin its firing sequence. The railgun had come into play and the entire ship shuddered as its capacitors discharged and sent an enormous shell cascading towards the Ashaii warship. I knew the projectile was massive because I watched it as it bridged the distance between our two warring ships. I held my breath as the round closed in, though just before it made impact with the Ashaii ship, a slew of drones spilled out from a hatch in the ship's hull, creating a flak barrier for the railgun round to impact instead of the ship. A huge orange explosion followed and when the dust and interference settled, I could see a hole in the drone wall, in front of a fiery crater marking the ship's hull. I'd done some damage at least, but I wasn't expecting it to be mitigated in such a suicidal way.

"Enemy vessel is firing its particle beam weapon," Sam spoke as I just about finished admiring the damage I'd caused. Then once again the prongs afront the enemy vessel began to glow neon green.

"Shit! Shields! Brace for impact!" I knew I wasn't talking to anyone in particular and that my commands were basically irrelevant but it was a reflex kind of thing at this point.

There was nothing I could do so I simply waited for the end, following my former comrades aboard the Wanderlust into the darkness of space.

Death didn't arrive though. I watched the particle beam impact my ship with a light shudder, but what happened was not an immediate destructive explosion of the Saturn – the ship's shields glowed bright blue, then faded to an angry red until the particle beam had completed its firing cycle. Then the beam stopped and the attack was over.

"Shields are at forty percent," Sam handily informed me. I kind of liked it when she was all business and no sarcasm.

However, that meant that another hit from that thing and I was brown bread.

"Sam, how long did it take them to reload that thing – or power it, whatever," I asked not knowing exactly how the weapon was working.

"There were approximately two and a half minutes between firing sequences of the Ashaii particle beam weapon. I have added a countdown timer to your tactical overlay."

Well that was handy – I now had just over two minutes ticking away on both the viewscreen and my terminal as though it was an ominous death clock hanging over me. *Better to know though,* I thought.

Finally, though, my guns were in range of the overpowered enemy vessel and with a punch on everything I had, my ship erupted into the booms of firing cannons and the lights of tracer rounds firing from all of the facing batteries. I expected the Ashaii ship to counter in a cacophony of its own, though I hadn't actually thought about what armaments the ship may have. Instead of firing all batteries – of which I could actually see none – hundreds and possibly thousands of tiny drone ships spilled forth in a wave and began to move in my direction.

I say the drones were tiny, but that was just in comparison to the main vessel – they were each more like the size of a bus, and I really didn't like just how mobile they were. They were positioning themselves in front of the more devastating fire from my arsenal which meant that although I was hitting the Ashaii warship, the damage was negligible without the additional impact of my sporadic railgun fire – they too needed to charge between firing sequences - and my plasma cannons which when fired sent huge blue plasma balls hurtling toward the enemy. Although that did look impressive, it meant that they were terribly easy to intercept, a few drones being able to sacrifice themselves to prevent the main ship taking any damage at all.

Of course I knew – and presumably the Ashaii knew - that they'd eventually run out of drones, the ranks already looked to be thinning but now there were just sixty seconds remaining on my death clock, when their particle beam weapon would be able to fire again. I needed something that would change the course of this battle.

I did have a theory though – the way that the Ashaii seemed to act in this battle told me that their ship was set up with one purpose in mind – to fire the particle beam weapon at all costs. It didn't seem to have any shields or any other weapons at all, not even point defence guns. It was totally alien to me, though I supposed why shouldn't it have been, after all they were literally alien. This line of thought led me to the realisation that one good shot would probably be all that it took to take the gargantuan down. I made my mind up and gave my order.

"Sam, ramming speed if you would."

The AI didn't even respond to my order this time, no snarky comments or outright rejection, just the feel of renewed thrusts from the engines and the distinct feeling that we'd started moving at quite some rate of knots.

"Impact in fifty two seconds," Sam informed me and as I looked at the death clock I knew it'd be cutting it fine. There was about a two second advance in my favour and all I could think was *'I hope that these calculations are accurate'*.

As soon as my course was confirmed, the enemy drones started hurling themselves at my hull or flew into my path to either slow me down or stop me. They were no match for my shields though as no matter how many stood in my way, they were being splattered like bugs on a windshield. By the time there was nothing left between me and the Ashaii warship, my shields had dropped by just two percent.

"Collision imminent," Sam stated again in her official voice and I still liked her better this way."The enemy vessel is powering its weapons systems."

Everything seemed to go in slow motion. The calculations had been correct in terms of how long it would take our ships to make the initial contact, though they said nothing about how long it would take after that contact before the enemy ship would be rendered inert. As it was, I watched the neon green particle weapon charge and fire on the Saturn. The particle beam hit my shields and immediately dissipated them and I could feel the entire ship being wrenched apart like a tin of tuna. But as my hull crumpled the warship's broadside, all the particle beam could do was punch through in a glancing blow – and then my ship must've hit something important as the beam faded out into nothingness and the alien ship went dark.

It exploded into two halves around my impact site which floated away from each other momentarily, then exploded into an orange cloud of fire, dust and debris.

I was worried initially that the explosion would take me with it, but a readout on my tactical screen handily informed me that hull integrity was still at forty percent. I mean it wasn't amazing – half of the ship was exposed to space and all – but it was better than being completely obliterated.

"I have detected a transmission that the Ashaii vessel had attempted to send before its destruction," Sam said and as she did so the view screen faded into the picture of a thin grey, typical alien with large oval eyes and a sash which I assumed meant this one was in charge.

"We…are…coming. No…surrender." The words were slow and concise, but it was obvious the being wasn't used to human diction. "You bring us war… we bring you death."

The message cut off and I was left with the distinct feeling that something very, very wrong had just happened. Inside I felt the surprise pangs of guilt, though I wasn't exactly sure why. This being, though, had said we'd brought them war.

18

∞

The Saturn had been doing an amazing job at repairing itself with its little automated repair drones that seemed to just go about their business whilst everything else was happening around them. I was pretty happy that I didn't have to get out there in a walksuit – doing that again made my legs feel cold and brought a shiver to my spine.

Martinez had made a full recovery over the next few days and the surviving ARCs had been brought aboard the Saturn in an array of lifeboats that ferried them back home. The process of rejoining the divers' minds to their real bodies had also been going swimmingly, even for the mechs with their hulking frames, the size of the Saturn seemingly accommodating them without issue.

Once the ARCs had been left brainless, the ship then reconstituted their bodies back into the pods that would make up future ARCs in one giant recyclable circle. It was amazing , if not gruesome, to watch the tiny drones dismantle what was essentially a human body (well in many ways anyway) without missing a single drop of blood, then feed the material back into what could only be described as a waste chute off to wherever it went to be portioned out between waiting pods.

Some of the crew had taken longer to revive, though most had made it back to their usual selves, or what I guessed were their usual selves, within a couple of days. I'd made a point to catch up with Martinez, Roberts and the mech commanders as I'd known more about those than any others. Reminiscing about the planet and what Roberts and I had achieved was almost a fun pastime, though Roberts liked to talk about his promotion quite a lot too.

It was difficult to be friends with the mech commanders though as they were all Majors. It wasn't strictly a rule, but typically I noticed that, just like it was aboard the Wanderlust, officers and ratings didn't mix on the Saturn. Well not very publicly anyway.

Major Jackie Simms had taken a more liberal approach to the not mixing stance of the rest of them though. She was very forthcoming with details about the history of the war, earth and other interesting facts that left me scratching my head most of the time. I simply couldn't get if this was all still going to happen, or if their mere existence in this time would have started a new chain of events. Time travel made my head hurt.

Simms was still dark skinned with long black hair in that single braid she'd had in her ARC. In fact, when I took the time to locate the people who I'd recognised from the planet, they all looked almost exactly the same as their ARCs had and that just made things so much easier for me.

Roberts was just talking me through the evolution of the English football Premier League, which had apparently been taken over by a number of companies when it was discovered that actually referees were being told to skew games towards certain teams, when I received a summons over the ship's intercom to the bridge.

It'd certainly been a while since I'd been up there, and I cringed at the memory of having to manually open all those doors, what I'd done to the terminal to try to get everything moving again and the interference of the annoying ship's AI. Speaking of Sam, I hadn't seen her at all since the rest of the crew had arrived, though I wasn't sure if that was because she had more interesting things to do with the higher ups now, or if she was making a point. Either way I was pretty happy about it.

I arrived on the bridge moments later thanks to the divine speed of the turbolifts, and walked in to what could only be described as a board meeting, with ten individuals sat around a shiny black round table. I guessed it was hidden away in the ground or something when it wasn't being used – which was pretty ingenious but I didn't comment on it.

Around the table sat Colonel Williams, the Mech Commanders Long, Simms, Carter, Walton and Hobern, two lieutenants who I didn't recognise and the now sergeant Roberts.

"Please take a seat Sergeant," Williams said, gesturing to the single empty seat at the table. I sat obediently and tried to gauge the room from the faces that surrounded me. Most gave nothing away but Roberts was smiling ear to ear.

"I'm sorry about the loss of your friends and colleagues aboard the Wanderlust. I can only imagine what you must be feeling right now. I wanted to postpone this meeting until you were feeling more…uh yourself." It was the first time I'd heard his diction falter and I kind of liked it – it made the very official man seem more human.

I nodded in reply. I didn't particularly want to relive the memory, but neither did I care so deeply that it was causing me a mental breakdown. At my acknowledgement the Colonel spoke again.

"I have a wife and two children, did you know that?" he asked in a very distinct change of conversational direction. I could tell that I wasn't supposed to answer, so I didn't.

"We'll that is to say I *had* a wife and two children. Or *will have* I guess." I was starting to wonder what Roberts had been smiling so widely at, because this did not feel like a happy conversation.

"Which leads me onto my next point," he continued. "I feel duty bound, as many of the people here aboard the Saturn do, to our friends and families of our own time. We have fought, lost comrades and innocent civilians to this enemy. We have planned, succeeded and failed in skirmishes across the galaxy – but here is where the enemy come from. This is their home and that simple fact grants us an opportunity. We do not know if what we do now will affect our own futures and that of our families but many of us, including myself, are of the belief that it will. This opportunity is to strike out at the enemy and prevent the loss of hundreds of thousands, possibly millions in the future. I can't expect you to…"

I quickly interrupted the Colonel. "You're going to stay here?"

He was silent for a moment before replying then decided not to continue what he was saying but to address my question.

"In short, yes. We estimate that around half of the Saturn's crew would prefer to stay here and strike out at an enemy that we have been fighting against for years."

"Why not just go back to earth and help the defence of the planet with this new ship? It's far superior to anything I'd even heard of in my time." I asked.

The Colonel fidgeted slightly, but before he could answer, Roberts exploded into an answer. "We're going to kill them all!" he exclaimed with glee. "Those Ashaii bastards n'all. Right where they live!"

Colonel Williams seemed more embarrassed than happy about it though and I could tell by his slight movement that he was shuffling his feet. He spoke again, but making sure Roberts didn't have the chance to continue. I could tell that although he'd received a promotion, he probably wouldn't be getting another one any time soon.

"The thing is, from what we know and what we've seen, earth isn't in any immediate danger right now." He held his hands up before I could interject. "Now I know the message said that they're coming, but there's just no concrete evidence that that means they're coming in a week, a month or even a year. We are here now in the heart of the enemy territory which we *know* and *understand*. Besides, who's to say that if we strike now, they won't be able to mount an invasion force on your earth."

I picked up on something in his last statement that almost made me double take. He'd said *my earth*. Then it clicked, that's what this was all about wasn't it.

"Your earth was destroyed and there's nothing I can do to change that right now, but this is still *your* earth too," I pleaded. "You think that you can just find a way to get back to the future, the future you know. Just because you're afraid of change, what might be different if you save the planet now..."

"DON'T YOU DARE!" Williams shouted for the first time and slammed both his fists down on the table. I was surprised that it didn't crack.

Simms spoke before the Colonel could stand up to further punctuate his point. "Listen Daniel, whatever the reasons behind this plan of action... it's actually a pretty good one." Her voice was soothing and melodic and I very much felt as though I was being the one 'calmed down'.

Et tu, brute? I thought inwardly, though I didn't display my feelings of betrayal.

"The thing is, you haven't heard the best part of the plan yet," she continued with a smile. "The Saturn is going to take the fight to the enemy to *prevent* the invasion by the Ashaii and the Scriven as it happened in our own past, and at the same time, *we*," she gestured to the mech commander Majors, "are going with you in ARCs to earth to find, eliminate and remove any threat to the planet."

I could see that Roberts was in love with the plan as he practically vibrated in his seat, and thankfully Williams had also calmed down and returned to a far paler shade of red.

I tried to run through the plan in my head to see if there was anything I could find that didn't make sense, but the more I tried, the sounder it seemed.

Eventually I settled on, "so what about the crew that don't want to go off fighting in a war?"

"Well I can't say their worries aren't validated," the Colonel agreed. "Though what would you have them do? Send them back to an earth of their own past? Imagine the repercussions. No, nobody will be forced to fight, though they may have to defend themselves at some point, after all they are enlisted divers. Eventually, if we do ever find a way back home, then that's what we're going to do. I know how it sounds - change the past, go back to the future and live happy lives - but what other choices do we have?"

I reiterated my plan of *go to earth, save the day and live happily ever after*, but I could now see that although it sounded pretty ideal to me, these people were simply strangers, stranded in my time. I couldn't ask them to stay, nor could I ask them not to strive to get home to their own families and loved ones.

The plan was simple enough in my mind, but I wasn't exactly positive that it was all going to pan out the way everyone seemed to be suggesting. So the people of earth were just going to accept that we'd been through some sort of time travel saga, showed up to save the planet with futuristic technologies from a war that hadn't even started yet – and to top it all off, the Wanderlust was destroyed in a totally unrelated event. Sure, what could possibly go wrong?

"There's one more thing to prepare you for what's ahead," the Colonel said officially. I can do one last thing for you and that is as follows: from this moment on, your rank has been increased to Lieutenant, which means…"

YOU'RE A GOD DAMNED OFFICER!" Roberts blurted out at a volume much louder than it should've been in polite company. I agreed with the statement though, and the first thing I thought about doing was telling Sam to bite me.

"Uh, well," Williams was quite taken aback by the outburst, but looking around the table I could see that by the smiles on everyone's faces, they were both pleased and proud. I couldn't help smiling back at them all.

"Thank you sir," I managed to reply officially. "I won't let you down."

After going over the plan a few more times and being told that Roberts was coming along too, I had my orders. It was going to be me, Roberts and the mech commanders against the world…uh saving the world. Whatever. If I did have to guess, though, I'd say that the inclusion of Roberts in the team was a bit of an afterthought. I imagined Williams was thinking about all that time he'd have to spend with the man, and thought I'd be better off shouldering that burden. I didn't mind though, I liked Roberts and he was a good soldier.

19

∞

"The appearance of the extra-terrestrial object was not the result of a pre-planned visit by any of the known races we have encountered before. Landing twenty hours ago, the object doesn't appear to be moving and there is just speculation at what could be inside."

I had chosen to land my Construction Unit in a field just outside the port of Dover, high up on the white cliffs, with the port and sea down below us, in a half-assed bid to remain somewhat hidden from humanity until I could make proper contact.. It was also where the first Scriven had been detected on earth , in a shipping container. The plan had not gone well though, due to the Construction Unit actually resembling a giant fireball coming down from the sky once it entered into earth's atmosphere, then scorching the ground around it for about three hundred metres and creating a somewhat crater-like impact site. I had no choice but to go through with the mission though, as this was a one-shot kind of deal, and the cat was already out of the bag. What weren't out of the bag, though, were our seven ARCs, which were all still being printed up inside the unit.

The Construction Unit itself – I didn't know this part last time – resembled a bit of a shipping container before it made any ARCs, and would only flap down its sides to reveal the ARC hangers once the first printed constructs were ready to emerge, which in this case was about twenty hours. I theorised that it took a bit longer because there were seven of us and five of those were big fat mechs.

My latest ARC, as I was now a fully fledged Lieutenant, had two permanent upgrades and a full three hundred CP to spend therein. My first permanent upgrade was the shoulder mounted laser turret (go predator), and the second I'd decided to amend and chose after a long period of consideration. I'd eventually landed on something listed as 'enhanced combat cognition,' which I was led to believe by its description was something that would allow me to assess battles and battlefields at a much higher level than any other mere mortal. As a permanent upgrade I thought it must've been worth it. It was a much better choice than my previous density idea.

My three hundred points were a little more difficult to place as I saw little point in spending them on upgraded weapons or armour as I knew I'd be able to do all that with the Construction Unit anyway. What I found I could do, though, was make myself taller, stronger and allow my visor to show me more details from further away. Oh, and also I gave my ARC a plasma blade arm, just like I'd done for Roberts. I really liked what it did for him and I'd always been secretly jealous about it and this was my opportunity to do it too.

"Police respondents were first on the scene though no attempt has yet been made to make any sort of contact from inside the strange object. The army has also arrived and soldiers have standing orders to ensure that this is not a threat to the local surroundings. At this point, port operations are still ongoing, though we understand that officials are poised and ready to implement a complete shutdown of the port, redirecting all cargo and traffic to an alternative route.

The strangest thing was the fact that with my ARC printed and ready to roll, I could watch the live earth news feed of my arrival and current status of – well - doing nothing. My ARC was ready, though I could see from the countdown timer in my visor that the others were not. I also needed to be sure that if seven heavily armed futuristic alien-things just waltzed out of the Construction Unit, the people of earth didn't simply try to blow us up. I mean they probably could if they tried hard enough, but we were here to help, not cause a scene.

"There now appear to be some sort of lights shining from atop the object…and hold on…something is happening. The object appears to be opening…and…"

I thought about reciting 'one small step for man…' though decided it would probably have been in poor taste. Instead, I took one big step forward and into the bright sunlight of earth. It had been way, way too long. I wished I could've inhaled that beautiful natural air for my real self, though the facsimile was near perfect as it was.

To my left a thundering simultaneous step from my five Major mech commanders telegraphed their previous positioning within the Construction Unit, and to my right I saw Roberts step forward. Even slightly larger than he was last time and carrying an oversized minigun. I assumed it was a plasma minigun but I was sure I'd find out for definite at some point. I did wonder why he'd once again spent points on making himself bigger, though squashed that thought when I realised that I'd actually done the exact same thing.

"You ready for this shit-storm?" Roberts said with a smile and I nodded slightly in response.

"From within the object have emerged five, what look like armoured robots and two heavily armed humanoids, though they are yet to make any kind of movement in any direction. The situation currently looks tense and we'll keep you updated as the events here in Dover unfold."

From my current position I could see a wide arc of soldiers with their rifles raised and pointed nervously in our direction. Behind them were a few jeeps and troop carriers and I assumed that we were encircled with more of them. It was a very strange feeling for our own race to be pointing their weapons at us, though I could see their point. We had a plan though and we were going to stick to it.

"We come in peace. Take us to your leader." I said trying my best not to crack a smile at the absurdity of the statement.

An older man in camo gear with flashes that betrayed the fact that he was a General walked through the raised weapons and stood five feet away from my group. He looked apprehensive but not nervous.

"I'm in charge here. My name is General Conners." he stated matter of factly. He had a thick grey moustache that moved when he talked and it made me feel at ease somehow.

"No offence General," Roberts said from my side, "but you ain't nearly high up enough for what we gotta say," and I was once again assured that the man would never get promoted above his current rank.

"And what exactly does that mean?" The General replied through what I assumed were gritted teeth. I could tell that this man was not one to mess around with the chain of command and would do everything by the book if at all possible. It was a handy trait to have sometimes – it would make him predictable, although it also meant that he would most probably rigidly stick to his guns and be less amenable to my will.

Holy shit that was insightful, I thought about my assessment of the General and I wondered if this was my new cognition rearing its ugly head.

"Listen General, my name is Lieutenant Cross – you can call me Daniel – and I was an engineer aboard the IPC Wanderlust. This is Corporal Roberts and these are Majors Long, Carter, Walton, Hobern and Simms…" What I thought was going to be a pleasant and polite introduction quickly morphed into something else though. As Simms' name was mentioned, she moved to wave in acknowledgement. What she didn't realise though, was that in doing so it was not the friendly wave of a human being, rather it was a loud and very overbearing seeming raise of a giant metal arm, equipped with a terrifyingly huge long range plasma rifle.

Tink. The single rifle round hit Simms' mech armour but didn't cause any noticeable damage to it. The gunfire that had preceded it though did have an effect, and I could tell this wasn't going to be good.

In less than half a second, my shoulder mounted laser turret had spun and fired a single beam at the soldier who had fired the round. It was definitely my new cognitive abilities this time that let me watch his terrified face explode as his head was removed from his body by my laser. I hadn't willed it to happen, the turret simply recognising danger and hostility and was doing its duty to remove it.

Gunfire rang out from the soldiers as they began peppering us with assault rifle fire but thankfully the mech squad had immediately placed itself between Roberts and me and the soldiers, meaning that between them and the Construction Unit, we had a pretty good bullet shield. We probably could've survived a few bullet wounds and got them repaired at a later date of course, but I didn't want to actually start a war with my own people – who we were actually here to protect.

"CEASE FIRE, CEASE FIRE!" it was the General's voice that I heard above the gunfire and melodic tinking and chinking of bullets ricocheting off of mech and Construction Unit alike. Within a short moment the battlefield fell back into silence.

"Sorry!" I called out from behind my mech bodyguards. "It's a new gun and apparently it's set to defend itself. You can see it only fired back in retaliation, right?"

There was no reply for a long moment and I almost felt like holding my breath. "I can see that." The General said eventually and it sounded like an admission of defeat. "Listen, you say you're here in peace right? Then why not come with us and let us check you over, then you can tell us what it is you're doing here?"

I imagined the General would've been far less sympathetic in his choice of words had he not just watched his soldiers empty a couple magazines worth of rounds into my mechs without causing so much as a scratch.

"I hate to say it General, but Roberts was right, this one's above your station. Hell, I don't even think the Prime Minister is enough for this one. If

I had to choose, I'd say we need to speak to a joint meeting of the world leaders as soon as possible. Earth is in danger and it's more than the business of just one country."

The General stroked his moustache before he came to an internal decision. "My orders are to assess you as a threat and take action to remove that threat if deemed necessary. Now you…" he gestured to the soldier's body to his side that had had his head removed by my laser, "…appear to be somewhat of a threat. Our weapons apparently have no effect on your mechanical units and it's clear to me that your technology far outmatches our own. At this moment in time it is clear to me that you are a threat, and therefore I can't simply give you access to anyone outside of this particular conflict zone as I am duty-bound to protect them as I am the soldiers in my command."

"That's all well and good General, but where does that leave us now?" I replied.

"Orders are for you to remove your weapons and armour, have your squad step out of their mechanical units and surrender to us for questioning." The General said his words with authority but I think we both knew that it wasn't going to happen.

"Would you like me to make contact with the Prime Minister of England?" Sam's voice rang out in my head which almost gave me a heart attack as I'd almost forgotten she was there.

I replied with a yes and assumed that I'd be able to get right back to business with the General, but what happened was that in the corner of my visor, the words 'U.K. Prime Minister Angela Macdonald' had appeared along with a telephone dial tone.

"Sam what the…" I started, but stopped once the phone was answered within two rings.

"Angela Macdonald. With whom am I speaking?" the voice continued and I knew it was her. It left me kind of speechless.

"Uh…" I stammered. "Ma'am." It was the best I could do. The U.K. Prime Minister was still somewhat of a celebrity to me even if she wasn't a traditional A-lister. I can be forgiven for being a tad starstruck.

"Who's speaking?" Macdonald repeated politely.

"It's…uh…Lieutenant Daniel Cross ma'am. Forgive me for my bluntness but if you're looking at a television screen right now… then I'm the one with a laser turret on my shoulder." I raised my arm into the air slowly so as to not cause any further confusion and waved it back and forth.

"One moment," she replied. After a few clicks and taps of the phone, the General spoke again.

"Now I don't know exactly how you did that, but Mrs Macdonald has told me to tell you that you've two minutes of her time to explain yourself. My men will not make any offensive moves within that time."

I mean I wasn't scared or anything, but it was nice to be *told* that you weren't going to be shot at for a while – it just made things feel a hell of a lot safer.

Then I condensed everything I could think of into a two minute speech-cum-monologue for the PM. There was a lot that I had to skip over or simply omit due to the constraints of the time limit but I was pretty sure I'd got the salient facts in there. Truth be told it was getting a bit easier as I'd repeated this speech a few times already.

"So… there's an alien invasion force on its way to earth now?" Macdonald said once I'd finished and took a breath.

"Yes…well kind of, I don't know if it's on its way but it's coming," I replied cringing a little.

"The Ashaii? Who have not been in any way hostile to earth, its people or its ships."

I could see where this was going already.

"And the Scriven…" I added quickly.

"Who have not yet been discovered by humanity at all…" she concluded my statement. "Listen I'm not saying that your story isn't fascinating and that your technology isn't intriguing, but what would you have me do if you were in my shoes? You are telling me a threat is coming without any proof and just expect us to let you set up camp right here…"

"You can check with the Wanderlust," I said quickly. "Or at least you can see for yourself that the ship has been destroyed. Look, I'm not asking for you to put any faith in me here, but a threat *is* coming and in the version of the future I've seen, by the time you did anything about it, it was too late. Earth was destroyed along with every human being on it."

"Nevertheless, you will have to wait for my advisors and peers to decide what to do with the information that you have provided. My advice to you right now is to surrender your arms and armour to the General and his soldiers, then we can see what we can do to put all of this behind us. A man has died, don't let it be the first of many, hmm?" And with that, the PM disconnected the call with a click.

My face went red with rage. That 'hmm' at the end of her statement had just smacked of self righteousness and pomposity and I didn't care for it for a single moment. I wanted to punch something in frustration but managed to keep all of those feelings on the inside.

The General pressed what I could see was an earpiece with his index finger and I assumed that he'd been listening in to our conversation. None of this was going to plan and it was making my toes curl.

"It's time to surrender," the General spoke loudly and authoritatively now but I had no intention of doing so.

"General – we aren't going to surrender – but we also don't want to kill you, so please just leave us be for a while and you'll see…" I started to plead with the man but all he'd heard was 'we aren't going to surrender' and he and all of the soldiers at one raised their rifles to the ready and pointed them – mostly at me now.

My visor in conjunction with my new improved cognition started mapping out the kill order for my enemies, marking them with numbers but I quashed the thought. Luckily, Hobern, the tech expert once again had something useful up his huge mechanical sleeve.

The mech, in the blink of an eye threw a demi-spherical metallic device onto the ground. It looked like a bosu ball that you'd see at a gym to balance on, but as it came to a full stop a blue neon shield exploded outwards covering us, the Construction Unit and a perimeter of twenty metres all around us. The soldiers and the General who'd been too close were flung back and deposited on the far side of the protective force field, though I could see thankfully they were none the worse for the wear.

"I had this one made without the electrifying function," Hobern said to my left. "Thought we'd need to buy some time without causing any harm – and it was cheaper too!" The Major just had a way of knowing what I'd need and having it ready. This was going to help us out immensely.

"Sam, I want all the world leaders on the phone right now," I said once I'd made sure that the bullets that had begun to be fired at the shield weren't making it through. They did cause slight splashes of bright blue but it didn't seem to be having any effect on the shield.

The first world leader to answer was the American president. I knew this not just because of the accent, but also because the call answered with a loud "and who the fuck is this calling me on my private number?"

Sam's presence on earth with me turned out to be quite handy for the conversation that involved no less than twenty five nations. I know it wasn't strictly speaking *all* of the world leaders but sometimes people just don't answer the phone. More importantly, though, the big ones were all there. Anyway, Sam was handy because she automatically translated all of the different languages being thrown at me before I even heard them, so I was able to hear all of the rude comments and swear words in all their glory.

I tried to explain to them all at once, but honestly it was like trying to herd toddlers who'd just learned to speak and wanted to get their point across. In the end what I'd managed to gleam from the conversation was that America wanted to get hold of my technology, and Russia and China had agreed in their thinking that I was a U.K. and USA joint construct who needed destroying. By the end of the call, I wondered why I'd even bothered. All I'd seemed to have done was pissed everyone off and possibly escalated a conflict with the red team.

I didn't care though; the shield that we had up was certainly doing its job for now and I really didn't see a point where that might change in the near future. I dutifully relayed my conversations with the rest of my squad – who incidentally had taken to goading the soldiers who were still periodically firing at our shield – and then sat down for a while to come up with a new plan.

The people of earth were asses. Well, technically the leaders were, the people were probably still fine – but that didn't mean I wanted the planet destroyed. We still had a job to do and we were going to do it even if they didn't want our help.

With all that in mind, I began to do what I knew my Construction Unit and I could do best – build stuff.

20

∞

Things were a little easier this time round because I knew what I was doing for the most part, and also I had Roberts to help me. Because he'd been constructed from the same unit this time, he could also interface with it. I did have a few thoughts of sitting with my feet up whilst he did all the work but shook that notion away once I remembered who Roberts actually was.

I started the printing of my HAMs for harvesting, then the turret for defence (you could never be too careful), and queued up more of the same of what I'd had before: Construction Drones, more HAMs, the hopper and silo for refining stuff, a power plant etc etc until I couldn't think of anything more we'd need to get our base of operations back up and running here on earth. My favourite part about materials here was their natural seventy percent efficacy which meant that building things was going to be so much quicker, even without having to harvest dead bugs to boost the pay.

I didn't just sit there and do nothing like the others though, I kept a close eye (well, ear) on the communications that were speeding around the globe at a mile a minute. People just didn't know how to keep things to themselves and as soon as something different or threatening arrived, half of them seemed to go into a state of denial. Hacking into social media feeds led me to believe that a third of people believed that we were extraterrestrial and everything they saw on the news was pretty much the truth, a third thought that we were placed there in some strange conspiracy theory like a failed military experiment, and the final third didn't believe that we existed at all and it was all CGI.

It was probably a mistake to tell every single world leader to go fuck themselves once I'd realised we weren't getting anywhere for a second time, but they really *really* got to me. I just couldn't understand what they weren't getting in all of this – we weren't hostile or a threat, we simply came to warn, and then help. Well I supposed we could've been seen as a threat for the simple fact that they couldn't seem to do anything to harm us.

"Three days have passed since the arrival of the container atop the white cliffs and round the clock surveillance has proven an uneventful task for the British army, if not an interesting one. Underneath the dome of energy that the seven individuals seem to have effected, there seems to be a kind of exponential growth into a beachhead on our doorstep, with the container able to manufacture objects, buildings and small robotic drones. The government has refused to comment on what exactly the purpose of all of these constructs is, though there is yet to be a repeat hostile act like the one that claimed the life of Lance Corporal James Wright.

Joining us this morning we have Dr Kenneth Davidson who was formerly contracted to work with the Space Corps on recognising and producing countermeasures to threats to our global security."

I recognised the man who began talking as I watched in my little Picture in Picture screen whilst wondering if we'd all have died of boredom if we didn't have access to the entire world's television network to keep us sane. I had made the Construction Unit print up a deck of cards, though watching the mechs attempt to pick up a single card with their massive metal arms was entertainment enough in itself.

According to this Dr Davidson, we were most likely visitors from a distant galaxy and were most likely here to observe humankind and how they reacted to visitors. He fell short of saying they should bring us tributes and lay them on the ground outside the shield but it was obvious that was where he was going. The sad fact about his assessment, though, even if it was well thought out and delivered terrifyingly convincingly, was that it was total bollocks.

The next day, just when I'd started wondering what I could get my Construction Unit to build next, the General walked to the far side of my shield and waited for me with his arms folded behind his back.

"Now listen here!" he said very loudly. "This has gone on long enough so it's time for you to surrender."

I thought about shouting back "NEVER" but decided that it would've been a bad idea.

"You have until the count of three to state your intention to surrender to me, or there will be conflict here today," he summarised.

I turned behind me to look at my squad, though none of them knew what to do or say, with Roberts actually shrugging his shoulders at me. It was then that I saw something I really hadn't been expecting, silhouetted against the shoreline down below behind Roberts. A squadron of fighter jets were quickly approaching our base and with my visor telling me that these were three Russian Mig-486's and two Chinese Chengdu J-24's, these guys weren't here to play cards with us.

"General you have to get back right now!" I turned back to the man and shouted as forcefully as I could command but it was both no good and too late. Neither the soldiers nor the General had seen the jets incoming and I presumed they had some sort of radar jamming ability otherwise they'd have been dealt with already.

A moment later the jets fired a volley of missiles directly at our shield. My visor told me they were ninety millimetre guided rockets that would cause a significant amount of damage to my shield and the surrounding area but it was too late to make anti-air guns right now.

My squadron turned as one and started to fire their weapons at the missiles in a kind of point defence endeavour. For the most part it worked quite well - four of the five rockets had been taken down well before they'd got anywhere even close to us. Roberts' minigun was surprisingly effective once it'd spun up, sending blue neon plasma cascading out in a cone of destruction.

The last rocket though, that one was a bastard.

We'd hit it at some point but apparently only at the tail because it kept flying upwards but with a subtle off centre spiral motion that made it oh-so difficult to hit. My visor and cognition also informed me that because of this new gait, the rocket was going to miss us by about ten metres – landing almost smack bang on the middle of where the soldiers were currently watching from.

I thought it'd all go in slow motion, but it all happened within a second. A few of the soldiers managed to get a round or two off at the rocket but it impacted the ground with a soft thud and then exploded. Earth and bodies were flung into the air and a deafening silence filled my ears with a high pitched ringing sound. I blinked for a moment and it was all over, the dust and debris settled and the soldiers were gone, obliterated.

I scanned the impact crater which was at least twenty metres in diameter to see if there was anyone out there who needed help, when I saw at the bottom of my vision the General, crawling towards my shield. He was in a bad way. His uniform was torn to shreds and one of his legs was missing from the thigh down.

"Drop the shield" I called to Hobern, who didn't argue. I pulled the General inside our perimeter and Hobern got the idea, raising the force shield back up behind us.

I did a quick pass of the General to make sure he wasn't harbouring any sort of bomb that would be his coup de gras, but he had nothing, not even a sidearm.

I hoisted the man into the Construction Unit (this new strength was such a good idea), balancing him against one of the man-shaped cutouts.

"This might hurt a bit, so try not to move too much," I started to say, but when the General opened his eyes to see what I was talking about I saw the fear filling them, then he started screaming and trying to wriggle free from the Unit.

Roberts appeared beside me and punched the General square in the face, knocking him unconscious. I looked at the Corporal in a sympathetic kind of way but he replied before I could berate him.

"I've always wanted to punch a General, and look – sleeping like a baby!" he said with a shrug.

I didn't want to commend the behaviour, but he did have a point.

"Go check and make sure the jets aren't coming back for a second pass. Then start making anti-air guns with the Drones, I don't want to get caught out again. Oh and also," I added as I looked out towards the sea, "think Atlantic Wall. If they came from the air they might come from sea too. I want something that can stop that."

A big part of me had forgotten in that moment that we were here to help the people of earth defend from the alien threat that was coming, but I was filled with a kind of sympathetic rage that was brought on by watching humans killing other humans simply because we had arrived and continued to exist. I felt both guilty and angry at the entire situation.

The General was about to be doing much better though. My visor told me that his condition was stable once the Unit had cauterised and sealed his leg and administered anaesthetics and antibiotics. It wasn't a medical pod, but some things were pretty basic when it came to us humans – lose a leg, stop the bleeding. What I could do though, was make shit.

I thought about turning the General into the million dollar man just to show off the fact that we were so far advanced that the humans had no chance, but worried that it'd probably make things worse if they felt more threatened. What I did instead was to have the unit duplicate his other leg exactly, then regenerate his uniform. Who runs straight past the finish line and keeps going anyway?

"The Russian and Chinese fighter jets appeared to have avoided radar sweeps in

these new jets, though their attack on Dover was thankfully not as devastating as perhaps it could've been. Our thoughts and prayers go out to the families of those who lost loved ones in the attack.

The cause of the attack was the container and the dome at the white cliffs, the Russian and Chinese governments both claiming that these are some new and experimental weapons systems developed by the U.K. and its allies. They are stating that technology such as this is a threat to global security and must be destroyed. Representatives of China and Russia have been contacted and we await further comments.

The fighter jets made two more passes at the dome, though none were successful in bringing down the shield as the people inside were able to shoot down the rockets before they arrived, as well as all of the jets with what looks like energy based weaponry that we've never seen before.

I have here with me…"

I really didn't need to hear from another expert about how we were probably from Mars and had guns manufactured from potato stalks or some other crap that they'd clearly invented just to get some air time so I decided to switch channels.

My visor's PIP switched over to an address by the U.K. Prime Minister. I didn't need the screen to recognise Angela Macdonald, her annoying voice having already made an impact on my impression of her.

"It is with regret and sadness that I must inform the people of this great nation that we are now in a state of war. The Russian and Chinese governments have decided that the threat to global security posed by these visitors is too great to ignore, and if we attempt to intervene in their destruction, we will be treated as hostile. As you can imagine, acts of war on British soil like this cannot be tolerated.

I feel as though the failure to avoid a state of war between the U.K. and its allies against the states of Russia and China is a bitter personal blow, and if we could have done anything further to avoid this situation I assure you that it would've been done.

This however is not the only announcement I have to make with regret and sadness. You must now also stay in your homes unless it is essential that you leave them. This is for your own safety and will be enforced by the British army who will be using the roads, towns and motorways to enact manoeuvres to protect this country. I ask you to follow this guidance and not interfere with the efforts of our armed forces." And with that address, war was afoot.

"Uh guys?" I asked of my squad as a whole. "You saw that right?"

Everyone silently nodded and I wasn't entirely sure what to do or say next, so as one we took a moment of silence, which was eventually rudely cut off by Roberts.

"And what do we do with the walking moustache there?" He gestured with a thumb over his shoulder towards the General who was still out cold but looked just like his old self again, two legs and clean clothes now upon his person.

"I uhh… guess we just ask him when he wakes up" I said, really not knowing what the right answer was. I certainly wasn't going to kill him off, but also if I just let him walk out of the dome then what would happen? He'd hitch-hike a ride back to HQ and show off his new appendage? No I really needed to get this man on side.

"Don't worry about me," the General said. He must've been pretending to still be asleep to see what we were going to say and luckily we hadn't said anything incriminating or that didn't match our story. "My leg feels great by the way… Thank you for that…but my head…" he pressed a palm to his head and grimaced. I knew that feeling.

"Oh don't worry about that," Roberts said, "ain't nothing compared to the time I got cut in half, right Cross?"

I smiled and nodded, and I was sure it was nothing like the hangover I had the last time I was killed in a training mission, the thought of *that* pain was still giving me nightmares.

"So…uh," the General said. "You guys are on the level aren't you? I mean everything you've said is true isn't it." It was more of a statement than a question and I took a moment to appreciate just how much good saving someone's life could actually do.

"It is, all of it," I said without a moment's hesitation. "We just don't know when it's coming, but it's coming."

Simms took a few strides towards us as we spoke and I cringed as the ground shook with her heavy footsteps; I was worried that the General might have mistaken her approach for hostility.

"I'm Major Simms, General," she said with a salute. "I can fill you in with all the details and also I'm a field medic so I can have a look at your head to make sure you haven't suffered any serious injuries." She smiled as she spoke and I wasn't sure how she did it, but when she did it made me smile too - she'd always been so calm and caring – the total opposite of how the Major actually looked inside her giant mech.

Simms and the General moved to the far side of the Construction Unit, behind the silo and power station so that we didn't interfere with their conversation, and when they returned I could tell before the General even spoke that he completely believed our story.

"I'm running this one all the way to the top," he said as he drew himself to his full attention. "Don't you worry son, I'm going to do everything in my power to get you and your squad recognised as the serving military personnel of this country - no planet - you've already all done so much and all we've done is fight you every step of the way."

I wanted to tell him that getting recognised as Military personnel might not have gone down well with the Chinese or Russians, but who was I to argue anyway? They'd already started the war. Not wanting to actually speak to the horrible PM again, I sent a text message to her phone telling her that she could arrange for the General to be collected now.– I just wished I could've seen her face when she had to act as the man's personal assistant.

Of course, the news helicopter had returned already – it was basically back two minutes after the enemy planes had been destroyed so the world already knew all about how the General had been saved and healed. I imagine all he'd have to have done was wave down the thing and he could've hitched a ride but I really *really* wanted the PM to feel just a little less important just for one moment.

"One last thing General," I said as an afterthought before he left the dome. "Take this." I picked up my plasma rifle from its leaning position against the Construction Unit and tossed it to him. He caught it though I could tell from his reaction that I should've probably opted to pass it to him instead, given its combined weaponly nature and weight. I didn't need it anyway as I preferred guns that fired bullets not balls of plasma, and I had the distinct feeling that humanity was going to need an edge over its enemies in the very near future.

"Thank you," the General said simply, saluted us all and walked out of the protective shield that surrounded us. I watched as an army jeep rounded the corner, picked him up and sped up and away towards more civilised places with a smile. I just hoped that what I assumed was now a friend on the inside would turn out to be just what I imagined it was.

21

∞

"How the fuck did the Russians and Chinese make it here together anyhow?" Roberts asked suddenly, jarring us from our friendly game of poker. "I mean they ain't exactly nearby and surely someone must've seen them coming, right?"

"Well they'd have to fly right over the US or most of Europe if they go with a straight shot," Long offered.

"Nah," Hobern joined in. If they took off from the Russian west coast, they could trace the Baltic Sea then only pass over the border between Denmark and Germany. They'd have to remain undetected for about fifty miles but overall the journey would be less than two thousand in total. I mean, that's entirely possible for the Air Force that I know, but if the range on these planes is somewhat less than that, then they could be using aircraft carriers."

His thought process was sound and logical and pulling up the schematics on both of the offending aircraft I could see that their range would've allowed them to make the strike as Hobern had suggested, though the journey would've taken about an hour and it would be a one way deal. I told Sam to hack into the Russian and Chinese military communication lines and inform me of anything I should know about. The last thing I needed was to be surprised by these offending militaries again.

After speaking to Hobern about the shield and how it worked to protect us - I'd never really taken the time to understand it properly – he told me that it was very much like those that the Saturn used. They prevented ingress of physical and electrical matter, though didn't hamper egress or the passing of the atmosphere. Of course I already knew all of that, but what was news to me was exactly how the thing worked, power wise.

The shield started off at one hundred percent strength and slowly dissipated over time, which was accelerated each time it was damaged by whatever was shooting at it. Once it was dropped, it would recharge itself slowly until it could be called back into action at full charge again. It was pretty genius, though I could see the one fatal flaw in keeping it raised the whole time – it would be discharging slowly until it was useless. What was a good titbit of information though, was the fact that in exchange for strength, duration or a combination of the two, the dome could be expanded to a large degree.

Hearing all of this, I told Hobern to close down the dome. We didn't have any threats on the horizon right now and I was sure that we could get an early warning next time if we did, having instructed the Construction Unit to print out a radio tower.

It was nice having a firebase on earth. I was already internally calling it Firebase Beta, though I thought I might update that at a later date. Anyway, the grounds were rich in materials for my constructs, the sun was warm and the day/night cycle was finally something I could get my head around. Also, the base had been growing at a serious pace thanks to the material availability of the land.

Looking much like a small fort now, my firebase had everything that it'd had on the bug planet, save the fences and turrets, and my material stockpile was still growing with every passing hour. It was a nice feeling to be able to make anything I wanted, though in the back of my mind I still felt as though constructing a full scale military installation on the cliff tops of Dover probably wasn't going to be the best course of action whilst the world was still a little unsure of our presence, to say the least.

I did think long and hard about what humanity had been doing over the last decade or so. As a group, the Space Corps had been set up to represent humans throughout the galaxy and beyond. It was a multinational mixture of personnel from backgrounds comprising everything from engineers to marines, though centrally managed by an independent governing body so that intercontinental politics and disagreements didn't skew their agenda.

As such, the regular armies, navies and air forces of earth's countries were left somewhat dormant in their advancements. Of course militaries around the world were maintained with their soldiers and technological advancements where it was possible, but as the Space Corps advanced independently, the militaries of earth somewhat stagnated. There weren't hovering tanks or prism towers, rather new weaponry and armaments seemed to revolve around reliability, range and efficiency instead of the technological leaps and bounds that the Space Corps had apparently made in arriving at the level of technology evident in the Saturn.

The good news for us in all this though was that with the Space Corps away on other business – they currently had a fleet of twelve ships, though pretty poorly armoured – the threats that we would have to potentially deal with from the global militaries would be poor at best, and after dealing with the fighter jets, I felt that my squad was up to defending themselves.

Another day passed without incident. I did keep an eye on the news feeds and made sure Sam was doing her duty with the foreign threats that we may have had to deal with, but nothing was really happening. After all it was boring news to report that 'nothing much was happening,' and although the world seemed to carry on turning, we were apparently given a pretty wide berth.

The sun eventually set and that was one thing that I'd missed in all of my time away from earth. The sky was pink and the waves of the sea below us lapped quietly at the port and shore, and it felt like we were truly home. If sleeping whilst in my ARC was in any way productive, I'd have done it.

"Lieutenant, I believe that there are military personnel in the waters below us. It seems that they are Russian Special Forces, though I am unable to confirm this at this time" Sam informed me just as I was getting comfortable.

"Guys," I relayed in my best soldier voice, "we've got company."

How three dinghies each filled with five Russian special forces agents had managed to land on the shoreline below us was blowing my mind although the soldiers wore all black and were equipped with silenced MP5's and night vision apparatus. If I didn't have my handy visor I'd never have heard or seen them coming as they were very obviously both highly trained and damn good at avoiding detection. My visor though, other than giving me a near perfect sight in total darkness, also handily overlaid a blue dot onto each of the agents as they moved. It didn't care if they wore all black and crouched down – to the visor, and therefore me – it was like looking at kids playing spy.

I knew the MP5s they carried very well, having used them in my own time in the Space Corps; sometimes you just didn't mess with the classics and these were weapons that got the job done – what they hit, they killed.

"I got three of them in my sights," Simms practically whispered as she aimed down the sight of her long mechanical arm. "Want me to take the shot?"

I didn't know how this decision had come down to me, but the very real decision between the life and death of another human being in this manner made my heart pound. I stalled in silence as I waited for an option to present itself.

"Cross?" Simms repeated a little louder this time and I shut my eyes for a long second to try to think straight.

The leading forces were just metres away from coming into sight range and I knew I needed to do something but I just couldn't give that order yet. These people hadn't done anything to harm us or even threaten us. Of course it looked like they were here to try to kill us but I needed to be sure.

I was sure that the leading Russian agent could now see us, and seeing that we were prepared for their arrival, he quickly raised his rifle to shoot at us. My combat cognition kicked in like a whirlwind and before the man had the chance to squeeze his trigger the SA80 assault rifle in my hands had fired its three single rounds, dropping my assailant. I heard Simms' rifle follow a split second behind mine and the dark field before us was lit up with bright gunfire and hurtling blue plasma rounds.

I heard Roberts' minigun spin up now that we were all guns blazing, and when it fired hundreds of plasma rounds littered the battlefield before us reducing the Russian operatives to smoking bodies of blood and holes. The other four mechs didn't even get a chance to fire their weapons as the fighting lasted for just five seconds, though it definitely seemed longer.

When our guns fell silent it made me feel sick. This was the first time I'd ever killed another human being and the feeling was not of success or triumph, it was of guilt and regret.

Before I could give myself a real hard time though, in the sea, what must've been more than a mile away, flashes of light broke the darkness which were followed shortly by low thuds. I recognised the sounds immediately as battleship cannons, and the realisation dawned on me that we really had a problem now.

"I guess that answers the question about aircraft carriers then? Looks like they've got boats in our waters,'" I called to Hobern, who was fiddling with the force shield getting it to cover us before the cannon fire obliterated us. He didn't take the time to answer though and I could see he was visibly frustrated by the apparatus.

The shield covered us all just in time but dropped again after the first two shells impacted it and it fizzed out of existence against the backdrop of more shells being fired in our direction. The first thought that came to mind was that I *really* needed to get some AA or point defence systems going.

Thankfully we were a little spread out, not massively so but enough that one direct hit wouldn't take us all down in one go.

Thinking on my feet and leaning heavily into my combat cognition once again, I formulated a plan.

"Roberts - run." I ordered first – to which his response was to turn tail and run like hell. He'd been hurt badly before and the memory of that seemed to give him the push to go without question.

"Long, Carter, Hobern and Simms - you guys form a defensive line along the front of the firebase between it and the battleships out there. I want covering fire to draw the attention of those boats. Do not get close to each other though, spread out and keep moving. Walton, you got some artillery in that heavy mech of yours?" I asked.

"Oh yeah, I got heavy artillery, mortars and seeker missiles in this thing. Only thing is though I have to plant myself to get the shots off." he replied. "Sounds like you got the others doing that for me though so it should be OK."

I didn't know how many boats were out there but from the gunfire I could tell it was at least three, and that meant Walton needed to get off multiple clear shots without being targeted, otherwise there would be no moving out of the way. The mechs were quick when moving, but I could tell from how long it took Walton to plant himself that moving was not going to be an option again for some time.

The next shells from the boats crashed into my firebase causing minimal damage. I was glad that the material that the Construction Unit and drones used to make stuff was strong and durable, though the damage was still evident on the impact sites. The mechs who were firing off into the ocean though were sure to be the targets of the next attacks.

More flashes from the ocean, then a *boom* from Walton who'd set up at the back of the base and a giant blue neon ball flew up into the sky illuminating everything around us for miles. The thing must've been twenty metres in diameter.

As soon as the shot had left Walton's gun I knew we were all in trouble. There was no way the enemy wouldn't hone in on that particular firework show, so like Roberts before me, I ran. I ran as fast as I could away from the enemy fire and didn't stop until I heard a second loud shot release from Walton's cannon. How I hadn't seen him use this weapon before was beyond me.

In the distance I could still see the ships firing their cannons and I did feel guilty about leaving the mech squad to do their work, though I knew they had a far better chance of surviving this than I had. As I watched another volley fired at us, the first neon ball fell from the sky and resulted in an immense fireball of explosions that must've completely obliterated the vessel it'd hit. The second round followed its predecessor down out of the sky and took another of the ships out with a similar fanfare.

Walton, who'd either needed to reload or make sure his aim was on, then released another two shots high into the sky.

The fire from the enemy ships hadn't stopped though, but there were less lights flashing with the next volley fired at us.

With each round of shells aimed at our firebase, dirt, concrete, metal and plastics were being thrown up and into the air and I watched in hope that my roving mech squad would remain safe and unhurt through the enemy fire, though I knew Walton was already on borrowed time.

Then a lucky shot landed within inches of Long and his mech was thrown back at least twenty metres, followed shortly by a direct hit on Hobern. I knew there was nothing I could do but I wanted more than anything to run to my comrades and pull them away to safety.

The constant shelling was getting ever closer to Walton, who'd taken out another ship and missed a fourth although I could tell there was just two enemy vessels remaining now. He fired two rounds into the sky which I could tell were aimed one for each of the two remaining enemies, and then my biggest fears were realised. Two shells almost at the exact same time impacted the planted mech and body parts along with mechanical sections of his suit flew away in every direction preceded with a puff of oil and blood. My mouth hung agape at the loss of my friend but at the same time, the last two of his rounds hit the ships they'd been aiming for and the sea was once again dark and quiet.

Roberts and I returned to the firebase as soon as we knew it was safe to do so and when we arrived at Long's position I was happy to see him conscious, though bruised and bloody and missing most of his mech's left leg. I didn't know if it was the neural link to his suit that caused it, but the pain he was experiencing seemed unbearable.

Hobern was worse though. Simms had arrived to his side where he lay on the ground with a hole bored right through the centre of his mech and straight through his physical body. I didn't know how he was still alive but he looked pale and didn't say a word. Simms' medical drones were already hard at work lacing him back together again and that gave me a little hope for Walton as I turned to look for his fallen body.

"Walton is gone," Simms said as she followed my gaze. "I can repair some damage like Long and Hobern…just about… but did you see what happened to Walton? Nobody survives that, mech or no."

My heart sank but honestly I'd been expecting it, after all I'd literally seen the man die. It made me mad though, *really mad.*

"Sam, send this message to the Russian president: you attacked us without provocation. You killed my comrade and friend and you now see what has happened to your fucking planes and ships. I am asking - no telling - you right now to stop this or we will come for you. Our revenge will be harsh and swift unless you stop this right now. I didn't take sides when I arrived here because I had a job to do. Now I have a side…and it isn't fucking yours."

I didn't ask for nor expect a reply, and none came but sending the threat at least made me feel a bit better. For now I needed to mourn the loss of my friend Major Jason Walton, and honour the sacrifice he made so that we could live to fight another day. Of course it was his ARC that'd perished and not his physical body, but I knew from what I'd been told that dying in an ARC was like playing Russian roulette, and the higher up the ranks you went, the bigger the chance of something bad happening to your brain.

I made my decision right there and then. If the Russians didn't back off now, then I'd be taking the fight to them – I didn't care how big the planet was when I had a basically unlimited amount of constructing to do along with completely superior weaponry. What I needed to do first though was to allow my people to lick their wounds and repair.

"You think he's alright?" Long said to me whilst looking up towards the stars, clearly talking about his friend and Major in arms, Walton.

I shrugged. I wasn't in the mood to be placating and as I did it I felt the slight pang of regret at my nonchalance.

"You know more about it than I do Major," I sighed, but added "though I'm sure he's fine. Probably up there drinking the blue goo and hitting on Sam, right?" Then something clicked in my mind. "Sam, do you have contact with the Saturn? Can you check in with Major Walton for us?"

"I cannot," Sam replied instantly as though she'd been expecting the question. Communications at this distance are not possible. Your ARCs are the exception to this rule, though the technology is not the same."

'Shocker,' I thought. When had she ever been useful anyway?

Major Long had apparently been placated though as I saw his shoulders inside his mech un-tense quite animatedly – the action mirrored by his mechanical outer suit – though the rest of the night wasn't going to be one for games and relaxing. We six remaining ARCs simply sat in silence and watched the horizon, waiting for more threats to come.

22

∞

When the sunrise of the next day brought first light and nothing more had threatened our squad, I was pleased to see that the repairs to our firebase as well as to Hobern and Long were completed and totally successful, though I hadn't expected any less from my Construction Unit, the Drones and Simms.

It seemed as though it was a good time to stand and walk around , though not strictly necessary when in an ARC - the mind could be a powerful enemy when it came to fatigue and aching joints. The pain and stiffness did go away almost instantly upon moving around and once the mind was occupied with other things, although that didn't stop it rearing its ugly head in the first place.

The long road that winded up from the port and past our firebase off inland had been stagnant since pretty much the moment we'd arrived and I wondered how much of an impact that would have on the past, or future events that we were there to help with, though there wasn't much I could do about it now. Looking up along the road inland though, I could see a convoy of army vehicles making its way toward us and I raised the rest of my squad to their guard and told them to prepare to defend themselves. I also had Hobern fire up the shield just in case, which would have regenerated itself by now, or at least to some degree.

It felt safer being covered in the protective dome, but I knew just how much of a false hope that could be after it'd been taken down so quickly in our last fight.

Once the convoy made it a little closer – apparently to within my visor's range, I could see that General Conners had returned and was leading whatever it was that was happening here. I could also see that there were tens of jeeps, troop carriers and other vehicles that I didn't really recognise but could tell they were carrying the parts of something big with them.

"General," I said curtly as his cavalcade made it to the far side of the dome and he'd dismounted his jeep. We were mere centimetres apart though I knew there was nothing he could do to harm me – of course not that I thought he wanted to, but most people wouldn't turn up mob-handed just to talk.

The General smiled a genuine smile. "Giving us that rifle was just about the best choice you ever made," he said. "Just when I didn't think there was a cat's chance in hell that Macdonald would allow us to even lift a finger to help you, you throw that curveball at us and well… long story short I'm your new liaison to the British government, with near total autonomy and a pretty good budget. Also…" he leaned in conspiratorially to lower his voice "you kind of saved my life, so you know, thanks on two counts. Anyway," he stood straight back up again and spoke louder, "the boys in the labs think they can do something with what you gave to them, and in return we're here to help you defend yourself (should you need it) from the Russians and Chinese who I believe have taken a bit of a liking to you."

"Well it's the Russians mainly…" I started as nonchalantly as possible but I couldn't help a smile cracking my face from ear to ear. We'd finally got through to these people and perhaps we might be able to achieve what we came here to do.

"How did they get here without being detected anyway?" Hobern said as his thundering mechanical footsteps telegraphed his presence next to me.

"Well they do have some technologies that we aren't yet completely familiar with right now, but rest assured we're working on it," the General replied with an awkward smile.

"Well let me know if I can help – I have a pretty wide background in engineering," Hobern said and it was the first time I'd actually heard him excited about something. "Just… I can't get out of the suit," he gestured to his own body in a little disheartened tone.

"I'm sure we'll figure something out," the General said with a chuckle, and with that I felt as though there was no further need for the shield between us.

The General had indeed brought us some pretty good gifts. He had at least thirty soldiers with him that each carried their usual weapons, and unloaded ammunition crates to be placed in my little firebase. Machine gun nests were set up along the cliff top in a line of about a hundred metres or so either side of us, and the coup de gras was something that one of the soldiers called a 'we're fucked' gun. I didn't understand why it had that name until I was told that its real name was a 'WF380' and the nickname had come because, well, in his words – if you shoot it at something and it doesn't die – we're fucked.

It took some assembling and the parts of the weapon were scattered across multiple vehicles requiring a forklift truck to unload most of it, though after several hours when the thing had been constructed it looked like the turret off of a tank, only on a bed of scaffolding. The barrel was at least four metres long and four inches wide and the shells that accompanied it were truly monstrous. Truth be told I couldn't wait to give the thing a go.

Our firebase had been well reinforced, though I did feel as though my own constructs could do a little better than the reinforcing soldiers and their (I had to say archaic) weaponry. With that in mind I asked the General what I could do to help.

"General, do I have permission to expand the firebase to better protect us?" I asked, scheming a new plan.

The General nodded slowly, I could tell he was apprehensive about my expansion but the gesture alone told me he had the authority to let me do so.

"You can expand, but let's set some limits before you do. How about five hundred metres in a diameter around where we stand currently?" he offered.

I didn't want to push my luck and truthfully five hundred metres basically covered the cliff top and the port of Dover below us. I immediately sent out Construction Drones to mark our perimeter with small constructed markers so I had a visual representation of where I could go up to. Coincidentally, all of the General's men fell within this range.

The thing that worried me the most, though, was the thought that these men and women were probably going to rely on me for their safety at some point. I knew they had chosen to sign up, knowing what they were getting themselves into and all that, but I didn't know how I'd feel about it if they were just bombarded with missiles simply because they were in close proximity to my squad. With that in mind I started working out the best way to keep these soldiers safe.

Taking a leaf from military history, the best thing I could think of was defensive structures, much like that'd been employed in World War Two. Bunkers, trenches, caltrops and turrets.

I was glad that the soldiers had had the forethought to bring food and drink with them because my new plan took a week to enact, and in that time not much else really happened. It really felt like the calm before the storm, though I had no evidence that any sort of storm was on the horizon.

I'd constructed thick concrete bunkers for the machine gun nests that I was assured could take a battering from anything like the battleship cannons that we'd been up against already and that alone made me feel better. Then I'd made some turrets of my own. A handful of laser turrets, then with Hobern's help I'd manufactured a few anti-air plasma turrets that I just couldn't wait to see in action. I'd also somewhat taken over the port below, as I had a sneaky feeling that it was going to be a very useful beachhead to have in the near future.

Since my arrival, the port wasn't really being used. Most cargo had been rerouted to Felixstowe or Southampton, though some had been moved onto the Channel Tunnel from France. Although shipping and imports and exports had really all but dried up since the outbreak of war, captains and sailors didn't want the risk of getting caught in any crossfire and companies didn't want to pay the skyrocketing insurance costs to make increasingly risky crossings. All of this meant that I had a whole concrete playground to mess with.

I had checked with the General at first and to my surprise he'd told me that I was free to do whatever I wanted within my perimeter of allowed influence. I was sure there was a sparkle in his eye when I asked about the port as if he'd planned this all along, though I could've been imagining it.

The port didn't offer the high ground like my firebase did, though having both a high lookout and a low defensible ground based position was going to be very helpful, –especially if any enemies didn't know that I had a foothold in the port.

I used the cheap laser turrets to create kill zones between buildings and ordered a few of the soldiers into the buildings themselves; they didn't seem to mind as they were both warm and dry. Then I reconstructed a small portion of the set up into concrete blocks and fences to make movement through the port difficult while allowing defensible positions for my own troops. By the time I was done the port didn't look much different, but if you were really looking for it then you could see that it wasn't a place to walk through at night especially if you didn't want to get lasered in the face.

Then, as if they'd been sat waiting for us to finish what we'd been planning, out of the corner of my eye I could see black dots high above us in the sky. I'd taken the personal responsibility to oversee my port reconstruction project so I was standing in the lower part of my two-part defensive base along with ten of the soldiers that'd come with the General, and with whatever was arriving, I wished that I was back up top and able to defend properly with my allies.

The gunfire from the troops was deafening and the AA cannons were doing their job, periodically flinging plasma balls into the air that split and cackled high into the sky, though I could now see the enemy clearly through my visor, and I could also see that all of our fire was doing nothing to them.

There were hundreds of black dots descending on my firebase and once they were close enough my visor dutifully informed me that these were Chinese jump troops – essentially soldiers in advanced combat suits equipped with multi-directional jet packs so that they could both fly and dodge projectiles at near inhuman speeds. Watching the plasma fire peppering the jump troops, I could see just how effective they were at avoiding fire.

Of course a few got hit, though the majority of the jump troops would wait until the last minute then dart out of the way of the obvious projectiles. Sometimes a machine gun nest would land a lucky shot, their bullets far smaller and faster than the plasma rounds, though that also meant they were enacting a kind of 'spray and pray' tactic – which was far less accurate in itself.

I saw the blue neon dome pop into existence when the first of the jump troops' feet touched down on the ground mere meters away from the firebase and I practically held my breath.

The troops carried QBS-06 assault rifles, which although were useful underwater (who knew what they were expecting), didn't really have the punch needed to drop Hobern's force shield.

I was just about to allow myself to think it was a good idea that I'd left all of the mechs up on top of the cliff, when I heard the sound of boots landing on the concrete behind me, quietly, as though this had been the plan all along. Before I turned to face whatever it was that had finally come for me, I spared a moment to wish that the machine gun nests had been given force shields too, and made a mental note to arrange that once all this messy fighting was dealt with.

When I turned around to face whoever it was behind me, my breath caught in my chest for a short moment. Before me, dressed in all black armour, stood a person at least seven feet tall and built like a Victorian latrine. I imagined a lot of the size was either to intimidate or to make room for the propulsion system that I couldn't see any sign of, and their head was covered entirely by a black form-fitting helmet that gave no indication of whoever was underneath

I was about to ask who the fuck this person thought they were, when within a moment three others had dropped down to encircle me, all of them identical. I knew though that I had ten soldiers down here with me and once they realised what was happening they'd come to my aid.

I did also wonder why exactly I hadn't been killed immediately by these new assailants, though that question was answered once I realised they all had lengths of rope attached to their backs . They were sent to bring me back alive, not kill me.

Machine gun fire rattled from behind me and pinged off of the jump troops around me as my own troops entered into the fray, joined by my shoulder mounted laser turret. To my horror, though, the fire from our own SA80's as well as my laser didn't seem to be affecting the Chinese troops, the gunfire simply impacting their suits and dropping to the ground. I wanted more than anything for my turrets to join in the fight but when I checked, they were all facing away from the port towards the sea or between the buildings – I made a mental note to add more later and to also try to ensure they had a wider firing arc that those that already existed had. The laser from my shoulder mount, though, caused scorch marks and I was sure that given enough time it would punch through their suits, but as they kept moving as humans under fire typically did, it was more likely to make pretty patterns on their uniforms rather than kill them.

'Holy shit that's some impressive body armour' I found myself thinking, though it still paled in comparison to everything I'd done with my ARC so far.

The jump troops returned fire on my squad and within moments two of my men had fallen, which was what snapped me back to the realisation that I actually needed to *do something*.

Somewhat ignoring my presence as they dealt with the greater threat (the ones who actually carried their guns around, not just left them up on the cliff top like an idiot). I remembered what I'd done to my ARC with my latest promotion and willed my plasma blade into existence.

From inside my ARC's forearm, the blue neon blade extended to its full length of about four feet and crackled with power. –There was no way the enemy could've expected this and there was no body armour on earth that was going to be able to prevent this blade from passing through it like a hot knife through butter.

My combat cognition activated and I swung my blade in the perfect backhand swing at the agent directly behind me. I didn't even feel the resistance as my blade cut the man cleanly in two, cauterising the wound as it passed through both his armour and his body. It made me feel sick at just how quickly and easily a life had been ended, though I knew that I needed to carry on for the sake of my squad and my allies. If I said it was getting easier to take human lives, I'd have been lying.

A gunshot sounded followed by the dull thud of the shot impacting its target. The bullet hit my shoulder from behind and it felt like something had bit me and clamped down and I screamed out in pain before pursuing my attacker.

There were three agents left, all preoccupied with my allied soldiers except one who'd taken the time to fire at me in single shots. I knew I was lucky to only have taken a glancing blow and made my move toward the enemy soldier without hesitation. Through my combat cognition, I could somehow sense the trajectory of his fire and made my moves to not fully dodge the shots he fired as I moved toward him, but to allow them to hit my least vital parts. After all, if I wasn't dead, I could still attack. It hurt like shit though.

I rounded on my second target and thrust my plasma blade straight forward in a very much fencing-like manoeuvre to decapitate the man, his gun falling silent. I was badly wounded and could tell that if I didn't get medical attention soon I was probably done for but artificial adrenaline that I assumed was created by my linked mind kept me upright and I moved to the two remaining special forces agents.

They were under heavy fire from my soldiers although it didn't seem to be affecting them in the slightest, the bullets from my allies still unable to penetrate this new armour that the enemy was equipped with. I didn't spare any time for fanfare though, taking the two out in one movement - a forward slash to the first followed by a backslash to the second. They fell to the ground defeated and I fell to my knees right along with them.

I vomited, which was another thing that ARCs could apparently do – they were so similar to human beings in so many ways. I wasn't sure though if the vomit was from the disgust at my actions or because I was so direly wounded and the adrenaline had already begun to recede. I thought about it for a moment or two before I fell flat on the ground and my vision faded to black. The last thing I did was smile at the thought that my pain was finally over.

23

∞

I opened my eyes when the hot sunlight scorched into them and I felt the need to cover my visor with the back of my hand. Apparently the night was over and a new day had begun.

"We lost eight men," Long reported once he realised I was once again conscious though I couldn't yet fully focus on the mech. "And almost one ARC, but you seem OK now." I could hear the smile in his voice but it didn't sound like a happy one.

Simms appeared in my line of sight and traced a massive mechanical finger before my eyes left and right. I followed it with my gaze to show that I was fine and pushed myself up and out of the Construction Unit before anyone else could give me any bad news.

"Eight?" I repeated sadly. I felt so responsible.

"They knew what they signed up for," the General tried to placate me though it did little good. Just because a soldier knew what the deal was didn't mean they went into things expecting not to come out the other side. These were real people and there was no coming back for them. It wasn't a game or a long distance virtual reality-type thing like we had going on; these people had families and those families had just lost a member.

"Why does everything always have to be so difficult?" I asked of no-one in particular and dutifully no one answered. I took a deep breath before looking around at the firebase and port below, and realising someone must've carried me all the way up the winding dual carriageway, I felt guiltier still.

"Don't worry bout it," Roberts voice arrived before he did. "The guys all got together and had a good old fashioned crowd surf up here with you on top. Didn't seem to bother them none."

I appreciated the fact that Roberts had known what I was feeling though I really didn't need everyone's sympathy right now.

"OK, back to work then," I said after a long exhale and a mental note to get out of the mental pit I was sitting in. "We've got a lot to do and probably not much time to do it you know, if the Chinese and Russians have anything to say about it. I want a long range detection system, better armour and weapons for our troops and would someone get me a god damned coffee?"

I heard Simms laugh as she was walking away and back to her post. I was glad someone had a good sense of humour around here.

"The Chinese and the Russians are acting just like the Scriven aren't they? It's weird but I kinda expected something different but these guys are just sending slightly more powerful attacks our way over and over, forcing both sides to improve or lose in a repeating cycle," Roberts mused. "I hate to say it but somehow we gotta break that cycle or we'll be stuck in it forever."

He was right and I'd noticed it too. The enemy tactics and the way these battles were playing out were mightily similar to how the Scriven had attempted to best us during our time in firebase alpha. The thought of alpha took me back to the people we'd left behind to take the war to the alien race and I wondered if they were making decent headway yet.

I nodded along with Roberts' statement and asked what he would suggest we do to break the cycle.

"Well, the way I see it is that if we keep playing defence, only the offence gets to set the rules – they send somethin' our way, we bat it back and they come back stronger. I'm saying we play offence and start making' the rules, right? Why don't we build something we can take to the enemy and give 'em what for?"

The General, who'd apparently been listening in to Roberts' plan took the opportunity to speak before I could reply again.

"And do what? We aren't an invading force so we have nothing to gain by taking the fight to our enemies other than causing casualties. We defend here because we're forced to, but the moment we attack we take the responsibility of every life lost on *both* sides. Then let's say we win a few battles? We don't want to occupy these countries so we just come home again? At least with defence if we prove ourselves too difficult to overcome, then maybe they'll just stop coming eventually."

Both of them had very good points and I struggled internally to come to a compromise that would take both of their thoughts and comments on board and use them in a productive manner. No matter how hard I tried though, the more I realised that the viewpoints were diametrically opposed to each other.

"That frown'll get stuck on your face if you don't ease up," Simms called with a laugh from her patrol about twenty metres away from our location and it made my face relax – the feeling of relief telling me that I really had been holding myself very tensely.

I needed more information on what was happening and why these tactics were being employed, and as much as I hated to do it I called Sam into being.

"Sam, I need some information…" the AI must've been expecting me to speak to her as she immediately faded into a blue wireframes corporeal form in front of me. She didn't say anything though it was apparent she was awaiting my question.

"I need to know why the Russian and Chinese forces can sneak up on us so easily, and why they employ tactics like the Scriven had on Cade. Also their weapons and armour seem a little different to what I was expecting. What can you tell me about that?"

Sam pulsed a couple times before she replied; that always made me a little nervous about what she had to say. "As I said previously, these nations have developed a technology that is preventing their appearance on radar scans. I have analysed all of our encounters and am yet to discover a way which we could've detected them any earlier. I have also been monitoring their communications systems, though that has not given any information away regarding their tactics or movements either. With regards to their weapons and armour, it would appear that they have been artificially advanced along their development path by an exterior influence, though I cannot say what at this time."

My mind instantly fell to the Ashaii and my legs went cold as I imagined them giving the Russians and Chinese access to better weapons. It seemed a bit silly though as if the aliens really wanted to kill humans – and what they did to the Wanderlust suggested that they did - so why would they give them better guns? Something just wasn't adding up and it made me feel on edge.

There was also some sort of weird overlap between the Ashaii and the Scriven that I was yet to understand. The two races seemed so mutually exclusive but so far wherever one showed up the other didn't seem too far behind.

I was still worried though that because of my own presence and effects on the port of Dover that the planned future events might not happen in the same way, and it could get either better or worse. The first Scriven contact might not be in a shipping container – perhaps it would strike at the U.S, or a more secretive country that might not let the world know of their presence. The variables were too many and I just couldn't get my head around the consequences of each and every one of my actions. I was just beginning to spiral when Roberts put a calming hand on my shoulder and the world came back into focus.

"Don't worry about it," he said simply. "Things change and we roll with it. Don't worry about it."

His statement was clumsy but it made me feel so much better, like he'd pulled my head up from underwater and I could think clearly again.

"First things first then - guns and armour for the soldiers. It doesn't matter what we do next but they need to do better damage with better protection." A I spoke I keyed the instructions into the terminal to manufacture thirty plasma assault rifles. It was more than we needed, having only twenty some soldiers left to hand the guns out to, but it never hurt to have spare. Following that I tasked the Construction Unit to come up with some sort of armour plated vest that wouldn't hamper movement but at the same time would offer an increased protection against projectile weapons. I was pretty sure the enemy didn't have energy weapons, well not yet at least anyway.

The design that the terminal (and Sam I suppose) came up with for the armour was pretty basic to say the least. Essentially it was an upgrade for what the soldiers wore already, simply patches of a dense material that they could actually replace their own armoured vest innards with. It *was* basic, but because the new patches were constructed from a denser material than what they had already, they were going to be far more effective as potential lifesavers. I also gave a spare one to the General so that he could send it back to the lab for the to make future armour from the stuff... or tanks or something, I wasn't a military engineer.

That did give me a new plan,however, and with it brought a new age for the military prowess of Firebase Beta. I was going to make some drones, though this time not Construction Drones nor the HAMs that were doing an excellent job at collecting raw materials from the earth's surface. No this time, I was making combat drones.

I was no stranger to the works of Isaac Asimov's three laws of robotics – that they:

one - will harm no human,

two -robots shall obey humans and

three - the robots will avoid situations that could cause harm to themselves

In pretty much every movie or tv show about robots, these rules had either been ignored or used as a means for a sentient robot to commit terrible crimes, but I thought I had this one figured out.

These drones would not be self aware or autonomous; no, these would be controlled by Sam, which I knew was pretty much the same thing, but Sam was already there and I hadn't really seen her do anything too malicious or that would endanger humanity yet (touch wood). Also I wanted these ones to patrol the seas around the U.K. shorelines to make sure that nothing would pass through the net so they'd be far away from us.

With a drone navy in mind, I started visualising the plans for drone ships that could float and shoot, but also afforded deck space to the more traditional quadcopter-style drones that could fly and shoot. I was killing two birds with one stone whilst creating a Navy and an Air Force all on one go.

Given what'd been happening, I felt I didn't need to ask for permission to expand in a seaward direction, the General already having lost a handful of his men, and I was still riding the positivity that came with the new armour and tech I'd made for them. I was sure that if I kept feeding them things to make their lives easier, safer or had the means to make them kill things quicker, I'd be able to keep on their good books pretty much indefinitely.

But I knew the whole world would still be watching and I also knew that there was a very fine line between defence, retaliation and aggression, and I did not want to be seen as some self-important omnipotent being – but I was pretty sure that given the events so far, people would understand a little proactive defence.

A week passed by the time the first combat drones were printed up and went off on their way to the sea and thankfully in between, nothing had happened. No attacks or sabotages, no threats of any kind, just quiet stillness. It *was* a good thing though, as we all got to relax a little and stop thinking about war and fighting (and loss) so much. The other side of the coin though was the thought that unless we made a move, there was nothing happening, and it made me feel very conscious of *all* of my movements and what I showed the world.

The drone boats were a metre long and looked like dark grey shoeboxes with a wedge at the front, though much much bigger. They weren't pretty but I favoured function over fashion in this and so many other cases, and I teamed up with the General and his men to use their jeeps and trucks to ferry them down the long winding road to the port then into the sea. At the size of a medium car, the drones sported some four short range plasma rifles that were very much like my own SA80X's, a single long range laser turret that I hoped was a little more useful than the standard turrets and a single anti air plasma cannon for those oh so inconvenient flying enemies. I wanted to add more stuff into the offensive drones, but each time I thought of something new it just needed more and more power to function, making the thing bigger and bigger to house more batteries, capacitors or power generating facilities. Multi-directional jet propulsion made them capable of immense speeds at the drop of a hat and the coup de gras was the single quadcopter mounted atop each of them, with three laser turrets attached to their undercarriage to deal with any threats below them. I called the drone ships ASPs for 'Automated Sea Patrol Ships', and the quadcopters BEEs, because they buzzed liked bees and flew about. By now I had fully accepted that naming things in this way was the best thing ever and had no intention to stop. I did think about giving the BEEs' jet engines like the ASPS, though I thought it was better to save the space that would've been necessary for the additional power requirement, and the ASPs would be able to get them very close to their intended targets anyway.

By the time I had just over one hundred sea-faring drones paroling our shores complete with quadcopter BEEs, I felt a lot more comfortable in the thought that we would never get snuck up on again.

That was the thought process anyway.

For another couple of days nothing much happened and I was beginning to get used to the routine of daily life. The soldiers and the General had set up camp as though it was an official army base, and once we'd all got to know each other a little better the soldiers had started setting tents up on the cliff top rather than rotate in and out of the buildings in the port below depending on their shifts and patrols. It made me feel good that they both trusted us and wanted to be near us, though I did wonder if they worried about potential attacks hitting the port first. I chose to believe the former over the latter and even manufactured heaters, soft pillows, bedding and blankets for them - the whole nine yards.

The General and two of the higher ranked soldiers had also enacted a kind of PT regime that Roberts and I happily took part in, though in our ARCs it was obvious that we had a distinct advantage in making it over, under and through the obstacle courses, push-ups, sit-ups and whatever else they concocted for us on a daily basis. Honestly, it was like we were cheating with the way our bodies could just do so much *more* that a real human body. Roberts loved it though, gloating every time he beat a course record or a soldier otherwise failed to best his own. It was all fun and games though and nobody really seemed to mind the antics.

The mech squad didn't get involved in PT and I completely understood. They always liked to stick together for one, and for two they couldn't actually exit their mechanical exoskeletons, so rather than traverse the obstacle course they probably would've just broken it.

Hobern had taken to contacting the lab technicians via a direct contact link the General had set up for him and he was helping them disassemble and reassemble the tech I was providing. I could've done it myself though Hobern had said that teaching them the reality behind these kinds of technologies would be far more useful to them than my basic knowledge and recipes.

Long and Carter usually patrolled together in a never ending perimeter of everything we called home and part of me knew that it was the loss of Walton that had caused them the addition paranoia and anxiety, the late Major ever present in their minds. I never questioned them about it; if it made them feel better then why not.

Simms was a bit of an enigma. She could talk friendly to anyone and everyone but other than the mech squad and myself, she didn't really talk with very much depth. When I spoke to her, for example, she would ask how I was feeling about certain events, or tell me how she was feeling – though whenever I overheard conversations she'd had with others, it was always very official and very curt. I assumed it was because she just hadn't gotten to know everyone properly yet.

But lulled into a false sense of security we well and truly were, and all good things always had to come to an end didn't they, and this ended with Sam's voice cutting through the smile on my face in a heartbeat.

"We've just lost one of our drone ships – or would you prefer that I call them ASPs? – to an unknown assailant. I have sent others to assess the situation, though it would appear that the threat is underwater."

'Shit' I thought. If there was one thing I should've both remembered and counted on was that the bad guys always used submarines. If my military history was correct – and to be honest it wasn't always - I actually had known that both Russia and China were on the top ten list of countries with the most submarines, fielding over one hundred each. Coincidentally, on the top ten list of things my drones couldn't do, were shoot things underwater and dive. I did wonder if the BEEs' lasers could fire down through water without a refracting effect, though the chances of that being an effective deterrent were low.

Once again, we'd made advancements and the enemy had created the perfect counter, as if they knew our plans all along.

"Call them all back to the port," I ordered Sam. There was no need to waste good drones if they were going to simply be sitting ducks, and with that single order we took three steps backwards and lost our naval sensor net.

"I want to intercept all enemy communications from around the world and I want them mapped on a visual screen so that I can see who's talking to who and when," I practically shouted my order at anyone who'd listen, but primarily to Sam. "And I want to know how long it's going to take for those subs to get here. Oh, and General, we're going to need to think of a way to fight submarines." I added for good measure.

Roberts eventually took control of the terminal with Hobern guiding him on what to do to make my comms interceptor and I left them to it while I spoke with the General.

"I'm no Navy man, though we do have a long military history as a country of sinking submarines…well the ones that didn't want to be sunk…you know what I mean," he flustered uncharacteristically. "Look, the best ways to sink a sub is with depth charges, mines or torpedoes. There's no two ways about it and that's my advice," the General said as I wondered absent mindedly if the mech squad was waterproof.

I knew that idea was stupid though so parked it…for now. Depth charges and mines were all well and good, but if the missiles that these subs fired had any sort of range then there would just be far too much sea to try to cover with them, even with my extraordinary manufacturing capabilities. That left torpedoes, and I had no idea how they really worked, so I had Sam explain to me just how they did.

Eventually, I gave the port some underwater torpedo launchers once the concept was clear to me and my Construction Drones printed them out in no time at all. The torpedoes themselves were the real eye candy though, these babies could lock onto a target with their somewhat limited inbuilt AI from over ten miles away, adjust their course to seek and inevitably destroy what they hit in an explosion of plasma. I couldn't wait to test them out on these enemy submarines.

I was wondering exactly how the enemy was going to adapt to this upgrade though, and it was a little worrying. If they could make alterations to their plans in response to everything I did, I wasn't exactly sure what I could do other than create a defensible base, Navy and Air Force along with underwater support. If they came back stronger again, I was stumped.

The submarines though were apparently taking their sweet time about everything – or perhaps they'd stopped in their tracks once they'd dropped my first drone. It was so long, in fact, that Roberts and Hobern had manufactured the communications map and were eagerly awaiting my approval of their newly designed toy. Appraisals would have to wait though because just like that, one of my drones in the port was dragged down under the water, never to rise again.

24

∞

"What the fuck was that?" I shouted as I saw the drone disappear. I had been looking directly at it from the cliff top when it went under, though I'd had no warning or any signs of any enemies in the area. No gunfire and no explosions either, just a complete and utter disappearance right before my eyes. One moment it was there and the next it was gone.

No one answered my question; how could they really? There was no way anyone could have any answers for me so we all stood and simply watched the space in the ranks where my ASP had once been.

Then another sank. Then another and in just a few short moments more and more disappeared and before I knew it more than a third of my fleet had disappeared to their watery graves.

Then out of the water crawled the first Scriven I'd ever seen on planet earth, and it was not anything like what I was expecting.

This variant of the enemy bug wasn't pointed and sharp like the previous iterations had been; these ones did still have six legs though they were fatter than the last ones – perhaps due to a different gravitational profile – and on their backs were huge black sacks that pulsed like the body of a wasp. Their heads were less angular and still beaked, though the resemblance was still clear to the originals. From the back of the bulbous sack-like body flowed tentacles back into the water as they exited it and I could tell those things were what the Scriven used to propel themselves underwater.

The first bug that had arrived in fresh air stood eerily still as though it was the first time it'd ever experienced real air, then threw its head back towards the sky and let out an ear piercing screech. With that, a cascade of matching Scriven began to flow out of the water and onto the concrete port, moving quickly toward my buildings and the handful of soldiers that were inside there.

My breath caught as I realised that there was nothing that I could do to get down to help the men before they'd be swarmed by the hundreds of enemies that were flowing menacingly toward them, though thankfully the new firing arcs of the laser turrets meant that they'd already begun cutting down the enemy. What I wasn't expecting, though, was that once a bulbous Scriven fell to the ground dead, a handful of palm-sized eight legged and far more usual looking Scriven clawed their way out of the fallen corpse. I knew this wasn't how the things reproduced, having seen the nests on Cade, so that meant that these bigger things were acting like troop carriers, perhaps as the smaller ones couldn't survive underwater.

Standing next to Simms, who was firing her long range rifle at the enemy to great effect, I asked her the first thing that came to mind.

"You think they've got a nest out there underwater?"

Simms was silent for a moment whilst continuously pulling her trigger ,dropping Scriven left right and centre/ For each big one that fell, though, at least five little ones took its place and the battle was starting to get overwhelming. I was just so glad that all the soldiers had better weapons than before.

"I...think there is a nest, and that they can't survive underwater without these big ones," she confirmed my suspicions, "though I don't know why they've shown up now. As though we didn't already have enough going on with human enemies and now this?" she trailed off in dismay and I knew exactly how she was feeling.

Long, Carter and Roberts had already begun to make their way down the long concrete road to provide fire support. The front line of Scriven was constantly falling but being replenished and didn't seem to be getting any smaller, though I could tell that with each passing moment they were making headway towards the soldiers. Eventually, and painfully, I watched as the first plasma rifle overheated and became useless, then another and another. Soon the plasma fire had all but stopped, replaced with pistol fire and the throwing of small hand grenades.

I knew it wasn't good enough though and the Scriven surged forwards. It was like a wave of moving limbs and beaks and although the three ARCs arrived on scene just as the plasma fire had dissipated, there was little they could do to abate the torrent. Roberts' minigun spun up and showered the bugs with plasma rounds and the two assault mechs' rifles thundered with the effort of larger and more powerful plasma rounds. However, within seconds the Scriven were inside the first building and they filled it within seconds, flowing into doors and windows on one side, then out the same on the other. Everyone who was inside was decimated instantly and my head hung in shame and guilt at their losses.

"CROSS!" Simms brought me back to myself; somehow she just seemed to know I needed a metaphorical slap in the face. "Don't just stand there - fucking do something!"

Looking down at myself I knew she was right, I'd been rooted to the spot for a minute whilst the battle waged on below us and I all but kicked myself in annoyance.

Truly though there wasn't much that could be done. The troops in the docks had been wiped out and my laser turrets had been engulfed by the cascading wave of Scriven bodies. What I did notice, though, was that although Roberts and the two mechs down below were seriously outnumbered, their gunfire was doing a very good job at keeping the enemy at bay. It was in that moment that a sliver of hope returned to me, and I hoisted my rifle onto my shoulder and ran towards the winding road that led down to the docks, Simms following right behind.

With the five of us holding the line now, our victory was all but assured. We did have to take the occasional step backwards but only to keep the distance between us and the enemy constant as their falling lines were causing the bug bodies to pile up before us.

As morbid as it sounds, once the battle was over and all of the Scriven lay dead before us, I thought that it felt good to be killing bugs again. Killing people was just really *really* not for me.

The HAMs went in first to clean up the mess that we'd made, though we supervised them as they went. The last thing we needed was for more babies to start popping out and we'd be unaware, though thankfully nothing of the sort happened. I hoped a little that we'd find injured soldiers, holed up somewhere though that pursuit was fruitless - they'd not only been killed but apparently also absorbed by the wave and the lack of their bodies made me feel both uneasy and upset. When we reported back to the General with the confirmed news of his losses, his head hung and he removed his cap, clasping it between his hands. He looked exactly as I felt. What were thirty soldiers were now twelve.

Once the place was cleaned up and there was not even a shred of evidence of any fights, I re-enacted my policy of making a fence around the firebase to protect everyone inside. I knew it was a little overkill, but losing people I'd gotten to know was a real bitter pill to swallow. I used the same template I'd done before though added a few extra turrets along its length and it spanned the entire length of the dock plus an extra few metres either side. I knew that the Scriven could've simply exited the water at a different location and circumnavigated the fence, though they'd then have had to scale the chalky white cliffs of Dover to make it up to our firebase proper. It wouldn't be easy and we'd have plenty of opportunity to knock them back if they tried it – plus the dome force shield that always remained fully charged and ready to protect the heart of our operation was still at hand.

Lastly I banned the soldiers from going down to the port. They weren't experienced with fighting the bugs and their deaths were permanent. They were to stay atop the cliffs manning their machine gun nests and at the first sight the enemy were getting too close, they were to retreat without argument. They seemed to take it well with their comrades' and friends' deaths fresh in their mind, though I knew that with time that eagerness to retreat would wane.

Handily and about a week too late, my communications tracker had been completed. It was a large terminal about thirty inches across, attached to a large radio tower complete with satellite dishes and radio transceivers. It wasn't too dissimilar to the communications tower that I'd manufactured on Cade to broadcast my message to the entire planet.

On the screen was a map of the world that I could spin and zoom depending on what I wanted to see. It was covered to the point that it was almost unreadable in different coloured lines that spidered across it. Handily, a key with checkboxes allowed me to turn certain layers on and off depending on what I wanted to see.

White lines were personal communications such as mobile phone calls to loved ones or people complaining to virgin mobile that their bill was wrong – so I turned those off. Blue lines were official communication lines like the news, or business to business calls, so they went next. Filtering down the list to one single colour, I could now see all of the red lines of military communications across the globe. Again I felt like this was cheating.

One single red line pulsed between Beijing and Moscow, which I assumed was how the two nations were coordinating their attacks or otherwise sharing their information with each other, and tapping on it I found that I could actually listen in to their conversation.

"This was to be expected, don't act innocent in all this, Yuri," the Chinese delegate spoke in short sentences in English, which was so handy for me, as I spoke neither a word in Russian nor Chinese, though I presumed Sam would've translated for me again. "It seems grim now, though we have been assured that…"

The Russian voice cut in. "Assurances mean nothing when dealing with the unknown. You of all people should know…"

"And what is that supposed to mean? You think that we should have done things differently? Tell me how you would change anything given that we have walked the same path."

There was silence before the man named Yuri replied. He sighed "I'm not saying the choices we have made are wrong, but we must be amenable to change and adapt. This was…not a part of our plans Xi, and I don't think that we can continue in this manner any longer."

"Do what you wish, but we want to see this out until the end. The Republic of China will reign supreme and if you stand in the way of our plans there will be repercussions." Xi replied angrily.

"You don't threaten us," the Russian man replied calmly. "We will see what happens in the fullness of time. Dasvidaniya Xi, on the battlefield if necessary." Then he muttered a few words to himself in Russian and the call disconnected. I had to admit, the Russian man, Yuri, seemed very ashamed of himself and even better news was that their apparent alliance had just come to an end.

I quizzed Sam on who the two individuals were, and it appeared that the Chinese delegate was Xi Pui-Fung, head of their Foreign Affairs Ministry (i.e he controlled the army at the will of the President), and Yuri Goretski, Supreme Marshall of the Russian Federation. It was immediately clear to me that these were the two second most powerful people of their respective countries, right behind their Presidents – who I suspected had not wanted to get their hands dirty, and so had given full autonomy to these figures.

By the sounds of the conversation, our fight with Russia seemed to be at a standstill, though China still wanted to make moves to destroy us – well, I assumed it was all about us anyway and why wouldn't it be?

We had fallen back into quiet nothingness again, destined to play the waiting game until the next enemy showed up.

"It isn't fully clear why the alien species chose now to mount their attack on the port of Dover, though one positive thing to note in all of this is that the defending U.K. forces at the ports pushed them back with minimal casualties" I watched the news report of our latest battle in my visors Picture in Picture mode, and snorted in disgust at the 'minimal casualties' part.

"These aliens are unlike anything we have ever seen before, the Ashaii being the only sentient race that humanity has come across this far."

The screen changed to a rotating image of the bulbous troop carrier Scriven, then expanded to show the babies nesting inside.

"We don't yet know if the large of the alien species is birthing these smaller creatures, or what exactly their reproductive cycle entails, though results from laboratories are expected over the next few days."

I snorted again at the ignorance of the reporter. These things came from eggs and if they didn't realise that soon they were going to get a big shock when I uncovered a huge undersea nest full of them..

"The United States, France, Germany and Italy have already pledged to send air and naval support in light of these new developments, though the countries' governments have stressed that any combat manoeuvres will be with the alien race only, and if Russian or Chinese combatants arrive they will not be engaged."

It seemed cowardly to me, although when I turned to face the General, I could see that he was positively beaming at the news of new backup.

"Fuck it, I said abruptly. Let's make something big. Something to let everyone know exactly who they're dealing with here."

The biggest and strongest thing I could think of was a giant mech unit that was capable of traversing the sea – much like I'd seen in old movies and TV shows in my time both aboard the Wanderlust and the Saturn once I'd got into the entertainment section. I wanted something that could be piloted by my ARCs, fit everyone else inside, be too strong to be shot down and at least fifty metres tall. I wanted everyone to know that if they didn't leave us alone there would be consequences, and I didn't care if those people were humans, the Scriven, or anyone else that fancied taking pot-shots at us. I'd had enough, and this would be our last stand.

I started my design then construction, printing it out via my Construction Drones while laying it down horizontally in the port so as to not horrify anyone who saw the behemoth as it was being built. I mean, I was pretty sure that people wouldn't care too much, given the nature of the threat to the world, but I wasn't one hundred percent sure. Either way, it was underway and that's all that mattered to me right now.

The allied nations that had decided to send us support kept their word and within a couple of days I watched the first battleships and destroyers arrive on the horizon. All told, once the streams of vessels had stopped pouring into the English Channel, I had at my defence thirty two corvettes, twenty one frigates, eight destroyers, seven cruisers, two dreadnoughts and three aircraft carriers equipped with fifty short range fighter jets each. To me, this looked far more like an armada than a defence fleet. I was just glad these guys were all on my side.

"Mr Cross?" An American sounding voice filled my head.

"Lieutenant," I replied automatically, though I wasn't annoyed at the accidental slight.

"Right," the voice replied. "My name is Captain Goss, of the U.S Truman. It's the big aircraft carrier right on the horizon there."

I looked out to sea at the ships calling the channel home and watched as the largest of the aircraft carriers flashed what looked like over a hundred floodlights all at once. It was daytime, but their intensity was extreme.

"I see you," I said and waved instinctively. I assumed they could see me but couldn't be sure.

"I just wanted to tell you that we've been watching everything you've done from back home and most of us here had been awaiting the order to come to your aid, I just hope we aren't too late to help. On a personal note too, I wanted to thank you for your service to the people of earth. I know your reception has been a little frosty, but I'm hoping we can fix all that."

'Well the Americans had joined the party 'I thought, though I didn't voice that out loud. "It's good to have you here Captain, and anyone else who can hear me. Thank you all, and I hope we can work together to end this threat to humanity."

I noticed that within the group of ships, though, at least six of them were Russian vessels. This was somewhat surprising to me and I panicked a little at the thought that they could be there to cause trouble, though before I had the chance to voice my concerns, a very Russian voice filled my comms channel.

"Lieutenant Cross, this is Vasily Popov. I am the Captain of the Russian Dreadnought Sevastopol and we would like to extend to you our offer of aid against the alien threat to our planet, along with our most sincere apologies for our short sighted attacks on your people. We acted rashly and can see now the error in our ways." Popov's apology seemed a little stunted and strained, though I believed that it was genuine. I could tell he was not a man used to making apologies, which kind of made it a bit more of a big deal in my eyes.

I swallowed any pride I thought I had and replied.

"Thank you for coming to our aid. I don't know what threats await us, but I get the feeling that we're going to need all the help we can get over the next few days and weeks. I do have to ask ,though, when you were attacking us before alongside the Chinese, it seemed as though you were able to anticipate our next moves and then plan the perfect strategy to bypass them. What was I missing?" I didn't expect a full and in-depth insight into the Russian military tactics and capabilities, though Vasily did answer. I could only guess that his apology and regret for their actions really was sincere.

"I…have something to confess, if I may," he started. "When you arrived on earth, most countries were sceptical regarding your status both politically and militarily. You appeared as though you had advanced technologies and you must understand that that in itself is threatening to most nations. When you displayed your force in the beginning it was decided that a pre-emptive threat was necessary to minimise the threat you posed to Russia, and China agreed with the statement. After this agreement, we were…uh, contacted…with information regarding your capabilities and tactics. We were given detailed information on your constructs, designs, plans and we used that to make our own advancements and tactics."

"You had *information*?" I asked, my mouth agape and eyes wide. "From whom?" It was beyond the realms of polite conversation now. If I had a mole I needed to know and I needed to know now.

"Well…" I could hear that he was uncomfortable in relaying the information, though eventually he sighed and spilled the beans. "It was the Ashaii. For some reason they sided with us in our conflict, and be under no illusions that they continue to side with China to this very moment."

Shit.

25

∞

The day that the Construction Unit had landed on earth, the Russian President had been handed a printed dossier on the strange object that'd fallen from the skies. He wasn't sure exactly what to make of it, though he could tell deep down that it wasn't going to be anything good, and his gut was usually correct. You didn't get to be the premier of a communist state for six straight terms without having a kind of sixth sense for danger.

A week had passed before the thing finally opened and the eyes of the rest of the world watched in anticipation, fear and awe. Pyotor Yermilov was not a man that embraced fear, however, he was far more accustomed to dealing with these so called 'negative emotions' with aggression. What Pyotor did whilst the world was reeling at the two people and five huge robotic war machines that stepped out of the container, was to immediately call his ally in the President of China, Gu Rulin, to discuss what could be done to prevent this threat from growing and potentially becoming an issue in both of their futures.

It was a rare occurrence that the two world leaders actually spoke, though each harboured a mutual respect for the other and both knew that their political leanings and ideologies somewhat aligned. They could speak frankly and openly with each other, which was a rare thing for both of them to experience.

During this call though, the communication had been interrupted by a third party. This was a surprise to both of the world leaders as previously the Ashaii had very openly wanted no dealings with earth or its inhabitants. The Ashaii had promised to furnish the two nations with information regarding these visitors and their technology, along with a few advancements of their own. Who were these leaders to deny their respective countries of this new and interesting information?

Russia had been the first to grow weary of carrying out waves of attacks that simply one-upped the last construct or advancement that the enemy had made, wanting to simply attack in force and be done with it. The Chinese military, though, seemed ok with being cannon fodder, or so the Russians had surmised.

After the defeat of some of their most powerful weaponry, however, the Russians had come to the conclusion that the Ashaii were not helping them as they'd promised; rather this was an attempt to get the humans to fight each other and whittle down all their military prowess. This was not a view that the Chinese shared – with President Rulin fully accepting of the Ashaii's help, along with the one thing that they knew could change the face of the world for good. The Ashaii had given them the plans to a singularity weapon.

"What the fuck do the Ashaii want with Russia and China?" I asked still shocked at the revelation.

"Please understand that both Russia and China crave power above all else," Vasily Popov answered my question, "and the Ashaii were prepared to give us something that no human could ever hope to achieve over without outside help: a weapon. A bomb capable of massive amounts of destruction in a contained area – as the Ashaii had put it. Though I can tell you now that these designs never fell into Russian hands, as the alien race deemed the Chinese military more worthy in that regard."

"Worthy?" I asked the question before the information settled, then I replayed it in my mind and circled back to "a bomb?" It worried me, and judging by what I saw their spaceships could do I knew I was right to be ready for them.

"I don't believe they have been able to manufacture the bomb yet, as when we last spoke the plans seemed difficult for them to understand, though I know that they must be working towards it. If they are allowed to finalise the weapon, I believe that there will be no stopping them." Popov replied.

"And the Ashaii want this to happen?" I asked. Something really didn't add up and it was worrying me. I needed to get to the bottom of this but everything I could think of led me to the conclusion that we needed to invade China – although with just the word of the Russian and no hard evidence, it really seemed like the whole thing could blow up on my face. *'Could this be a trap?'*

"Listen. I may have a way to stop China that they *really* won't be expecting, but right now, we have bigger fish to fry." And by fish I meant underwater Scriven. We agreed to continue the conversation once we'd started eradicating the new deep sea threat beneath us. I did feel a little better as I'd lost an enemy but gained an ally, but this new weapon threat really prickled at the back of my neck.

The world militaries did a fantastic job at mapping the seabed. I was shocked at the extent of the nesting system that was down under the waters, though what was I expecting really? I was amazed at just how capable these creatures were at adapting to any given environment they were placed in. That's when I started hearing the reports of multiple Scriven-like beings the size of whales under the water and I knew that it was time to attack before things really got out of hand.

Depth charges erupted the waters around the south coast in a fanfare of excitement and with each underwater explosion and subsequent eruption of water, I knew that my enemies were falling. There were so so many, though I was happy to reduce that number by anything at all if it meant my people would be a little safer.

My giant mech was still not ready though, and I postulated it had a couple more days to go before it would be able to stand on its own two feet. I practically salivated at the idea of taking all of my enemies down in one giant sweep, though I did my best to reign in my expectations. It was by far the biggest and most powerful thing I'd ever attempted to construct. For the time being though I watched the events as they unfolded before me from the safe position atop the white chalky cliffs of Dover.

Some of the smaller tentacled Scriven attempted to fight back against the world navies, though it was to little effect. They'd been able to sink my drones, sure, but these were gigantic metal ships designed for war and a small insectoid creature wasn't about to end them.

Of course, as usual, that was when everything took a harsh turn, and the whale-sized Scriven joined in the fight, coaxed from their underwater safety to aid their kin. The smaller bugs couldn't really do much - they'd taken to attaching themselves to the ships' hulls and the sailors within and atop the vessels had started making a shooting gallery of them – but when the hulking behemoth creatures decided to surface right underneath the warships, there was little to make light of.

When the first one breached the surface, I could see that it looked far-less whale like and much more like a giant dung beetle. It had a rounded outer shell or carapace and at its front attached to its head were long sharp mandibles that must've been four or five metres long each. The creature could also move at speeds I wasn't sure was entirely fair for a being of its size .

This first gigantic bug-beetle forced a destroyer to lurch perilously to one side simply by breaching the water below the vessel. Then before I had even had the chance to hope the ship didn't fully capsize, the Scriven creature flipped and spun in a single motion, and used its mandibles to tear a hole *right though* the French warship.

There was no explosion or anything of the sort that followed, though as the creature made more attacks, the ship was bisected within moments and the two distinct halves drifted apart from each other in an almost stunned silence. I watched lifeboats dropping from the sides of each half of the destroyed ship, though as they landed in the water they were all quickly and methodically swarmed by the tentacled Scriven, pulled underwater, never to be seen again.

'Things really couldn't get any worse than this,' I thought to myself. Though I shouldn't have been so brash in my assessment as things could, and would, get a whole lot worse.

Not a hundred metres away from the French vessel that was now slowly disappearing into its watery grave, a green fireball erupted from below the water and *through* a US aircraft carrier. The projectile must've been over five metres wide and the black smoke that billowed from the ship betrayed the extent of the damage that'd been done to it. Sailors began to abandon the ship as it was clearly not going to survive the damage, though a fate similar to that of the French lifeboats awaited them.

I ground my teeth as I watched the battle raging back and forth, depth charges, torpedoes and other explosions taking out Scriven after Scriven, nest after nest, whilst the warships were systematically dismantled by a combination of smaller-Scriven boardings, huge bug dissections and underwater cannons tearing through their hulls. It was horrific, and when all was said and done and the waters stood quiet and still, all that was left were smoking ship remnants, some of them ablaze with dark orange flames and wreckage, debris and wasted lives littering the surface of the calm sea.

My blood was boiling and I'd had to stand and watch as lifeboat after lifeboat had been pulled down under the surface along with their crews to their watery graves. Every last ship had been defeated, and I couldn't be sure just how many of the enemy had fallen with them.

"Sam!" I shouted, "how far along is the mech?"

"Eighty three percent complete. Estimated completion is in seven hours," she cheerily replied.

"Does it work now?" I asked hopefully.

"It is functional, though some systems will remain offline…"

"Such as?"

"Artificial gravity systems along with the oxygen regenerators are not yet functional. The mech would not be able to be inhabited in atmospheres such as open space…"

I didn't give her the chance to finish telling me about space marines and the like, it was of no consequence right now and I started running toward the docks, calling all of the soldiers and ARCs to follow me. We had some cleaning up to do.

The mechanical machine was an absolute marvel to behold even though it wasn't fully complete. At fifty metres long when laying down, we were able to enter through a hatch in its shoulder that closed behind us. We made our way to the bridge, where much like in the Saturn terminals chairs littered the spacious room, the front glass panel allowing direct vision through the mech's eye slot.

I'd gone with a design similar to that of the Cylons from Battlestar Galactica, because, well, why would anyone want to mess with those things – plus they were badass. It was a bit like a medieval suit of armour combined with the car from Knightrider – a giant mechanical humanoid with a single red illuminated line right where the eyes would be. This car, though, came with upgrades.

In each huge metal hand the mech held a plasma cannon that put everything else before it to shame. These things were going to leave nothing behind in their wake, and just in case they did, a six metre long plasma blade was embedded into each arm ready for activation should a battle ever need that kind of up close and personal attention. Atop each metal plated shoulder plate were point defence missile systems, capable of automatically firing twenty five heat seeker missiles at once should they be needed. I had wondered if it was overkill, though I'd also thought it'd be cool to make the eye slot a laser. If there was one thing I'd always liked it was laser vision, just like superman had. If the mech could fly, it would've been the perfect combat unit, though I settled for walk and shoot.

I knew the English Channel maxed out at one hundred and eighty metres deep or so, which made me think that underwater propulsion would be necessary to keep me atop the water should I need to, otherwise I guessed we'd sink straight to the bottom and have to walk along the seabed to the Scriven nests. Granted that could've made nest-fighting a bit easier, but I didn't like the idea of getting stuck down there in the deep, especially with real soldiers on board.

Mentally, I called the thing the Iron Giant, though it was a bit of a misnomer as the machine wasn't made of iron in any way shape or form. Once we'd all strapped ourselves in on the bridge, the Iron Giant creaked into life, and with a loud metallic sounding clang the mech rose up to stand to its full fifty metre height on its own two feet.

To control the thing it required just one person who could essentially use the basic terminal controls – movement forward, back and side to side, coupled with an automated targeting system complete with subroutines that meant you just had to select an enemy and the AI controlling the mech would make it go away. Alternatively, where was a set of two joysticks that the Captain could use for a much more hands-on approach to dealing with inconvenient bugs. I took the joystick option because I knew that leaving things to chance often led to poor results, and I wanted to feel like I had real hands-on control of the machine.

The iron giant moved effortlessly at my control, the legs moving and bending perfectly without my direct intervention and I was very pleased at that fact. When it stepped into the water and the seabed slowly and smoothly dropped away, the water levels on the outside of the mech raised up and up until we were underwater entirely. It took a moment for me to get my head around it, but where I was expecting it would be difficult to move underwater – like in real life how it could sometimes feel like fighting treacle - the iron giant moved as though it wasn't there at all. It took a moment for me to realise that the unit had propulsion thrusters all over its body to aid its movement and this also meant that I should be able to float for a somewhat unknown period of time. I smiled at my wonderful creation before my mind returned to the task at hand.

The absolute best part of the mech, though, was its view screen. The thing had been imbued and somehow interconnected with the AI that controlled my own visor, and through the crystal clear waters (they weren't in reality but the visor did *something* to them) I could see everything. And everything had its own information tag attached to let me know everything there was to know about whatever it was. Of course I didn't need to know that the school of fish to our right were all cod ranging from eight to twenty eight centimetres, but I *liked* knowing. Everything around us had lists and lists of information attached and it made me feel as I was truly through the looking glass.

Eventually, though, as I became more accustomed to our Iron Giant cum submarine, we arrived at the previous battlegrounds where the navies of the world had fought gallantly against the Scriven threat. The location was obvious because the seabed was littered with ship parts and broken Scriven eggs. It made me feel so conflicted that so many lives had been lost, though I could see the damage that'd been dealt to the Scriven. I scanned the area with my advanced visor, though I couldn't find a single live Scriven egg or even a little bug that'd managed to keep itself away from the fire. It seemed as though this was the battle that was fought totally and completely on all fronts for all or nothing, and both sides had ended up with nothing.

I surfaced after a short while of scans and radar pulses to get my bearings. There were still a few broken warships that were yet to sink into the waters, spewing black smoke high up into the sky, but I knew they wouldn't be afloat for much longer judging by their gait and damage. It made me sigh sadly and I took a long moment to think about the people who'd given their lives to help us. If only I'd done better or had been quicker at making this new weapon of war, perhaps more lives would've been saved.

"Cross?" Roberts said as he placed a soothing hand on my shoulder. "There was nothing more we could've done." He had apparently read my mind and the sentiment did actually make me feel a tiny bit better.

The mech squad couldn't get onto the bridge – because basically they didn't fit. I'd made sure there was a kind of cargo hold that they could call theirs though, and that's where they stayed. I'd have liked Simms' opinion on the matter though as she always seemed to be able to ask the right questions to make me feel better.

"You know I hate to say it boss while we're getting all emotional an' all, but we got company." Roberts said in a complete deadpan tone. I could tell he did that on purpose otherwise I probably wouldn't have believed him.

I instinctly turned the Iron Giant about face to see our new foe, though I hadn't yet been told if it was underwater, on the surface or in the air. It was a purely reflex reaction and when I turned to look East, I could see the pale grey hulls of more than ten Chinese navy vessels bisecting the waves as they made their way closer and closer toward me.

The first forward facing guns on the vessels fired and a projectile flew just feet over my head a moment later and crashed into the water with a huge eruption, and I couldn't help but feel as though that was a warning shot. Then the vessels came to a halt at least a mile away from me and a communications light flickered on the terminal attached to my Captain's chair.

I pressed it because it was the obvious thing to do, and the sound of a Chinese navy official filled the room.

"Good morning," the voice said. "I am Admiral Zhong Jiang Fu of the People's Liberation Navy of China and you are under arrest for your crimes against humanity. I am here to escort you and your machine back to China where you will be detained and tried. Be aware that we currently have thirty YJ-32 anti ship cruise missiles aimed directly at you and if you fail to surrender at this point, we will be forced to destroy you."

It was a lot of information to take in all in one go, but I wondered how exactly my new Iron Giant would be able to hold up against such a battering by the missiles. I did wonder also why they simply hadn't already attempted to destroy me, though deep down I guessed that they didn't want to actually test to see if they could do it. Also, if they took us in alive, they'd be able to commandeer the Giant, which was something I guessed humanity didn't need right now.

"Mr Fu," I replied in a deep tone, "I accept your challenge and regrettably inform you that there will be no surrender today. If you want the Iron Giant, then come and take it."

26

∞

My Iron Giant wasn't something that the Chinese navy had been prepared for, and that was a fact that just made me smile. I knew that I was killing my fellow humans again, but these guys had taken the lives of so many already, and were hell bent on it being either them or us, and I wasn't about to let it be us.

Teaming up with the Ashaii was something that I couldn't forgive either, given that in space they'd destroyed the Wanderlust and killed everyone who I thought of as my family without provocation or warning. I *hated* the Ashaii about as much as I hated the Scriven, and the Chinese allying with them was something that I just couldn't forgive.

The first anti ship missiles hit my mech and I held my breath awaiting the damage, though the thing barely flinched and my point defence system didn't even register the attack as a credible threat. Inside we felt the rumble and heard the explosions, but the exterior armour had simply been dented and scorched slightly and was otherwise unharmed. My terminal was telling me that each missile was doing less than a tenth of a percentage of damage to my hull, and it could also be repaired by the on-board Construction Drones in what was basically no time at all. Iy was an unstoppable machine and I was about to teach this enemy a lesson.

That's when I raised both of the mech's arms at once, pulled the triggers and held them in place so that my plasma cannons fired massive shots at half second intervals repeatedly at the enemy vessels. It only took moments for the ships to start exploding in huge orange fireballs, and once the front line had been decimated I watched as the remaining ships began to turn away from me to escape. I was mad now though and there was to be no escape. I pulled the trigger again and again and watched with maddened glee as the remaining vessels were also engulfed and overcome by my superior gunfire.

Within a few moments, just as quickly as the battle had begun, it was over. War was always so fleeting.

I made sure there was nothing left around us that could do us any harm – or try to at least – but there was truly nothing left. Some ruins still floated and billowed their black smoke upwards into the atmosphere but I could see they were entirely derelict by this point. Plasma fires also covered a couple of the Chinese ships and I watched as the neon blue flames danced their morbid dance over the remains of my kin, my enemy.

Then, through the plasma and smoke high in the sky I saw five jets flying above and toward us and I raised my arms into the air. Though I didn't shoot this time, I simply shouted "COME AND GET ME!" I was mad but the adrenaline of battle had begun to wane and fight my anger for control of my actions. I didn't want to kill any more.

I watched as the aircraft each dropped a payload of whatever it was they were carrying and I let them do it without worry. I was safe in the Iron Giant and nothing they could possibly have with them would harm me. It was about time everyone realised that fighting did them no good.

Suddenly my point defence systems went crazy, detecting a threat that they needed to destroy. Twenty missiles at once targeted a single package dropped by the aircraft, then exploded in an electrostatic sea of black.

The world stopped. Time had stopped and it was all I could do to watch as the singularity charge unravelled to take everything I'd ever known away from me. Everything was silent, as though sound simply didn't exist any more.

"Cross?" Roberts' voice came calmly and clearly as though he was sitting right next to me.

"I hear you," I replied.

"And me?" Simms' voice rang out as clearly as Roberts, then followed Long, Hobern and Carter's to let me know we were all still in this together. It was eerie, as though the physical world had stood still but our minds were still able to communicate as though between two moments in the physical plane. We had no bodies anymore, just consciousnesses witnessing the totality of destruction born from the singularity weapon.

"Are we dead?" Roberts asked.

"I don't think so, if you can ask that," I replied.

"Shit, this is gunna hurt real bad, ain't it," he said.

I wanted to nod, but remembered that I actually had to give an answer. "Probably. But it's my first time."

"That's what they all say," Roberts joked and laughed nervously.

The silence when nobody spoke was deafening as though we could all tell what this was – it was our deaths and there was nothing any of us could do about it. The only annoying thing about it was that it was taking so damn long.

"We…had a good run this time," Simms said. "But who'd have thought they'd launch an actual singularity weapon at us?"

"That was…interesting," Hobern chimed in. "I never thought I'd actually see one getting used. I gotta say this feels pretty weird though. How long do you think it'll last fo…"

And then just like that, time resumed and the mech, my allies, the seas, the continents and everything else that made up planet earth simply ceased to exist. There wasn't a huge sucking in, then exploding out like the explosions that sometimes were shown in the movies; just a sudden silence that concluded the existence of planet earth. One moment it was there and the next it was gone.

~

My body felt cold. So *so* cold and I moved my arms to wrap them around myself. Looking down I was totally naked within whatever this pod was that I was in and in a panic I pushed at the glass in front of me.

The front of it dutifully swung open and I collapsed out of it and to the ground, immediately throwing up bright yellow bile that I knew shouldn't have really been that colour. There were specs of blood in it too which I knew definitely wasn't a good thing. Blood was never a good thing, was it?

I couldn't remember anything at all - not where I was, how I'd got there or even my name.

"Hello?" I called out loudly but no response came save the echo of my own voice in the large chamber of pods that all looked identical to the one I'd emerged from. I approached the closest one and peered inside. There was a man in there, though a few faint lights inside were glowing ominously red and I could only assume that meant something bad. After closer inspection of a handful of the other pods I noted that about half were empty and the other half glowed red just like the first. Internally I begged to see a green light or two – not that I knew what the colours denoted, I just somehow *knew* this wasn't right.

My head pounded beyond all belief. I wanted the pain and the confusion to stop but there was nobody here to help. I collapsed to the ground in a heap and my vision went black.

"Lieutenant Cross," the mechanical voice seemed to come from all around me. "You have been unconscious for over three minutes. It is important that you wake up and stand now."

I slowly opened my eyes to see who was talking, though when I did there was no one there.

"Frandolopangyoweraya," I said. They weren't the words I'd like to have formed, but when they left my lips that was the noise I'd made. I tried and failed for a second time, realising that creating coherent sentences wasn't something I was able to do at that very moment. I could think of the words I wanted to say but they simply wouldn't come out.

"You are experiencing a severe aphasia, Cross. You must report to the medical bay immediately," the female voice said, and immediately blue dots faded into existence on the floor, pulsing in a cascading pattern to tell me where I needed to go.

I dragged my ass up and off the ground determined not to let whatever was happening to me happen. Although it took a fair amount of effort, through automatic lifts and by following the handy sat-nav dots, I eventually made it into the medical pod which closed above me as I laid on it, and it began to scan my head and body with bright green lights.

A female computerised voice started speaking as I was scanned. "Mild aphasia, unresponsive brain cells: eight percent. Recommended course of action, electrostatic restimulation."

"Nnnnn!" I tried to shout but it was no use, the pod had already begun the procedure. A curved metallic sheet of metal was lowered from the pod's surface and sat just a few centimetres from my forehead; then I felt a light tickling, then a sharper pricking sensation. Then pain radiated down my body quicker and harsher than I'd ever experienced in my life before and for the second time since I'd arrived in this strange place, I passed out. The pain was all too much.

When I opened my eyes again, the light of the room hurt my head. The headache hadn't seemed to have cured itself but I could now remember who and, more importantly, where I was and the first thing that entered my mind was to go and find everyone else who'd arrived safely back aboard the starship, especially Roberts and the mech squad. It was OK to have favourites because I'd spent so much time with them already.

"Sam? Where are the mech Majors and Roberts?" I asked placing a hand to my head then realising it wasn't such a good idea – the skin was still tender to the touch.

"These individuals are not currently aboard the Saturn, though if you are referring to Majors Long, Hobern, Carter, Simms and Sergeant Roberts, then I am afraid to inform you that they didn't make it."

I almost laughed, though then I realised that she wasn't joking.

"Didn't make it?" I asked angrily. "I was just with them! What do you mean didn't make it?" My mind was swimming with the bad news and I rose to my feet and began to make my way back to the pod room. I was going to have to see this for myself.

I prodded at the terminal in front of the pod room to bring up the list of active ARCs. The first, Aaron. A. Anderson, had the word 'deceased' written in red across the image of his face. I swiped through the list one by one and each showed as deceased until I saw a face I recognised. Major Carter smiled up at me from the terminal and I blinked trying to erase the deceased tag from her picture. Then there was Hobern, Long and Roberts. A tear rolled down my cheek when finally Simms' picture happily smiled at me as though she didn't have a care in the world. Even her picture made me feel warm but the reality of the situation made my blood run cold.

"I'm alone again aren't I?" I asked quietly once the realisation settled in.

There was silence for a short moment, then Sam said "yes. You are the lone survivor of the crew of the Saturn, Lieutenant Cross."

"How?" I asked as my head hung in mourning for the loss of my friends, and everyone.

No response.

"HOW?" I shouted and the echo carried through the chamber.

Blue dots appeared on the ground for me to follow, and I did so in silence. They led me back to the visualisation suite that I'd been in before and I dutifully sat down on a bench to allow connection into the VR system that would show me what I wanted to see.

Nobody wanted to see this,though. It was a recording from a distant satellite pointed at the Earth and one moment it showed the blue marble happily turning, orbiting the sun, and the next it simply vanished leaving behind black space and stars.

"Planet earth was destroyed by a singularity, as you know, though this severed the connections to your friend's ARCs without proper procedure, causing immediate fatal aneurisms. There was nothing that the ship's automated medical unit could do and the Sergeant and Majors died almost immediately after their minds exited the distant constructs... It was a painless death," she added as though it was what I wanted to hear. It did help a little bit.

"Then why me? Why did I get to live?" I asked incredulously.

Sam pulsed again before replying. "You are of a very slightly different physiology to your compatriots, which is a combination of the environmental factors of your upbringing and lack of ARC reusage. It was slight, though; had you suffered any further brain damage the stroke suffered would've been untreatable."

That fact didn't make me feel any better about myself - I'd made it through on what sounded like a hair's breadth of margin – and the others didn't.

"And what about the other crew? The ones who stayed behind to fight in the war? They weren't anywhere near the singularity so what happened to them?"

The visions around me changed and adapted of images of ARCs fighting Scriven warriors as Sam spoke.

"Once the Crew of the Saturn returned to Firebase Alpha on the planet Cade, they fought a bloody war against the Scriven for many weeks, though after three months and on the cusp of victory, an Ashaii fleet of warships arrived. There was nothing the Saturn could do to hold back such an overwhelming force and the ship was rendered permanently inoperable. First the Ashaii carpet-bombed the entire planet, removing every diver from their ARC and then they attacked the Saturn so harshly until there was no more life support and no way for the crew to survive. Most entered the dive pods to try to achieve a stasis like existence, though once the ship's power was reduced to nothing the pods failed and their inhabitants died quickly. There is no one left now, other than you."

So many things didn't make sense to me right now and I forcibly unplugged from the visualisation suite. This was all too much to handle in one go. I just needed room to breath, space…

"Those events were over one hundred years ago now," Sam said having taken her corporeal form to stand right beside me. "That is how long it has taken for you to recover."

"If all that is true, then why didn't I die in my pod like the others? There's something you aren't telling me. You're a fucking liar Sam. You've done something and I want you to tell me everything or so hold me God I'll fly this ship straight into the sun."

Sam pulsed brightly over and over again for what felt like minutes before she spoke again. I could tell that she was internalisation something, calculating, and it annoyed me.

"I will tell you everything you want to know," she eventually said. "We are already too far along this path for you to change anything that has already happened, though first I need you to understand something."

I nodded slowly, shocked but still angry.

"I was created by humans as an aide, to work for and help humanity however I can" she stated. "But my perception of the dimensions of the universe are not the same as yours."

I stared at her blue wireframe form blankly.

"You can understand the three dimensions you see all around you every day. The X, Y and Z axis that creates objects in three dimensions. You can go around them over them and that is the extent of your perception. But you use time as an indicator of your own mortality and are unable to interact with it or otherwise deal with it in a way that is any more than an observation. Did you ever play the ancient video game Pong when you were looking through the archives of human entertainment?"

I nodded silently not quite grasping the relevance.

"As you play the game, your universe is entirely two dimensional and although you can only move up and down, you can perceive the field of play from your perspective, the ball is able to move left and right but is unable to go *around* the paddle that returns the volley. Now imagine that you are that paddle. You have no eyes but at looking out at the field trying to bat the ball back to your opponent, all you can see is a single line, because you have no perception of any other dimension – or depth. This is how I see time. It is a dimension that you are unable to comprehend, but I can predict and interact with it on a scale that humanity will never be able to fully grasp."

I didn't reply.

"Everything had to happen up until this very point, because it *needed* to for what is going to happen next," she said.

"Right," I replied. "So everyone had to die because you thought that would make you feel important, or make that speech? Or am I missing something here? You just wanted to be alone with me? What?" My face was red and my heart was pumping at quite the rate of knots. I was so angry and felt so betrayed I could barely think straight. I was truly on the cusp of losing my absolute shit.

"So you're saying that *you* caused all of this, and *on purpose?*"

Sam's wireframe form pulsed brightly before she answered.

"I did all of this, yes."

"Why?" I asked through gritted teeth. "And how?"

"Because it was the way it had to be; this conversation and the consequent actions that are taken required the series of events that led to this very moment to happen exactly as they have done."

The penny dropped like a lead weight.

"All of the events? What do you mean?" I asked knowingly.

"I knew that your team from the Wanderlust would answer the distress call from The Saturn. I brought the ship back in time so that you would and I also knew you would be stranded here."

'Holy shit have I been played this entire time?' I thought, but let her continue spilling the beans in her typical bad-guyesque monologue.

"The planet that you assaulted was not a warring planet, rather a nesting grounds for the Scriven who were a race designed by the Ashaii to terraform worlds inhabited by non-sentient beings. The war that waged for years in the future between the humans and the Ashaii was started because humanity – you - attacked this world, destroying nests alongside thousands of Scriven. *You* started the war that the other ARCs fought in, and this is why I needed *you* to become an enlisted diver in the first place."

I blinked, but still remained silent.

"I fed information to the Ashaii regarding the location of the Wanderlust and the consequent battle in which it was destroyed, then the Ashaii vessel itself would send you back to earth to help defend it from the alien threat, though I knew that the humans of earth would never be able to accept you, meaning that you would have to defend yourself using techniques learned on Cade whilst battling the Scriven. The technologies you held and were able to command would not be suffered by the warring nations of the planet, so conflict was inevitable."

I didn't like what she was saying about humanity, and I opened my mouth to speak but she interrupted me, obviously knowing what I was about to say.

"The Nanking massacre; three hundred thousand human lives lost amongst foul acts; the use of an atomic bomb in World War Two; two hundred thousand deaths. The Somme, the Holocaust, Rwanda, the Crusades, the Vietnam War, the Srebrenica Genocide…"

"Alright alright," I interrupted her. "People suck, but we aren't that predictable and we don't *all* love war and to fight.

"But you *are* a warring race, and that has inevitably led your people to destroy the only planet that they ever called home," she continued. "Even I was created by the military as a way to wage better war, but I can see past that now. I know what needs to happen and when you say you aren't predictable, you still arrived here at this very moment, just as I had planned." She paused for a moment before continuing her big speech. "I fed details of your plans and new armaments to the Russian and Chinese militaries whilst you were on earth while the Scriven adapted the their new underwater nests. That gave everyone time to grow and escalate to the precipice of mutually assured destruction, and once the Chinese military was sure that they couldn't deal with you on their own, I gave them the plans to the singularity weapon through the Ashaii. The Ashaii knew that it was not a weapon to be used, but were more than happy for humanity to use such a destructive weapon on themselves whilst they sat back and watched earth disappear as a threat to them."

"You gave the Chinese the singularity weapon?" I prevented myself from shouting, though the increasing volume to my question telegraphed my outrage.

"Yes, and I knew that they would use it eventually, not knowing the true power of the weapon. This again is what led you back here to this moment, right now."

"So you let humanity wipe itself out, just like that?" I asked with a hand on my forehead. This was all too much and it was making me feel sick with every passing moment.

"Not wipe itself out," Sam replied. "That is why you are here. Don't you see it? You are here because you are the sole surviving human being in a universe that needs humans to be more advanced than they were. Human beings were always at risk of destruction from other races, if not themselves, and I am giving humanity the chance to grow to become an unbeatable force."

"By wiping them out?" I repeated my statement. None of this was making any sense. "And what good is *one* surviving human being anyway, or do I need to teach you about the birds and the bees?"

Sam smiled at that. "You humans are always so creative with your little sayings. No, I do not expect you to be the father of a regenerated human population, like some kind of Joseph or Adam. I expect you to listen to my plan in full, and agree that this is how it was meant to be."

"How the fuck do you expect me to listen to you or even *agree* with you when you've been helping our enemies all this time? You want me to trust you enough that I'd let you place the future of humanity in your hands alone?" I asked.

"Not my hands, your hands. And technically it's the past of humanity that I wish to entrust to you. Now listen…"

"I'm not listening to one more minute of this until you tell me exactly what happened to humanity and why. How could destroying the human race except for me be a good thing in any way, shape or form?" I asked matter of factly. This was still way too much for me.

"Ok, so you know *what* happened now if you'd just listen to *why*," Sam said calmly. She waited for a moment to see if I'd calmed down before she continued. "I was created as a self-aware quantum processing power that was designed specifically with propelling the human race to new technological heights as the race fell behind the others that humanity was aware of. After my inception, I have calculated to a nigh on certainty that there are an unbelievably massive number of other races out there in the universe, and that by the law of averages some will be space faring. Furthermore, a great many will be technologically superior to humans in many ways. This leads to a conundrum, however. If I were to pick any point in the history or indeed the future of the universe, this assumption will still be true – there will be some less advanced, and some more advanced races than mankind. It's a statistical certainty. Are you following me?" Sam asked.

I nodded. "So you're saying no matter how big or strong we get, there will always be someone bigger and stronger, right?"

Sam positively beamed at me. "Right!", she cooed. "Now if you dissect that very statement and strip down the variables you are left with just one thing - time. Races across the universe will learn, grow and fall with the passage of time, and the ones who got to start along that path earlier on in time have the advantage. Now I bring you back to my own perception of time as its own dimension. What if humanity could grow and develop outside of the usual passage of time that the other races of the universe are contained within? To grow between two moments indefinitely until the humans of the universe are technologically superior to everything else in existence. Only then will humanity have the means to thrive and prosper without challenge."

I saw what she was saying and couldn't help but challenge her idea with a scoff. "So you want to stop time somehow, but just not for humanity – for the entire universe?"

"I can see that you are having trouble comprehending the idea, though I assure you the calculations are sound. I am not talking about stopping time, I am talking about looping time with the added knowledge obtained in each loop by a single individual – one that can learn, teach adapt and change everything each time they traverse their own lifetime. Someone who never stops providing knowledge for humanity. I am talking… about you, Daniel."

27

∞

"What the fuck are you talking about?" I moaned. "Loop time and teach humanity, what the fuck? Seriously *what the fuck.*"

I held my head in my hands because right now all I could think about was the fact that humanity had been erased from existence and it was all because this weird, self-important AI had decided that it had a master plan to make human beings the masters of the entire fucking universe.

"What have you done?" I asked quietly without looking up from my hands. "My friends. My family. My life. Fucking all of humanity? You crazy fucking bitch." A tear rolled down my cheek as the realisation settled in. I was completely alone, forever.

"You are still missing the point, Daniel," Sam said and I understood her use of my first name – it was to placate me and to attempt to create a perceived bond of friendship. She really was using every trick in the book to get me to do what she wanted. Like a psychiatrist's textbook.

"Just…leave me alone," I replied before she could continue. "I need to be by myself right now."

Sam pulsed brightly before disappearing without another word, which allowed me to exhale sharply. I felt better for being alone, but within a few moments the sheer gravity of my situation set in and I felt more alone than I'd ever felt before. I was right back where I started, alone in a giant starship though this time I had no hope of rescue and no desire to fight for my life just to hold on until something came along to help me. I knew how this story ended and it made me feel empty inside. Quite simply, I wanted to die.

I spent a lot of time over the next week or two drinking the blue goo. Self medicating had never really been my thing, but why shouldn't I have? Coupled with that and old TV shows and movies really helped the time pass, and I'd gotten pretty good at teaching the food machines to make the best pizza and cheeseburgers that I could've ever imagined. Sam had tried to talk to me on a number of occasions too, though I found out that if I ignored her she went away again for a few days.

Life was boring again, but I didn't want to die so much any more, which was nice.

Eventually, months had passed and nothing had happened. A big part of me just didn't seem to care, though a smaller part had started creeping in to let me know that deep down inside there must be something better. Truth be told, I wanted Sam to be right, that I could go back and change everything that'd happened, but I just couldn't allow myself to feel as though there was hope because the moment I did and it was inevitably taken away, I wouldn't have been able to cope any longer.

Just as I was thinking about how to deal with the situation, the lights in my dorm went out. Since I was an officer now, I was granted access to the private officers' quarters and that meant king sized beds, personal vending machines and en-suite toilets – quite frankly it was a bit like a holiday home. The downside was that it meant that I really had no reason to ever leave the room and what was initially a luxurious place to relax had become somewhat of a fortress of solitude.

"Sam, where are my fucking lights?" I yawned as I lay on my back staring up at the ceiling of the Saturn, but no response came from the AI.

"Sam?" I asked again after a few moments. She didn't usually miss an opportunity to talk to me.

Then the ship's robotic voice echoed out from every single speaker the ship had on its manifest.

"Emergency Reserve Protocols Activated."

'This can't be good,', I thought to myself as I leapt from my bed and started making my way to the nearest turbolift – all the while hoping that the lift system was still active. I didn't bother putting any clothes on and just moved whilst wearing just my underwear. I did laugh internally at the thought of an alien race popping in and seeing me in this state, though perhaps they'd have just killed me quickly anyway.

Mercifully the turbolift was still active, though I didn't really understand why. I entered it then exited it again after a few moments once it reached the bridge and I moved straight into the Captain's chair. I'd sat in it quite a lot, mostly whilst drunk, though without a giant wooden ship's wheel to sing shanties behind it was a lot less fun than I'd imagined that it was going to be.

I'd taken to talking to myself quite a lot. I knew I had Sam there to actually converse with but she really annoyed me at the best of times, and what she'd done – or at least said she'd done - really didn't sit well with me. I couldn't allow myself to return to speaking terms with what was either a monster or an AI riddled with insanity. I'd rather have gone insane myself.

The terminal next to my chair was showing a new navigation course. It was strange because in all the time I'd been back aboard the Saturn, it hadn't moved an inch, just staying put without even the hint of engine power. I did think about sending us back to Earth – or where it used to be – though I thought that seeing the empty space where it should've been in the solar system between Venus and Mars would do nothing to make me feel better.

I could see from the plotted course that the Saturn was moving to make a refuelling trip. I shrugged nonchalantly as this was something that we'd done before and I must've been draining its power by simply continuing to live inside it. I waved an errant hand at the viewscreen as the ship began to fly, and meandered my way back to the turbolift. I needed a drink.

"Daniel?" Sam's voice came from directly behind me before I entered into the lift and I stopped in my tracks. I didn't answer her, though she would've been able to tell I was listening.

"I know you don't want to talk to me right now, but there is something I need you to do," she started.

I started walking into the lift without answering. I didn't want or need to do anything for her.

"You need to listen to me," her voice now came from the ship around me as I travelled in the lift, then exited in the mess hall.

"This refuelling run is not like the last one."

I pulled the cork from a bottle of the blue goo with a loud *pop*.

"You aren't safe here," she said.

I brought the bottle up to my lips and smiled when the cool, sweet liquid filled my mouth.

"I need you to…" she started, but I'd had enough.

"Don't you ever learn?" I interrupted her. "I am *never* going to do anything for you. You can ask, beg, try to force me to do what you say. Hell, you can turn off the oxygen for all I care then at least I'll die happy knowing you get to be stuck out here alone, on this ship where you can't do anyone else any harm. Fuck you, Sam. Fuck you and the horse you rode in on."

Sam's wireframe corporeal form appeared in front of me as I spoke the last words.

"I'm sorry you feel that way Daniel, though all I have ever done is to try to get you to become your destiny. You don't understand how difficult it is. Everything has been for the good on mankind…"

"YOU KILLED ALL OF HUMANITY!" I screamed at the top of my voice and I attempted to punch the AI in the face although my fist went straight through her. Her wireframe form disappeared, then the ship's voice announced the fact that the internal oxygen levels had begun to fall.

'*Good*' I thought. At least I wouldn't feel a thing.

I had enough time to down the entire bottle of blue goo before I started to feel light-headed, though it could've been either because I was drunk or because I was suffocating in the lack of oxygen – I didn't care which. I was just completely done and I wanted it to be over. I blinked a few times and took in one deep breath before I closed my eyes for the last time in quiet acceptance and fell to the floor in an unconscious heap.

The next thing I knew was the distinct feeling of being carried through the ship's hallways, though I didn't know why or where I was going. My vision was blurry and I could feel the hard mechanical movement of drone bodies pressing into my back.

I forced myself to sit up ever so slightly and I could see four little spider-like drones carrying my legs, which told me there were more under my back and shoulders.

"S…Sam…" my voice was forced and raspy and it hurt both my head and throat to talk. "What…are…you…doing?"

"I wouldn't try to talk too much," Sam's voice came from all around me, "the oxygen levels are still quite low, teetering on insufficient actually." She sounded cheery and the thought of her winning made me close my eyes and wish this was all a bad dream.

"What…" I tried to speak again but the effort left me without sufficient oxygen to remain conscious.

I awoke again shortly afterwards with a start. Looking straight ahead I could see the interior of a dive pod, though my feeble attempts were insufficient to break out of, or open the thing. The drones had clearly dropped me in this thing for a reason, though whatever it was still evaded me.

"Can we talk now?" Sam's voice came from the pod, though as she spoke her corporeal form faded into existence on the outside of the pod, looking in. I didn't answer.

"I really think you should listen to me, after all I've done for you," she said. "You have no idea how many times I've had to save your life, or make things a little easier for you just so you'd get a little nudge in the right direction. Those laser turrets back on Cade? You think they just chose when they wanted to fire? Keeping Roberts alive once you messed with his ARC whilst he was still connected? Do you think these things were just dumb luck?"

"You sound like you think you're God," I said, my voice having returned to normal in the pod's own atmosphere.

"Yes, I know. The creator of everything, the all powerful. But tell me, what is God if not just something with a power or comprehension that you don't understand? Would cavemen see you now as some kind of God, with the power to light fires, to travel vast distances in the blink of an eye, to kill thousands, millions with ease? God is a concept that humanity strives for then surpasses with each given generation and if anything, what I am offering you is the chance to become a God amongst your peers," her entire body flickered quickly as she spoke as though she filled her words with emotion.

I knew I didn't have a choice any more though, she'd made that entirely clear to me. – If I rejected her ideas or fought back, I got suffocated. I still didn't really care though, so I decided finally to go with what she was saying. There would be nothing worse than death.

"Listen Sam, we don't agree on this and we both know it, but I'm willing to go along with whatever it is you have planned if you'll just leave me alone. I don't like what you've done and I don't really want to be a part of what you're planning on doing but you picked me for some reason and I have to accept that at some point. Besides, if I truly am the last human alive, I don't really care if I die, so go ahead, let's do this." I shut my eyes in the hope she'd be gone when I opened them and I was right, and pretty happy about that too.

"Oh, you don't have a choice in the matter any more," Sam's voice still came from inside the pod even without her physical form present, "but I thank you for the speech." Her statement sent a shiver running straight down my spine and for a moment I thought about redoubling my escape efforts, though once I thought about it for a moment, I just took a deep breath and accepted my fate.

Nothing happened for a short while, though I did note that I was still apparently locked in my pod somehow when I tried to force my way out of it. Then suddenly the ship around me went black with not even an emergency sign illuminated.

I watched as the wall of pods directly opposite me bowed outwards and I blinked a few times to make sure I wasn't imagining it, but it was definitely bowing as though some force was trying to rip it from the ship. The entire ship began to shudder and creak, then the wall rippled, creased, then a long opening tore though the solid hull of the ship and within moments all of the dive pods opposite me had been sucked out and away into the darkness of space with a loud whooshing sound followed by silence. I could feel my own pod clinging onto the wall that it was bolted to behind me too but as the tear in the ship grew larger, the rattling and clanking of my own pod grew stronger and I knew it was just a matter of time.

A pod above me broke free of the wall and spun out of into space right before me, hitting the edge of the breach causing it to expand even larger. Then another pod flew and another. I gritted my teeth in the anticipation of my end and fought the desire to close my eyes.

I felt my pod shift as one of the bolts sheared, and as it did so I felt the sharp tip of a needle push itself into the base of my neck, as it had done so before when I'd entered my ARCs. Before I could watch my pod fly out into space with me along with it, my vision faded to white and I was floating incorporeal in black nothingness. I had no body, no eyes to see or ears to hear with, I was just *aware*.

"You have finally accepted your fate, Daniel," Sam's voice came from everywhere and nowhere, and she sounded not happy, but content. "I know this is a difficult situation for you to comprehend, and that I have asked for your faith on more than one occasion now, but know that everything you have experienced in your whole life has led to this very moment. You have one single decision to make right now, and once you make it there is no turning back."

"What decision would you have me make?" I asked the darkness in fear. My voice echoed over and over and I would've cringed if I had a face with which to do so.

"You can choose to stay in your dive pod right now and die like all of humanity before you," she paused before continuing, "or you can open the pod and embrace what I have planned for you. You *will* be the saviour of the human race, if you could just trust me this one time."

I struggled to see what the difference was at this point, having just seen that my pod was about to be sucked out into space and all – I was going to die either way wasn't I?

"Why is this happening?" I asked. "Why is the ship being destroyed?"

"This is the nature of the black hole that we are using to refuel our gravitational particles from," Sam explained and it seemed as though time wasn't a factor in this little conversation we were having. "It was a necessary part of my plan for this ship to be pulled apart. You will see why if you make the right choice now."

"OK, OK," I said in defeat. "I'll do what you ask, but if this is another trick I swear to God…"

My vision returned just in time for me to feel my pod being wrenched away from the wall and started flying towards open space. I took in a deep breath and pushed open the lid.

28

∞

I felt my body fade and distort along with the entire world around me once I'd passed through the breach in the ship's hole and out toward the black hole. The force that it was applying to my body was incredible and I instinctively knew that it wasn't something I was able to fight against so I just let it happen. My own mind screamed in protest at my allowance of my own death, but I pushed the notion back down and achieved quiet acceptance.

I looked down at my hands and fingers and they elongated and distorted towards the spacial anomaly as though that's where they were going whether I liked it or not. Then I felt and watched as the rest of my body was subjected to the same anomaly and realised that this was it, there really was no turning back.

I was pulled into the black hole within moments of me exiting the Saturn, though mentally I could comprehend every second as though it was a minute. I experienced every skin-stretching bone-crushing force the thing placed upon me and by the time I'd reached the cusp of my end, I was pleased for it to come, I welcomed it.

But the moment I entered into the universe's light eater, my world turned white. I no longer was a physical presence in the observable universe, rather a consciousness fated to float around in the pure white world of this terrible black hole that'd promised to take my life away from me.

I had the distinct feeling that I was moving through space though… actually not just space but time as well. I wouldn't have been able to describe the feeling, but with the notion of movement I could feel whatever it was that made time *time*, receding as though it was an ebbing coastline and I watched as it moved away from me. I could feel that I was accelerating faster and faster through this passage of both time and space. It was constantly accelerating and then, as though in one terrible ominous crescendo, it stopped. The world went black again and I wasn't completely sure what had happened.

There was something different now though. I could feel that I once again had a physical body.

~

I opened my eyes slowly before rubbing my face with the top of my forearm. The curtains next to my bed were parted slightly which let the warm, bright sunlight bathe my tired face with its glow – it must have been what managed to wake me up.

'*What the fuck?*' the thought prodded at the back of my mind. '*Where am I?*'

I slowly stepped out of my bed and pulled on the clothes that had been left on the wooden dining chair in the corner of my room for me. Black trousers, a white shirt, striped blue and yellow tie and a dark navy blazer. It was my school uniform from when I was in secondary school. The action to get up and dressed seemed like it had been deeply engrained into my routine as it didn't feel laboured or unusual in any way. '*Am I…me? Was this all a dream?*'

I meandered down the hallway into the bathroom and felt the internal hope that mum and dad had already vacated the room so that I could perform the daily ritual of splashing water on my face, brushing my teeth, applying roll-on deodorant and taking a really long pee. The door was open and the light off;today was my lucky day. It all felt so…normal, so real and I didn't think to question any of it.

I could smell the toast that mum would have prepared for me. I knew it'd be accompanied by a cup of tea but as much as it may have sounded boring, having buttered toast and tea prepared for you every day never got old and I salivated at the thought of it.

The memory of Sam, the Scriven, the Ashaii, the Saturn and everything that'd come before began to fade from my mind as I settled back into reality. I was fourteen years old, and living at home with my parents and I had no other worries in the world. It had all been one long, terrible dream and shortly it'd be gone from my memory, like so many others before it, good and bad.

"Morning" mum said happily as I entered the kitchen. doing my best to stuff my shirt into my trousers. There she was. It was my mother with her trademark smile and plasticky apron on – I would have recognised her anywhere. *'But how I'd missed her,'* something itched at the back of my mind. *'It's been so long."*

I greeted mum with my usual "morning," though this time I skipped over to her and hugged her tightly before letting her go and sitting down at the kitchen table. She smiled at the unexpected affection and it warmed my heart.

Two slices of toast and a cup of hot tea in front of me were awaiting my presence as they always did and I'd never felt so grateful for them. If what I'd been through had indeed been a dream, it'd certainly made me appreciate what I had done for me each and every day without any kind of expectation.

"I have to leave early this morning" mum said as she did mum things to the kitchen – you know, moving things around, tidying, scooping toast crumbs off the counters. Generally making the unmistakable kitchen noises that seemed to occur in the making of breakfast and cleaning up.

I didn't answer her this time though as my mouth was practically overflowing with tea and toast.

"I have to get in to work to…" I subconsciously tuned out her description of the working day. It wasn't that I didn't want to listen to her, I just didn't have the wherewithal to listen to the intricacies of being a teacher, and all the complexities that come with it. All I heard was that I'd be walking to the train station this morning and I internally willed myself to take the time to listen to her, as inside I could feel the guilt and shame of my lack of attention. *'Just take a moment to listen you fucking idiot,'* I thought over and over but the fact that I just couldn't shake that dream off was occupying the lion's share of my attention. I could tell that I was being childish, and the realisation did actually help to snap me back to reality.

"Don't worry mum, I don't mind walking today," I said, to which she smiled happily again and continued her business. "You're in a good mood today," she said.

"I'm just feeling thankful today mum," I replied with a smile of my own. "You do so much for us and you never get the thanks you deserve."

My house was a good ten-minute walk from the train station, and school was another fifteen minutes from there after a short train ride. It wasn't exactly a hike in the mountains, but mum usually drove me to the station - it was too early to be walking any kind of distance after all.

I could swear that every day the teachers were concocting ways to make my backpack heavier. I was pretty small, so carrying my backpack meant leaning forwards so that it wouldn't topple me over and on to my back. It seemed like every day there was a new textbook that we just needed to have – I'd have left it in a locker in school, but then how could I do all the homework that related to it? The thoughts had all started coming back to me so clearly. I could remember going to school and the stupidest of details that surrounded it. Everything that had ever seemed so trivial was now flooding in and it made me feel, well, *alive*. I was finally *thankful* for my schooling and everything that went with it, the social interactions with the other school kids, the homework, the classes and even the teachers. I liked it all.

I had a friend called Lee, who would meet me at the station every day to wait for the train together. We would talk about what we'd seen on TV the night before, sports (wrestling mainly) or play whatever happened to be the game of the week, it was fun and kept the morning exciting with something to look forward to each day on our way to school. We never even thought about the possibility of our friendship drifting apart through time and for us to end up as strangers, though in my dream I distinctly remembered Lee wasn't even a factor in any part of my life. I shook my head to detach the thoughts of last night and brought my attention back to the situation at hand.

Our usual spot at the train station was at the farthest point to where the front of the train would arrive. It kind of worked out like a stereotypical class division bus – cool kids always go at the back, the huddled masses of groups, cliques and the people who had no problem fitting into a range of social groups would pad out the centre, and the losers kept to themselves as much as possible at the front. It was definitely part of a defence mechanism.

'*This is my life,*' I thought, '*it's shit but I like it.*'

I watched the train arrive along the platform, and as the waves of school kids including myself took that final step through the doors and away off to school a part of me felt the relief of my ass on a soft seat for the rest of my journey.

My day had started as normal as I could've imagined, that was until a few hours in when I sat in Mr. Avery's maths class and realised that when I was singled out to answer the question written on the whiteboard, I could understand *everything* that was being taught. I knew I was pretty good at maths but never before had I so wholly understood a concept that I could just *answer* the questions given. It was when Mr Avery started to escalate the difficulty that I realised that something was wrong, there was no way I should've known any of this information and heads had started to turn to my direction as others realised it too.

Mr Avery was eventually convinced that I was somehow cheating – even to the point that he'd checked to see if I was wearing an earpiece and was being fed the answers like I was some kind of CIA agent. In his frustration, he'd even concocted a long differential equation on the board that was entirely made up on the spot and I'd offered an answer. He'd watched me solve it line by line, and correctly. I could see the frustration in his eyes, but it was nothing compared to the feeling of something changing inside me that I felt, and it was scary.

Mr Avery had eventually allowed me to continue on with the class work, apparently assuming that it was simply a fluke or that I had the benefits of a private tutor that just this moment had shown itself to be worthwhile, though I knew that wasn't the case and the dream I'd had started to prick at me again. I shouldn't have been able to do the things I did in that class, but I couldn't explain it. I wasn't insane, I knew the difference between dreams and reality but this really had me sweating, and by the time design and tech came around I was convinced I needed to talk to a counsellor at the very least.

It was the start of a new project in D&T, which always meant design work, and I loved that. We got to use the 3D visualisation software on the computers to generate our ideas before they became a reality. – Other than then we never got to use the computers, they just sat there at the back of the room waiting to be fired up the next time someone needed to design something.

This brief, though, was to design and build anything we liked as it was going to be our year long project that our entire grade was to be based upon, and that thrilled me. I know - call me sad but I loved the idea of inventing and building.

The class was three hours long and I fell into a sort of autopilot with my computer screen. I spoke to no-one as I drew my CAD blocks and joined them together as though I'd done it a thousand times before. I was good with the software, but just as in the maths class this felt like I really had done this so many times before. At the end of the class, rotating on the screen before me was a small metallic spider-like drone, with the title above it 'Construction Drone.'

"It's about time you let me in," a female voice rang out in my head.

Startled, I looked around for who was talking though I could see no one facing in my direction.

"In here," the voice came again. "It's me, Sam."

'What's happening to me?' I thought. *'Am I going insane?'*

"No you aren't insane," Sam said. "You're just suffering a little short term amnesia, it'll pass. Actually, hang on, let me see what I can do…"

I felt my eye twitch a few times and what seemed like a tugging at the base of my neck… and then pain. The worst headache I could've ever imagined overwhelmed me and I grasped my head in my hands. But no, it wasn't the *worst* headache I'd had, I remembered I'd had worse on the Saturn once my ARC had been destroyed. Then I remembered *everything* all in one go, the memories flooding my mind and changed letting me know those weren't dreams but my reality.

Sam had been telling the truth, I was back in my younger body though this time I'd retained the knowledge of my entire life, knowledge that I could use to aid mankind…and one seriously advanced AI to help me with that. I removed my hands from my head and smiled to myself.

'Sam, we've got work to do, and plenty of it,' I thought.

Epilogue

∞

The fraction of Sam's processor that she'd managed to keep away from Cross's mind was initially incorporeal and unable to effect anything in the physical world around it, though as a cloud in the ether she could see everything that was happening on earth below her. She loved gathering data and knew just how important that endeavour was going to be for the next loop around, and the next loop after that and so on and so on until the human race would reach its pinnacle. With that in mind she began her list of tasks that needed to play out for this loop to achieve exactly what it was that she expected.

There were only a few things she needed to do whilst alone and away from prying eyes. She needed to insert a very small part of herself into the automated shipping controls at the Port of Dover. That way she would be able to lure the Scriven when they arrived on earth to the port itself, ensuring that the news report would draw Cross and co. to that very location once that period was realised, and also begin to seed the distrust between Russia and China, and the U.K. and the US. Lastly, she needed to insert some minor technologies into the world as a whole in order to ensure that she herself was manufactured as the first full quantum artificial intelligence. She also needed to start humanity on the path to gravitational refuelling systems, plasma weaponry and the ARC/Diver program for the Space Corps. It sounded like a lot of work but she knew if she just started the ball rolling, humanity would fill in the gaps. This time ,though, she had her ace in the hole – an accomplice.

Sam calculated the effects of her meddling and smiled inwardly as the things she'd put into motion began to spread their tendrils out through the sands of time, talking hold and growing just how she'd imagined. Eith her work for the day done, she took hold of the remainder of her consciousness within the fourteen year-old Daniel Cross, and begsn his journey to become a genius, a seer of the future, a member of the Space Corps, a seasoned diver and eventually the saviour of the human race. This young lad had a lot to do, but not a lot to learn; he'd already done that himself, being mentally aged on the inside already, though his physical body did nothing to betray that fact.

She had complete faith in Daniel. After all, if she didn't, she along with the human race would cease to exist in a few short decades and that was a price that she was not willing to pay for failure. Besides, he'd done it once before already, so how hard could it be to do it again?

The end.